Acclaim for Tamera Alexander

"Tamera Alexander takes us to the Civil War battlefield with a vivid yet sensitive portrayal of war and its aftermath. With warmth and grace, she shows us hope and faith at work in the midst of suffering. The beautifully-drawn characters and rich history in *With This Pledge* work seamlessly to demonstrate that Christ's love and romantic love can triumph even in our darkest moments."

—Lynn Austin, bestselling author of *Legacy of Mercy*

"Tamera Alexander has once again given readers a beautifully written story full of strong characters and tender romance—all while staying true to the actual history of the people and events she describes. From the horrors of war to the hope of blossoming love, Lizzie and Roland's story will live in my heart for a very long time."

—Anne Mateer, author of *Playing by Heart*, on *With This Pledge*

"Based on actual events surrounding the Battle of Franklin in 1864, Tamera Alexander vividly captures the resilience, strength, and ultimate hope of those men and women who endured this dark chapter in American history."

—Joanna Stephens, Curator, The Battle of Franklin Trust (Carnton), on *With This Pledge*

"I thoroughly enjoyed *Christmas at Carnton*! This tender love story between two wounded people whom God brings together for healing is a book readers will enjoy anytime—but *especially* at Christmas!"

—Francine Rivers, *New York Times* bestselling author of *Redeeming Love* and *A Voice in the Wind*

"With heartwarming humor, romance (and recipes) to savor, Tamera Alexander delivers a sweet, second-chance love story between a widow and a wounded soldier. A wonderful Christmas gift for readers everywhere!"

—Julie Klassen, bestselling author of *The Ladies of Ivy Cottage* on *Christmas at Carnton*

"History, hardships, and a heroine, *Christmas at Carnton* offers a new perspective of the home front during the Civil War in Tennessee. Thank you, Tamera, for honoring our site."

—ELIZABETH R. TRESCOTT, COLLECTIONS MANAGER, THE BATTLE OF FRANKLIN TRUST: CARNTON AND CARTER HOUSE

"*To Wager Her Heart* is a wonderful historical romance . . . Alexander has certainly done her research in this lovely Belle Meade Plantation inspirational romance!"

—*RT BOOK REVIEWS*, 4 STARS

"A vivid glimpse into Nashville's history, *To Win Her Favor* is excellent historical romance with a gentle faith thread that adds depth to the tale, proving once again that you just can't go wrong picking up a Tamera Alexander romance!"

—*USA TODAY*

"Strong characters, a sense of the times, and the themes of love, friendship, and the importance of loyalty and determination make this a triumph. It will be popular not only with Alexander's many fans but also with readers of Judith Miller and Tracie Peterson."

—*LIBRARY JOURNAL*, STARRED REVIEW ON *TO WIN HER FAVOR*

"Alexander continues her ode to the magnificent Belle Meade Plantation, using it to illustrate questions of race, faith, and loyalty that continue to haunt today. Richly drawn secondary characters add depth, humor, and a sobering perspective on how Reconstruction affected racial relations, social status, and economic fortunes. Fans will appreciate and applaud the smooth merging of social commentary and a sweet love story."

—*PUBLISHERS WEEKLY* ON *TO WIN HER FAVOR*

"Already a *USA Today* bestseller, this novel draws a fresh thread in this author's historical fiction tapestry. Tamera Alexander's painstaking research into the people, places, and times of which she writes is evident on every page, and she depicts the famous residents of postbellum Nashville with great detail and even greater affection."

—*USA TODAY* ON *TO WHISPER HER NAME*

WITH
THIS
PLEDGE

Books by Tamera Alexander

The Carnton Novels
Christmas at Carnton (novella)
With This Pledge

Belle Meade Plantation Novels
To Whisper Her Name
To Win Her Favor
To Wager Her Heart
To Mend a Dream (novella)

Belmont Mansion Novels
A Lasting Impression
A Beauty So Rare
A Note Yet Unsung

Timber Ridge Reflections
From a Distance
Beyond This Moment
Within My Heart

Fountain Creek Chronicles
Rekindled
Revealed
Remembered

Stand-alone Novels
Among the Fair Magnolias (novella collection)
The Inheritance

WITH
THIS
PLEDGE

TAMERA ALEXANDER

THOMAS NELSON
Since 1798

With This Pledge

Published in Nashville, Tennessee, by Thomas Nelson. Thomas Nelson is a registered trademark of HarperCollins Christian Publishing, Inc.

Scripture quotations marked NLT are from the *Holy Bible*, New Living Translation, copyright © 1996, 2004, 2015 by Tyndale House Foundation. Used by permission of Tyndale House Publishers, Inc., Carol Stream, Illinois 60188. All rights reserved.

Scripture quotations marked NASB are from the New American Standard Bible®, © The Lockman Foundation 1960, 1962, 1963, 1968, 1971, 1972, 1973, 1975, 1977, 1995. Used by permission.

All other Scripture quotations are from the King James Version.

Excerpts from *A Christmas Carol* appear in chapters 13, 29, and 35. *A Christmas Carol* by Charles Dickens was first published in England in 1843 and is in the public domain.

Thomas Nelson titles may be purchased in bulk for educational, business, fund-raising, or sales promotional use. For information, please e-mail SpecialMarkets@ ThomasNelson.com.

ISBN: 978-0-7180-8185-0 (HC Library Edition)

Library of Congress Cataloging-in-Publication Data

Names: Alexander, Tamera, author.
Title: With this pledge / Tamera Alexander.
Description: Nashville, Tennessee: Thomas Nelson, [2019] | Series: The Carnton novels; book 1
Identifiers: LCCN 2018037968 | ISBN 9780718081836 (trade paper)
Subjects: | GSAFD: Love stories. | Christian fiction.
Classification: LCC PS3601.L3563 A44 2019 | DDC 813/.6--dc23 LC record available at https://lccn.loc.gov/2018037968

Printed in the United States of America
19 20 21 22 23 LSC 5 4 3 2 1

In memory of all those who fell at the Battle of Franklin, and for the ones who either tended their wounds or helped usher them Home.

I lie awake thinking of you,
meditating on you through the night.
Because you are my helper,
I sing for joy in the shadow of your wings.
I cling to you;
your strong right hand holds me securely.
Psalm 63:6–8 NLT

Know therefore that the LORD your God, He is God,
the faithful God, who keeps His covenant and His lovingkindness
to a thousandth generation with those who love Him
and keep His commandments.
Deuteronomy 7:9 NASB

Dear Reader,

The journey you're about to embark upon is drawn heavily from the pages of history and from the lives of people who lived through the events portrayed in this novel. I am deeply honored to have been given the privilege to write about both. But along with that honor comes a weighty responsibility to accurately convey the events that took place. This is the story of what happened on the evening of November 30, 1864, at Carnton Plantation in Franklin, Tennessee, following the tragic five-hour Battle of Franklin, in which nearly ten thousand soldiers were either killed, wounded, or captured, and how the people who lived at Carnton dealt with the aftermath.

To that end, I've written this novel with a careful consideration of history—including oftentimes disturbing descriptions of combat—coupled with a deep desire to weave a compelling story of hope. Because hope is what I experienced time and again as I pored over the history of these events. I read literally thousands of pages of historical and personal accounts through which we can witness, with awe-filled admiration, the courage and strength that characterized these men and women.

My thanks go to the staff at Carnton for allowing me access to their extensive historical resources, with special appreciation to Joanna Stephens and Elizabeth Trescott for answering countless questions with never-failing patience. I also extend my gratitude to David Doty, the great-great-great-great-grandson of Captain Roland Ward Jones, the last wounded Confederate soldier to leave Carnton following his convalescence—and one of the main characters in this novel—for sharing his family's personal history, including the love letters between Roland and Lizzie. This novel is all the richer for our phone conversations and email exchanges, David, and for the many pictures you've shared. *Thank you.*

Finally, to you, dear reader, thank you for entrusting your time to me. It's a gift I treasure and never take for granted. Perhaps we'll cross paths at Carnton one day soon. I hope so. And as you walk the hallowed grounds of the battlefield, as you tour the rooms and hallways of Carnton and view floorboards that still—over a century and a half later—bear the bloodstains from that fateful November night, I trust you'll gain, as I have, a deeper appreciation for the sacrifices made by the men and women who were there—most of whom will remain unknown to us.

But some we do know. And this is their story.

With fresh eternal perspective,

Tamera

CHAPTER I

NOVEMBER 30, 1864
CARNTON PLANTATION
FRANKLIN, TENNESSEE
21 MILES SOUTH OF NASHVILLE

"And this, children, is a drawing of the Great Pyramids of Giza in Egypt. Which is a very long way from Franklin, Tennessee." Lizzie read fascination in young Hattie's eyes, and in those of Sallie, the cousin visiting from Nashville. Yet seven-year-old Winder only stared glumly out the window.

Lizzie lowered her voice. "This pyramid here is where a mighty Egyptian pharaoh, or king, and his queen are buried. And it's full of secret rooms."

Winder's head whipped back around. "Secret rooms?"

She nodded. "Archaeologists recently discovered some new rooms in the upper portion of the pyramid. They'd been hidden for centuries. See this drawing . . ."

As she continued teaching, she glanced at the clock on the side table, expecting Tempy to bring the children's midmorning refreshment anytime now. A summerlike breeze fluttered the curtains on the open jib window leading to a second-story balcony, and the sunshine and warmth beckoned them outside. Perhaps she would take advantage of the beautiful weather and conduct the afternoon classes under the Osage orange tree out front. After so many weeks of rain and cold, the mild weather was a welcome change. Especially for the end of November.

A few moments later she heard Tempy's footsteps on the staircase. "Thank you for listening so intently, children. And for your excellent questions, girls. And now it's refreshment time!"

Tempy knocked twice on the door, then entered. "Mornin', little ones!"

Winder hopped down from his chair. "What are we havin' today, Tempy?"

Lizzie cleared her throat and gave him a pointed look.

"I mean . . . Thank you, Tempy, for whatever it is you made," he corrected, still trying to peer up and over the side of the tray.

Tossing him a wink, Tempy set the tray on the table. "I made y'all some cinnamon rolls this mornin', Master Winder. You go on now and help yourself. And get a glass of that milk too." She included the girls in her nod, and the children took their snacks and hurried outside to the balcony overlooking the front yard. "Miss Clouston, I brought you one too, ma'am."

Lizzie accepted the roll and took a bite, then sighed and briefly closed her eyes. The bread, still warm from the oven, all but melted in her mouth, the buttery icing slathered on top a concoction of sugary goodness. "Oh, Tempy, these are even better than usual. Thank you."

"My pleasure, ma'am." Tempy eyed the globe on the table and shook her head. "Look at all them places. Hard to believe all that's out there somewhere."

Lizzie heard something akin to yearning in the woman's tone. She'd noticed Tempy gazing at the globe before, but without comment. Mindful of any icing on her fingers, Lizzie turned the globe to show North America, then pointed to Tennessee. "That's where we are right now. And this"—she turned the globe again and pointed to the northeast corner of Africa—"is where these pyramids are located." Lizzie held up the image and gave a condensed version of what she'd taught the children. "It's in a place called Egypt."

Tempy eyed her. "You tellin' me a fancy king's buried in that thing?"

Lizzie nodded. "Along with his queen."

"Mmmph . . . It don't look so far away on this ball, but I'm guessin' it'd take us a while to get there."

"Yes, quite a while. And we'd have to traverse an ocean in the process." Lizzie drew an invisible line from Tennessee across the Atlantic Ocean to the general region of Giza.

Tempy shook her head. "So much world the good Lord made. Wonder how he ever thought it all up."

Lizzie moved her finger a little to the right, knowing Tempy would appreciate this. "Do you see this tiny portion of land here?"

Tempy squinted. "Yes, ma'am. But only just."

"That's Palestine. The part of the world where the Lord was born and where he dwelt during his life here on earth."

"Pal-es-tine," Tempy repeated slowly and said it twice more as though wanting to feel the word on her lips. "I was told he was from a place called Bethlehem."

Lizzie nodded. "You're right, he was. Bethlehem is located in this area."

For the longest time Tempy studied the spot on the globe, then traced an arthritic forefinger over it, her expression holding wonderment. And not for the first time, Lizzie felt a firm tug on her conscience.

By Tempy's own admission, the older woman had been at Carnton for nigh onto forever, serving as the McGavocks' cook. Lizzie had often wanted to ask Tempy about her life here. About this war. And about being the only slave left behind when Colonel McGavock sent the other forty-three south three years ago, far from the reach of the Federal Army that would have freed them.

She felt certain that Tempy would have leapt at the chance to learn her letters, but teaching a slave to read and write was against the law. Here in the South, at least. The Emancipation Proclamation, issued by

President Lincoln nearly two years ago, hadn't made much difference in that regard. So Lizzie had never offered. And in the eight years she had lived and worked here at Carnton, she'd never confided in Tempy her opinions on slavery. She'd never had the courage. After all, slavery wasn't a topic a "properly bred" woman deigned to broach. And certainly not with a slave.

And what would stating her differing views have changed? Nothing. Lizzie held back a sigh. She was a governess, not a landowner. She couldn't vote. She wasn't even mistress of her own home—yet, at least. She had no voice. And sharing her opinions would have only driven a wedge between her and the McGavock family, which was a relationship she cherished. Being so forthcoming might well cost her the position here, and that was something she could ill afford, especially now with the war on. Still, even when considering her reasons, she felt a sense of shame.

She wondered sometimes if she shouldn't have gone north all those years ago when she'd first considered it. She could have found a place with a family in Boston or Philadelphia, surely. Yet that would have meant leaving behind her family, her friends, all that was familiar. So she'd stayed, and tried not to dwell on what she couldn't change.

"You teachin' them children 'bout all them places, ma'am?" Tempy glanced at the globe.

"I'm doing my best. Although with so pretty a day, it's difficult to maintain their attention."

"Days like this don't come round too often, 'specially this time of year."

Lizzie dabbed the corners of her mouth, checking for icing. Then she lowered her voice, mindful of the open jib window. "I'm thinking of moving outside for a while so we can enjoy the sunshine."

"If you want, ma'am, I could fix you all a picnic lunch and you could eat out there."

Lizzie nodded. "That's a wonderful idea! I'll use that as an entice-ment for them to remain attentive until then."

The promise worked like a charm. Following a delightful lunch, the children helped clean up the picnic without complaint. Winder needed a little prompting, rambunctious boy that he was. Still, he pitched right in when asked. Lizzie sat on the blanket beside Sallie watching as Winder and Hattie chased each other beneath the shade of the Osage orange tree. A wave of affection for them swept through her, nearly stealing her breath. She'd known Hattie before the girl had turned two. And Winder she'd known since birth. She loved them as though they were her own.

The warmth within her faded by a degree. Someday, Lord will-ing, she and Towny would have children of their own. A flicker of guilt accompanied the thought of Towny. But as she always did, Lizzie tried to set it aside. After all, women married for a whole variety of reasons—money, prestige, social standing, security. So was marrying for the hope of having children really so bad?

She studied the bare ring finger on her left hand and thought of what Towny had said in his last letter almost a month ago. The next time he saw her, he'd written, he had something special to give her. She wondered if it was his mother's ring. Having known his mother, Marlene—God rest her soul—Lizzie found the thought endearing. Then again, having known Towny's parents and the close relationship they'd shared, she only hoped that *if* Towny planned on giving her that ring, she would prove worthy of it.

It would be wonderful to see him again after all these months. Would he be much changed? Would he consider her so? Had his intent to marry her waned in any way? Did he ever entertain the same ques-tions about their future as she did? A warm breeze rustled the leaves overhead, and Lizzie checked the chatelaine watch pinned to her shirt-waist. It was later than she'd thought. She ushered the children back into the schoolroom upstairs and was closing the door behind her when Tempy caught her attention.

"A letter come for you, ma'am. From your Lieutenant Townsend." Tempy handed it to her. "I hope he's all right. He's such a good man."

Your Lieutenant Townsend. Tempy had taken to calling Towny that in recent months, but the term still struck an odd note within Lizzie. "Thank you for bringing this to me. And yes, he *is* a good man." She checked the date stamped on the envelope. Only a week ago. Mail delivery had been quick this time. She wondered where he was.

"He'll make you a good husband too, ma'am."

"Yes. Yes, he will," Lizzie answered. She'd told herself the same thing many times.

Tempy tilted her head and studied her in the manner she sometimes did. A manner that always caused Lizzie to ponder whether the woman could read every blessed thought in her head. And, even more, if Tempy questioned whether Lizzie herself was as well acquainted with those thoughts as she should be.

"Well, enjoy your letter." Tempy dipped her head and took her leave.

Lizzie closed the door and laid the envelope on the table's edge. It would have to wait for now. The first hour passed swiftly as they reviewed grammar lessons, then transitioned to penmanship. Hattie and Sallie both possessed a beautiful hand. But Winder's cursive, bless him, looked more like chicken scratch. Lizzie sat with him while he painstakingly practiced each letter, then she whispered, "Well done," and tousled the hair on his head. She did love a good challenge. Next they moved to arithmetic. Lizzie wrote addition problems on a slate, and each child took a turn solving two or three. Arithmetic was Winder's favorite subject, and to Lizzie's joy he excelled in it. Finally she set them to working problems on their own and reached for Towny's letter.

She opened the envelope. Only one sheet of paper within. Her gaze scanned the page, and her eyes widened. He'd been brief, but not evasive. Quite the contrary. Lizzie felt her face go warm.

Dearest Lizzie Beth,

    I'm counting the days until I see you again and sincerely hope that that number will be a small one. I've taken to dreaming of you in recent days and those dreams are so real I can almost feel you beside me. To say I'm eager to make you my wife would be a dilution of my fierce affections. It would be like saying that Tennessee summers can be a mite warm. Yet as warm as we know those summers to be, they are nothing compared to the fire that burns within me for you, and that seems to grow stronger with each passing day.

Lizzie looked up to see if the children were watching. Then she realized how silly that was. As though in watching her read the letter, they would somehow be made privy to its contents. She fingered the high collar of her shirtwaist and continued.

Tucker's Brigade is being ordered farther south, but I pray we make our way back to Franklin soon. Hopefully by spring. I want us to be married as soon as possible, Lizzie. That is my wish and I hope yours is the same. I apologize for my brevity, but I must see this posted before we move out. Please pass along my kindest regards to the McGavocks and their children. When you see my father, please inform him that his son is well, is fighting for the land he cherishes, but misses home and all the treasures it holds. Namely you, my dearest Lizzie.

Most affectionately yours,

Towny

    Any question about whether he'd changed his mind about their pending nuptials had been erased. And once again Towny had managed to surprise her. She'd last seen him in January, when he'd asked her to marry him. To say she'd been surprised then as well was an understatement. One minute they'd been walking back from town after a visit with her family—discussing the war and how he'd managed to secure a brief furlough home—and the next thing she knew, he'd turned and grabbed hold of her hands.

"I know this seems sudden, Lizzie, but I've been thinking about it for some time. I think I've loved you since I first laid eyes on you that day at the mercantile. You with your brown hair in pigtails, eating a peppermint stick. You would hardly look at me, until I did a somersault with no hands." His boyish grin held traces of youth. "Once we're husband and wife, I know we can make a good life together. We already know each other at our best and worst, and that gives us a great advantage over most couples. So please, say you'll be my wife? At least consider it?"

She had agreed and then sought her mother's counsel, only to discover that Towny had already asked her father's permission for her hand, which he had heartily given. Her parents were overjoyed. And looking at it practically, she'd realized Towny was right. They did already know each other very well. And they were both twenty-eight years old. It was well past time for her to wed. No one else had sought her hand in marriage, and she had no reason to think that would change, especially with the war claiming the lives of so many men.

But the real reason she'd agreed to marry Towny—the reason she'd not shared with him—made her feel false inside. She wanted children of her own, and the time for that to happen was swiftly passing her by. She smoothed a hand over her midsection. Soon Hattie and Winder would be grown, and she'd have to move on to another house to raise someone else's children. Either that or become a burden to her parents. So . . . she'd said yes.

And she *was* terribly fond of Towny. She could honestly say she loved him. Not, perhaps, in the way she'd always imagined she would love a husband. But love could grow from friendship. Or so she'd been told. And she and Blake Rupert Townsend—or Towny, the nickname she'd bestowed upon him as a boy—had been the best of friends since childhood. So she'd given him her pledge. And Towny *would* make a fine husband. She'd thought so for many years. She'd simply never imagined he would be hers.

Lizzie folded the letter and put it away, then checked the time. She'd allow the children another five or ten minutes to complete their tasks. In the meantime, she'd fetch the novel she'd left in Winder's bedroom down the hallway. She intended to start reading it to them tonight before bedtime. She'd saved it specially for this time of year.

"Miss Clouston," Sallie said before Lizzie shut the door.

"Yes, dear?"

"Could you help me with this one before you go?" The girl pointed to her slate.

"*Would* you help me," Lizzie gently prompted. "And yes, I'd be happy to help you. But I want you to try to figure it out first on your own. I'll prompt you if you begin to do it incorrectly. And feel free to work the problem aloud, if that helps you."

She smoothed a hand over Sallie's long blond hair and gave her an encouraging nod, then tugged a strand of the equally long golden hair of Clara, the porcelain doll the child took with her everywhere. Sallie grinned and set to work, whispering faintly to herself. Following a recent buildup of Federal troops in Nashville, Sallie's parents had asked the McGavocks if they could bring Sallie to Carnton for a few days to keep her distanced from the war. It was nice to have an additional student to teach, and since Hattie and Sallie were close cousins, they were enjoying every moment together.

Sallie finished working the problem and peered up.

"Well done!" Lizzie whispered, and the girl's eyes sparkled. "By working it aloud, you were able to do it all by yourself. Now see if you can complete the rest, and I'll be back shortly."

Lizzie closed the door, then waited a few seconds to make certain Winder didn't start jabbering at the girls the way he sometimes did when she left the room. But blessed quiet reigned, and she sighed. Days like these were what governesses lived for.

She headed for Winder's room across the hall, then remembered she'd left the blanket they'd used for the picnic folded on the front porch. Best get that first. She descended the staircase to the main floor and heard the clock in the family parlor chime. Two o'clock. She might dismiss the children early today and they could all take a walk down to the Saw Mill Creek, or maybe even into town to get penny candy at the mercantile. They could stop by her parents' house for a quick visit too, and—

The front door flung open and Lizzie stopped short, her heart skipping a beat. A soldier strode in. A general, she thought, judging by his uniform. Scarcely pausing, he focused on the staircase and strode in that direction.

"May I help you, sir?" She didn't recognize him, yet he did look familiar to her somehow.

Without a word, without even looking at her, he started up the staircase. Lizzie glanced into the side rooms for Colonel or Mrs. McGavock but didn't see them. So she followed the man upstairs, where he hesitated only briefly before heading into the guest room and stepping through the open jib window onto the second-floor gallery porch that spanned the back of the house. He walked as far as the northwest corner of the porch, then stopped and stared out across the fields.

Lizzie stood just inside the guest bedroom, at odds about what to do. Her main concern was for the children's safety—and clearly they were not at risk. But what was the man doing, simply barging into a home like this without asking permission? Without even a greeting? Perhaps he knew Colonel and Mrs. McGavock, but still . . . common decency should prevail.

Seconds ticked past. She finally went as far as the window and peered out, wanting to see what he was looking at. And her heart thudded a heavy beat.

Scarcely a mile away, Federal troops were gathering en masse around the Carters' house. *Thousands* of them. She'd never seen so many soldiers in one place. She stepped out onto the porch for a better view. Earlier that morning, she and Mrs. McGavock had seen several hundred blue coats headed up Columbia Pike. That wasn't unusual, considering that the US Army had occupied the town of Franklin off and on for nearly the past three years. They'd held the city of Nashville too, almost since the war started. So both she and Carrie McGavock had simply assumed the soldiers were on their way there. Either that or to nearby Fort Granger, a Federal outpost some two miles away. But what Lizzie saw now . . .

Why so many soldiers? And what were they doing? Constructing fortifications of some kind, it looked like. In a crescent shape just south of the Carters' home. She hoped Fountain Carter and his family were all right. Something glinted in the sunlight and she took a few steps closer, then stopped. Even without field glasses, she could see numerous cannons being situated along the crest of the hill.

The general suddenly turned, his features fierce, and retraced his steps. Lizzie followed him downstairs, where he strode through the open front door and down the front steps, and mounted a stallion. She paused in the doorway and stared after him as he rode south across the fields.

"Was that a soldier?" she heard behind her. She turned to see Tempy, folded picnic blanket in her arms.

"Yes. But I don't know who it was. He never gave his name. He simply barged in without even knocking!"

Footsteps sounded, and Colonel McGavock emerged from the farm office.

"What was General Forrest doing here?" he asked.

"General Nathan Bedford Forrest?" Lizzie responded.

At his nod, she looked back outside. No wonder the man had looked familiar. She'd seen his likeness many times in the newspaper.

"I have no idea, Colonel. He simply walked in, went upstairs, looked out over the porch, then walked back out again. He never said a word. But I know what he was looking at. Federal troops are gathering around the Carters' house. Far more than what Mrs. McGavock and I saw this morning." She instinctively lowered her voice in case the children were listening from above. "It appears as though they're putting artillery into place."

The colonel's eyes narrowed, and he headed up the stairs. "Please keep the children inside for the remainder of the afternoon, Miss Clouston. And focused on their studies."

"Of course, sir." She and Tempy exchanged a look.

Lizzie left the novel she'd planned on getting from Winder's bedroom for later and returned to the classroom. She instructed the children to open their primers, then turned in her chair to glance out the partially open jib window toward the front of the house. But she saw nothing out of the ordinary.

"Hattie and Sallie, please turn to page seventeen. Winder, please turn to page eight. You may begin reading while I review your arithmetic problems."

Lizzie was halfway through checking Hattie's work when she realized she'd been staring at the same problem for the past five minutes. She couldn't seem to concentrate. What were so many Federal soldiers doing at the Carters' house?

A knock on the door made her jump. The door opened, and Mrs. McGavock stepped inside. Lizzie rose. Visits from her employer during lesson hours were rare.

"Is everything all right, Mrs. McGavock?"

But she could tell from the woman's furrowed brow that it wasn't. Mrs. McGavock quietly greeted the children, then discreetly motioned for Lizzie to join her on the balcony. Lizzie stepped outside and, for the second time that day, a sinking sensation pulled her heart down in her chest. In the distance, no more than two miles away, a massive sea of butternut and gray moved steadily forward. Like a great crest of an ocean came wave after wave of men, already in their divisions, it appeared, with flags flying. Lizzie's pulse edged up a notch.

She looked in the direction of the Carters' house but couldn't see it from the vantage point the front balcony afforded. "Surely they can see the Federal Army up ahead. Waiting for them."

Mrs. McGavock nodded, her expression grave. "The colonel isn't certain what's happening. But he did hear yesterday that the bridges across the Harpeth are all impassable due to the recent rains."

"So you think the Federals tried to cross but couldn't?"

"I don't know what to think, Lizzie."

Lizzie looked over at her. She considered Carrie McGavock a dear friend, but rarely did her employer use her Christian name. Lizzie checked the watch hanging from her shirtwaist. Half past three.

Mrs. McGavock turned. "I'd like for you to take the children down to the kitchen. Get them settled there with their studies, and perhaps give them something to eat." She offered a faint smile. "A treat will help keep them occupied."

"Yes, ma'am. I'll do that right away."

Wanting to reassure her, Lizzie tried to maintain a smile. Many years ago a matronly aunt had told her mother, *Lizzie's a quiet thing, Sena. Sweet enough, but I declare if that girl can't seem to hold a smile.* Lizzie often wondered if that statement had been a self-fulfilling prophecy. Either way, it was the truth. She returned to the classroom, pressing a forefinger to her lips while Mrs. McGavock made a quiet exit. "Children, I want you to gather your books and slates. We're going to have our afternoon lessons in a special room of the house."

Winder's eyes widened. "Is it a secret room?" he whispered, his chin dropping a smidgen as he peered up at her. "Like in that triangle place you showed us this mornin'?"

"No, it's not a pyramid. Not even a secret room. But it *is* a secret where we're going." She gathered her things and gestured. For effect, she opened the door slowly and peered out, then motioned for them to follow quietly.

The girls giggled as they moved down the stairs to the entrance hall, then to the dining room. The bi-fold doors separating that room from the farm office were open, and through the window, in the distance, Lizzie spotted the Southern army advancing.

"Hurry along now," she whispered and encouraged the children to precede her down the short flight of stone steps to the kitchen.

"We're goin' to the kitchen?" Winder asked, obviously nonplussed.

Lizzie shook her head. "Follow me!"

Tempy looked up from where she stood at a worktable mixing something in a bowl. She must have caught the look Lizzie sent her because the woman only smiled at the children as they passed, then raised her brows when Lizzie retrieved an oil lamp from the hutch.

"All right, children . . ." Lizzie nodded toward the larder and summoned a conspiratorial tone. "Remember I told you that the rooms in the pyramid have no windows? We're going to go inside the larder and pretend that we're in a pyramid!"

Hattie and Sallie looked at each other and grinned. Winder, however, stopped dead in his tracks.

"I got in trouble for goin' in there last time, Miss Clouston. Mama said I ate too many of Tempy's tea cakes. And it took forever 'fore I could have 'em again."

Lizzie's heart warmed as she remembered that incident. How she loved this boy. "It's all right, Winder. We have your mother's permission to go inside, I promise. Come along."

She opened the door and a bevy of scents reached out to them— fresh ground flours and meals, an array of spices ranging from cinnamon to nutmeg to oregano, and above it all the sweet scent of dried apples, peaches, and pears. Tempy worked tirelessly when it came to storing up summer fruits and vegetables, and was equally skilled at turning those stored goods into culinary treasures.

Lizzie placed the oil lamp on the stone floor. "Have a seat, children." She sat on a barrel of molasses, her mind racing.

Sallie sucked in a breath. "I forgot Clara! May I go back and get her, please?"

Hattie jumped up. "I'll go with her. We'll be like those explorers you told us about!"

Lizzie held up a hand. "I'll go get Clara. Meanwhile, I want you three explorers to discuss what you think it might be like to be inside a pyramid in one of those rooms. Each of you write down three things you might see or feel or smell while in that room. Then when I get back, we'll share our lists with each other."

The children nodded, though Sallie didn't look quite as convinced.

Lizzie reached behind her for a tin. "And of course every explorer needs nourishment." She removed the lid and held out the container.

"Tea cakes!" Winder yelled and grabbed two, then paused and looked up at Lizzie, who gave an approving nod.

After serving the girls and seeing her three charges settled, she slipped from the larder and closed the door behind her. Tempy stood staring out one of the kitchen windows.

"Miss Clouston, you best come see this."

Lizzie joined her and saw two large groups of Confederate soldiers moving their way. Trees lining the serpentine brick walkway out front blocked the rest of the view. "Yes, Mrs. McGavock and I saw them earlier, before I brought the children downstairs. I wanted to say something to you but couldn't. Not in front of them."

"What's goin' on, ma'am? Why's that army marchin' this way?"

"I don't know. But from what I saw earlier, there are just as many Federal soldiers holed up over by the Carters' house."

"Oh great God be with us all," Tempy whispered.

Lizzie said a silent amen. "I need to run upstairs and get Sallie's doll. Would you keep an eye on the children for me until I get back?"

"Yes, ma'am. I surely will."

Lizzie hurried up the steps and through the dining room and started up the staircase.

"Miss Clouston . . ."

She turned to see Mrs. McGavock peering out the front door, which stood slightly ajar. Reading the woman's expression, Lizzie joined her. "The children are safe, ma'am. They're in the kitchen with Tempy, and—"

Mrs. McGavock opened the door the rest of the way and Lizzie fell silent. Despite her feelings about this war, the sight spreading out before her was spellbinding. That great sea of butternut and gray they'd seen from a distance earlier advanced toward them in columns that seemed to stretch out forever across the Harpeth Valley, nearly two miles wide. No sound jarred the tranquil afternoon other than that of the soldiers' rhythmic footfalls and the occasional trill and chatter of a barn swallow. Most of the soldiers looked so young, and they marched with spirits high and rifles at the ready straight across Carnton's fields and front lawn as the warm Indian summer day drew to a close.

On closer inspection, Lizzie realized that some of them weren't carrying rifles. While it was common knowledge that the Southern army was less adequately equipped than their Northern counterpart, seeing that fact evidenced so crudely in the weapons some of the soldiers wielded was sobering, to say the least. Pitchforks, knives, pickaxes, even shovels. And it only added to the measure of the almost tangible grit and determination she could feel with each forward step the soldiers took.

"The mighty Army of Tennessee," Mrs. McGavock said softly, her voice a mixture of pride and dread. "Twenty thousand men, the colonel tells me."

While Lizzie was stirred by the sight and shared the sense of dread, she couldn't share the same sense of pride. Because for all the reasons given to support the Confederacy's cause—states' rights, economic concerns, protection of home and land, and families' futures—they all seemed to lead back to the continuance of slavery. And though she had yet to voice her opinion in this household, she was very much in accord with the North on that count. In the same breath, she only wished it wasn't taking a war to find some semblance of common ground.

Carrie McGavock stepped outside onto the front portico, then descended the steps and followed the brick path to the front gate. Lizzie shadowed her steps.

The neat columns of soldiers briefly broke ranks as they circled around the house, marching in quick time straight toward the mass of entrenched Federal troops waiting for them just south of the Carters' house. Lizzie studied the men's faces as they passed. Fierce determination marked some, weariness and fatigue others. Then she heard it. Music. From somewhere within the throng rose the South's oh-so-beloved "Dixie." She spotted the brass band as they marched past, the fading rays of sunlight reflecting off their instruments. After "Dixie" came "Bonnie Blue Flag," then "The Girl I Left Behind Me." The latter tunes seemed far too rousing and frivolous to accompany an army's charge, yet she heard some of the troops singing along as they—

A stray gunshot sounded from the advancing forces, and she and Mrs. McGavock both turned and hurried back toward the portico. When they reached the steps, they heard someone calling out to them.

"Ladies! Please, I must prevail upon the house!"

Lizzie turned to see a man hurrying up the brick walkway.

Mrs. McGavock took a step forward, squinting. "Reverend Markham? Is that you?"

The man's steps slowed as disbelief clouded his features. "Caroline Elizabeth Winder?" His voice held disbelief. "Could the woman before me be the same young girl I knew back in Louisiana?"

A slow smile curved Mrs. McGavock's mouth. "She would be one and the same, Reverend. Except it's Mrs. John McGavock now. Those closest to me call me Carrie. And it's been several years since I was that young girl. And since our paths have crossed."

"Yes, it has been." He looked over at the soldiers still pressing forward. "Or several lifetimes, it feels like."

The tender understanding in Mrs. McGavock's expression rendered any verbal response unnecessary. Footsteps behind them drew their attention. "Reverend Markham," Mrs. McGavock continued, "allow me to introduce my husband, Colonel John McGavock."

Following swift introductions, a pause settled in, and Lizzie detected a subtle change in the reverend's demeanor.

"Colonel McGavock, Mrs. McGavock, I need to inform you that your home has been designated the division field hospital for the wounded of Loring's Division. On behalf of General Hood and the great Army of Tennessee, we're grateful for your devotion to the Confederacy and to your fellow countrymen." He solemnly extended his hand and Colonel McGavock shook it, and in doing so accepted the selection of his home without hesitation. But what else could he do? Armies never requested. They took. Even when it was *your* army.

"Reverend, our home is yours," the colonel responded. "We'll make ready as best we can in the time that we—"

From somewhere behind them, a cannon boomed. Its echo thundered across the valley. A high-pitched whistle set the very air on edge, and just as Lizzie looked west toward the Carters' house, an explosion rocked the ground beneath her feet. Instinctively, she ducked. Her whole body tensed.

"Ladies—" The colonel took both her and Carrie by the arm. "Back inside the house."

As though that cannon blast had been a signal, an eruption of artillery fire exploded in the distance behind them. Halfway to the door, Lizzie glanced back at the reverend but found he was already running for the gate. She was nearly inside the house when she heard it . . .

An eerie screech, unearthly and primal, rising like a phantom chorus from the Confederate soldiers. The air trembled with the sound of it. Amid volleys of musketry fire, the squall rose in a fearsome swell over the valley, and her spine tingled with a prickly chill. The Rebel yell. She'd read about it, had heard men speak of it, but had never heard it herself.

Hearin' it will strip the courage clean outta your backbone, a man once told her. And though she'd questioned it then, she believed it now. How could an enemy hear that and not shudder?

Close on Colonel and Mrs. McGavock's heels, she raced to the family parlor to peer out the window to the fields behind the house. Fire and smoke poured from the Federals' entrenchment line as though they'd unleashed hell itself on the Confederate Army advancing across the open field. Men were cut down by the dozens midstride, rifles not yet raised to shoot. Still the Rebels surged forward. But it was too far an expanse to cross. The field was too deep.

Lizzie pressed a hand to the windowpane, unable to breathe. *It's too far. Turn back!* she screamed on the inside. But by some depth of courage and strength of conviction she'd never known, the men pressed forward, stepping over fallen brothers, pitching forward only to struggle to their feet again. Pushing, pushing to make the Federal breastworks. Smoke and fire soon engulfed the valley.

"Carrie! Miss Clouston!"

Lizzie turned to see the colonel pushing furniture up against the wall. His wife ran to help him.

"Where are the children?" he asked.

"In the kitchen with Tempy," Lizzie answered.

He nodded. "We need to make room for as many men as possible. Carrie, you and Miss Clouston work together down here. I'll go upstairs and do what I can there."

Lizzie grabbed hold of one end of an upholstered settee, Mrs. McGavock the other, and they hefted it up against the wall. They moved a marble-top table and wingback chairs to the side of the room, then did the same with the furniture in the best parlor. And all the while, war raged on the other side of the wall.

They hurried to the dining room next, then emptied the table of dishes Tempy had already set for that night's meal and shoved them into the sideboard.

Breath coming hard, they crossed into the farm office. Mrs. McGavock went immediately to the Grecian rocking chair, and Lizzie read her mind. The chair was a gift from the late President Andrew Jackson to the colonel many years earlier and held great sentimental value.

Lizzie grabbed hold of one side. "Why don't we take it down to the kitchen? Then the colonel can decide what to do with it later."

"Very good."

They managed to get the chair down the steps, but maneuvering the last turn into the kitchen presented a problem. Tempy rushed to help, and between the three of them they managed it. Lizzie looked over to see the children standing in the doorway of the larder. Wide-eyed uncertainty etched the girls' expressions, while curiosity painted Winder's.

"Winder says there's fighting outside," Hattie said, looking between her mother and Lizzie.

"I only told her 'cuz it's true!" Winder responded, making a beeline for a window.

Lizzie caught hold of him. "Children, I need you to stay in the larder awhile longer." She looked to Mrs. McGavock, wondering if she wanted her to stay here or go back upstairs with her.

Mrs. McGavock's gaze shifted to Tempy. "Tempy, I want you to stay with the children until Miss Clouston returns. She and I have a few more things to do upstairs. But I'll send her back soon," she added, her tone growing more maternal, as though she'd intended the last comment for the children's sake as well.

Lizzie gave each of her charges a quick kiss on the head and guided them back inside the larder. Just before closing the door, she pointed to the tin of tea cakes and winked.

Back upstairs, she worked furiously alongside Mrs. McGavock to move things out of the way, making room for what was to come. And somewhere between the cannon blasts and rifle fire she caught the faintest strains of the Confederate brass band still playing in the distance.

Hands on hips, Carrie McGavock paused in the entrance hall. "I wish we were better equipped to help them—had more to offer in the way of medicinal supplies."

But when the front doors burst open a moment later and stretcher bearers began carrying in the wounded, Lizzie realized that nothing could have prepared them for what crossed that threshold.

CHAPTER 2

For all the death she'd seen in her life, Lizzie had never seen anyone die. She cradled the bloodied cheek of the smooth-faced soldier before her. He was only a boy, no more than thirteen years old—scarcely half her age. And as he took his last ragged breath, she would've sworn she felt the tug of heaven's tide drawing him home. But it was his final words, whispered with such urgency, that wedged her heart in her throat. The scream of artillery shells and thundering cannon blasts shook the very air around her, and it sounded—and felt—as though the world were coming to an end.

She looked again into the young boy's countenance and found it growing steadily paler in death. Even as her heart broke further, she wrestled with what to do with his final words. Perhaps if she could learn where he—

Sharp commands issued from the entrance hall, and she turned to see more stretcher bearers pouring through the front doors with more injured men. The wounded already crowded the best parlor and spilled over into the farm office across the hallway. Their wails and moans tore at her.

How could these men still be drawing breath with bodies so broken, shattered by artillery and rifle fire? They'd been shot, bludgeoned, gouged, and bayonetted. Most clutched their sides and abdomens, others their heads. One man sat leaning forward in a wingback chair groaning and holding his arm tight against his chest. Only, upon closer inspection, Lizzie realized that the appendage he held so tenaciously was completely severed. She steeled herself. Not one to swoon, much less faint, she gripped the edge of a small table, needing to feel something solid.

The pungent haze of spent gunpowder, campfire smoke, and blood was inescapable, as were the odors of sweat and unwashed bodies. Soldiers called out for their mothers, for their sweethearts, for a drink of water. Others cursed the Yankees with language so foul Lizzie felt each word like a pinprick. Still others prayed in piteous voices to be relieved from their awful suffering. And during it all, surgeons moved among them, dressing wounds and shouting orders.

"Bandages! We need more bandages!"

"Move this soldier upstairs!"

"Morphine! We need morphine!"

"Miss Clouston, you think Lieutenant Townsend is somewhere in this army of men?"

Lizzie glanced behind her to see Tempy standing with wads of fresh bandages in her arms. She took a steadying breath. "No, Tempy. Thank goodness, he's not. In his letter today, he wrote that Tucker's Brigade was being sent south of here. Away from Franklin."

Towny hadn't told her precisely where his brigade was being ordered, of course. The soldiers were always mindful that mail could be intercepted by Federals. When she first read of his being sent farther south, she'd felt a touch of disappointment. Now she was grateful beyond imagining.

"Well, thank you, Jesus, for that," Tempy said softly, then deposited the fresh bandages on a side table. "I best get more of these, Miss Clouston. Looks like we'll be needin' them."

Lizzie knelt to help the next soldier, a young man lying on the floor clutching what remained of his right arm.

"I think I'm done for, ma'am." He groaned, his eyes glistening with emotion. "Them Yankees done managed to kill me."

"Not yet they haven't," Lizzie said softly and attempted a smile. "And we must work to keep it that way." She pushed back strands of hair from her face and checked the makeshift tourniquet corded tightly around the corporal's upper arm. Deciding she could do no better, she focused on the deep gash on his lower leg instead.

"Federal got me with his bowie knife, ma'am. He was swingin' it wild."

Lizzie winced. "I can see that."

"You think one of them docs can save it?" He took a sharp breath. "My leg, I mean?"

"Why you wantin' to keep that leg of yours, Bowman?" The soldier lying next to him grinned even as he clutched his own abdomen, his shirt soaked through with blood. "You know you never could dance worth a lick!"

Both soldiers laughed even as their eyes told the truth of their pain, and Lizzie recalled how Towny and other boys she'd known used to jest at the most inopportune times.

She retrieved a nearby basin of water and rinsed out a bloody cloth. "I'll clean the wound as best I can, Corporal, then bandage it. One of the surgeons will need to look at it later, as well as see to your arm."

She worked hurriedly, mindful of other soldiers who needed tending. The continuing barrage of rifle and cannon fire, plus what she'd witnessed earlier when peering through the family parlor window, painted an all-too-vivid image of how these men had sustained their injuries. She'd counted nearly a dozen surgeons working either inside the home or out in the yard. They'd offered the household little instruction on how to help, so Lizzie simply did what she knew.

Through the years she'd watched her father in his pharmacy in downtown Franklin, so she had some knowledge of the primaries in doctoring. Whenever the town's physician was otherwise engaged, people turned to druggist Edward G. Clouston for help. Lizzie had actually entertained the idea of following in her father's footsteps when she was a girl. Either that or becoming a doctor. Until she'd realized that such opportunities were rarely open to a woman.

So while she didn't possess any truly *special* gifts—not like singing or playing the piano or being especially adroit at knitting or sewing— her ability to memorize was exceptional. So she'd become a teacher instead.

"There you go, Corporal." She gently but firmly tugged the knot to secure the bandage. "Now try to rest. A surgeon will be by soon, I'm sure."

"Thank you, ma'am." He clenched his jaw tight, his eyes glazing. Perhaps due to the loss of blood, or shock. Or both.

Lizzie moved to help his friend and applied pressure to the abdominal wound until a corpsman finally arrived. She rose carefully, her legs aching from kneeling so long. She counted thirty men in the best parlor alone. With scarcely any space to walk, she stepped over the soldier she'd finished tending to help another whose arms were badly injured.

Most of the men, beards all wild and wooly, were ill-clad for winter and barefoot, the soles of their feet cut up and bruised. Some had fashioned shoes from threadbare gunny sacks and odd bits of cloth. But the dried blood caked on the bottoms of their feet revealed what little protection their ingenuity provided. Over the last three years she'd read accounts of battles in the newspapers—some overly graphic, or so she'd considered them at the time. But now she saw that the journalist's pen—and her own imagination—had grossly failed to depict the awful truth. This war was exacting far too high a price. From both sides. And slavery stood at the center of the debate.

Yet she knew it wasn't that simple. Towny and his family had never owned slaves, yet he'd been one of the first to sign up to fight. *What is a man supposed to do, Lizzie, when an army shows up to occupy his land? His home? His possessions? He fights, that's what he does!* Towny's eyes had blazed with conviction that night.

Even though she hadn't agreed with his decision to join the war, she could better understand fighting in defense of home than she could fighting for ideals and values she considered wrongheaded and vile. For years they'd read in the newspapers about a divided Congress striving to reach a compromise, but by 1860 any whiff of a settlement seemed all but dead. Eleven seceded states later and this war was born.

When the McGavocks entertained, Lizzie was sometimes invited to join them for dinner, depending on who their guests were. She'd heard every argument in support of states' rights along with the need to rein in President Lincoln's overreach in government. But even the argument about states' rights boiled down to a state's right to maintain the institution of slavery. Her own father, who owned slaves, had sided with the Confederacy. She'd attempted once, at the outset of the war, to share her differing opinion with him, but he swiftly and firmly put an end to that conversation. So she held her tongue.

She looked around the parlor. Most of the men appeared to be in their late teens to midtwenties. She doubted whether any of them had ever owned slaves, much less extensive property. After all, if a man owned more than twenty slaves, like Colonel McGavock, he was released from the obligation to fight, because the Confederacy needed food for the army and relied on those plantations and estates to contribute it. No, the men in this room looked more like farmers, laborers, railroad workers, perhaps accountants or mercantile owners. She guessed that most of them simply woke up one day to find a war on their doorstep.

She finished wrapping the wounded lieutenant's arms, tied off the bandages, and moved to help the next man.

Colonel McGavock's connection to the War Department kept him well informed, and based on what he'd shared with her and Mrs. McGavock earlier that week, the Army of Tennessee, under the command of General Hood, was the last standing army for the Confederacy. General Lee and his men were still besieged by General Grant in Virginia. So that meant the men in this house and those wounded yet still alive on the battlefield a short distance away were the Confederacy's last hope.

But with the Confederate government all but bankrupt and the Federal Army outnumbering the Southern forces by almost three to one, it seemed a dim, if not already dying, hope at best. A hope that Lizzie could not support, much less champion, no matter her love for family and—

"Miss Clouston! Your assistance is required!"

She looked up, a blood-soaked cloth in her hand, to see one of the surgeons making his way toward her across the crowded parlor, his focus intent.

"We need assistance in surgery, ma'am. Colonel McGavock suggested you might be of aid."

She hesitated. "I'm . . . most willing to be of any help I can, Doctor. But I've not been trained in the specifics of—"

"Have you ever administered chloroform? Or ether?"

"No, sir. Though I have read accounts of such."

"That will be sufficient, under the circumstances. I'll guide you through the rest. The most important thing—" He looked her square on. "According to the colonel, you possess a stalwart constitution and are a compassionate woman whose sensibilities will not be easily offended by the aftermath of war."

Despite her unsteadiness a moment earlier, Lizzie nodded, finding "the aftermath of war" a rather sanitized description for the carnage all around them. "Colonel McGavock is gracious in his assessment, Doctor. But in this regard, I do possess a sturdy constitution."

"Then tonight you're a surgical assistant, Miss Clouston. There are at least forty men upstairs on the second floor, with at least that many waiting outside, and more to come. They need surgery now or many of them are going to die. Keeping the men sedated during the procedures is crucial to saving as many as we can." He leaned closer, his voice lowering. "For as long as the chloroform holds out."

Sobered yet further, Lizzie nodded. "Of course. I'll come upstairs straightaway."

The surgeon left the parlor and she shadowed his path, mindful of where she stepped. She spotted attendants loading the deceased onto stretchers before carrying them outside, and she hesitated, recalling again what the young boy who'd died in her arms had whispered.

With no time to spare, she crossed the room, wiping the blood from her hands on her apron. She hastily searched the boy's clothing, his desperate tone so clear in her memory. *I done grieved over h-how I left things 'tween us, Mama.* His thinning voice had faltered. *But I didn't take it with me like I said. I-I left it. Buried. Way back on our land. 'Neath that ol' willow. And now . . . somehow it makes dyin' easier knowin' you'll have it.*

What did that mean? *Knowin' you'll have it.* Have what? Oh, that she'd had time to ask him, but he'd slipped too swiftly beyond the veil.

His shirt pocket proved empty, but his pants pockets yielded a thin stack of envelopes bound with string both horizontally and vertically, as one would tie a package meant for posting. Only the string was tied in a knot, not a bow. Next she withdrew a pocketknife absent its inlaid ivory, an oblong stone with a well-worn surface, and a page torn from a Bible and folded with care. *The Book of Psalms*—she glimpsed the heading at the top, along with a name scrawled in poor penmanship—*Thaddeus*.

With a last look at his youthful face she said a prayer for his mother, wherever she was, then stuffed the items into her skirt pocket. She traced the surgeon's steps into the front entrance hall, where the ache inside her deepened.

Every spare space in the front hall and farm office was filled with bleeding, dying men. Every niche and corner was occupied, the thick floorcloth and fine upholstered furniture soaking up their blood. Even in the shadows beneath the stairs, soldiers sat slumped against the wall like wounded animals gone off by themselves to die. Stretcher bearers continued to carry more men up the stairs, struggling beneath the weight of their task. Feeling as though she'd walked into some horrible nightmare, Lizzie briefly squeezed her eyes tight and opened them again, half expecting to see the home as it had always appeared, pristine and in order. But the scene remained unchanged. Then rising above the cacophony of chaos and death she heard familiar words.

"'The LORD is my shepherd; I shall not want. He maketh me to—'"

The ragged voice broke, and Lizzie turned in the direction of the shuddering sigh that followed.

Not too far from her, a soldier sat slumped against the wall, his head bowed, the front of his shirt soaked through with blood. "'. . . to lie down . . . in green pastures. He leadeth me . . . beside still waters.'"

The man grimaced and clutched his belly, yet continued to recite, his voice halting. Lizzie hurt for him and was grateful when she saw an attendant bend down to help him. Whispering a prayer for him, for all of them, she managed to pick her way to the staircase.

Hand on the stair rail, she'd started up when she felt a tug on her skirt and looked down.

"Please . . ." A soldier, his voice raspy, rose up on one elbow, a jagged gash on the side of his head and his tattered trousers of home-spun butternut stained a deep crimson. Hand trembling, he held out an envelope. "Would you see that . . . this gets to my daughter?"

With a grimace he fell back, and a fresh flow of blood seeped from the hastily applied field dressing on his leg. Lizzie tucked the envelope into her skirt pocket and carefully edged back his trousers to inspect the wound.

She clenched her jaw. Needing something, anything, to use as a tourniquet, she spied a decorative silk cord looped around a vase on a nearby table and grabbed it. She wrapped the cord around the man's upper thigh and pulled taut. He let out a groan. His face went ashen.

Lizzie knelt over him, willing him to stay conscious. "What's your name, soldier?"

"Pleasant—" He gasped. "Captain Pleasant Hope, 46th Tennessee Infantry."

She gripped his hand. "That's a fine name, Captain Hope. I'll keep your letter in my care. And *if* the time comes, I'll do exactly as you've asked. But until then, I need you to—"

An explosion shook the floor of the house, sounding closer than any of those previous, and for an instant everyone held a collective breath. Lizzie instinctively looked into the family parlor at the clock mounted on the wall to the right of the fireplace. A quarter past five. Only an hour had passed since the first exchange of gunfire? It felt like forever. How long would the battle last? Surely with night falling the fighting would end. It would have to. How could they fight when they couldn't even see each other?

She looked back down. "As I was saying, Captain Hope, I need . . ." Her words trailed off. The captain's eyes were still open, but his gaze was dull and fixed, his hand slack in hers. Lizzie pressed her fingers to the side of his throat, then slowly released her breath. "I'll do as you've asked, Captain Hope," she whispered and gently closed his unseeing eyes.

"Quickly, gentlemen! Bring them inside!"

Hearing Mrs. McGavock's voice, Lizzie looked back to see her employer directing yet another wave of stretcher bearers through the front double doors. Beyond them, darkness had indeed fallen and taken with it the unseasonably warm temperatures. Replacing the warmth, a chilling wind swept into the entrance hall as though to remind them that December was mere hours away.

"The farm office is already full," Mrs. McGavock continued, "as are the best parlor and family parlor. But we still have space. Put them in the dining room. And in the family bedrooms upstairs."

Mrs. McGavock's steady tone carried authority worthy of a general's rank, and the men obeyed without question. Lizzie's gaze briefly met hers and so much was said in their wordless exchange.

Bracing herself for what awaited upstairs, she continued up the steps toward—

"Mama?"

Lizzie turned back and spotted Winder standing in the doorway of the farm office. Her spine went rigid. What was he doing out of the kitchen! And Hattie and Sallie stood huddled close beside him.

Lizzie cut a hasty path back down the stairs and across the entrance hall, eager to usher the children back to where they belonged. She scanned the foyer for Colonel or Mrs. McGavock. And where was Tempy? She'd promised to keep the children with her. Yet the children weren't Tempy's responsibility, Lizzie knew. They were hers. She was their governess, after all.

She grasped little Winder by the hand. "What are you all doing up here? I instructed you three to keep to the—"

"They're bleeding so bad," Hattie whispered, tears pooling. "*All* of them."

Winder looked beside him. "'Course they're bleedin'. They been shot by them dang Yankees. I told you that's what we were hearin' from the kitchen."

Lizzie squeezed his hand. "Winder, don't speak in such a—"

"Miss Clouston—" Sallie tugged on Lizzie's sleeve. "I'd like to go home now, please." The girl's chin trembled and her already stricken expression grew more so.

Lizzie placed a hand on her slender shoulder, thinking about how Sallie's parents had brought her here to keep her safe from the war. But how could anyone have predicted this?

"I'm afraid going home isn't possible right now, Sallie. But I will see you all safely back to the kitchen. Where you were supposed to stay until I returned to—"

"Miss Clouston!"

Recognizing the deep voice, Lizzie straightened and looked behind her, cringing. Severity darkened John McGavock's expression, and she rushed to explain. "Colonel McGavock, sir, I'm so sorry. It was my intent that the children remain in the kitchen, away from all this. But I should have taken better care to—"

"Miss Clouston," he began again, his tone hinting that excuses would not be brooked.

Lizzie briefly bowed her head and prepared herself for the uncustomary reprimand, hating that she'd disappointed him.

"My dear woman, this is not your fault. I, too, wish there were a way for these children not to see this. But this has been brought to our door—with the Lord's knowledge, I must believe. And there is no escaping it."

She realized she'd been mistaken. It was anguish, not anger, that shadowed his gaze.

"So let us help them navigate this terrible journey." He peered down at Hattie, then at Winder, and lastly at Sallie, his wiry gray beard brushing the edge of his vest. "Would you not agree, Miss Clouston?"

Her throat tightened with both regret and relief, and she nodded. She trailed her employer's focus to the children and, even now, saw in their expressions that this "terrible journey" was already burning through their innocence, an innocence she would have fought fiercely to protect for a great many years longer. But Colonel McGavock was right. This was their world, for better or worse. The world in which they would grow up. However much she might wish it were not.

"Thank you, Colonel McGavock," she whispered. "For understanding."

Impressed with the need to be upstairs, she also knew she couldn't leave the children alone. But what to do with them in such a situation? Then a thought came. "Colonel, the soldiers are thirsty. If you'll permit me, I'll fetch pails and ladles, and the children can help distribute water and tea to the men."

The colonel nodded. "Excellent idea, Miss Clouston. But I'll see to the children for now. Dr. Phillips is waiting for you. Your talents will be better utilized alongside him and his colleagues. I've already assured him you're more than up to the task."

Hoping that would prove true, Lizzie climbed the staircase, mindful of the wounded leaned up against the wall and of the soldier below still struggling to recite the psalm. But when she reached the second-floor landing, she spotted a surgeon in one of the bedrooms, bone saw in hand, feverishly cutting on a soldier's arm, and her confidence ran screaming.

CHAPTER 3

Lizzie's body flushed hot, then cold. Prickles of sweat broke out on her arms and legs. She breathed in and out. *I am of stalwart constitution. I am of stalwart constitution.* The air was considerably cooler on the second floor, and she soon realized why. The jib window leading to the balcony from the schoolroom at the far end of the hallway was open, as were all the windows that she could see. She welcomed the chill.

Similar to downstairs, the wounded lay everywhere. She stepped mindfully among them, their piteous groans and pleas echoing those of their comrades on the floor below. She looked to the left first and checked for Dr. Phillips in the McGavocks' bedroom, then crossed the hall to the guest quarters directly opposite, where the scene beyond the open windows brought her stock-still.

The fields stretching northwest behind the house, where the McGavock property joined that of the Carters, were engulfed in flames. Fires billowed high like scalding tongues reaching up into the dark night sky. She saw a flash of light in the distance and heard an explosion, the reverberation reaching the wooden planks beneath her feet. Her chest ached. *Lord, when will this end?*

The groans of the injured pulled her back, and seeing no sign of Dr. Phillips, she continued down the corridor to check Hattie's room on the right. She turned toward Winder's bedroom across the hallway and found her attention drawn to a soldier lying on the floor. Why he, in particular, drew her focus when there were so many others, she couldn't say. Then it became clear. Though seriously injured— the bone of his right thigh laid bare and the flesh on his left torn to ribbons—he maintained a demeanor of calm. He didn't thrash or moan or cry out like the others. He didn't curse or weep. His face—what little she could see of it past the full, unruly beard—was pale, yet betrayed no sign of suffering save the slightest corrugation of his brow and the thin white line of his tightly pressed lips.

Perhaps the man was already dead and his body had begun to—

His eyes fluttered, then slowly opened. He stared upward for the longest time, then took a measured breath. His gaze settled on her. "Are you among the living, ma'am?" he asked, his deep voice languid and graveled. "Or the dead?"

Despite the serious nature of his question, Lizzie felt her mouth briefly curve. "I am among the living, sir. As are you." Though for how much longer he would inhabit this realm, she couldn't say. Surely the sands of his hourglass were nearly spent. She knelt beside him. Seeing him more closely, she realized he was older than most of the other soldiers she'd seen. Her age at least, if not a few years older. "You're at Carnton, the home of Colonel John McGavock. In Franklin, Tennessee," she added.

His eyes closed briefly again. "The handsome estate we passed some time earlier. On our way into battle. I remember . . ."

His lucidity confirmed, she took note of the stripes sewn onto his jacket. "What is your name, Captain?"

"Roland Ward Jones, ma'am. First Battalion, Mississippi Sharpshooters. Adams' Brigade." He started to move his arm and grimaced.

Lizzie reached out, wondering how to help him, when she saw that part of his right hand had also been torn away, the remaining flesh singed and blackened with spent gunpowder. She felt a stab of sorrow for him, wondering again how he was abiding the pain, much less how he was still alive.

"Miss Clouston! You're here."

She looked up to see Dr. Phillips, who promptly knelt beside them and began assessing the captain's wounds. Lizzie read the surgeon's expression and knew the news was not good.

"Captain, grapeshot has mangled both of your thighs. Your right is shattered, and your left is badly shredded. Grapeshot also took part of your hand, I see."

Something in the doctor's manner, in his tone, gave Lizzie the sense that the two men knew each other, or at least had met before this moment. The captain's expression—still calm and focused—didn't alter when the surgeon gently gripped his shoulder.

"Captain Jones, there's an excellent chance that I can mend your left leg. But your right . . ." He leveled his gaze. "I'm afraid the only course of action there is to amputate, as I'm certain you've already ascertained. And even then, taken together, the extent of your injuries may yet prove fatal. I'm so sorry."

The words, kindly delivered and without a stroke of hesitation, felt like a knife plunged into her chest, and Lizzie clenched her jaw to quell the emotion. She didn't know this man, and death hovered in every corner of the house. Yet she couldn't help but feel for him, having come so far and having endured so much. Then to receive such news.

"You are right, Doctor," Captain Jones replied, wincing as he covered his shattered hand with his whole one. "But I don't intend to have that leg cut off, and—"

Lizzie wouldn't have believed it if she hadn't seen it. But a slow-coming smile—one that touched the intensity of his gray eyes first—passed over his face.

"—I don't intend to die, sir. So I want to hold on to what is left of me."

Dr. Phillips shook his head. "One's intentions can only carry them so far in life, Captain Jones. And while I deeply appreciate your bravery and all you've done for the Confederacy . . ." He paused. "Your skill in marksmanship and your war record are campfire fodder, as I'm guessing you're already aware."

Lizzie watched the captain's smile fade.

"But the severity of this particular leg wound is such that it's simply not possible for the limb to be salvaged. Much less for me to guarantee that I can sustain your life. Though I'll do everything I can."

"I'm not asking you to sustain my life, good doctor. That is a feat only the Almighty can undertake. What I'm asking is that you patch me up as best you're able. *Without* taking my leg."

Seconds passed and Lizzie waited, looking between the two men.

With great effort the captain extended his good hand, and Dr. Phillips, briefly closing his eyes, finally accepted.

"We'll get some morphine into you, Captain, then bring you back shortly. I'll give you all I've got within me. But if I determine that the only chance for you to live is to take your leg, then by God Almighty . . . I'll take it."

Lizzie accompanied Dr. Phillips into Winder's bedroom but felt someone's attention and glanced back. Captain Jones was still watching them, an attendant with a syringe at his side, and she thought again of his comment. *I'm not asking you to sustain my life, good doctor. That is a feat only the Almighty can undertake.* That was precisely what she'd been thinking at the time.

She admired the man's courage and his will to live, especially in the face of such suffering. But it would take nothing short of heaven's intervention for that to happen. She tilted her head in silent acknowledgment, and though she detected no change in his expression, she somehow sensed a reciprocation.

Both windows in Winder's bedroom had been thrown open, and a stiff, cold breeze billowed in, making it even colder than outside in the hallway. Though the room faced the front of the house and the battlefield lay to the back, the sound of artillery still boomed through the open windows, the scream of bullets traveling across the open fields to ricochet off the surrounding hills. And still the explosions came. With each one she imagined yet more soldiers being blown apart. Just like the injured, bleeding men who occupied Winder's bed and the chairs by the brick hearth, and who either sat or lay on the floor, watching Dr. Phillips—and her, now—as each awaited his turn.

A shirtless soldier lay on a makeshift operating table—Winder's bedroom door, she realized, balanced on two sawhorses—and she moved closer to stand beside him. It took every bit of her concentration not to look at his arm—or what was left of it. Artillery of some sort had all but shattered his elbow.

The soldier shivered, likely from the trauma and the chill. Or maybe he was thinking about what was ahead. He peered up at her and managed a smile of sorts, his face upside down to hers. "You're a mite kinder to the eyes, ma'am, than them docs are."

Perceiving a generous nature, Lizzie leaned closer, reminded of her brother, Johnny. Younger than her by only a year, Johnny and she had grown up being especially close. Last she'd heard, his regiment had been sent to South Carolina. She prayed he was safe and unharmed. This man was younger by a few years, she guessed, and she so wanted to put him at ease. Never mind that her insides were quaking.

"And I'm inclined to believe, soldier, that someone has already been administering chloroform in my absence."

He laughed, or tried to. The sound came out hoarse, and she recognized the fear in his eyes. She also saw Dr. Phillips in her peripheral vision, readying his instruments—a bone saw on the table—and she reached for strength beyond her own.

"I've got a letter, ma'am," the patient continued, "in my shirt pocket over there—"

"I'll see to your letter for you," she said. "Should that time come." She gently touched the soldier's temple, much as she did Winder's when he fell and skinned a knee. "What is your name?" she asked, instinctively moving her hand to shield his vision from the bone saw and other instruments, as if he didn't already know what was coming. Same as every other man in the room.

He swallowed. "My name's James, ma'am. Second Lieutenant James Campbell Shuler." His composure faltered as uncertainty flooded his eyes. "Fifteenth Mississippi Infantry, Adams'—" His voice broke, and he grimaced. "Adams' Brigade."

Lizzie nodded. The same brigade as Captain Jones, she noted, then saw that the doctor was ready. "My name is Miss Clouston, Lieutenant Shuler. And Dr. Phillips here is going to take excellent care of you."

"Take that cloth and bottle there, Miss Clouston," Dr. Phillips instructed in his kind but forthright manner. "Hold the cloth over the patient's nose. Like this . . ." He demonstrated. "Then slowly—*very* slowly—drip the chloroform onto the cloth. You need to saturate the cloth while also not dousing it too quickly. Remember, we need to use that sparingly. And stop when he goes limp. When the bottle is empty, refill it from the can of chloroform on the floor there. Now, soldier—"

The doctor reached behind him for a glass Lizzie hadn't noticed before.

"—Colonel McGavock, the generous owner of this estate, has donated several bottles of Tennessee whiskey. And each man who lies on this table gets a shot if he wants one. So would you care to—"

"Yes, Doc, please. I would."

With Lizzie's help, the young lieutenant rose up slightly, accepted the glass, and downed the amber liquid in one swallow. He leaned back again, his expression one of gratitude. Lizzie eyed the bottle surreptitiously.

The doctor set the glass aside. "When we administer the chloroform, you might feel like you're going to suffocate at first, Lieutenant. But I promise you won't. Just breathe through it, son. If I can save your arm, I will. And if I can't, I'll make it quick and clean. And Miss Clouston here will make sure you're not awake for any of it."

Judging by the volume of Dr. Phillips's voice, Lizzie gathered the instructions were meant for everyone in the room, not only Lieutenant Shuler. The young man stiffened his jaw and nodded, then looked up at her, and she felt a weight of responsibility along with the threat of tears. But she wrestled them back, knowing that to shed even one would only add to the already enormous burden these men carried. And giving in to tears might somehow undermine the confidence they had in this surgeon. A confidence they needed and that she sorely wanted to share. The clock on the mantel sounded and she looked up.

A quarter of six.

She tented the cloth over the patient's nose, recalling what she'd read about this procedure some time ago in one of the military publications Colonel McGavock received. She carefully tilted the bottle of chloroform as the author of the article—and Dr. Phillips—had instructed, aware of the slight tremor in her hand. And of the lieutenant watching her.

She willed a steadiness to her voice. "Breathe deeply, Lieutenant Shuler. I'll be right here when you wake up."

Two minutes later the lieutenant noticeably relaxed. Two minutes more, and he went limp.

The surgeon immediately set to work examining the wound and probing for shrapnel. Three oil lamps lined up on Winder's dresser beside the makeshift operating table cast a burnt-orange glow, and the trio of flames flickered and danced as the breeze rushed across the clear glass chimneys.

Atop the dresser was the novel she'd placed there earlier that morning, and in her mind's eye Lizzie could see Winder as he'd stood only hours ago buttoning up his shirt. He'd yammered on and on, enthusiasm building, about the book she'd planned to begin reading to the children at bedtime.

A Christmas Carol by Charles Dickens. Or the title Winder found much more intriguing, *A Ghost Story of Christmas*. She'd read the opening sentence to him and he was hooked, as she knew any seven-year-old boy would be. She'd been saving the book for this time of year. But needless to say, they would not begin reading tonight.

Dr. Phillips reached for the scalpel. "Time is crucial, Miss Clouston. We have a lot of men and only so much whiskey and chloroform. So keep a close eye on his respiration."

"Yes, sir."

Lizzie told herself to look away, but couldn't.

The doctor made a deep incision above the point of injury and cut through skin and muscle clear down to the bone, leaving a flap of skin on either side. He tied off the arteries and scraped the bone clean, then reached for the bone saw. The sight of blood had never bothered her, but the first pass of the blade sent a shiver through her that she felt to her core.

She broke out in a cold sweat and angled her body toward the window, grateful for the icy wind on her face. She filled her lungs with it. Yet she still had to keep watch on the rise and fall of the soldier's chest, which meant seeing the doctor's movements from the corner of her eye. As if hearing the sound of what he was doing wasn't enough.

"Colonel McGavock tells me you're the children's governess, Miss Clouston," Dr. Phillips said, never looking up. "So you're a teacher by training?"

"That's right," she whispered, surprised her voice held. She took a deep breath and feared this might push her beyond her capabilities.

"Well, as a teacher, I'm assuming you're versed in several languages. I know some Latin, of course, but that's where my fluency in languages abruptly ends."

Lizzie dared glance back. Did the man seriously think this was the time for conversation? He looked up at her and smiled. A quick gesture, scarcely there before it was gone again, and he'd refocused on his work. She realized then what he was doing. This was for her benefit, not his.

"Yes, Dr. Phillips, I'm versed in several languages. Latin and French, and some German. Though my German is rusty from disuse."

"And I believe I detect a soft Scottish burr to your voice on occasion."

She nodded. "My father was born in Scotland. He tried his best to pass along his accent to me when I was a 'wee bairn.'" She spoke the words with the lilt of her heritage. "But my mother is from Kentucky, so his efforts were thwarted from the outset. My father's a druggist here in Franklin, and I've worked for the McGavocks for almost eight years now. They're more like family to me than employer."

"They seem like a fine family, Miss Clouston. Would I be correct to assume, taking into account your father's profession, that you know your way around a medicinal cupboard?"

"You would. My father taught me a great deal, which has come in handy being a governess."

"I would imagine."

He continued to speak, telling her how he'd chosen medicine as his career. She appreciated the opportunity to focus on the ease and confidence in his voice, and she drew strength from it.

After a moment he paused and leaned closer to examine his progress. "When the bones splinter, they shatter into hundreds of sharp little pieces, like knives. Hence, the minié ball striking a bone doesn't permit much debate about amputation. And a minié ball—or grapeshot, for that matter—to the gut is almost always fatal."

It occurred to her then that all the soldiers she'd seen who'd suffered abdominal wounds were on the floor below. Now she could guess why, and she found herself grateful in a way she hadn't been before that men such as Dr. Phillips knew how to mend and sew the body back together again. Odd how war had a way of leveling out life. Of making what once seemed so important—such as propriety and decorum in conversation—not quite so significant. And in turn, it made what truly mattered—people, taking care of one another, *life*—of utmost urgency.

Sweat poured from the doctor's face as, with a muted *thud*, the appendage fell to the carpet. It was a sound similar to Winder's dropping his ball on the floor. A sound Lizzie had never paid much mind to before, but would never forget from this day forward.

With a tool resembling a scalpel, only thicker, he continued his labors while Lizzie noted a difference in the patient's breathing.

"Now to sew him up and we'll be done." Dr. Phillips gestured. "Miss Clouston, he's beginning to—"

But she already had the chloroform and cloth in hand. She arranged the cloth over his nose and counted. Soon the lieutenant went limp again. Her sensibilities sufficiently numbed, she watched the doctor cover the remaining stump of bone with skin and muscle tissue before expertly suturing it closed.

He stood back and wiped his brow with the back of his sleeve. "We leave a drainage hole. Because if the wound doesn't heal properly and gangrene sets in, then we risk the sutures bursting. And a second amputation might be necessary."

She nodded. "I've seen gangrene before."

"At this stage, a surgical fever is our worst enemy." Dr. Phillips motioned to attendants in the hallway, and Lieutenant Shuler, who was slowly coming to, was carried and laid on the floor by the hearth. Lizzie looked at the clock on the mantel.

Almost six o'clock. It had taken scarcely more than ten minutes for the surgeon to remove the lieutenant's arm. She looked around the room—so many men—besides those waiting in the hallway. She glanced behind her and saw Captain Jones where he still lay on the floor, unmoving. His eyes were closed. She hoped he hadn't—

"Miss Clouston."

At Dr. Phillips's voice, she looked back to find that another soldier was already atop the table, shirtless and waiting. Cloth and chloroform in hand, she administered the anesthetic, her loathing for this war increasing with every passing second.

Roland drifted on a wave of morphine, welcoming the drug's power to relieve the pain, if only for a little while. He heard a sound, moving toward him from far away . . .

A child's laugh. *Lena.*

Her girlish giggles tugged on heartstrings already worn thin and stretched to near breaking. As long as he lived, he'd never forget the music of her laughter. Too much time had passed since he'd been home. Since he'd seen her and Susan. He hoped they were faring well in his absence. That they weren't having to do without. Memories of his and Susan's final night together during his last furlough—nearly a year ago now—drifted toward him. He could see her face, so beautiful, smiling up at him as she lay in his arms.

"I knew you'd come home to me," she had whispered. "As I begged of you so many times in my letters."

"I will always come home to you, Weet. Always."

She'd smiled at his use of the playful nickname he'd given her, and then—

Before the memory was fully formed, another came rushing forward. Overbearing and unwelcome, it attempted to displace the former. But he shoved it aside, not willing to allow it, despite its insistence. Instead, he clenched his eyes tight and drew the thoughts of his wife and child close, guarding them as though he were guarding his life. Because he was. They were his life.

But gradually the memories began to break apart, as they always did, until finally they scuttled and scattered beneath the weight of the unrelenting truth. The breaking wave of loss washed through him again. His eyes began to burn, whether from reality or the remnants of the choking smoke clouding the battlefield, he couldn't say. He knew Susan and Lena weren't home. And yet they were. Only not a home he'd ever visited.

While part of him wished he could join them, he couldn't forget what had happened on the battlefield after he'd been shot. Then he heard her. He heard Weet's voice. It was impossible, he knew. But . . .

"Susan," he whispered. "My love . . . Are you there? Are you and Lena—"

"Captain Jones," came the reply. "Can you hear me?"

Disappointment knifed deep, severing the echo of Weet's precious voice. Roland slowly opened his eyes to a murky wash of darkness haloed by golden light. He blinked, trying to clear his blurred vision and half wondering if he were slipping through the shroud of this life and into the next. Then shadows draping strangely familiar ceilings and walls took on gradual clarity, and he remembered where he was. Carnton . . .

He'd been here before. A year or so back, maybe. Had delivered supplies to the kitchen with a fellow captain and sharpshooter. Slowly, as his thoughts cleared, his surroundings began to register with him. As did the pain.

The piteous moans of soldiers around him encouraged the groans harnessed deep inside his chest to strong-arm their way out. But he pressed his lips tighter and clenched his teeth until he feared his jaw might break from the effort. He couldn't do that to his men. They looked to him for courage and strength. He couldn't fail them now. Only, how many of his men were left? How many had—

"Captain Jones," the soft voice said again, closer this time.

Then he saw her, the woman from earlier, holding up an oil lamp.

"Can you hear me, sir?"

"Yes," he ground out, his composure slipping. He tried to swallow, but his parched throat denied the effort.

"Here—" She held a cup to his lips and he drank.

The cool wetness slid down his throat, reviving his voice while also awakening his senses to the crushing pain in his legs and right hand.

"Dr. Phillips will be back in about ten minutes, Captain Jones. You're next in line for surgery."

Then he heard it—the rumble of artillery. He took a steadying breath. "They're still fighting."

"Yes," she whispered, her simple response weighed down with meaning.

"What . . . time is it?"

She looked across the hallway. "A quarter till eight."

Roland closed his eyes, and emotion escaped their corners and edged down his temples. The battlefield—a mile and a half of wide open plain, a longer distance than George Pickett's famed charge at the height of Gettysburg—had been a slaughter pen of smoke and fire. In full view of the enemy. And with no way to penetrate the Federal earthworks, or so it had seemed. Yet somehow at least one division had. He'd witnessed it through the smoke and haze after he'd been shot. What had first been an advancement through a hail of bullets and cannon fire had turned into a savage brawl. A ferocious melee of men bludgeoning, gouging, and bayonetting each other to death around what had appeared to be a cotton gin. But as more Federals had joined the fight, the tide had turned, leaving his Confederate brothers nowhere to retreat. Roland gritted his teeth.

As the reddish sun had dipped beyond the hills in a sea of molten bronze, men had been mown down, wave after wave of infantry advancing gallantly only to wither beneath the onslaught of long-range artillery fire. The three-inch ordnance rifles and twelve-pound Napoleons had torn gaping holes in Loring's Division until body upon body was piled up in the trenches. So many of them men he'd fought with for the past three years. All gone now. As was the dream of the Confederacy.

Heaviness filled his chest. He'd seen the battlefield, what they were up against. And to believe that the South still stood a chance was a fool's errand, or worse. In his gut he knew the truth—no matter how much he didn't want to accept it.

"I need you to do something for me, Miss—"

"Clouston, Captain. Miss Elizabeth Clouston."

"Miss Clouston," he repeated, pushing through the drug-induced fog hazing his mind, searching for a way to phrase his question in a manner that would compel her to say yes. Because even from what little he'd observed of her behavior thus far, instinct told him she would keep her word. "Do you . . . believe in signs, ma'am?"

Her brow knit. "In signs?"

He held her gaze, keen to its slightest alteration. "You remember what I told the doc earlier, about how I don't intend to die. Leastwise, not tonight."

She nodded. "I remember, Captain."

"Earlier, after I'd been shot. I was lying facedown in the dirt. Felt like my whole body was on fire, and ten thousand flying bullets plowing the ground around me. But then, when I turned and looked up . . . I saw the autumn moon, Miss Clouston. Full and clear. Over my right shoulder."

Her eyes flickered with acknowledgment, and he felt the scant hope within him begin to stir.

"Don't get me wrong, ma'am. I—" Stabbing pain shot down the length of his left leg then back up again, taking his breath with it, and the urge to cry out nearly overwhelmed his resolve. He pressed the back of his head hard into the carpeted floor and drew in air through clenched teeth.

"Why don't you rest, Captain. You can tell me all this after the doctor—"

"No, ma'am." His breath came heavy. "I've got to say my piece now. While I can."

She lifted the cup for him to drink again, but he shook his head.

"I don't hold to superstition. Be it about a new moon or any other kind." He rushed to get the words out. "And I don't think that just because I saw that moon over my right shoulder I'm going to live. I've never believed in luck, ma'am. I think things happen for a reason." He took a breath. "And as I lay there watching good men die all around me, with those bullets raining down yet no more of them finding their way into me, I reckoned God was telling me I stood a chance. That I would make it through this."

She opened her mouth to say something, but he hurried to finish.

"I've seen these surgeries more times than I care to remember, and I've got a good mind how this will go. With the doc, I mean. Dr. Phillips is a good man. One of the best. But he's got way more men than me to deal with and not near enough time. He's got a hefty respect for gangrene too, which I share. But I don't want to lose my leg, ma'am. The doc's already going to take most of my hand."

He slowly lifted his right hand and held it before his face. Though he'd already examined the damage, seeing it again—and with her looking on—somehow made it worse. The appendage, all torn and bloodied, fingers broken and blunted, felt almost foreign to him, like it belonged at the end of someone else's arm. Not his.

"But my right leg . . . I aim to keep it, ma'am. Same as my left. So I'm asking you, Miss Clouston, if you'll be my voice in there. When the time comes and he reaches for that bone saw—which he *will* do— would you do that for me? I need you to promise me you'll do that."

She frowned, then briefly looked away. "Captain Jones, I don't feel as though I'm qualified to question the doctor's decisions. If he thinks that—"

"It's got nothing to do with being qualified, ma'am." He grimaced, the grapeshot lodged in his legs acting like hot pokers, branding him clear to the bone. "It's *my* leg. *My* life. And that's what I choose. And with everything in me, I believe the Almighty's on my side in this one."

The room began to sway. And though he was flat on the floor, he was gripped with the sensation of falling. He reached out with his good hand to grab hold of something solid—and she clasped his hand between hers and held on tight.

"It's the morphine, Captain. Close your eyes and rest. Dr. Phillips is back now, so we'll—"

"Not until you promise," he whispered, his voice hoarse. He tightened his grip. "Promise me, ma'am. Give me your word. *Please*."

He saw the stretcher bearers coming for him, heard the urgency in his own tone, and saw the conflict warring inside of her. She looked at him, biting her lower lip until it went nearly white. Then she nodded.

"I promise, Captain Jones. I'll be your voice. And you will keep that leg."

CHAPTER 4

"You know how this goes, Captain Jones." Dr. Phillips leaned over the operating table, his apron stained and bloodied. "I'm confident I can salvage your left leg. And I'll do all I can to save your right."

Cloth and chloroform in hand, Lizzie looked down to discover the captain staring up at her, pain riddling his gaze. But in the depths of those discerning gray eyes, she saw the reflection of the promise she'd made. But why had she made it? Even as the words had slipped past her lips moments earlier, she'd doubted whether she'd have the courage to fulfill the pledge. Dr. Phillips was the one with authority here, not she. Then, in a blink, Lizzie imagined another man lying before her.

If this were Towny, if he'd been wounded and had made this same request of someone, would she want that person to keep their word? To do their best to see that Towny's wishes were obliged? Knowing the answer to that question, she met Captain Jones's gaze with unflinching conviction and nodded.

"Yep, Doc. I know how this goes." The captain's gaze shifted. "But remember what we talked about earlier. When Miss Clouston was with us." He shot her a quick glance. "You recall what my wishes are, sir. Those still stand."

Dr. Phillips's eyes narrowed slightly. "When I became a doctor, I took an oath to—"

"I know all about that oath, Dr. Phillips. And I respect your honor and your word that stands behind it. Now please, sir, I'm asking you to respect mine."

The thrum of noise in the room fell to a hush, and Lizzie looked over to find soldiers watching them, staring at the doctor and the captain.

A muscle flinched in Dr. Phillips's cheek as he poured whiskey into a glass and handed it to the captain who, like the men before him, downed it in a single swallow. Lizzie could all but taste the liquid fire at the back of her throat, and though she didn't customarily partake of such spirits, she was beginning to wish she did.

The captain trained his focus on a point somewhere above her head, and the surgeon's curt nod in her direction told Lizzie what to do next.

She tented the cloth over Captain Jones's nose. "Take steady breaths, Captain," she said softly. "You may feel as if you're going to suffocate at first. But—"

His gaze locked with hers, and she would've sworn she felt something pass between them.

"—I assure you, you won't," she finished, sensing the surgeon's eagerness to commence. "I'll be here the entire time. And I'll be here when you awaken."

She gave the captain an almost imperceptible nod, and he closed his eyes. A scant handful of moments later, and his body went limp.

Dr. Phillips began cutting away the shredded remnants of the captain's trousers with scissors, and Lizzie confined her gaze to the captain's face. Thankfully, his once-white long-sleeved shirt, now gray, possessed length enough to maintain his decency—and to allay her momentary discomfort.

The doctor tended the captain's left leg first, probing for pieces of grapeshot and cleaning out the wound. Lizzie had read about grapeshot. But she'd not seen its results up close. Not like she had seen damage from a shotgun. Thanks to her brother, she'd learned how to hunt and shoot at a young age. Not that he'd had to twist her arm to learn. While she did know how to knit, quilt, and sew well enough, she'd always been less fascinated with the pastimes assigned the gentler sex and far more enamored with those of the opposite.

At ten years of age, she routinely hunted with Johnny and their father. By thirteen, she and Johnny would strike out by themselves, and they rarely returned home empty-handed. So she'd witnessed firsthand the damage a shotgun was capable of inflicting. But grapeshot . . . The mass of small iron balls and slugs—resembling a cluster of grapes when assembled—was packed tightly into a stand before being rammed down the barrel of a cannon tube. Upon firing, the stand of grapeshot exploded, sending ammunition in all directions, increasing the likelihood of hitting the target. And when that target was a man—Lizzie tightened her jaw and reminded herself to breathe—the metal balls ripped through the flesh like a butcher knife through fine silk, making the grapeshot devastatingly effective. Especially at close range.

She detected a shift in Captain Jones's breathing and tented the cloth over his nose. Then slowly, very slowly—*drip, drip, drip*—she added more chloroform, and his head lolled to one side again.

He had strong facial features and was a handsome man in a rough, rugged sense. All except for his gray eyes, which had revealed a kindness that brooked no argument, and that thoroughly convinced the onlooker of his honor at first glance.

She observed Dr. Phillips as he sutured and prayed for him, for Captain Jones, and for all the men filling this house and the grounds outside. Through the open window to the backyard she could see lanterns dotting the lawn. The wounded kept coming.

The surgery took longer than she'd anticipated, and she detected fatigue in Dr. Phillips. In the way he paused to roll his neck and shoulders and in the darkened half-moons showing beneath his eyes.

She'd overheard soldiers speaking earlier and learned that for the better part of the past week, the Army of Tennessee had slept little and eaten less. They'd marched the near 250 miles from Atlanta up through Georgia and into Tennessee to the town of Columbia. They'd covered ground quickly in order to catch up with the Federal Army with the hope of flanking their troops and drawing them into battle. When Hood's forces arrived in Spring Hill, a town that lay only ten miles southeast, by yesterday evening, Hood had apparently given orders to cut off the main road so the Federals couldn't push on toward Nashville. He wanted to fight them then and there while the Rebels had them boxed in on either side. But from what she could decipher by listening to the soldiers' discussions, the plan to capture General Schofield's army had apparently come unhinged. Somehow Schofield managed to move his army past them unmolested, straight up the main road during the dark of night. Two of the soldiers said they'd actually seen regiment after regiment of Federal soldiers quietly passing by them not three hundred feet away. But they were only privates, they said, and since they'd been given no orders to attack, they stayed by their fires and did nothing. Hence, General Schofield's army had arrived first in Franklin earlier that morning—and the die had been cast. The soldiers described General Hood as being enraged when he learned about the missed opportunity.

Not for the first time that evening, Lizzie thought of Fountain Carter and his family and hoped they were safe and far from the dangers of battle. But if they *were* still in the house, she prayed the Federal officers who had most likely taken quarter there were treating them well.

She sent up prayers for her parents and siblings who lived near downtown Franklin too. They were a safer distance away and well behind the line of enemy cannons, but still . . . Knowing her parents, she knew they were worried sick about her and the McGavocks. She'd send them word at first opportunity. But first, to make it through this night.

"I'm finished with this leg, Miss Clouston."

Pulled back to the moment, Lizzie nodded.

"Now for the right leg." The doctor gestured. "I'll move to the other side of the table. And I'll need you to hand me my instruments, if you would."

Lizzie stepped to one side to make room for him to pass, all while keeping close watch on Captain Jones.

"If you see an attendant, Miss Clouston, we need more bandages and suture thread. We're nearly out."

"Yes, sir. I'll keep watch."

But mostly Lizzie watched the doctor as he examined the captain's right leg.

"Straight forceps." Dr. Phillips pointed, and Lizzie placed the surgical instrument in his palm.

As the doctor extracted the grapeshot, Captain Jones's breathing altered for a second time. Lizzie administered more chloroform, and he soon drifted off again somewhere beyond the confines of Winder's bedroom. Maybe, as earlier, he was dreaming of home.

He'd called out for Susan. His wife, Lizzie presumed. He'd also whispered the name Lena. Their daughter, perhaps. Or his sister. Did Mrs. Roland Jones know where her husband was right now? Doubtful, given the soldiers' care not to include details in their letters that might give the enemy a foothold.

What would Captain Jones's wife say about her husband's decision? Would she be for it or against it? Keep the leg? Or amputate?

Even without the benefit of knowing her, Lizzie felt secure in her speculation that the woman would want whatever stood the best chance of keeping her husband alive. Whatever would enable him to return to her. Much as she herself wanted Towny to return safely home. Only—a twinge of something tugged at her, an emotion she couldn't quite identify—wanting your husband to return to you and wanting him to "return safely home" weren't quite the same thing.

Dr. Phillips's heavy sigh drew her attention, and she looked up.

He shook his head. "Even if I set the bone and suture the torn tissue and muscles, that leg will never be of use to him again. There's too much damage. And choosing to leave so injured a limb intact means it will only atrophy with time. And long before that, the severity of the wound will most certainly invite gangrene."

She'd known the surgeon for scarcely more than four hours, yet already she'd learned to read his expressions. The deep furrows in his brow did not bode well. Sadness, even remorse, swept his countenance, and he rubbed the back of his neck as though weighing his options—and not liking any of them.

He held out his hand. "Scalpel."

Lizzie didn't move.

"*Scalpel*, Miss Clouston."

"You . . . can't take his leg, sir," she said softly. "You know what he told you."

The doctor stared, clearly unaccustomed to being challenged. "I told the captain I would do my best. Which I have done. There's no surgeon alive who could save this leg. It's too far gone. Now, hand me the scalpel. And the bone saw."

Feeling almost as though she were outside her body, watching her own actions, she shook her head. "No . . . Dr. Phillips. I cannot." She hurried to explain. "I gave Captain Jones my word that I wouldn't allow you to take his—"

"You gave him your word," he repeated, leveling a stare. "You don't even know this man, Miss Clouston. I do. For the past three years I've patched up his wounds. I've shared his campfire at night as we've written to our wives, all while praying this war would come to a swift and victorious end. I've seen him advance on the enemy with courage and determination that inspired his entire regiment. So please understand that I am not making this decision lightly. He will die if I don't take off this leg, and he may yet die even if I do. But his chances for recovery are far greater if I amputate. Now hand me the scalpel."

The words crackled with warning, and only then did Lizzie realize the room had gone silent.

"Dr. Phillips," she began, surprised that the trembling in her hands hadn't yet reached her voice. "You are a most gifted surgeon, that is undeniably clear. And that you care for these men is clear too. But it seems only fitting that a soldier—especially one as dedicated as you know Captain Jones to be—should be able to choose the manner in which he dies. And though I am no doctor," she added, "judging from the severity of his wounds, he should have met his Maker on the battlefield tonight. But he didn't. And he believes the Almighty's hand was in that. So please"—her throat tightened with fatigue—"I ask that you honor this soldier's request . . . sir."

Dr. Phillips held her gaze, his own stony and unrelenting. Then he looked briefly at the room full of soldiers. And though she didn't turn to see them, she sensed they all agreed with her.

Finally the doctor nodded. A short, unconvincing gesture. "Needle and suture thread, Miss Clouston."

Lizzie gave him a weak smile.

"Don't see this as a victory, ma'am. That pledge you made has likely sentenced one of the finest soldiers I've ever known to an agonizing death."

CHAPTER 5

Two stretcher bearers carried Captain Jones to Winder's bed and carefully laid him down. The captain didn't so much as stir, his coloring still far too pale. Watching him from across the room, Lizzie prayed that the doctor's prognosis would not come to pass and that the autumn moon Captain Jones had seen—the same moon whose silvery light spilled in through the open window—would indeed prove to have been a prophetic sign of some kind. However unlikely that possibility seemed at present.

Lizzie squeezed her eyes tight and rubbed her temples, a dull headache starting at the back of her head. Then, remembering, she called to one of the stretcher bearers.

The young man looked back. "Ma'am?"

"We need more bandages and suture thread, please. We're almost out of both."

"Sorry, ma'am, but there aren't any more bandages. We've checked with the other docs for suture thread too. But they're out, same as y'all."

Dr. Phillips joined them. "You've spoken with the surgeons outside?"

"Yes, sir, Doc. They've already taken to cuttin' up the patients' shirts or coats, if they have 'em. And they're usin' that to staunch the blood and wrap the wound."

"But it's so cold outside." Lizzie frowned. "They need their coats."

"Better bein' cold, ma'am, than bleedin' to death." The attendant gestured toward the hallway. "The Negro woman from downstairs set off to ask the owners of the house if they have anything else we could use. She hasn't come back yet."

Lizzie stepped forward. "I can tell you where to fetch more materials for bandages. If you'll take the stairs down to the entrance hall, then go through either the dining room or farm office on your left, you'll see a short staircase leading down to the kitchen, located in the east wing. Cross the kitchen to the narrow staircase and—" Seeing the confused look on the young man's face, she turned. "Doctor, if you'll permit me, I'll fetch the materials myself."

"Go." Dr. Phillips nodded. "Sam here can fill in for you while you're gone. But please, ma'am, don't delay."

With a last look at the captain, who had yet to stir, Lizzie maneuvered her way through the men lying on the bedroom floor, then through those in the hallway. She'd almost reached the landing when she spotted Tempy bustling up the stairs.

"Tempy! I'm glad to see you. I'm headed to my room to get the extra blanket to cut up and use for bandages. Do you know of anything else we can—"

"We already doin' the same thing down below, Miss Clouston." The older woman's breath came hard. "Scavengin' from everywhere. We done used all the old linens, the napkins, most of the towels. Missus McGavock sent me up here to fetch all the sheets. She tol' me to get the colonel's shirts too, along with her day dresses." Tempy leaned in, her brown eyes going wide. "She even said to fetch her underclothes!"

Working in tandem, Lizzie and Tempy hurriedly gathered the sheets from the family bedrooms, which were all filled with wounded men. Thirty soldiers in each room, at least. Then they collected several of Mrs. McGavock's dresses and her undergarments, and carried the bundles of clothing and linens downstairs to the kitchen, where they hurriedly cut them into strips. Slicing through the finely woven fabrics didn't feel quite real—until she saw Mrs. McGavock's best Sunday dress in ribbons on the kitchen floor.

Then Lizzie remembered the blanket in her own room and climbed the narrow staircase to get it. Her bedroom was dark and the air chilled, but she didn't bother lighting a lamp. She opened the door to the wardrobe and retrieved the blanket from the top shelf, then grabbed her three remaining day dresses from the hooks. Thinking of how much Mrs. McGavock had already sacrificed, she reached for the two scarves hanging there as well, then closed the door to the wardrobe. Her gaze fell to the trunk at the end of her bed, and she paused. But no. She couldn't use that. No one would expect her to do such a thing. *Better bein' cold, ma'am, than bleedin' to death.* If it were Towny who was wounded and needed surgery . . .

Her unyielding response to that silenced all internal quibbling. Lizzie opened the trunk and gently lifted the paper-swathed bundle on top and carried it back down to the kitchen with the rest.

But when Tempy saw her unwrapping it . . . "Oh no, ma'am! Not that, Miss Clouston. You been workin' on this for months now. Your Lieutenant Townsend, he wouldn't be wantin' you to—"

"What if Lieutenant Townsend is somewhere injured tonight, Tempy? Wounded and needing surgery? What if there was nothing to be used for him?" Her eyes flooded, but she drew in a fortifying breath and held up the simple white cotton dress, the pale pink flowers she'd sewn along the waistline nearly disappearing in the dim lamplight.

She laid the dress out on the kitchen worktable and held the scissors poised to cut, wanting to remember it. "I can make another one," she said, more to herself than aloud. "Lieutenant Townsend and I aren't planning on being married until after the war is over anyway."

"Which might be soon, from what I been hearin' the soldiers say."

Lizzie looked up.

"I heard 'em talkin', Miss Clouston. They say the Army of Tennessee is takin' a real lickin' tonight. We got near three hundred men here in the house. And that ain't countin' all them others out in the yard, in the barn and outbuildin's. And they tell me there's hundreds more lyin' dead on the field, ma'am. And even more dyin' out there as we speak. Both ours and theirs."

Lizzie briefly closed her eyes, and a single tear slipped past her resolve. "And knowing that, Tempy, makes what I'm about to do feel so much less significant by comparison."

She sliced across the carefully stitched hem of the garment all the way up through the bodice—a clean, even line—imagining how the delicate pink roses at the waist would soon be turned to crimson.

It took surprisingly little time for the two of them to reduce the stack of fine shirts and dresses, including the blanket, linens, and undergarments, into strips for bandages. They divided them into two baskets.

Rubbing her temple, Lizzie indicated for Tempy to precede her up the short flight of kitchen stairs. "I'm going to get a drink of water, then I'll be right up."

Tempy nodded. "You can take yours on upstairs, Miss Clouston. I'll make sure the rest gets handed out on the main floor and then outside. I got a mind where we can get some suture thread too, but I got to check with the colonel first." Tempy climbed the stairs, her soft tread a familiar sound.

Lizzie set aside her basket, fetched a glass, and filled it with water from the pitcher on the counter. She drank, willing the ache in her head to subside. She glanced about the kitchen, at the orderliness of the pots and pans hanging on the wall, the various cooking utensils nestled between them. Then her focus moved to the fire burning low and white hot in the hearth. How quiet, how peaceful it was down here in comparison to upstairs.

Although she could still hear the faint hum of chaos that resided only steps away in the main rooms of the house, this wing of the home that housed the kitchen—part of the original house Colonel McGavock's father had built near the turn of the century—felt like another world away. It was still. And quiet. Death did not reign here. Nor did pools of blood puddle on the stone floor.

The knot wedged tight at the base of her throat threatened to break loose, same as it had all evening. But she wrestled to hold it in check, knowing that if she gave in to it now, the tears would be impossible to stem. The time for that would come soon enough.

MOMENTS LATER, LIZZIE passed through the farm office, then the entrance hall, the basket of bandages on her hip. She noticed that several of the wounded men she'd seen earlier in the evening were no longer there. And still the stretcher bearers came and went through the front door, bringing in the wounded as quickly as they carried out the dead.

She looked down the hallway. Though she couldn't hear his voice, she saw the soldier who'd been repeating the Twenty-Third Psalm, head bowed, his lips still moving.

"Oh God . . . ," came a twisted cry from another room. "Give me forty grains of morphine and let me die!"

Drawn by the desperation in the voice, Lizzie peered into the dining room and saw an officer lying on the floor. She wondered why he was calling for forty grains of morphine when two grains was a regular dose. But as she drew closer and saw the extent of his injuries, she knew why, and had trouble containing the tide of emotion rising inside her.

"That's Colonel Nelson of the Twelfth Louisiana," a voice said beside her.

Chin trembling, she turned to see another of the surgeons.

"Both of the colonel's legs were crushed by a cannonball, and his gut is riddled with grapeshot."

"Nothing can be done?" she whispered.

He shook his head.

"And no morphine?"

He winced. "We're running very low. We need to save what we have for the men going under the blade. Who stand a chance of living."

She nodded, loathing that such a choice had to be made.

"I've tried speaking to him," the doctor continued, "but he's out of his mind with pain."

"Give me forty grains of morphine," Colonel Nelson called out again, his eyes sinking deep into his head, exhaustion and pain contorting his features. "Oh, can't I die? My poor wife and child. What will become of my poor wife and child!"

"They brought him in here to die," the doctor said, respect deepening his tone, "due to his rank and fine military record. It seemed wrong to his men to leave him out there in the cold. And while I know it's most difficult, ma'am, it's truly best if we both continue where we can to nurture life instead of courting death."

Her throat aching to the point she could scarcely breathe, Lizzie nodded and hurried up the stairs with the basket, Colonel Nelson's pleas fading in volume but not in her memory. But when she reached Winder's bedroom, she stopped stone-still, certain her legs were about to buckle beneath her.

Captain Jones still lay in the bed where she'd left him—but with a cloth draped over his face.

CHAPTER 6

What had she done?

Lizzie felt the basket of bandages slipping from her grip and set it at her feet. She stared at the still form on the bed. She'd been so certain, so convinced by the captain's own confidence that it had apparently blinded her to what an experienced surgeon had known was best. She heard her own voice again as she'd taken a stand against Dr. Phillips's advised course of action.

Men had died all around her that night, were dying still. But in none of those other deaths had she been complicit. A wave of nausea swept through her, and she grabbed hold of the doorjamb.

"Miss Clouston! You're back."

She turned and saw a blurred image of Dr. Phillips standing by the operating table, the young attendant beside him still filling in for her. Scalpel in hand, the doctor gestured to the basket at her feet. "You're just in time. I'm nearly done here."

Lizzie lifted the basket that felt twice as heavy as before. And though her thoughts swirled and collided, the only words she could hear in her mind were, *I'm sorry. I'm sorry. I'm sorry.*

The attendant eagerly surrendered the chloroform and cloth, and Lizzie stood staring down into the boyish face of a young soldier whose left leg now lay separated from him in a basket on the floor. "Too much," she heard herself whisper, feeling a shaking starting deep inside her. "They've given too much." She swallowed. Brother fighting brother. Countryman fighting countryman. All the bloodshed and killing. For what? When would it end? She thought she was going to be sick.

"Miss Clouston, the chloroform."

Lizzie blinked to refocus and tented the cloth over the boy's nose. With each *drip, drip, drip* of the anesthetic, she saw blood. The blood these men—and boys—had spilled. Suddenly it didn't matter that she didn't agree with their reasons for fighting. Anger festered up inside her. How had the country come to this fatal brink? For all her training as a teacher, for all her learning, she had no answer. She had no idea—no power to wield—that would bring this war to an end. She tried to pray, but no words came that adequately conveyed the turmoil inside her, all around her.

She looked down at the young soldier before her and thought of his mother, whose heart would ache the first time she saw her son again, his body broken. Yet that mother would rejoice that her precious son was still alive. A joy that Captain Jones's wife would never experience.

"This is the last of the thread." Dr. Phillips finished suturing the wound and bandaged what was left of the boy's leg.

Lizzie felt the doctor's gaze on her and knew what he was waiting for. "I'm sorry," she whispered, making herself look into his eyes when it was the last thing she wanted to do.

He frowned. "You're sorry for what, Miss Clouston?"

She shook her head. "I should have allowed you to do what you knew was best, and now . . . Please forgive me, Dr. Phillips. I demonstrated poor judgment in taking up Captain Jones's cause. He was under the influence of morphine, and I"—she glanced back at the bed—"I should have taken that into account. I'm deeply sorry for my part in what happened."

"Captain Jones?" he repeated. He followed her gaze to the shrouded figure on the bed, then just as swiftly trailed back again. "Oh . . ." He sighed. "That's not the captain. Captain Jones is on the floor in front of the fire."

Lizzie searched his expression. Then, needing to see for herself, she stepped through the maze of men lying on the floor to the other side of Winder's bed and—a hiccupped breath escaped her lips—there was Captain Jones lying before the fire, his eyes closed. But the rhythmic lift and fall of his chest chased away her misgivings until guilt fled without a backward glance. Watching him, knowing the extent of his injuries and the pain he'd already endured, and would yet endure, she could all but feel his determined nature. The same determined nature that had convinced her to say yes when he'd asked for her pledge. She felt someone behind her and turned to see the doctor.

"He said the bed felt foreign to him after all these years of sleeping on the ground, so the stretcher bearers moved him down here."

Lizzie felt a rush of hope. "So he's going to be all right, you think?"

"No, Miss Clouston." His voice went somber. "I still do not think the best decision was made in Captain Jones's regard."

She swallowed.

"It goes against everything I've spent the last near twenty years studying and practicing, to not do everything I can to save a life. But," he added, briefly looking away, "my dedication to saving lives can sometimes blind me to doing what is right. Which is what you were doing, Miss Clouston. You are right—a soldier should be able to choose whether or not to keep his leg, even if that decision may cost him his life. If the captain does die, ma'am, you will not be responsible for his death. Nor, in truth, will I. Though I will carry the burden of my decision in that moment to my grave." He looked past her to Captain Jones. "You championed the wishes of a soldier in a moment when I needed to be reminded of what he wanted, not of what I thought was best. And if I may say so, Miss Clouston, you championed him exceedingly well."

Lizzie offered a dim smile. "Thank you, Dr. Phillips. But if he *does* die, know that I, too, will carry a portion of that burden for the rest of my days." She looked back at the captain. His eyes were still closed. Only then did she notice he clutched a piece of paper to his chest.

"Miss Clouston!"

Lizzie spotted Tempy standing in the doorway holding a cup and went to meet her. Lizzie looked inside. "Is that—"

"Suture thread, ma'am. Horsehair suture thread." Tempy beamed. "I had to get permission from the colonel first, to relieve his fine horses of their tails. But he said, 'Do it now, Tempy!' So I did. I boiled 'em up and they're ready for sewin', ma'am." Tempy pushed the cup into her hands and turned to leave.

"Dr. Phillips," Lizzie called, gently taking hold of Tempy's arm.

"What do we have here, Miss Clouston?" The doctor examined the contents of the cup.

"Genuine horsehair sutures, sir. Thanks to Tempy here."

He looked up. "And they're already boiled and ready to use?"

Tempy briefly bowed her head. "I took some outside to the other doctors too, sir."

Dr. Phillips nodded. "Well done. Now let's get back to work."

Lizzie gave Tempy a parting smile, then felt a light pressure on her arm.

Tempy looked up at her. "You doin' well too, Miss Clouston," she whispered, then glanced beyond her to the surgical table. "You doin' real well."

IT WAS HALF past nine when Lizzie first noticed it—a strange stillness moving toward them from the darkened fields outside. "Do you hear that, Doctor?"

"Hear what, Miss Clouston?"

She turned her face into the icy breeze blowing through the open bedroom window. "The silence."

Scalpel in hand, he stilled. His head came up slowly. His eyes narrowed. "No cannon fire."

"No gunfire either." She looked back. "Do you think it's over?"

He stared out the window, his expression a wash of cautious hope.

"I don't know. But let's pray to God it is." With a sigh, he returned to his work. "Let's finish up here, then I need to get some coffee and take a quick walk outside to check the progress with the other surgeons. I won't be but a few minutes, then we'll continue. If you're able."

Lizzie nodded, the headache from earlier still lingering. But at least it wasn't getting any worse.

Once Dr. Phillips finished and the stretcher bearers moved the soldier back to the floor, Lizzie checked on the wounded in the room, among them Captain Jones. His eyes were closed, but his steady breathing answered her most crucial question. She might have considered him asleep, if not for the firm set of his jaw. Despite his full beard, wild and unkempt, she could see the tension in him. Still, she wasn't eager to disturb him on the outside chance he was managing to find some rest.

She silently tallied the number of men Dr. Phillips had operated on since she'd begun assisting him. She counted twenty-one. Twenty-one men, all of whom had lost at least a portion of an arm, leg, or hand. Or combination thereof. And Dr. Phillips was only one of the near dozen doctors operating here tonight.

A book on the same table where the doctor's instruments lay drew her attention. *Manual of Military Surgery—Confederate Army*. She retrieved the book and opened the cover. 1863. Recently published. And it was illustrated, she noted with some trepidation as she flipped through the pages. The book was divided into chapter headings. "Surgical Diseases." "Gunshot Wounds." "On the Arteries." "On Amputations." And more.

She swiftly turned to the section on amputations and began reading the detailed description of the surgery she'd just witnessed Dr. Phillips performing. Each step was described in fastidious detail. But having experienced the surgery up close made reading the text definitely less impactful. She closed the book and looked about the room, still having difficulty accepting what was happening.

The grim realities of war simply would not meld with life as she'd known it within the walls of the McGavocks' home for the past several years. Yet every step she took, the carpet beneath her feet saturated with blood, told her she wasn't dreaming. And somehow she knew that the life and world she'd known were gone forever.

The groans and cries from the men continued to tear at her. There was so little she could do for them compared to their needs. She looked over to see Captain Jones's eyes open.

She knelt beside him. "Captain," she whispered. "Is there anything I can get you, sir?"

"A pint or two of Tennessee whiskey," he answered without hesitation, and a couple of the soldiers around him offered a hearty "Amen!" He looked over at her and gradually focused on her face. "But I'd be most grateful for a drink of water, ma'am."

Lizzie nodded. "Water, I can do."

She fetched the pail and ladle that Tempy had left in the hallway a moment earlier and spent the next several moments slaking Captain Jones's thirst along with that of the other men in the room. She couldn't fathom the pain they were enduring.

"Miss Clouston . . ."

She turned back. "Yes, Captain Jones."

"If you have a moment, ma'am, I'd be most grateful if you'd read this letter aloud to me."

"Of course." She set aside the bucket and pail.

Winder's Poynor chair, which sat in the corner, and which was named after the local craftsman who'd made it, was constructed for a young boy Winder's size, but had proven sturdy enough for her on several occasions. And since that was the only unoccupied chair in the room, she retrieved it and situated it beside the captain.

She took the piece of crinkled stationery he held and gently smoothed the paper on her skirt, then scanned the heading.

To Lieutenant R. W. Jones
Nashville, Tennessee
c/o Captain P. R. Leigh
of the Oakachickamas
Mississippi Volunteers

She recalled him saying earlier that he was from Mississippi. And a sharpshooter. She glanced down at his bandaged right hand, wondering which was his trigger finger. The forefinger on his left hand? Or the one that had once been on his right? Then it occurred to her . . . Lieutenant?

The letter must have been written before he'd been promoted to captain. She checked for a date and . . . sure enough. *December 11, 1861.* Almost three years ago. Which was a bit odd. She'd naturally assumed the missive would've borne a more recent date. She held the letter up to read.

"'My own Roland,'" she started softly, speaking loudly enough for him to hear while hoping others nearby could not.

"The long looked-for letter (for it seems an age to me) has come at last. I knew it was not negligence or forgetfulness on your part that deprived me of the pleasure of hearing from my absent Roland, as his last words were 'Weet, I will write as soon as I reach Nashville.' Roland, it's hard to be separated from you. I know full well that duty alone and a high sense of honor that ever prompts you to act has forced us thus apart."

Lizzie glanced up at him midparagraph, making sure he was still awake. Not only was he awake, but his expression held a longing that stirred within her a touch of envy toward the woman who was the recipient of this man's loyal affections. Sweeping aside the unexpected thought, she continued reading.

"Life here at Oak Hill is scarcely bearable without you. The house itself seems to mourn your absence along with me. I sent you a leaf clipped from my geranium that was given me by Bettie Cooke. It is growing very prettily. Write and—"

"Please move to the next paragraph, Miss Clouston."

He apparently knew the letter by heart, Lizzie noted, then did as he asked.

"How many sermons have you heard since you reached Nashville? I suppose you attend church regularly. Sister Ruthie and I walked to the garden to gather you a few flowers. On our return, we received a considerable fright from the alarm of fire. I ran as fast as I could for a few minutes, but soon found it was only soot burning in the chimney. You may be sure we felt relieved. You would have laughed could you have seen me running and screaming at every step. I am not as fleet as I once was."

Lizzie felt a little smile tug at her mouth and looked up to see the same on his. It felt good to share such a moment in the midst of deep shadows and pain.

"'How I wish you could be with us this quiet evening,'" she continued, reading a little ahead and finding it impossible not to compare the tone of her own letters to Towny with that of this letter from Mrs. Jones to her husband.

"What a vacancy caused in my heart by your absence could be filled were it in your power to form one of the circle around our fireside. I listen every evening after the train cars pass down below for your footstep on the front porch; could I but hear it what pleasure it would bring. I must cease my communication with you for tonight. Good night, and a thousand kisses to my beloved Roland. With the sustaining hope of seeing you home soon, I remain your loving wife . . . Weet."

Lizzie sat for a moment staring at the unique name and letting the beauty of the words and their sentiments sink in.

"Thank you, ma'am," he whispered, emotion in his voice.

"It was my pleasure, Captain." She folded the letter and handed it back to him, debating whether or not to say anything. Finally, sensibilities won out. "You must miss your wife very much, sir. As she obviously misses you."

He didn't look at her. He just kept staring above him at some place on the ceiling. "I miss her more than you know, Miss Clouston. More than I ever thought one person could miss another and still be drawing breath. But it's not—"

A commotion from downstairs echoed up the staircase, and Lizzie thought she heard a few men whooping and hollering.

"The Yankees have tucked tail and run!" a man shouted from below. "And General Hood says he's going to take his army to Nashville and whip General Thomas and his men to a pulp!"

"Did you hear that, Captain? They're saying the Federal Army has retreated."

Hearing what sounded like disbelief in Miss Clouston's voice, Roland knew that if he were to be anything less than straightforward it would be dishonest. Because he knew the truth of how this war would end, as should any man who'd been on that field tonight. And anyone who believed otherwise was either a fool or a foolhardy dreamer.

"While I loathe being the one to dash a spark of hope, Miss Clouston . . ." He paused, his legs throbbing with pain and the ache in his head—from the chloroform, he guessed—still disrupting his thoughts. "What I witnessed tonight was not a retreat. And from surveying the Federal Army's breastworks this afternoon from atop Merrill's Hill, then again tonight a fair piece closer up, I have a difficult time reconciling this news with what we experienced. As much as I know this will pain you to hear"—he lowered his voice—"I believe the cause for which we've been fighting was lost tonight."

Saying the words aloud all but choked him, and her injured expression conveyed her sense of loss as well. Perhaps he shouldn't have spoken so freely with her. How long had it been since he'd actually talked with a woman? It was a welcome change, that went without saying. But conversing with Miss Clouston was a mite different from the exchanges he'd grown accustomed to having over the past three years.

"My apologies, ma'am. I didn't mean to—"

"No apology required, Captain." She briefly looked down at her hands clasped in her lap. "And I believe you may be right."

What strength this woman possessed. Even in the face of pending doom for the Confederacy, she bore herself with quiet dignity and grace. "I have seen things today, tonight, that even in my worst nightmares I had not begun to imagine. I am no longer naive about war, Captain. Although up until about five hours ago, I very much was. I want to know the truth of what happened out there today. So please, continue."

Roland looked up at her, knowing there was still a depth of naiveté within her that she would even make such a request after everything she'd already witnessed. And yet her need to know, to understand, was one he could well comprehend.

Seeking to ease the ache in his back, he shifted slightly, and the pain in his legs catapulted to a level that caused his head to swim. He sucked in air through clenched teeth, the white-hot stabs of pain worse now than before the doctor had operated.

He teetered on the brink of consciousness, part of him wanting to give in to it and let it drag him under full and deep, far away from all this. Away from a world that was changing in ways he'd already begun to imagine—and didn't like. In truth, the changes scared him. Yet the other part of him knew that God wasn't finished with him here yet. No matter that he and the Almighty hadn't been on the best of speaking terms of late.

CHAPTER 7

"Captain Jones, are you all right?"

A gentle pressure on Roland's arm registered with him—such a contrast to the bolts of fire shooting through his veins—and he latched onto the comfort her touch and voice afforded.

He grimaced. "I'm all right. But I think I've learned my lesson about trying to move."

"What else can I do for you, Captain? Tell me."

He swallowed. "You're doing it right now, ma'am. Just give me a minute."

Slowly, much too slowly, the pain leveled out again and returned to a constant ache. Miss Clouston held the ladle to his lips and he drank, water dribbling down into his beard. He felt so weak, so helpless. Like a prisoner in his own body, a slave to his wounds. Yet in the same breath, he was grateful to be alive.

"Miss Clouston, ma'am?"

Without moving his head, Roland peered in the direction of the door and spotted the older Negro woman he'd glimpsed before.

Miss Clouston rose. "Excuse me a moment, please, Captain."

The two women lowered their voices, but the sound still carried.

"I got pots with beef bones in 'em simmerin' on the stove, Miss Clouston. I'm waterin' down the broth to make it stretch, but at least it's somethin' warm to fill their bellies. Missus McGavock wanted me to tell you. We figured we might use the water pails to serve it up, seein' as we don't got enough cups to go round, not even with usin' Missus McGavock's fancy ones."

"That's wonderful, Tempy. It should be a few minutes yet before

74

Dr. Phillips returns. So let me finish with things in here, and I'll come down to help."

"I seen Dr. Phillips in the backyard just now, ma'am, helpin' one of them other docs. There's a colonel, a big boulder of a man by the name of Farrell, havin' both his legs took off under the Osage orange tree. They havin' some kind of trouble, I heard 'em say. I didn't stop to find out what." She shook her head. "It's grim work they doin', but I guess it got to be done."

Miss Clouston said something in response that Roland couldn't make out.

As she made her way back across the room, she whispered encouragement to the wounded she passed. And everywhere her gaze touched, she left kindness. The soldiers responded to it too. And whether Miss Clouston was aware of it or not—and Roland felt certain she wasn't—their gazes followed her. Much as his own did now.

She settled back onto the child's chair beside him. Expectation filled her expression, and a pretty brown curl escaped the hair knotted at the nape of her neck.

"I'm sorry for the interruption, Captain. You were telling me about what you saw this morning. Atop Merrill's Hill."

Not really wanting to, Roland reached back for the thoughts he'd gladly laid aside. "The Federal Army beat us to Franklin today by several hours. So by the time we got here, they were well entrenched and fortified. They'd been busy little beavers, as one of the officers standing beside me said." He thought of Daniel Ranslett, the fellow captain and sharpshooter who'd accompanied him to Merrill's Hill. Ranslett was a fine officer and a crack shot, and hailed from around these parts. He hadn't seen Ranslett since they'd gotten separated on the battlefield, and he hoped his friend had made it through. "So judging from what I saw before the battle, and then what I observed in the midst of that cauldron of smoke and fire after the battle began . . ."

He briefly shut his eyes, and images rose to his mind; images he feared were so fiercely burned into him that he'd never again close his eyes without seeing them. Confederate brothers piled one atop the other like snowdrifts come winter. Men who'd been shot and killed while in the act of reloading their muskets, firearms and ramrods still in their grip.

"There's no way the Federals tucked tail and ran, ma'am. They were ready for us. We came at them on an open field with daylight still stretching, so they could see us every step of the way. Even when the sun had dropped behind the hills, their artillery lit up the night sky above. They'd dug ditches and piled up breastworks three feet high in some places and had capped them with head logs."

Delicate wrinkles knit her brow. "What's a head log?"

"It's where you take a tree trunk or a branch, as big as you can find, and heft it to the top of the pile of dirt. Then you dig out a little of the dirt to create a peek hole beneath it. Enough to fit the barrel of your gun through. The top of your head is better protected that way as you take aim."

She nodded, her expression smoothing.

"Their line of entrenchments stretched for a good two miles in a sort of crescent from the Harpeth River on the southeast part of town to the bend of the river to the northwest. We counted six artillery batteries from atop the hill earlier in the day and thirty-eight Napoleon guns."

"Cannons," she said quietly. "I saw those earlier today too. From the second-story gallery porch on the back of the house."

He nodded. "Looking across the field, we could see the sun's last rays gleaming off their bayonets. General Schofield's men had polished them up special for us."

Her expression sobered, and he knew she was trying to picture the scene. A scene he refused to paint in its truest colors. Not to a woman. Besides, he'd had enough talk of battle for two lifetimes. He had something else he wanted to say to her.

"I've been meaning to thank you, ma'am, for what you did. Lieutenant Shuler here gave me a full accounting of how you championed my cause when the doctor aimed to take my leg." Roland nodded toward Shuler, who was lying near him. "Shuler said he'd put you up against General Schofield any day."

"It's true," Shuler piped up. "She told Doc Phillips just how it was, Captain. And she didn't back down either."

Roland smiled. "I don't doubt it. Even in the short time I've known this lady, I've learned she has a verbal arsenal of sufficient variety at the ready."

"A verbal arsenal?" she repeated, brows arching. "I'm not certain I should take that as a compliment." But the sparkle in her eyes said differently. She gave both him and Shuler a look of feigned scolding, and Roland would've sworn from the young lieutenant's grin that Shuler had been given another dose of morphine. Miss Clouston's kind and calming demeanor had a definite tonic to it. And those deep blue eyes didn't hurt either.

As innocent an observation as it was, he realized it was the first time he'd truly taken notice of a woman since Susan's passing nineteen months ago, almost to the day. And the noticing felt traitorous to his wife's memory. Thinking of his precious Weet again, and of Lena, an aching sense of loss moved through him. *I listen every evening after the train cars pass down below for your footstep on the front porch; could I but hear it what pleasure it would bring.*

He knew the words of that letter almost by heart. He should have been there with them. If he had, maybe he could have prevented what had happened. A gnawing pain rose up inside him, a pain that had nothing to do with his physical injuries, yet felt just as real and raw. And he questioned, as he had many times before, the cost of his decision to leave behind his family to go and fight. To serve beneath a leadership he'd questioned more times than he could count—especially when serving under General Hood.

From the moment he'd learned about Mississippi seceding from the Union, he'd known he would take up arms. What honorable man wouldn't defend his state, his home and land, his family? But while he was away defending them from the Federals, another enemy, unseen and even stealthier, had invaded their home and stolen his life away. He squeezed his eyes tight, the mixture of anger and loss causing them to burn. Grief coupled with regret had a way of bending even the strongest man's knees, and there were moments, like now, when he was certain he'd be crushed beneath the weight of it.

Which was why, as he'd been lying on the battlefield, feeling the lifeblood pour out of him, he'd been ready—even eager—to join Susan and Lena in the hereafter. Until he'd looked up to see that big autumn moon. Then he'd known, even while part of him longed to die and be done with this world, that it wasn't his time yet.

"And though I'm certain Lieutenant Shuler embellished the exchange with Dr. Phillips far more than would align with the truth—"

Roland blinked, only now hearing what Miss Clouston had been saying. She glanced back at him.

"—I'm grateful that the doctor listened, and that what you wanted done—or not done, in this case—was affirmed. However . . ." She rose, looking pointedly at his right leg. "The doctor is already concerned about gangrene. As am I. So we'll have to make sure to keep the wounds clean."

Roland managed a nod, his emotions shredded about as badly as his legs. "I'll do my best, ma'am."

"This is a good-tastin' soup, ma'am. What is it?"

Touched by the sincerity in the young soldier's tone, Lizzie refilled the ladle and held it to his mouth—his left arm amputated just inches below the shoulder, his right bandaged and immobile in a remnant of what had once been one of Mrs. McGavock's foundational garments. She wondered what the corporal would think if he knew a woman's chemise was holding him together. "It's warm bone broth. Colonel and Mrs. McGavock are working to have something more substantial for you all tomorrow."

He looked up. "Don't rightly see how that could be, ma'am. This is the best-tastin' thing I've had for as far back as I can string my thoughts together."

Touched by his gratitude, Lizzie received similar comments from the rest of the men she served on the second floor. Since Dr. Phillips wasn't back yet, she returned to the kitchen and refilled her pail with broth, then retraced her steps upstairs.

Not particularly hungry, she knew she needed to keep up her strength, so she filled the ladle to almost full and drank the warm broth, feeling it travel all the way down. Though it didn't begin to compare to Tempy's beef soup with vegetables, the brew put something on her stomach, which was good.

She still couldn't believe that Captain Jones had actually admitted to her that he thought the Confederacy was going to lose the war. She'd seen the struggle in him to even say the words aloud. And she'd struggled to keep her true feelings hidden. She only prayed that the captain was right and that this war was almost over.

She served the wounded men bedded down in Colonel and Mrs. McGavock's bedroom and those few on the second-story gallery porch outside, the night having turned bitter cold. After filling her bucket again, she served the soldiers in the guest room, then started into Hattie's bedroom, only to discover Hattie and Sallie already there with Carrie McGavock. The three worked their way through the maze of wounded men scattered among Hattie's childhood—her dollhouse with porcelain dolls sitting leaned up against it all wide-eyed and watchful, the cradle nestling her stuffed bear, the diminutive table and chairs where Hattie served tea to imaginary friends. Sallie held the bucket with both hands while Hattie dipped the ladle in and carefully lifted the broth to the soldiers' mouths. Mrs. McGavock spoke with each and every man she passed, touching their heads, their shoulders, giving comfort as only a mother could give.

Lizzie stood for a moment, watching. How would this night change these dear girls? How did a nine-year-old cope with something like this? And how could she, as the family's governess, ever find a way to explain it all? To help them navigate their way through the indelible memories that would shape not only who they would become but how they perceived the world. Namely, their Northern neighbors.

Having no answers, only more questions, she crossed the hall to Winder's bedroom. Her gaze was drawn to Captain Jones as soon as she entered the room. But apparently he'd finally drifted off to sleep. The rest would do him good.

Every soldier offered broth drank it hungrily, then looked up at her as though she'd bestowed upon them the elixir of life. With everyone fed—*fed* being a generous term—she knew she should go look for Dr. Phillips to see if she could assist him. Colonel and Mrs. McGavock and the children were seeing to the men inside the house, and there was nothing else she could do for now. Her arms and legs ached, and her body longed for rest, but she had only to look around her to be reminded of how grateful she should be. How grateful she was.

She checked on Captain Jones one last time. Still sleeping soundly. She set the pail of broth beside him, thinking of the letter from his wife. The beautifully phrased sentiments. And the love behind them.

A vacancy caused in my heart by your absence . . .

I listen every evening after the train cars pass down below for your foot-step on the front porch . . .

. . . a thousand kisses to my beloved Roland.

While she thought about Towny often and hoped he was well and wanted him to return, could she say she'd experienced a "vacancy in her heart" due to his absence? Or that she listened every evening for a footfall on the porch while praying it was him? And about those thousand kisses . . .

Towny had kissed her. Once. The January morning he'd left to return to his brigade. It had felt a little odd kissing him, but she reasoned that was because she'd never been kissed. So the experience was new to her. Everything would be new to her.

Her thoughts flew back across the years to her twelfth summer when she and her mother had been sitting on the front porch shelling beans one afternoon. "Kissing and all that such is something husbands and wives do, Lizzie. Some more often than others. But you shouldn't fear it, because it isn't unpleasant. Not once you're accustomed to it."

In the years since, Lizzie had acquired considerably more knowledge on the subject, thanks to her friends who were already married. But something about the wording in Susan's letter tugged at her, naggingly so. And as Lizzie stared at Captain Jones—at the strength in his features, his well-muscled shoulders and arms—she found the thread of her thoughts taking a decidedly more intimate turn. She quickly turned away and busied herself by adding two more logs to the fire, then watched the flames crackle and pop as the wood ultimately surrendered to the heat.

With time, she would come to feel for Towny what Captain Jones's wife obviously felt for her own "beloved Roland." Lizzie nodded to herself as though that confirmed it. Once she and Towny were married and had consummated that relationship—a shiver went through her, though whether pleasurable or not she wasn't sure—her feelings would change. They would grow; at least that was what others had said. So there was no more reason to wonder or worry about "kissing and all that such." Determined to put that thought behind her, she left the room without a backward glance.

As she descended the staircase and passed through the main entrance hall, she heard Colonel Nelson still crying out, his pleas now peppered with expletives. The poor man. She questioned whether such language was part of his usual dialect or merely a response to the pain. With a hasty prayer that the children wouldn't hear, she paused in the doorway of the dining room. Petitioning the Almighty to heal was quite familiar to her, but given what she knew about Colonel Nelson's condition, praying for healing didn't feel thoroughly honest. So she gave voice to the soft whisper in her heart instead. "Lord, please take him home. Relieve him of this torture and take him home."

Minutes later, as she left through the back door, she paused, wondering if the soldier who'd been reciting the psalm was still—

But he was gone. Only a bloodstain on the wallpaper testified that he'd been there.

Heart heavy, she heard the clock in the family parlor strike midnight—and Colonel Nelson's agonizing cries only grew louder.

CHAPTER 8

Lizzie paused on the crowded back gallery porch, her eyes swiftly adjusting to the torch- and lantern-studded darkness beyond—and her chest clenched tight. The view from the guest room window on the second floor hadn't revealed the entire truth. Wounded men filled the back lawn, the outbuildings, the barn, the empty slave houses. As many men as occupied the house, even more were out here. Everywhere she looked, men lay on the cold, wet ground, either awaiting a doctor's care or recovering from it—or no longer in need of it. And as if the men who'd lived through the battle hadn't already suffered enough, icy rain and sleet now pelted down from the dark night skies.

Like the soldiers inside, these men were ill-clad for such temperatures. Most had no coat. No blanket. Many were without shoes and socks. Lizzie looked heavenward, ashamed of the questions foremost in her thoughts yet unable to quell them. And though she would never give voice to them lest anyone else hear and judge her, the questions rose silently, even demandingly.

Why? And where are you in all of this?

She didn't doubt that God was watching. That he was present. That he saw every man and even knew each of their names. She'd walked with the Almighty long enough that he'd proven his presence to her time and again. And yes, this was war. And in war, as despicable as she found it, men died. And each death was tragic. But what she couldn't reconcile was why so *many* had to die. And so brutally. How many ways would men devise to kill each other? How many more fathers, brothers, sons, and husbands would be sacrificed before this war ended? Before some sort of agreement or compromise was reached?

Slavery *had* to be abolished. There was no question. But at what cost would this nation dictate that that end would come?

For nearly four years now this conflict had been tearing the country apart. What was it Towny had written in a recent letter? Something about how, when his regiment had reached the border of Tennessee, they'd seen a sign that read "Tennessee—A Free Home or a Grave," and they'd all let out a cheer as they passed.

But as she looked out across the sea of broken and lifeless men, she didn't see a free home. All she could see were graves waiting to be dug. Hundreds if not thousands of them, considering those dead or dying on the field. And as she thought of Towny again, she was so grateful his orders with Tucker's Brigade had taken him far from Harpeth Valley and the town of Franklin.

She searched the yard for Dr. Phillips and finally spotted him beneath an oak tree near the smokehouse speaking with another surgeon. She made a path for him, head down to shield her eyes from the sleet and hugging herself for warmth. Dr. Phillips chose that moment to look up. And when he saw her, he shortened the distance between them.

"You don't need to be out here, Miss Clouston. I'll be back inside shortly."

"I need to be of assistance, Doctor. Wherever that may be."

He hesitated. "The men out here could use something warm to drink. The Negro woman has been serving them, but there's only one of her and—"

"Tempy," Lizzie supplied. "Her name is Tempy, Dr. Phillips. You met her upstairs."

He looked at her, then slowly nodded. "Yes, Miss Clouston. Tempy. She's been—"

"Say no more, Doctor. I'll be back with more broth in a few moments."

Lizzie wove a path through the wounded men to the back door of the kitchen, irritated by the surgeon's common oversight. How did a person get to the point where he considered others lesser than himself based solely on the color of one's skin? She didn't know Dr. Phillips well, by any means. And he might not hold to the common view about slaves. But he'd obviously made no attempt to even remember Tempy's name. And this after all Tempy was doing to help.

As soon as Lizzie opened the back kitchen door, the savory aroma of beef broth greeted her, and she found Tempy at the stove using a large measuring cup to scoop the broth into pails.

Tempy looked up. "Land sakes, ma'am, you done look frozen clean through."

"I'm fine. Cold and tired, but fine." Lizzie moved close to the brick hearth, relishing its heat and that from the stove. She shivered in response. "Everyone on the second floor has been served. So I'll help with those outside."

"You best have yourself a cup of this first."

"I had some earlier, thank you. I'm fine."

Tempy looked at her, her expression saying she begged to differ, but she said nothing more.

Once they'd filled several pails, Tempy slipped a ladle into each. Lizzie reached down to pick up two of the buckets, but Tempy waved her off.

"Not 'til you eat a bite of somethin' solid, ma'am. Here, take this."

Lizzie looked down at the piece of cold cornbread in Tempy's hand, and her stomach stirred with hunger. But how could she eat when so many others were suffering and going without? She shook her head. "I'll eat later."

Tempy didn't move. "Miss Clouston, I know the look of bein' worn. And I'm tellin' you, ma'am, you best eat somethin'."

Lizzie's eyes filled. But she shook her head again. *I can't,* she mouthed.

Tempy leveled a stare. "You takin' care of lots of people tonight, ma'am. And you starvin' yourself just 'cause they can't have any of this right now ain't gonna help 'em. No, ma'am. It's gonna hurt 'em. 'Cause if you go down, who's gonna carry the weight you been carryin' here tonight? Nobody. That's who. We each got our jobs and we got to do 'em." She dipped an edge of the cornbread into the warm broth and held it out again. "So come on now. Eat it fast, so we can get back out there."

Feeling scolded, yet lovingly so, Lizzie looked at the bread in Tempy's hand, then took it and ate. The day-old cornbread tasted like the finest of fare, and she realized how often she ate without thought. With only the most fleeting sense of gratitude. Even when Colonel McGavock said grace before a meal. Seeing herself and her abundance of blessings in light of others and their lack carved out a deeper awareness inside her, and a depth of appreciation she'd not known rushed in to fill the space.

"Thank you, Tempy."

"You welcome, ma'am."

Lizzie's gaze brushed hers, and she thought back to yesterday morning when Tempy had studied the globe with such curiosity and longing. That moment seemed another world away now. Yet Lizzie still felt that tug inside her, and she wished she could offer Tempy what she was offering Hattie and Winder. An education. The power of knowledge to change yourself and the world around you. Only, here in Franklin, Tennessee, that wasn't allowed. Not yet. Not for someone like Tempy.

Lizzie bent down to pick up the pails of broth and saw the hem of her skirt soaked six inches deep in blood. A price the soldiers in this house had willingly paid for what they believed in. What price was she willing to pay for what she believed? Something locked tight deep inside her slowly opened and began to unfurl. Her heart started pounding.

She turned and looked at Tempy. "How would you like to travel to those places you saw yesterday morning? Those places on the globe."

Tempy stared at her. "What you mean, ma'am?"

Lizzie set her pails on the floor. "What I mean is . . . Would you like to learn to read and write? If you knew how to read, you could travel to all of those places and learn so much about the world God made, all without ever leaving Carnton. Because you could read what other people have written. People who've been to those places and who tell you what it was like."

Tempy frowned, then glanced over her shoulder. "What you doin' askin' me all this? This ain't somethin' that can happen, ma'am, and we both know it. First, 'cause the law says I can't. Second—" She briefly bowed her head. When she looked up again, defeat shuttered her gaze. "'Cause I'm older than them hills out there, Miss Clouston. I reckon I'm too far gone for you to teach me, even if people said you could."

Lizzie took the pails from Tempy's grip and set them on the floor beside hers, then she grasped Tempy's hands—her own so pale and colorless, Tempy's so dark and work-worn. "And I reckon that you're going to be an excellent student."

Lizzie managed a smile, but Tempy pulled her hands away.

"You don't know what you sayin', ma'am. Even if I did want to be learned by you, what would the colonel say? And Missus McGavock? They wouldn't take to it. Not one bit. And if anybody else learned what we was doin' . . ." She shook her head, fear displacing the defeat in her expression.

"The world is changing, Tempy. Right before our very eyes. I don't believe it's right, what they've done to you. What they do to Negroes. I never have. I believe we're created in the image of God. *All* of us. And while I'm so sorry the men in this house and those on the battlefield are suffering, I'm grateful beyond words that the North is winning this war. Or at least they appear to be. Because this needs to end. And I'm sorry, so sorry that I've never said anything to you about this before now." Ashamed, she bowed her head.

But Tempy gently lifted her chin. "You think I don't know how you feel, ma'am? That I don't see the difference in you?" The older woman shook her head. "You done forgotten that first day you come to Carnton all those years ago?"

Lizzie looked at her.

"You and me, we was standin' right over there." Tempy pointed toward the back door in the corner. "I'd done took my own wash off the line from dryin' and was takin' it upstairs when you said, 'Let me get that for you.' And you done toted that basket up them steps for me to my room." Tempy's chestnut-colored eyes softened. "Ain't nobody ever done that for me before. So don't you go thinkin' that I don't know who you are, ma'am. 'Cause I do. I always have."

Lizzie met her gaze full on. "So are you saying you'll let me teach you?"

A flicker of trepidation shone in Tempy's eyes again, then that flicker slowly warmed to joy. "I reckon if you can abide tryin' to teach an old woman, the least I can do is try to learn."

OVER THE NEXT hour, Lizzie and Tempy served the steaming buckets of broth to men on the back and front lawns, while the surgeons performed amputations on makeshift operating tables set up beneath the trees. As Lizzie moved among the wounded, she did her best not to focus on the appendages piled as high as the tables.

Whenever her gaze connected with Tempy's, they exchanged knowing looks. Lizzie was thrilled at the prospect of teaching her. Which, oddly enough, these soldiers were partly responsible for. Because in seeing their sacrifice and courage, she'd found a measure of her own. And since Tempy's room was next to hers on the second floor of the kitchen wing, they'd have the privacy they needed.

"Miss Clouston!"

She glanced up to see Dr. Phillips and an attendant striding toward her. Dr. Phillips took the buckets from her and handed them to the young soldier.

"Miss Clouston, I need your assistance, please."

Lizzie followed him to the shelter of the back porch, where he turned.

"I've just received word that an ambulance will be arriving any-time." His voice lowered, and he briefly looked away, the muscles in his jaw cording tight. "It's carrying four of our generals who were killed in battle tonight."

"Four?" Lizzie looked up at him.

"Actually, five were killed, I've been told. But one of them was taken to another field hospital to be treated and died there. I don't know who they are yet, but every man here who's able will want to pay his last respects to these leaders. So we'll lay out their bodies on the back gallery here. I haven't been told the extent of their injuries. But I'd be greatly obliged, Miss Clouston, if you'd help make these men as honorable in appearance in death as they were in life."

Still absorbing the news, Lizzie nodded. "Of course, sir."

Moments later, a four-wheeled ambulance pulled to a stop in the side yard. The driver, a middle-aged soldier, set the brake and climbed down, then spoke in hushed tones to Dr. Phillips. Two younger ambulance corpsmen climbed out from the back, their expressions somber.

She didn't recognize the first officer they unloaded from the back of the ambulance, so marred with dirt and blood was the man's countenance. But the second, she did. General Patrick Cleburne.

She'd seen the young Irishman's likeness often in the newspapers alongside reports about the war. Reporters described him as quiet and soft-spoken, but possessing an undeniable air of authority and competence. Towny, an admirer of the man, had told her that Cleburne was the highest-ranking military officer of foreign birth in the Confederate Army. And judging by the pained expressions on the faces of soldiers already looking on, to say General Cleburne was beloved by his men would be an understatement.

Dr. Phillips returned to her side. "Brigadier General John Adams," he said solemnly, watching along with her as the corpses were carried to the rear gallery and gently laid beneath the western windows. "Major General Patrick Cleburne. Brigadier Generals Hiram Granbury and Otho Strahl."

All names she knew. All names any Southerner would recognize.

"And I was told just now," the doctor continued, "that the fifth was General S. R. Gist of South Carolina." Defeat burdened his deep sigh. "When you're finished, Miss Clouston, please meet me back upstairs, and we'll continue with the surgeries."

Feeling that ever-present weight growing heavier inside her, Lizzie nodded, then went inside the house to fetch fresh cloths and a bowl of water. When she returned to the back gallery, men were already gathered around the bodies of the generals. Some hastily wiped away tears. Others worked to choke them back.

One of the ambulance corpsmen who'd helped transfer the bodies to the porch stood close by, his cheeks streaked with dirt and emotion. "I'd be obliged if you'd allow me to help you, ma'am."

"Of course," Lizzie whispered and dipped a cloth into the water. She wrung it out and handed it to him, and he began wiping the dirt and blood from General Adams's face. After a moment, he looked over at her as though asking what he should do next.

Lizzie paused from smoothing the damp cloth over General Cleburne's face and beard, and positioned Cleburne's hands one atop the other over his abdomen. The young corpsman did likewise with Adams. The two of them worked silently as soldiers looked on.

General Cleburne's gray coat was unbuttoned, his white linen shirt beneath stained with blood on the left side. He was in his sock feet, his boots apparently having been stolen. By a Federal soldier, she reasoned. Because none of these Southern sons would have so dishonored the man. His sword belt was also missing. Another trophy of war, perhaps.

Lizzie determined that nothing could—or should—be done about the blood on their uniforms. Any attempt to disguise that would feel like a diminishment of the sacrifice they'd made. Especially General Adams, whose body had been pierced with at least nine bullets. General Cleburne, from what she could tell, had suffered a fatal shot directly to his heart. General Strahl's bloodstained uniform bore three bullet holes. And General Granbury's bore at least that many.

"Here you go, ma'am."

Lizzie peered up to see the second ambulance corpsman holding a kepi.

"This cap belonged to General Cleburne, ma'am."

She nodded and took the kepi and laid it on his chest. She recalled the description Captain Jones had painted of the battlefield as he'd surveyed it yesterday afternoon, and the image brought a measure of dread. She couldn't begin to imagine marching, much less running headlong, into a fortified line of guns, bayonets, and cannons all aimed at the very heart of the field upon which she trod. And yet these men had done that very thing. The shuffle of feet drew her focus upward, and she saw a heavily bearded officer cutting a path through the men who, once they saw him, saluted and made way.

"General Govan," they whispered as he passed.

Govan kept his gaze straight ahead and nodded to Lizzie. "Ma'am," he said in a deep, even voice, then looked down at the generals. He stood at attention, eyes glistening, then slowly lifted his bandaged right hand and saluted. He held the posture for a long moment, and no one moved. Once he brought his hand down, he looked around.

"I had the honor of serving with these four fine men, as did many of you." His voice carried in the night. "Yesterday afternoon, before General Cleburne took to the fight, I turned to him and said, 'Well, General, few of us will ever return to Arkansas to tell the story of this battle.' To which Cleburne replied with words I'll never forget, words that are indicative of the man he was. General Cleburne said, 'Well, Govan, if we are to die, let us die like men.'" For the first time, Govan's voice wavered. "And die like men these officers did."

The general moved to stand at the foot of each body and saluted each fallen soldier in turn. The wounded who were ambulatory followed suit. Others saluted from where they stood leaning up against the house or from where they sat, and Lizzie gained a deeper sense of the camaraderie that war forged between men.

Still, injustice burned within her at the grand scale of senseless death and bloodshed. And while General Cleburne's words—*let us die like men*—held the most honorable intentions, she would rather he had lived like a man. That they all had lived.

The back door opened, and she heard two distinctive chimes from the clock in the family parlor. Two o'clock in the morning. Chilled near to the bone, she gathered the cloths and bowl and went inside.

She deposited the items on the floorcloth beside two empty buckets, then started for the stairs. She spotted Mrs. McGavock kneeling to offer a soldier a drink, and wondered if the young man had any idea who was serving him. He might be aware that Carrie McGavock was the wife of the property owner, but did he realize what a treasure this woman was?

As Mrs. McGavock rose, her attention shifted to Lizzie, and she gestured that she wanted to speak. Lizzie met her halfway, only then seeing that the hem of her employer's skirt was also stained with blood, just like her own.

"Miss Clouston, I've heard that we lost several generals tonight in the battle. And that the bodies have been brought here."

Lizzie relayed the sad details, feeling the woman's deep sigh.

"So much death and suffering," Mrs. McGavock whispered. "Too much." She grasped Lizzie's hand. "My dear, you're working so hard. Perhaps you should slip away and get some rest. Just a few moments at least."

"I wouldn't be able to sleep, ma'am. Not with so much to be done and still having breath within me to do it. Which I know is something you can understand."

Tenderness filled her employer's eyes, and Carrie nodded. "The colonel and I have moved a few of our belongings into the bedroom beside yours, so we'll be staying in the kitchen wing with you and Tempy. For a few days, at least." Her voice lowered. "I think it's best to have some distance from all this for the children. And for us as well, until life returns to normal." Sadness moved into her expression. "If 'normal' is something that will ever return to this house. Or to those of us who will live through this night." She gave Lizzie's hand a parting squeeze, then returned to her task.

Lizzie watched her go. Here she'd finally gotten the courage to offer to teach Tempy, only to hear that the McGavocks were moving into the bedroom beside theirs. Not ideal, to say the least. But they would find a way to work around that. She started up the stairs, then paused.

Above the moans and pain-induced mumblings of the wounded, she sensed a sudden quiet. Already feeling the truth resonating inside her, she turned and walked into the dining room where Colonel Nelson lay in quiet repose. For all the suffering he'd endured, he now looked as though he were merely sleeping, so natural was his expression. "You finally have the peace you sought," she whispered and pulled the thin blanket up to his chest.

She walked up the steps, the staircase leading to the second floor seeming taller and longer than usual. Her eyes felt heavy and irritated from lack of rest, and she wished she could curl up into a tiny ball, go to sleep, and then awaken to discover this had all been a horrible dream.

But seeing Dr. Phillips standing beside the surgical table, another soldier lying before him, she knew she wasn't dreaming. And sleep was a long way off.

A FEW HOURS later as the sun peered up over the horizon, Lizzie watched the dawn transform the dark night sky into a golden wash streaked with pink and violet. Her gaze skimmed the hills to the distant east as morning stretched out across the highest treetops. The iced bare winter branches sparkled like diamonds in the distance, and she sighed. How could so beautiful a morning follow so tragic a night?

As Dr. Phillips sutured the remains of another soldier's arm, Lizzie shifted her weight, her feet throbbing in her boots, her lower back aching. A handful of soldiers in the room, Captain Jones among them, had slept fitfully off and on through the night, while the rest hadn't slept at all, pain their constant companion. She was grateful when Dr. Phillips suggested they take a short break.

"I need to grab more coffee, ma'am, and speak with the other surgeons about where we are with remaining patients."

Lizzie nodded, then crossed the distance and collapsed onto Winder's tiny chair and unlaced her boots. She would've liked to have removed them, but the condition of the carpet made walking in stocking feet inadvisable. How would they ever get this much blood out of the carpet? Was it even possible? She doubted it. And it was like this in nearly every room of the house.

Scarcely able to keep her eyes open, she drew her knees to her chest, rested her head on her arms, and was instantly, blissfully adrift. But even in sleep, she still heard the echo of what the young soldier Thaddeus had said to her.

"Miss Clouston."

Lizzie tried to shut out the voice, but it grew insistent.

"Miss Clouston."

She lifted her head and blinked. It took a few seconds to focus. "Yes, Dr. Phillips?"

"With first light the ambulance corpsmen found more wounded on the battlefield, ma'am. A brigade that fought on the western flank, and they need our help."

Lizzie rose, unsteady on her feet, then realized her boots were still unlaced. She sat back down and tied them, aware of the doctor gathering instruments and stuffing them into his leather satchel.

"George?" came a hoarse whisper. "George, are you there?" Captain Jones, eyes clenched tightly, thrashed his head from side to side. "I can't find you, George. Where are you?" His voice grew desperate, and he stretched out his bandaged hand as though trying to grasp something only he could see.

Lizzie knelt beside him. "Shhh, Captain, you're dreaming," she whispered and laid a hand to his forehead. "Everything is going to be—" His skin was like fire. His shirt was drenched. "Dr. Phillips! Come quickly!"

In a blink, the surgeon was at the captain's side. He examined the sutures, then took the captain's pulse. His head came up slowly. "It's what I feared. It's surgical fever."

CHAPTER 9

Lizzie took in a breath, reality hitting her like a physical blow.

"But it may not be gangrene," Dr. Phillips added hurriedly. "Sometimes a patient will have a fever following surgery that's only temporary, so let's not jump to a false prognosis."

Lizzie knew his intent was to hearten her, but the very fact that he had warned against this outcome left his encouragement hollow. "I'll get some cold water and cloths."

He nodded. "And I'll check the other men for fever."

Lizzie fetched the things from the kitchen and met Dr. Phillips on her way back upstairs.

"I examined the other men." He paused at the bottom of the staircase. "There's no more fever. Not yet, anyway. I administered laudanum to the captain and left the bottle on the hearth, in case he grows more restless. It won't do for him to thrash about in his condition. He can have another teaspoonful in three hours. More, if you deem it necessary." He glanced past her toward the open front doors where an ambulance waited. "I'll be back as soon as I can. Dr. Clifton and I are going to see about the men in Tucker's Brigade."

"Tucker's Brigade?" Lizzie frowned.

"Yes. I mentioned the wounded men still on the battlefield. A great many of them are from Tucker's Brigade."

"But that's not possible, Doctor. Tucker's Brigade was ordered south."

"They were, until General Hood ordered them back here two days ago. Tucker and his men marched without stopping and arrived just before the battle commenced. From what I've been told, they suffered great losses. Many were killed. Either that or captured and taken prisoner to Nashville."

Lizzie could scarcely breathe. *Towny* . . .

"Dr. Phillips," an attendant called. "We need to go, sir."

"I'll be back as soon as I can, Miss Clouston. Take care of Captain Jones. And try to get some rest yourself, if you can. We have a long day ahead of us."

Lizzie watched him leave, his image blurring in her vision. Towny was *here?* She pressed a hand to her midsection and searched the faces of the wounded men in the entrance hall, then the ones on the stairs, all while praying that her dearest friend was still alive.

LIZZIE BATHED CAPTAIN Jones's face and neck with cool water. She unbuttoned his shirt, plunged the cloth into the basin again, and rubbed his chest down. Disoriented with fever, he attempted to push her away time and again, but she persisted, her focus torn between her obligation to care for him and her desire to get to the battlefield. And to Towny.

"George," the captain whispered, his expression pained, his breath coming in short, ragged gasps. "George, where are you?" His face suddenly contorted. "I'm sorry, Weet. I'm so sorry. It's my fault. It's all my fault."

Lizzie leaned closer. "Captain, if you can hear me, you *must* lie still."

He pushed her away again, harder this time, and Lizzie checked the clock on the mantel. Over two hours had passed. She reached for the laudanum. It took several attempts to get the dosage of medicine through his parched lips, but she finally managed it. Even with him wounded and fevered, the captain's strength was formidable.

"Weet," he whispered after a moment, his voice thick with longing.

"I miss you . . ." He took a deep breath and tears slipped from the corners of his eyes. "George . . ." He mumbled something unintelligible, then gave a deep sigh.

Lizzie laid a hand on his forehead. Still warm, but a bit cooler to the touch, she thought. What did the captain feel so at fault for? And who was George? His son, perhaps? She continued to apply cool compresses, grateful when the laudanum finally took effect and he began to rest easier. *God, please let him live.*

Even as the words formed inside her, she knew the silent plea was intended for two men.

For Captain Jones, because she would feel responsible if he died, all due to the promise she'd made him. But not only that. She stared at his rugged features. She didn't understand it, and even the silent admittance brought her some discomfort, but she felt tied to him somehow. The more she thought about it, she realized the connection she felt was likely due to the letter she'd read from his wife. The private nature of the missive had given her insight into the kind of man Captain Jones was, and the kind of marriage he shared with his wife. That had to be it, she told herself, still not fully convinced. But thinking it made her feel better.

And the plea was also for Towny. He was the closest friend she'd ever had. When something happened, either good or bad, he was the one she wanted to share it with first. Tempy was right. He would make a good husband. She only hoped she would make an equally good wife. She was determined to be what he needed, even while not quite knowing what that meant. But first, she needed to find him.

Footsteps sounded behind her, and she turned. Her eyes widened at what appeared to be an apparition bathed in light standing in the threshold of the doorway. But an apparition wouldn't possess discernible footsteps, would it?

"Miss Clouston?" a soft voice inquired, and the apparition stepped from the swath of sunlight into the room. "I'm Sister Catherine

Margaret. Mrs. McGavock suggested I come upstairs and see if you need any assistance. The other sisters and I are here to help in whatever way we can."

A trace of humor edged up the corners of Lizzie's mouth. "Sister Catherine Margaret, that's most kind of you. But can I say . . . When I first saw you standing there, I thought I might be seeing a ghost. Or should I say an angel."

Warmth filled the woman's eyes. "While I'm neither, my dear, you could say that I'm most definitely in league with the latter."

Lizzie liked her instantly. And saw the opportunity for what it was.

She gave Sister Catherine Margaret a quick summary of the men in the room, along with instructions in caring for Captain Jones, who, though his fever hadn't yet broken, didn't seem to feel quite as warm to the touch as he had earlier.

The nun picked up the cloth and dipped it into the water. "Rest assured, Miss Clouston, I'll keep careful watch on them while you're gone, and will stay here until you return."

Lizzie instinctively wanted to hug the woman, but she wasn't certain whether nuns hugged. So she settled for a gentle touch on the arm instead and headed for the stairs. Then she paused in the doorway and looked back, feeling the weight of death in this house and willing the captain to heed her silent warning.

Don't you die on me, Captain Jones. Don't you dare die on me.

"MA'AM, IT'S NOT a good idea for you to go out there. You don't know what you're gettin' yourself into. It's nothin' that *femi-nine* emotions should ever have to reckon with."

Lizzie looked up at the driver seated in the ambulance, reins in his grip. "I appreciate your concern for my femi-nine emotions, Lieutenant—" She raised a brow in question.

"O'Brien, ma'am."

Lizzie gave him a single nod, impatience and fatigue stiffening her spine. "Lieutenant O'Brien, but I have spent the better part of the past fourteen hours assisting Dr. Phillips with amputations upstairs. I've lost count of the number of limbs I've seen sawn from men's bodies, then have watched their faces as they've awakened from surgery to see the body they've known forever altered. Along with the life they knew and the future they'd hoped for. So while I appreciate your concern for my emotional well-being, I intend to get to that battlefield whether you allow me to ride along with you or force me to walk afoot."

Lizzie clenched her jaw tight, the tangled knot at the base of her throat all but choking her. But if there was one man here she would not cry in front of, it was this man. Not with the weight of condescension in his gaze.

Lieutenant O'Brien eyed her, then shook his head, murmuring a profanity. "You can't ride up here with me. It's against military regulations. Climb on up in the back, and I'll take you. But you'll have to walk back on your own steam. I'll be loaded with wounded."

"Thank you, Lieutenant O'Brien." Lizzie pulled her cloak closer about her and walked around to the back of the canvas-enclosed wagon and climbed in, surprised to see the same young man who'd helped her prepare the generals' bodies for viewing.

Recognition registered in his eyes as well, and he scooted over on the bench seat to make room for her. No sooner did she sit than the wagon lurched forward. The ride was rough and jarring over the frozen, rutted field. But with her feet already aching, she was grateful not to have to walk. The dirt-stained canvas stretched taut over bowed wood shielded from the wind, yet made it impossible to see what lay ahead. As Carnton grew smaller in the distance, Lizzie felt a degree of her bravado shrinking as well.

She'd hastily searched every room of the house, then both the front and back yards and the outbuildings, looking into the face of every wounded or dead soldier, praying she wouldn't see Towny's among them. And she hadn't. But that meant one of three things. He was still on the battlefield—either dead, or alive but wounded, or he'd been captured and taken prisoner to Nashville. As much as she didn't want to discover that he'd been taken to a Federal prison—she'd read accounts about those dreadful places in the newspapers—at least he would still be alive.

The temperature was bitter, and she tucked her hands into the folds of her cloak to try to keep warm. She felt a bunching beneath the woolen fabric—and remembered the items in her skirt pocket. She reached inside, and her fingers touched something cool and hard. Thaddeus's stone. She held it in her palm, then rubbed her thumb across the well-worn surface, imagining he'd done the same. What kind of boy had he been? Focused and eager to study? Or mischievous and adventure-loving like Winder? What color were his eyes? She couldn't recall, but wished she'd paid closer attention. What she did know was that he'd died far too young.

Why had he been on that battlefield? Did his mother sense yet that he was gone? She'd heard of mothers being able to feel such things across the miles, being so connected to their children. A connection Lizzie couldn't begin to understand, but prayed that she would, one day.

The wagon jolted to one side, and she gripped the seat just as a certainty gripped her. She would find Thaddeus's mother. She would tell her what her precious son had said and how he'd died in her arms. That he hadn't died alone. And Lizzie knew where she would start her search too. With Colonel McGavock. If anyone had ties with the War Department, he did.

Sooner than she expected, the wagon slowed and came to a stop. She tucked the stone back into her pocket and—even in that scant passing of seconds—realized that Lieutenant O'Brien had likely been right. Because though three of her senses were rendered helpless as she sat there in the wagon—a chilling breeze billowing the canvas, her fingers white-knuckling the bench seat beneath her—the sounds and smells permeating the air stirred an uncanny fear inside her.

And when she climbed down from the wagon and peered across the vast open valley, she would've sworn the devil had taken full possession of the earth.

CHAPTER 10

What indescribable fury wrought this unspeakable destruction ...

Trembling, part of her wanting to run, yet unable to move, Lizzie stared across the acres of carnage, locked in the grip of the unimaginable. She clamped her hand over her mouth to silence the sobs clawing their way up her throat as tears spilled down her cheeks. The dead lay everywhere. The ground so thick with them, a person could have walked all over the battlefield upon dead bodies without ever stepping on the ground. And their postures—she swallowed, tasting bile—inconceivable even in death.

"Here, ma'am. You'll need this."

Lieutenant O'Brien, his expression neither punishing nor self-congratulatory, held out a handkerchief, and she saw he already had one tied across his nose and mouth. She took the kerchief and held it to her nose. But it barely masked the thick smell of blood and death prevalent on the breeze, despite the freezing moisture that had settled over the valley during the night.

The lieutenant and two corpsmen started toward the field, and she followed, not knowing where to begin her search for Towny. Not even in Dante's darkest nightmares could he have imagined a scene such as this. In some of the hastily dug ditches, bodies were stacked seven deep. Many men were left standing, their corpses supported in an almost upright fashion by the dead who had fallen first. Two soldiers, one dressed in gray, the other blue, were fixed in the act of bayoneting each other, the blades still buried deep, their rage and agony frozen in their expressions. Lizzie turned away, but there was nowhere to look to escape the fury and death.

She attempted to step over a body, but the ground was slippery from the night's frozen rain and sleet and she went down hard. She scrambled to get up, and in the process fell again. It was then she realized, looking down at her hands and the handkerchief in her grip, that it wasn't dew beneath her feet, but blood. Blood pooled so thick the ground's thirst had been slaked until it refused to drink any more. She finally managed to stand. Wiping her hands on her skirt, she heard a sigh from one of the bodies beneath her and she scurried backward, desperate to put distance between them.

"It happens," she heard behind her and turned.

The young corpsman who'd shared his bench seat with her in the ambulance pointed toward her feet. "They're dead, but once you move the bodies, the air trapped in the windpipe sometimes finds its way up. Scared me right sorely too, first time I heard it."

Lizzie nodded, realizing her hands were shaking. "I-I didn't know that. Thank you."

"Who is it you're lookin' for, ma'am?"

Lizzie wondered how he knew she was searching for someone, until she saw the answer mirrored in his gaze. It seemed to say, *Why else would you be out here?*

"I'm looking for my fiancé, Second Lieutenant Blake Townsend. He was—*is*," she swiftly corrected, "in Tucker's Brigade."

The young man turned and pointed across the valley where a gentle rise in the land obscured the remainder of the field from view. "Tucker's Brigade was part of the western flank, so you'd do best to head over that way. That's where most of the wounded men still are. We got the wounded through here last night."

"Thank you." She paused. "What is your name?"

"Private Rogers, ma'am. Albert Rogers."

"Thank you, Private Rogers, for your help. My name is—"

"Oh, I know who you are, Miss Clouston. Every man at Carnton knows your name. Mrs. McGavock's too." For the first time, the young man smiled. "Everybody back there's sayin' that if they had to get all shot up, they're mighty glad it got to be around Carnton."

Lizzie felt the warmth of his smile in her chest. "Thank you again, Private." She nodded and walked on toward the west side of the field, stepping on the ground whenever she could, and cringing and stepping as gingerly as possible when she couldn't.

The corpses of horses redirected her steps more than a few times, and she instinctively checked to make sure a rider wasn't trapped beneath and somehow still alive. Close by lay a Confederate colonel and a Federal major, their positions indicating they'd slain each other with pistols. And not three feet from them was a commander lying facedown, his sword in one hand, hat in the other, as though he'd been surging forward, rallying his troops, when death took him.

On the scant parcels of ground not cradling the dead, the earth resembled fields recently raked or harrowed. She remembered what Captain Jones had said about ten thousand bullets plowing the ground around him. It was a wonder he—or anyone else—could have lived through this. And yet men had. And, she hoped prayerfully, Towny would be among them.

As she ascended the gentle rise of land, she could hear the now all-too-familiar moans of the wounded. When she reached the top and the valley began to gently slope back down, spreading out before her, she saw hundreds of wounded men scattered among the dead and dying. The scene caused her to view the number of men convalescing at Carnton in a different light. The men groaned and begged for water, and she chided herself for not giving this undertaking more forethought.

Infirmary corps worked their way among the soldiers, stopping to give aid to some while carrying others away on stretchers. Fires still burned here and there on the field. Whether started by intention or lingering from the battle, she didn't know.

She spotted townspeople, no doubt looking for someone as she was, picking their way across the valley. She peered down the pike and spotted even more people coming. Women and children in droves. She prayed for the children, that God would somehow protect them from being scarred by what they would see.

She continued on, searching the faces of the deceased, praying she wouldn't recognize any of them. Only yesterday these men had been living, breathing, conversing, some even jesting with each other and singing along with the band as they'd crossed the fields on their way past Carnton. On their way to die. If she could have spoken with them before the battle, she had no doubt they would have told her they were ready and willing to die for the Confederacy, for their families, for their convictions. Yet she couldn't help but wonder . . . With the benefit now of looking back on this life from eternity, would they still think the sacrifice worth it?

She knew her personal loathing for this war influenced her perspective, but she had a difficult time believing that all of these men had died with honor. Because surely the honor in giving one's life for a cause could not be measured solely by the act of laying down one's life. The pages of history were rife with people who had willingly died in the name of despicable convictions and beliefs. So how did one make sense of all this death?

Both sides had committed atrocities. Both sides believed God was on their side. Both sides had families waiting at home. Families who, for scores of men on this field, would never see their father, husband, son, or uncle again. The weight of the question bowed her head. And she soon realized it was impossible to answer without having known each man's heart.

But God knows.

The thought came like gentle thunder, and she slowly lifted her head and stared across the valley. Her throat filled with unshed tears. Each man lying dead on this field had had his reasons for joining the war. And although God seemed another world away right now, and had for some time, he knew the heart of every one of them. She believed that even when the world—and everything around her—told her otherwise. So as she continued on, looking for the one face she prayed she would not see among the dead, she silently honored in her heart every man she passed, those dressed in blue and those in butternut and gray, even while wishing they hadn't had to kill each other.

West of the pike lay the locust thicket where she and Johnny had hunted together as children. But the thicket looked more like a forest of toothpicks now. The trees, once twelve inches in diameter at the stump, either stood stripped bare of their leaves, limbs, and bark or had been struck by so many bullets they'd toppled beneath their own weight.

She passed another ditch piled high with mangled bodies and was several steps past when she thought she heard something. She turned back to listen, recalling only too well what Private Rogers had told her. Apparently having been mistaken, she moved on.

There it was again. An almost inaudible moan. She retraced her steps to the ditch.

"Hello?" she said softly, too softly. So she said it again, louder this time. And someone answered. Someone from beneath the pile! Heart racing, Lizzie turned back and spotted a corpsman about a hundred yards away. She cupped her hands around her mouth. "Help! I need help over here! Someone is still alive!"

The corpsman lifted an arm and called something back to her, but he was downwind so she couldn't hear him. He turned to another man a ways behind him, and together they came running. Lizzie tried to pull one of the bodies off, but the weight was too much for her.

She leaned down close to the ground. "If you can hear me . . . help is coming!"

A muffled response. Perhaps weaker than before? She couldn't be sure.

The first corpsman reached her, his breath heavy. "You think somebody's alive under there?" He began hefting the bodies and laying them to the side.

"Yes, I believe I heard a voice calling out."

"We checked all these ditches through here earlier."

The second corpsman arrived, and working together, the two men removed the bodies down to the last layer. And sure enough, when they'd hefted a particularly large man off the pile, a young soldier lay at the bottom, faceup, his skin pale and eyes glassy, and with a nasty leg wound. Grapeshot, Lizzie felt certain, based on the damage. But he was alive.

She climbed down into the ditch. "Do either of you have any water?"

The second corpsman had a pack with him, and he handed her a canteen. Lizzie uncorked the cap and held it to the soldier's mouth. He gulped the water down.

"Take your time. Little sips. You can have more." Judging by his lean physique and the fine smattering of fuzz on his jawline, she guessed him to be around fifteen or sixteen years old. On closer inspection, she saw a bone in his leg was shattered, so she knew what fate awaited him.

"Did . . . we win?" he asked, looking up at her.

She brushed the matted hair from his forehead. "You fought bravely. All of you fought *so* bravely."

He seemed to understand her meaning and didn't ask again.

"We'll go fetch a stretcher, ma'am, and get him out of here."

Within minutes they returned and transferred him to the stretcher—a painful process. And when the young soldier reached out to her, Lizzie gladly took hold of his hand. They lifted him from the ditch, and when they started in the direction of the ambulance, Lizzie gave his hand a final squeeze. But his grip tightened on hers as tears welled up in his eyes.

"Thank you, ma'am. For hearin' me. If you hadn't come out here today—" He didn't finish his sentence. He didn't need to.

On a whim, Lizzie leaned down and kissed his forehead, emotion blurring her vision. "Thank you for your courage and your bravery."

Weary beyond anything she could remember, she continued toward the western flank, one foot in front of the other, searching the faces and stopping twice—heart in her throat—to turn over the bodies of two particular soldiers. From the back, they had looked so much like Towny. When she spotted Dr. Phillips up ahead tending the wounded, she knew she was getting close to where Tucker's Brigade had fought.

But it was the soldier he was tending, the one leaned up against hastily dug earthworks, who truly captured her attention—and caused her to quicken her pace.

CHAPTER 11

When the soldier turned and looked her way, Lizzie knew. "Towny!" She hurried as fast as she could, thrilled when she saw that he could stand, and even more so when he closed the short distance between them.

"Lizzie!" He wrapped her in a hug as familiar as home and as comforting as a feather bed come winter, then quickly drew back. "What are you doing out here?"

"I'm looking for you! I didn't know until this morning that your brigade was called back to fight." She looked down at the bandage on his arm. "Are you all right?"

He shrugged in typical Towny fashion. "Bullet passed straight through. The doc over there fixed me right up."

"Dr. Phillips," she said, looking beyond him to where the doctor stood.

Towny glanced between them. "You two know each other?"

"Indeed we do." Dr. Phillips nodded. "We've become rather well acquainted over the past few hours. I'm with Loring's Division. Loring's wounded are being cared for at Carnton, and the McGavocks have graciously been helping tend the injured. Miss Clouston has been assisting me in surgery. And doing very well, I might add."

Towny looked down at her, his expression a mixture of pride and regret. "I'm sorry the war's come to Carnton's door. But I'm not surprised at Miss Clouston's abilities, Dr. Phillips. Or the McGavocks' generosity. I've grown up knowing both for as long as I can remember." He pressed a kiss to the crown of Lizzie's head.

Lizzie caught the somewhat curious look the doctor gave her as he began gathering his instruments. She started to explain that Towny was her fiancé, but somehow the moment and setting didn't seem quite right.

"Take care of that arm, Lieutenant." Dr. Phillips gestured. "It needs time to heal. And again, I admire you for staying with your men last night. I'm sorry so many were lost."

Towny's expression sobered. "I am too, Doc. Thanks for stitching me up."

Once Dr. Phillips was out of earshot, Lizzie peered up. "I'm so grateful you're alive, Towny."

"Me too." He stared out across the field. "For a while there last night, I wasn't so sure I was going to be. It was . . ." He blew out a breath, his chin trembling. The haunting descriptions Captain Jones had shared with her that morning were clearly written in the lines of Towny's face.

It had been almost a year since they'd seen each other last, but he looked considerably older, and the customary sparkle in his eyes had dulled. How very much war stole from people. And not only in the cost of lives, though that was tragic enough. All the lost years that could have been spent together, the innocence of children shattered, the children who would never be born, the deep scars that battle left on the land.

He sniffed, then looked over at her. "How are you, Lizzie? I mean . . . beyond the last day or so."

"I'm well enough. Weary at present. But well."

"And your folks?"

"They've been well too. I'm going by their house on the way home to check on them, and to let them know I'm all right. I'll likely stop by the Carters' later and check on them too. They'd all more than welcome a visit from you if you're able to come along."

He glanced away again. "I'd welcome that, but I need to stay and help bury the men from my regiment. We're going to start here soon enough." He gestured behind him to a small group of men seated around a fire, every one of them bandaged up and beaten down.

"Of course." She nodded. "I could stay with you and—"

He shook his head. "As good as it is to see you again—and it *is*—it's hard to see you here. It's not right for you to be here."

She wanted to tell him that there was no protecting her from the war. Not anymore. That when men decided to take up arms, they thrust every woman and child into the fray as well. Different battlefronts, most certainly. But a battlefield all the same. Yet she knew that wasn't what he needed to hear.

He took hold of her hand. "I've thought of you so much during these last months, Lizzie Beth. You're what's kept me going. I'm so eager to get back here. To start our life together as man and wife."

He intertwined his fingers with hers, and Lizzie stared at their clasped hands, waiting to feel something more than the warmth of friendship. Especially when he brought her hand to his mouth and kissed it. She definitely felt something different then, but it was the opposite of what she should have felt. An emotion more disconcerting than moving. She recalled the intimate turn her thoughts had taken when she'd recently been watching Captain Jones, and that recollection only fed the seed of doubt taking deeper root inside her.

She realized Towny was watching her, waiting, and she knew she needed to say something. "I've missed you too. And I'm so glad you're all right." True statements, both of them. Yet judging by the longing in his gaze, it wasn't what he'd hoped to hear.

"Are you okay, Lizzie? Are . . . *we* okay?"

"Of course," she said hurriedly, the uncertainty in his expression too much to bear. She worked to lighten her voice. "Will I see you again before you leave?"

He hesitated, then nodded. "I'll do my best to call on Carnton before we pull out."

She noticed it then, the scarf around his neck, the one she'd knit for him the past Christmas. She gave it a tug. "I see you're still wearing it."

He looked down and smiled. "I've hardly taken it off since you gave it to me. It's like carrying a piece of you with me everywhere I go."

The silence stretched between them, and as he looked at her she sensed an ocean of words wanting to spill out from him. Yet she hoped he would stem the tide. Because once they were let loose, the words wouldn't ebb quickly. And this was not the place or time.

She stood on tiptoe and kissed his cheek. And to her surprise, he hugged her tight again. The way he'd held her the day he'd buried his sweet mother all those years ago. Like she was the last thing he had on earth.

"I love you, Lizzie."

Warmth sprang to her eyes. "I love you too, Towny."

He pressed a firm kiss to her forehead, then walked back to join the other men.

Gathering her emotions, Lizzie picked her way north across the field in the direction of town, hopeful of finding more wounded men among the dead. But with each step she took, that hope drained away.

Up ahead, still some distance away, lay the Federal breastworks Captain Jones had told her about. The formations were exactly as he had described. Well built, seemingly impenetrable from this perspective. At least three feet wide in some places and at least that many feet tall, if not more. How could anyone approach that barrier with guns flashing and cannons firing from behind and hold any hope of living? She paused for a moment and looked behind her to the south. Such a wide-open field. No place to hide. So vulnerable. Exposed. She briefly closed her eyes, still able to hear the crack of rifle fire and the explosions of cannons. And standing here now in the midst of the destruction, she could not envision charging across this valley toward an army entrenched behind those walls. The mere imagining sent a shudder through her.

"Ma'am?"

Startled, Lizzie turned to see Lieutenant O'Brien approaching. She hoped he didn't ask for his handkerchief back. She'd lost it somewhere along the way. "Yes, Lieutenant?"

"I know you got a mind of your own, ma'am, and you can do as you please. But I'd feel wrong within myself if I didn't warn you away from going any closer to the Federal line. There ain't much left of the men who got that far."

Lizzie swallowed hard. "Thank you, Lieutenant. I'll heed your counsel. And am grateful for it."

Changing course, she headed due east, intent on taking the long way around to town, when she saw a soldier in the distance, sitting astride a horse. The man was full-bearded with a long, tawny mustache, and if her vision wasn't playing tricks on her, he was absent a leg. He had an air about him too. Melancholy, without doubt. But also contemplative.

"Lieutenant." She glanced back. "Who is that man? On the horse?"

O'Brien gave her an odd look. "That'd be General John Bell Hood, ma'am. Commander of the Army of Tennessee. Or what's left of it."

Lizzie felt surprise register in her expression. The lieutenant must have seen it too, because he nodded.

"Rumor is he told General Cheatham he'd rather fight the enemy where they'd been fortifying for eight hours, instead of Nashville, where they'd been fortifying for years." O'Brien let loose a stream of tobacco juice. "Little good that did him."

He walked on, and Lizzie slowly looked back at General Hood. And though she hadn't taken a single step, the knowledge O'Brien had given her changed her view. She continued on, General Hood not far from her path. He continued to stare across the fields as though she were not even there. Some might call her twisted, but she wanted to see close up the kind of man who would send twenty thousand soldiers across an open field to almost certain death. And if not to death, to hellish rage and mutilation. That didn't feel like war to her. That felt like something very different. And very wrong.

She passed him, half expecting him to look her way. But he didn't. And though she couldn't be certain, she thought she saw his face damp with tears. Yet no amount of tears could right this kind of wrong. But—she paused and looked back across the field—how could anyone in their right mind view this cauldron of inconceivable fury and call it right? Much less worth it.

Roland felt like he'd been dragged by a horse over rough terrain for twenty miles. Every part of him hurt. His head throbbed. And he wondered, not for the first time, if he'd done the right thing in insisting the doctor allow him to keep his leg.

"Captain Jones, how may I make things more comfortable for you, sir?" Sister Catherine Margaret bent over him.

"Well, Sister . . ." He grimaced. "Unless you have a full flask hidden somewhere in that habit of yours, I'm guessing not much."

That earned him a grin, as he'd thought it would.

She made a tsking sound. "If only you hadn't stipulated 'full,' Captain Jones, I might have been able to comply."

Roland managed a slight smile. Just what he needed. A nun with a sense of humor.

Sister Catherine Margaret disappeared from view, then returned with a bottle of laudanum. He gratefully accepted the medicine and the glass of water to wash it down, then closed his eyes and willed himself to think of home. Or what used to be home.

But instead of the gently rolling hills of Yalobusha, Mississippi, and the house he'd built for Weet and Lena, other images crowded in—the barrage of rifle fire, grapeshot cutting his legs to pieces, the deathly whistle of a cannonball right before it—

Roland opened his eyes wide, preferring the company of pain to being forced back into that nightmare again. A frontal assault over a near two-mile open expanse before a well-armed entrenchment. He'd questioned General Hood's orders as soon as they'd come down. Same as he had in Atlanta. Not to the commander's face. Hood had been holed up on Winstead Hill with his senior officers. So Roland found General Cheatham, who'd also been studying the Federal Army's position, and shared his concerns with him.

"I don't like the looks of this fight either, Captain Jones. They have an excellent position and are well fortified." Cheatham had mounted his horse and ridden off with the intention of conveying those opinions to General Hood, to try to dissuade him. But Hood's orders remained unchanged.

Roland made an effort to set the thoughts aside, having learned that little good came from rehashing what couldn't be changed. Sister Catherine Margaret or one of the other nuns had closed the windows in the room, but the drapes remained open, and he could see it was getting dark outside.

His shoulder muscles ached, and he longed to shift positions on the floor, but he didn't dare, remembering the outcome of his last attempt. Maybe once the laudanum took effect again, he could manage it. At least his fever had broken. That was something. That portion of early morning was hazy to him, but he did remember seeing Miss Clouston hovering over him, pressing cold cloths to his face and neck, hearing her voice from what felt like a long distance away. He'd instinctively reached out and tried to grasp her hand, but she'd been just beyond his reach.

Footsteps sounded in the hallway, and he looked toward the door, hoping to see her. But it was the older Negro woman who entered the room, carrying a wicker basket on her arm. He caught the scent of freshly baked bread, and his hopes rose even as his stomach rumbled.

What was the woman's name? Miss Clouston had used it that morning when the two women had spoken at the door. He could almost remember it.

She made her way to his side of the room and leaned down. "Care for a hoecake, sir? They're warm from the stove and slathered with butter."

"I'd be much obliged . . . Tempy."

The surprise on her face matched his own at his memory. She smiled and pressed not one but two warm hoecakes into the palm of his left hand. He ate the cakes stacked together so as not to draw attention to her generosity and closed his eyes as he chewed. The cornbread tasted like home, comfort, and Sunday mornings. And bacon. She must fry hers in bacon grease like his own dear mother did.

He needed to write to his mother and sisters at first opportunity. Tell them what had happened and that he was going to be all right. At least, he thought he was. He also wanted to ask them to send George. If ever there was a time he needed George, it was—

"Tempy, you've been busy!"

Hearing her voice, Roland opened his eyes and looked toward the door, and felt as though the sun had risen for a second time that day.

CHAPTER 12

Roland would be hard-pressed to explain it, but the sight of Miss Clouston lightened his burden somehow. It was foolish, he knew, and felt disloyal to Weet's memory, which he never wanted to be, but he'd missed the young woman. Missed her calming nature and the way she brightened the room just by being in it. Miss Clouston accepted the hoecake Tempy offered her and ate it in three bites. Nothing pretentious about the woman either.

Her gaze soon sought his out, and it did him good to watch the tentative smile that briefly curved the corners of her mouth. As she crossed the room toward him, she greeted the other soldiers, something almost reverent in her manner. The way she gently touched their shoulders or brushed the hair back from the foreheads of the younger boys. The loving touches of a mother. Or a sister, perhaps. Although he doubted any soldier in this room viewed Miss Clouston through either of those lenses. And he'd guarantee that every one of them welcomed her attention as much as he did. But it was the tiny chair right next to him that she claimed.

"Captain Jones, you look as though you're feeling better than you did this morning."

"I am, ma'am. For the most part." It wasn't the whole truth. But being up closer to her, he detected weariness in the half-moon shadows beneath her eyes, and a weight on her slender shoulders he didn't remember. And he didn't wish to add to it. "How are *you* faring? We're all just lying around up here. You're the one doing the work."

She smiled with her eyes. "I'm well enough. I went to see my parents this afternoon to make sure they were all right."

He raised his brows, and she nodded.

"They are. Mama said a few of the buildings downtown had been set ablaze last night. Some of the stables and the old Fellows Hall. But the fires were quickly extinguished."

He frowned. "Your parents live in downtown Franklin?"

She nodded, and he suddenly had an inkling as to the weariness he'd detected in her. He knew this area fairly well, his division having encamped outside Nashville before. And he'd studied a detailed layout of Franklin before the battle yesterday as tactics were being discussed. The only way to get to town from Carnton was either to walk directly across the fields or to take Lewisburg Pike. Either path would have taken her directly across the eastern flank of the valley—and the aftermath of the battle. It wasn't weariness he saw in her; it was horror. And shock. The hoecakes in his stomach went sour.

"I wish you hadn't gone there." He kept his voice soft, still hoping he was mistaken in his conclusion. But the watery truth in her eyes told him he wasn't.

She opened her mouth to speak, but nothing came out. She turned away from the room and toward the hearth, and bowed her head.

Struggling to contain his own emotions, he felt fatigue move through him. Not so much physical—although there was that, most certainly, aided by the laudanum—but fatigue of heart. Of soul. He was weary of this war. He'd witnessed more killing, by his own hand and the hands of others, than a person ever should. But seeing war's brutality through a woman's eyes—the price it exacted—made him think of Weet and the times she'd begged him to come home, both in her letters and during the two visits they'd shared since the war began. Her tears and pleas had moved him deeply. The memory of them still did.

But in the end, considering the US government's determination to mandate how the South would live and conduct its business, he'd felt as though he'd had no choice but to defend hearth and home. To defend his land, his family's honor, and their future. He'd attended the Charlotte Democratic Delegation in April of '60 where he'd prayed some semblance of peace would come through negotiation. But when a backwoods congressman from Kentucky, one bent on abolishing slavery, won the Republican nomination, he and everyone else in the South knew what was coming down the pike. And sure enough, Abraham Lincoln won the White House. But before Lincoln could take office, seven states seceded, Mississippi being second among them. Then on the heels of Fort Sumter, four more states followed suit. What gave a man—or a government, for that matter—the right to tell its people how they were going to live? To simply come in and take away a man's livelihood, his ability to provide for his family? Roland's chest tightened with emotion.

He'd counted the cost before entering this war, and had decided it was a price he was willing to pay. But hindsight was challenging that original conclusion. Because what he saw so much more clearly now was that when a man decided to stand firm on a conviction or belief, it was never he alone who paid, but everyone who knew and loved him.

He looked at Miss Clouston, her head still bowed. Debating with himself, he finally reached over and gently covered her hands on her lap. She didn't pull away.

"Every man out there yesterday knew the likelihood that he would die, ma'am. We all went in having accepted that."

She slowly met his gaze. "I know, but . . ." She firmed her lips, her chin trembling. "I saw the Federal entrenchments. And they were just as you described. What I can't understand"—she briefly closed her eyes—"is how you all saw that and yet still chose to charge across that field to . . ." Her voice broke, and she simply looked at him, her gaze communicating what she could not.

"For love of home and family," he said softly, guilt tugging hard at the irony of that conviction. He'd left those he loved in order to defend them. Only to have them die while he was away.

For the longest time she stared at him, then gave him a tentative, watery smile and nodded. Reluctantly, he withdrew his hand.

A moment passed, and she blew out a breath and wiped her cheeks. She sat up a little straighter, the strength of character he'd first seen in her last night returning. But having glimpsed the vulnerability behind it, however briefly, made the resiliency he saw in her now even more of a treasure.

"This morning, Captain, when you were with fever, you kept asking for someone named George. You said you couldn't find him."

"Really." He narrowed his eyes. "I said that?"

She nodded. "Is he a member of your family? Or a friend?"

Roland thought about her query before answering, having had time to consider how integral a person George had become to him through the years—which he wouldn't have expected, considering each of their positions—and how all that was set to change once the Confederacy fell. "He's both, I guess you could say. George is my manservant. And a most trusted one. He's been with me since we were children. I intend to send for him."

Her eyebrows rose slightly. "George is a slave."

She said it matter-of-factly, yet he sensed a hint of question—and perhaps disapproval—in her tone, if he wasn't mistaken.

"That's right." He eyed her. "What? You don't consider us Mississippians cultured enough to have manservants?"

The look she gave him said she wouldn't be so easily baited. It also confirmed the disapproval he'd glimpsed seconds before. "It's not that. I simply didn't—" She straightened, then glanced about as if concerned others might overhear their conversation. "I simply assumed George was someone else. Do you own many slaves?"

He held her gaze, hearing polite yet undeniable censure this time. "Seven currently. That number was considerably higher before the war. But the last letter from home informed me that six more have run off."

She didn't say anything. Aloud, anyway. But whether the woman knew it or not, her eyes communicated plenty. He knew there were pockets of abolitionists all over the South. Counties in the middle of slave states that had voted against secession, and that had even given aid to the Federals. But to find one of those persons here, on an estate such as Carnton, and at the home of such a prominent plantation owner as Colonel McGavock—now that was surprising.

"You said you intend to send for George?" she asked, obviously desiring to change the subject.

Roland hesitated, not as eager to brush it aside as she was. Especially not with her. He found himself wanting to know more about her. More than she apparently was willing to reveal. And to think he'd thought her sorrowful over the Confederate States being poised on the brink of losing this war. Yet considering the present company around them and feeling the laudanum slowly working its way through his body, he simply nodded. "I hadn't planned on it, but now that this has happened"—he gestured to his legs—"I'll need help being transported to the nearest Federal hospital. Wherever that is. Usually with wounds so severe, I'd have to stay behind, which would mean being taken prisoner by the Federals."

She frowned. "But the Federals have left. They've gone on to Nashville, I hear."

"Yes, for now. But they'll be back. Fort Granger, one of their outposts, is only a short distance from here. And the US Army still occupies Nashville, remember. Nashville's the second most fortified city in the country, with Washington, DC, being the first. So rest assured, they'll be back. Over the next day or two, every soldier who isn't able to walk his way out of here with what's left of the Army of Tennessee will become a prisoner. The Federals will likely take those men to either a hospital in Nashville or a prison up north."

She stared. "You state it so matter-of-factly."

He managed a shrug. He felt anything but cavalier about the

prospect, especially considering his injuries—and his own options if George couldn't get here in time. "It's war, Miss Clouston. And there are protocols. Besides, I've been taken prisoner before. Although, having experienced that, I'm none too eager to repeat it."

Her brow furrowed. "When was that? And where?"

"At Shiloh. Back in April of '62. I got exchanged pretty quickly, though, so I didn't have it rough for long. Not like some others. The men who were badly wounded, even those sent to the Federal hospitals, a lot of them didn't make it."

Without warning, the muscles in his back went from aching to screaming, and he sucked in a breath. He needed to move, no matter the resulting pain in his legs. "Miss Clouston, would you be so kind as to help me change positions?"

"Of course. Where is it hurting?"

Where does it not hurt? he wanted to reply, but didn't. "My lower back, mainly."

She knelt behind him on the floor. "What if I were to slip something beneath your neck? Something like"—she glanced around, then reached for something under the bed—"this." She held up a stuffed bear. "Winder hasn't played with him in ages, and I think it will provide the support you need."

He grimaced. "Whatever will stop the pain."

She slid her hands beneath his head, and although her touch felt heavenly, he braced himself, the mere anticipation of more pain causing him to break out in a cold sweat.

"Relax, Captain, and let me do the work. I haven't lost a head yet." She peered down at him, a smile curving her mouth.

Roland tried to return it but couldn't.

She gently lifted his head and slipped the stuffed animal beneath his neck. Roland gritted his teeth, waiting for the pain in his legs to escalate—but it didn't. In fact, after a moment or two, the spasm in his lower back began to subside. Eyes closed, he released a held breath.

"Better?" she whispered.

"Oh yes, ma'am. Thank you."

His eyes watered with relief, and he lay there for a moment reveling in the sheer absence of at least a portion of the pain—and in the softness of her hands on his body. He opened his eyes and found her staring down at him. But as soon as his gaze connected with hers, she looked away.

"Miss Clouston?"

Roland turned his head in the direction of the tentative voice and spotted a little boy peering wide-eyed into the room from the side of the doorway. Judging from his expression, the lad was hesitant to enter.

"Winder . . ." Miss Clouston rose and went to him.

She knelt down and must have asked him a question because the boy nodded, his eyes fixed on hers. Miss Clouston tousled his hair and lifted him into her arms. He hugged her neck tight, then held on as if that were second nature to him.

Miss Clouston took him around the room and introduced him to every soldier by name and rank until they finally came to him.

"And this, Winder, is Captain Roland Jones, from Mississippi. Captain, this is Master Winder McGavock, Colonel John McGavock's son—and my all-too-grown-up seven-year-old charge."

"Nice to make your acquaintance, Winder." Roland saluted the boy with his bandaged right hand, which drew an instant grin and a salute in return.

Winder's attention shifted. "You found Horace!"

"Yes, we did," Miss Clouston interjected. "He'd somehow been stuffed beneath your bed." She gave the boy an admonishing look, which the child pretended not to notice. "But when I was looking for something to serve as a pillow for Captain Jones, Horace immediately crawled out and graciously agreed to help."

"Which," Roland added, "has earned him a special citation of merit medal that I'm certain he'll share with you."

The boy's brows shot up. "Can I see the medal, Captain?"

"*May* I see it," Miss Clouston gently corrected.

"Sure you can. It's over there in my knapsack in the corner. It's in the inside pocket."

She lowered the boy to the ground, and Roland caught a glimmer of delight in her expression. Perhaps he was making up ground for her earlier disappointment in him. Odd that he cared so much about her opinion. But he did. Winder retrieved the knapsack and joined them again. Miss Clouston took a seat on the child-size chair, stifling a yawn, and Winder cozied up beside her.

Feeling another wave of the laudanum's effects and grateful for it, Roland nodded. "It's just inside the pocket there. But you must hand it to me first, Winder, and let me formally present it to you and Horace."

Winder did as instructed, soberly handing the contents to Roland, who made a show of clearing his throat.

"Master Winder McGavock, it is with greatest honor that I confer this citation of merit upon you and Sir Horace the Bear for your generosity and service to the Army of Tennessee." Roland would've sworn he saw the little boy's chest puff out with pride. "And specifically to you, Winder, for your kindness in sharing your bedroom with all of these soldiers. And your bear with Captain Roland Ward Jones, First Battalion, Mississippi Sharpshooters, Adams' Brigade."

Winder's eyes lit up. "You're a sharpshooter?"

Roland held a forefinger to his lips. "I still need to confer your medal," he whispered, able to sense the boy's excitement. "Hold out your right hand, please, Master Winder."

Winder complied, and Roland placed the "medal" into his tiny palm.

The boy studied it, then looked back. "Looks kind of like a button to me." A touch of suspicion colored his tone.

And Roland didn't miss the *Aha—he caught you!* expression on Miss Clouston's pretty face. But he forged on, still remembering what it was like to be a boy.

"That's because, Winder"—he motioned the lad closer, lowering his voice—"these medals are largely given in secret. They're made to be sewn onto a young man's coat. Do you see the eagle on the front?"

Winder nodded, studying it up close.

"That's a symbol of courage and honor. And it's there as a reminder to whoever's wearing this that *he* is a man of courage and honor. Because real heroes don't have to wear big shiny medals on their chests to show others who they are or to prove themselves worthy. No, sir. Real heroes are the ones who do what's right even when no one's looking, and who give up something for someone else even when it costs them dearly. Like you've done with your bedroom. And like Sir Horace here is doing by serving as my pillow."

Winder looked at him, then to the button, then back to him and leaned down and hugged Roland's neck. "Thank you, Captain Jones." He straightened. "I'm gonna ask Tempy to sew it on my coat right now!"

"We might want to wait until tomorrow to ask Tempy," Miss Clouston said. "She's been very busy today cooking and taking care of everyone in the house."

Winder hesitated, then finally nodded. "Yes, ma'am." Then just as quickly, his focus shifted, and he pointed to Roland's bandaged right hand. "Does that hurt?"

"Winder . . . ," Miss Clouston quietly corrected.

"No, that's all right." Roland held up his hand, its bandaging leaving no question as to the absence of his fore, middle, and ring finger. "It doesn't hurt too badly right now. But it did sting an awful lot when it first happened."

"Did the doc give you back your fingers after he cut 'em off?"

Roland enjoyed the look of horror on Miss Clouston's face.

"And *that*, Master Winder," she said, rising and nudging him toward the door, "will be all of the questions for tonight. Captain, we bid you a good evening, sir. I need to get the children to bed. But either

Sister Catherine Margaret or one of the other nuns will be here with you all throughout the night. Some family members and neighbors have come to help as well. I hope you're able to get some sleep."

"Thank you, ma'am. I hope you rest well too. And while I wish I could award you a citation of merit as well, I fear, madam, that the medal fine enough to reward you for your courage and honor has not yet been forged."

She held his gaze for a beat, then quietly dipped her head and left the room hand in hand with her young charge. Roland watched her go.

An abolitionist at Carnton. Though not an outspoken one, it would seem. He wondered if the McGavocks knew. Somehow he doubted it, based upon Miss Clouston's quiet nature. But as he'd learned in his life, still waters ran deep. And given enough time, even the smoothest river could carve through rock.

He'd encountered people of similar opinion to Miss Clouston before and—especially considering the outcome of the battle last night—was all but certain that the North would win out in the end. Because the Confederacy was on its last leg, for lack of a better term. A condition he knew a little something about. If the North did win this war, changes were coming, and he'd had plenty of time in recent weeks to contemplate them. And it unnerved him, though he didn't like to acknowledge it. He didn't know what that new world would look like. He only knew it would look vastly different from this one.

It also meant he'd likely lose his estate. *Oak Hill.* Then again, he'd already lost what was dearest in this world to him. Losing his home and even the family land would pale in comparison, if not for his continuing duty to care for his mother and unmarried sisters, along with his aunt and young female cousins from Georgia, who'd recently sought refuge at Yalobusha after Sherman had finished his work in Atlanta. Plus, there was George and his family and the remaining slaves. No, he had to find a way to keep the estate. To keep their home.

He closed his eyes and struggled to picture both Susan's and

Lena's smiles, which were becoming less and less clear to him with each passing day. He hadn't been back home since he'd gotten news of their deaths. He wasn't even there when they'd been buried. His eyes burned with emotion. Because he'd been away fighting. Fighting to keep them safe.

CHAPTER 13

Lizzie ushered Winder down to the kitchen where Mrs. McGavock, Tempy, and Hattie sat at the table in the corner looking as worn and weary as she felt. For a half second she wondered where Sallie was, then remembered that the girl's parents had traveled down from Nashville earlier to take her home.

"Hot cocoa?" Tempy offered, half rising.

Lizzie shook her head. "No, thank you, Tempy. All I want is my bed."

"Can I sleep with you tonight, Miss Clouston?" Hattie asked.

"Me too!" Winder pleaded, tugging on her hand.

But Mrs. McGavock shook her head. "Children, we'll make you a pallet upstairs as we did last night. Miss Clouston needs some time to—"

"It's fine. Truly. They're welcome to stay in my room with me, if it's agreeable to you and the colonel."

"You're certain, my dear?"

"We'll be fine in my room. And you'll be right next door in case they need anything." Lizzie bid them good night, then remembered. "I went to see my parents in town to tell them about what happened here and that we're all right. They're well too. Papa's busy delivering what medicine and supplies he has. Mama's helping as she can."

Carrie nodded. "I imagine they're helping many."

"They send their greetings to you and the colonel." Lizzie didn't want to deliver this next news. "I also stopped by the Carters' house on my way back."

Carrie leaned forward. "How are Mr. Carter and his family? I believe the grandchildren were there this week too. Were they overrun?"

"They're mostly all right. Now. And yes, Federal officers took over the house for their quarters. The Carters were holed up in the basement during the fighting. His daughter told me that bullets started flying in, breaking through the windows."

"Was anyone hurt?" Carrie asked.

"No. They stuffed coils of rope into the openings. But there were twenty-four of them down in that basement in the dark from the time the battle started until early this morning. Mr. Carter and his eldest son, his daughters and his nine grandchildren, along with their slaves and the Lotz family. They said they thought the battle would rage on forever. There must be a thousand or more bullet holes in the house and the outbuildings."

Carrie shook her head. "God bless them."

"There's one more thing." Remembering the heartbreak in Fountain Carter's eyes, she had a hard time speaking. "Mr. Carter told me they found his son Tod less than two hundred yards from the house. He was shot several times. He's badly hurt and delirious. A doctor extracted a bullet from his head, but the family hasn't been given any hope for him to live."

Her own eyes glistening, Carrie bowed her head. "I'll make a visit tomorrow and see what I can do for them."

Lizzie trailed the children's path up the narrow staircase to the three bedrooms situated directly above the kitchen—Tempy's, hers, and a third bedroom that usually remained vacant. But not tonight.

She felt as though she were groping her way through a thick fog. Every muscle in her body ached with fatigue, and her eyes burned from lack of sleep. She found the children's bedclothes in the third bedroom at the end of the hall, along with Colonel and Mrs. McGavock's trunks that sat near the foot of the bed. Odd how life oftentimes came full circle. This had been the colonel's room when he was a young boy. No doubt it held special memories for him.

Even now, with hog killing day a good two weeks ago, the strong aroma of salted pork—ham shoulders, roasts, fatback, and bacon—seeped through the shared wall with the smokehouse on the other side. She was grateful now that the colonel had taken advantage of November's especially cold weather to organize the hog killing earlier than usual. They would need the extra meat to feed the soldiers for however long they were here. Which wouldn't be long, per Captain Jones.

She shouldn't have been so surprised to discover he was a slave owner. He was older, in his early thirties, she guessed, and seemed to be a man of means. Or had once been. No doubt the war had significantly reduced his financial holdings, much as the McGavocks' wealth had been affected. Although, as far as she knew, the McGavocks were still comfortably well off and were still very generous with that wealth. But the prosperity of these large estates had been built on the backs of slaves. So what would the McGavocks do after the war? How would their lives change? More importantly, how would Tempy's life change? She massaged her temples, more tired than she could ever remember being.

"What are you going to read to us tonight?" Hattie asked after changing into her nightgown.

"Oh, that Christmas book. You promised!" Winder piped in, still clutching his "medal" in one hand. "The one with ghosts! And that bad man."

Lizzie added more wood to the low-burning fire in the hearth, having known this moment would come. "I'm sorry, children, but the book is back in Winder's bedroom. However . . ." She spoke over their disappointed groans. "I've read this book numerous times and happen to have some of the opening paragraphs committed to memory."

Instantly their groanings ceased, and they climbed into bed and beneath the covers. In moments like these, Lizzie was grateful for her knack for recollection. *Like flies swarmin' to warm honey,* her father always said in that Scottish brogue of his. *Any bit of knowledge comes close enough to my sweet Lizzie, it's stuck fast and done for!* She could read something once and pretty much commit it to memory. Though how much she could depend on her recollection tonight, she didn't know.

She settled on the edge of the bed, the softness of the mattress and her pillow beckoning. But she still needed to change from her soiled shirtwaist and skirt into her gown after the children were asleep. She would love a hot bath too, but that would have to wait.

"*A Christmas Carol,*" she started with as dramatic a flair as she could muster. "By Charles Dickens."

The siblings glanced at each other, smiling, and Lizzie marveled again at how resilient children were.

"Are you going to do the voices?" Winder whispered.

"Of course she's doing the voices," Hattie countered. "She always does the voices."

As was customary, Lizzie waited until they were absolutely still before she started. "'Marley was dead: to begin with. There is no doubt whatever about that.'"

Winder's eyes gained a spark, while Hattie's widened.

"'The register of his burial,'" Lizzie continued, "'was signed by the clergyman, the clerk, the undertaker, and the chief mourner. Scrooge signed it: and Scrooge's name was good upon 'Change, for anything he chose to put his hand to. Old Marley was as dead as a door-nail.'"

"When's the part with the ghost?" Winder whispered.

To which Lizzie merely raised an eyebrow. His mouth flattened to a thin line.

Lizzie continued narrating, but after a few moments, being so tired, she felt certain she was forgetting sentences here and there. "'Oh! But he was a tight-fisted hand at the grindstone, Scrooge! a squeezing, wrenching, grasping, scraping, clutching, covetous, old sinner!'"

Winder beamed. Hattie bit her lower lip.

Her memory fading, Lizzie closed her eyes to concentrate. "'Hard and sharp as flint, from which no steel had ever struck out generous fire; secret, and self-contained, and solitary as an oyster. The cold within him froze his features, nipped his pointed nose, shriveled his cheek, stiffened his gait; made his eyes—'"

Lizzie looked back and, just like that, discovered both children fast asleep, eyes closed, little mouths slack. She released a long sigh. *Thank goodness.* She tilted her head back and angled it from side to side, the muscles in her shoulders corded tight.

Knowing how Winder would feel if he lost what Captain Jones had "conferred upon him," she gently pried open the boy's palm and placed the brass eagle button on her bedside table. Clever thinking on Captain Jones's part. He was a most kind and caring man, and articulate in conveying his thoughts.

For love of home and family, he'd told her.

He'd no doubt been thinking of his wife when he'd said that earlier. Which, knowing that, made Lizzie feel even more uncomfortable because of her response to him when he'd briefly touched her hand. The captain had been attempting to comfort her, she knew. An innocent gesture on his part, and scarcely more than other soldiers had done in conveying their thanks during the past hours. But when he'd covered her hands with his and looked up at her—she stared at her shadowed reflection in the mirror on the wardrobe door—something had stirred inside her. A longing, a desire akin to a thirst begging to be quenched. The mere memory of it caused her breath to quicken.

But Captain Roland Jones was a married man, and she was betrothed. And while that alone was more than enough to give her pause—and make her rethink the amount of time she spent with him—what added to her anxiety was her attraction to him. To his easy smile and kind manner. And those intense gray eyes. Why couldn't she feel those things for Towny? Would she ever feel them?

Towny was her dearest friend. She'd known him since they were nine years old, and she'd always looked up to him, admired him. Her love for him *would* grow into something deeper, she simply had to trust in that. She was going to marry Towny, and they would be happy together. They would have children, and he would be a wonderful father. And in the near future, she hoped, Captain Jones would be returning to his wife. If what he'd said held true, he would first be sent to either a Federal hospital or prison. For his sake, she hoped it was the former, and that his manservant, George, arrived in time to help. She rose and crossed to the washbasin, eager to dismiss the doubts.

She poured tepid water from the pitcher into the bowl and washed her hands and face. Checking again to make certain the children were asleep, she quickly disrobed, ran a damp washcloth over her neck and chest, arms and legs, then donned her gown, shivering, her body chilled and goose-fleshed.

She unpinned her hair and ran a brush through just enough to smooth out the tangles—never mind the usual 150 strokes—and turned down the oil lamp and climbed into bed. Or tried to. Winder was already sprawled out on her side, so she carefully scooted him back over and climbed in beside him.

For a moment she simply lay still, relishing the softness of the feather mattress beneath her and the gradual lessening of tension as her tired muscles began to relax. She heard the creak of wagon wheels from outside and thought of all the wounded men lying on the floors in the house or, worse, on the cold, hard ground in the yard. And all those still on the battlefield.

A barrage of images burned into her conscience pulsed one after another in the darkness before her, and she shut her eyes tight, not wanting to see them. But still they came, along with fresh tears. Beyond exhausted, she soon realized sleep was keeping its distance, so she rose, turned up the oil lamp, and reached for her skirt.

She withdrew the contents from the left pocket, knowing that somewhere Thaddeus's mother was waiting for word from her precious son. Perhaps she was scanning a newspaper even now, praying not to find his name on the latest list distributed by the War Department. It was odd. She'd begun to refer to the boy by his first name, as though the two of them had formally met during his lifetime, instead of during his final moments. She fingered the stack of envelopes—three in number—still bound with string, then her focus centered on the knot.

People usually tied bundles of letters with a bow so they could be reread more easily. The knot represented such permanence, such a firm decision, she was hesitant to cut it. It was one thing to be given a letter to be passed along to someone else, but to knowingly open a letter without its having been entrusted specifically to your care was something else entirely. And yet Thaddeus was dead. These letters might contain information that would help her reach his family and give them the message he'd spent his last breath leaving.

She retrieved her scissors from her sewing basket and positioned them over the string, debating, legitimate reasons for why she should cut it flitting through her mind. And yet the knot finally won out. She laid the scissors back on her bedside table alongside the letters. Thinking better of leaving the letters out, especially when sharing a room with the children, she tucked the thin stack safely in the drawer of the bedside table.

She picked up the pocketknife next and, with her forefinger, traced the empty slot where the inlaid ivory had once been. She fingered the worn oblong stone again, but it was the page torn from the Bible that drew her most. She carefully unfolded it. Printed along the top, beside his scrawled name, was *The Book of Psalms.*

Growing chilled, she slipped beneath the covers of the bed, the warmth from Winder's little body radiating heat into hers. She turned the torn page from the Psalms over in her hand. Several of the verses were underlined. Counting front and back, the section contained chapters 62 through 67, along with the first verses of chapter 68. She'd read through the Psalms many times, so some of the verses were familiar to her. *But why this single page?* she wondered. She gave the chapters a quick perusal, then refolded the page and tucked it next to the letters in the drawer and withdrew the contents from her right skirt pocket.

She held the envelope to the lamplight, remembering its author with vivid—and painful—clarity. There was no address on the front, but the envelope wasn't sealed, so Lizzie withdrew the single piece of paper and unfolded it. She was relieved to find a name and address at the top of the page, and beneath that, *For our child.*

She felt herself holding her breath as she read.

Dear Child,

It is with pleasure and delight that I write you a few lines, which will be the first letter you will ever receive, and one, too, which I hope you will preserve until you can read it. By the misfortunes of war, I have been separated from your mama, but by the blessings of God, I hope to soon return to you, never more to leave you, until death shall separate us. My dear and only child, be a good girl, ever love and obey your affectionate mama, and don't forget your first letter writer, who has not nor never will forget you, who daily prays to God, in his infinite mercy, to spare, bless and protect you amid the troubles of this world, and should you live to become old, may God bless you and prepare your soul in this life to go to that happy world after death.

Your father,

P. M. Hope

Lizzie pressed a hand to her midsection, the ache inside her growing until she couldn't contain it. Choking on a sob, she laid the letter aside and reached for her pillow. She pressed her face into its softness to muffle the cries, then curled onto her side away from the children, not wanting to awaken them.

After what seemed a very long time, her spirit and body spent, she gave herself over to sleep, willing it to take her away from all this. At least for a little while. As she drifted on the edge of consciousness, she prayed for the wounded, for the town of Franklin, for Towny . . . and for Captain Jones. All the while listening to the muted weeping coming from the bedroom next door, followed by the deep timbre of Colonel McGavock's voice that let her know he was comforting his wife.

But it was Thaddeus's youthful features and the pleading in his voice that wove in and out of her dreams.

CHAPTER 14

The next morning Roland sat on the bedroom floor, the wall at his back for support, and read the contents of the field orders for a second time. He struggled to reconcile General Hood's message with what he knew firsthand to be true.

December 1, 1864

General Field Orders, Hdqrs. Army of Tennessee
No. 38
Near Franklin

    The commanding general congratulates the army upon the success received yesterday over our enemy by their heroic and determined courage. The enemy have been sent in disorder and confusion to Nashville, and while we lament the fall of many gallant officers and brave men, we have shown to our countrymen that we can carry any position occupied by the enemy.

By command of General Hood:
A. P. Mason, Assistant
Adjutant-General

"'That we can carry any position occupied by the enemy?'"

The audacity of Hood's statement issued late yesterday afternoon, in light of the battle's outcome, nearly burned a hole in his chest and mirrored the bewilderment in Lieutenant Waltham's expression.

"I know." Waltham settled on the floor beside him and glanced at the soldiers lying close by, as if questioning whether he could speak freely.

"It's okay in here, for the most part." Roland surveyed the room, the tension among the men noticeably higher today. And with good reason, considering that eleven more soldiers—two in this room alone—who had seemed on the mend had died during the night from their injuries. That, and they'd gotten word that the Army of Tennessee would soon be moving out. Colonel McGavock had graciously agreed to send the telegram Roland had written his mother requesting she send George posthaste. But he held little hope that George would arrive in time. "Most of the men in here would agree with us, Waltham. Except for Taylor and Smitty across the room there." He noted the two men deep in conversation by the door. "In their eyes, General Hood can do no wrong."

Waltham gestured to the field order. "It's as if Hood was watching a whole different battle."

"Or more like he's trying to cover his own backside after what happened on the way here this week."

"You think he used the battle here in Franklin to try to get back at Schofield for what happened in Spring Hill?"

Roland sighed. Waltham was a fine lieutenant, but he was a good deal younger and still looking for a way to make sense of all this. Something that was difficult enough to do with life in general, much less with war.

"It's only my opinion, Waltham, but I think Hood is desperate, and looking to make up ground wherever he can. He was furious when Schofield managed to get his army past us in Spring Hill. It shamed him." Roland briefly closed his eyes, having gone over these scenarios at least a hundred times. "I think he's still bruised over how Sherman bested him in Atlanta. And remember, Hood and Schofield go back a ways. They were classmates at West Point in '53. Schofield graduated near the top of his class, Hood at the bottom. So I think what happened last night was part battlefield strategy and part personal pride."

Waltham leaned in. "A lot of the men think Hood never should have attacked, Captain Jones. That he should have moved off to the east across the Harpeth River and flanked Schofield out of his breastworks."

Roland shook his head. "With as wide open as that field is and with the Federals commanding the high ground, Schofield would've seen any flanking and would've started moving out. I overheard this morning that the existing bridges across the Harpeth were impassable due to recent rains. All except for a railroad bridge. From what I can piece together, once Schofield arrived in town Wednesday morning, he quickly discovered that the river was too deep to ford. So he set a detail to planking up that trestle bridge as fast as they could. It wouldn't surprise me to learn that he was already moving his supply wagons across the Harpeth even before we charged."

Waltham stared. "So you're saying you think Schofield was already planning to leave? That he hadn't intended to fight?"

"I'm saying I think it was his intention to get to Nashville that night. Which he did, as we now know. Dr. Phillips was here awhile earlier and told me he'd gotten word from General Cheatham that the Federal breastworks were abandoned by midnight after the battle. Schofield left behind their dead and severely wounded and hotfooted it to Nashville."

Movement at the door drew his attention, and Roland looked over, hoping. But it wasn't Miss Clouston.

She hadn't been in yet this morning, which struck him as odd. Yet a lot more people were tending the wounded in the house today—the nuns and several neighbors were helping. Maybe Miss Clouston was assisting Dr. Phillips in another area. Or maybe she was seeing to the children. She was the governess, after all.

"Maybe if we'd waited," Waltham continued. "Maybe if General

Hood had given time for Stephen Lee's corps to catch up with us. Lee had the artillery, after all. You think that would've made a difference?"

"I trailed that rabbit too, Lieutenant, but my gut tells me no. Think about it. It took us nearly two hours to get Cheatham's and Stewart's corps onto the field and ready for action. By then it was already four o'clock. It would've been well after sundown before Lee could've gotten his men positioned. And I got pretty close to those Federal breastworks. I don't think our artillery would've had much effect on them."

"So you're saying it was suicide from the very beginning?" Defeat weighted the younger officer's voice.

"No, I'm not saying that at all. Whenever a soldier offers up his life for his country, for what he believes is worth dying for, I'd never call that suicide. That tarnishes the man's sacrifice, and the honor that first led him to fight. But what I am saying is that I've had plenty of time to lie here and think back through things, wondering had we done this or that, might it have turned out differently. Maybe if Hood had directed the main assault against some other part of the breastworks, we could have penetrated the Federal line better than we did, however briefly. But again, Schofield had the advantage of higher ground, Waltham. He would've seen it coming, and he would have quickly adjusted. What I think really happened . . ." Roland leveled his gaze. "I think Hood looked across the Harpeth Valley, saw the Federal Army within reach, maybe even saw Schofield himself. And Hood wanted to get him before Schofield had a chance to slip away again. So he took that chance."

"Which cost us seventy-five hundred of our men," Waltham said, his voice thinning. "A *third* of our army, Captain Jones. They say near two thousand are lying dead on the field. Or were. They've been burying them since yesterday. It's just not right."

Roland shook his head, aware of Taylor and Smitty and another soldier whose name he didn't recall talking amongst themselves and looking his way. Then he saw her. Miss Clouston walked into the room, and he felt a measure of the weight lifting from deep inside him.

With a basket on her left arm and coffeepot in hand, she began serving the men. She looked more rested this morning. She'd pinned her hair up again, but he could already see a few rebellious brown curls working their way free. He waited for her to look his way. Willed her to. But she didn't.

"I'm sorry about what happened to you, Captain Jones."

Roland glanced back to see Waltham staring down at the worn soldier's blanket that covered his legs, empathy shading his features. Thanks to Sister Catherine's ingenuity, he now wore an older pair of Colonel McGavock's britches—cut off up high on the leg—so he could remove the blanket without fear of offending any of the females in the house.

"Thanks, Waltham. You too. Grapeshot?" He motioned to the young lieutenant's right arm, bandaged at the elbow following the amputation.

Waltham nodded. "I was out early this morning trying to shoot, but . . ." His laughter had a flat edge to it. "I couldn't hit the broad side of a barn. And that's not an exaggeration."

Roland held up his right hand. "It's not like I could do much better."

"I've seen you shoot with your left, though, Captain Jones. There's hope for you yet." A shadow passed across Waltham's face. "Have the doctors said anything about you walking again?"

Roland stared down at his legs. "Not yet. Doc Phillips hasn't given me much hope for even keeping this one long term." He gently touched his right leg, working to appear more optimistic than he felt. "I aim to prove him wrong."

Waltham rose to his feet. "If anyone can, Captain, it's you. And I'm not the only one who holds that opinion, sir."

Moved more than he cared to admit, Roland nodded. "Thank you, Lieutenant Waltham."

Waltham saluted him and Roland returned it, then held out his left hand. Waltham accepted it, then turned and left.

Always keen to Miss Clouston's whereabouts in the room, Roland glanced back in her direction again. But she still didn't look his way.

If he didn't know better, he might think she was ignoring him on purpose. And when she came within three of feet him and still didn't make eye contact, he was certain of it.

"Good morning, Miss Clouston," he offered.

Finally she turned. "Captain." A stiff smile not hers by nature briefly turned her lips. "How are you this morning?"

Roland eyed her. If this woman ever decided to try her skill at poker, she'd get fleeced the very first hand. What he didn't understand was *why* she was attempting to ignore him.

"I'm doing all right, Miss Clouston. How are you, ma'am?"

"Oh, I-I'm well." Her gaze was flighty and landed anywhere but near him. "Would you care for a soda muffin and some coffee?"

"I'd be much obliged." He held out the tin cup Sister Catherine Margaret had left with him, and she filled it. "Thank you. That bread sure smells good. I guess that's more of Tempy's cooking?"

"Actually . . ." She handed him a warm muffin, a flicker of uncertainty shadowing her eyes. "Mrs. McGavock and I baked these this morning, what with Tempy being so busy with the laundry and cooking up several pots of broth."

Roland took a bite, then raised the muffin in a mock toast. "Delicious! My compliments to the cooks."

A hint of pleasure brightened her expression. "Thank you. I actually wasn't sure if they would be any good or not. They're only soda muffins. But with trying to feed so many, we had to do something fast."

"Well, as I said, they're delicious."

She didn't respond, only stared at him, and he would've given much to read her thoughts. To know what was going on behind those eyes that could sparkle like sunshine through stained glass when she laughed. At the moment they resembled more the deep blue of a late summer night sky. Enchanting and fathomless.

"You're sitting up," she finally said, her voice soft. "That's good progress."

"I suppose." He raised a brow. "But at this rate it'll be Easter before I'm able to walk again." It was humbling to realize how he must appear in her eyes. So broken and crippled. But he still had breath within him. That was something. "I just hope that Dr. Phillips will . . ."

From the corner of his eye, he spotted Winder tiptoeing across the bedroom, apparently trying to sneak up on Miss Clouston. Mischief colored the boy's expression, but considering the basket of muffins and pot of coffee Miss Clouston held, Roland thought it best to warn her. He gave her a quick wink. "Don't turn around just now," he whispered, "but you're being stalked."

Her eyes widened in conspiratorial fashion, and she braced herself.

"*Yeeeeah!*" Winder squealed, then let out a high-pitched yelp and grabbed her about the legs.

With surprising—and impressive—agility, Miss Clouston slid the basket handle farther up her arm, transferred the coffeepot to her left hand, and tickled Winder in the ribs with her free hand until the boy dissolved into a pile of giggles.

"That . . . *tickles me!*" he managed amidst laughter.

"Well, that's what a young man gets for sneaking up on his governess!" Miss Clouston's laughter was light and airy, and Roland noticed that several of the wounded men who'd been sullen and keeping to themselves now wore hints of smiles.

Laughter was a powerful medicine. Much like the quiet charm and tender compassion of this beautiful woman. She was Southern through and through, except for her undisclosed abolitionist leanings. Which he was eager to explore once opportunity allowed.

She looked down at him, and something about the way she tilted her head made his heart give an odd double beat.

"Men of the mighty Army of Tennessee!" came a booming voice, and every gaze turned toward the doorway, Roland's included. Standing in the hall was General Cheatham, his face like stone.

Chapter 15

"To every Confederate soldier within earshot of my voice . . ."

Lizzie sobered at the presence of the commanding officer, and Winder did the same, pressing into the folds of her skirt. All conversation fell silent. Even the ever-steady cadence of moaning and groaning quieted. The general's voice, steeped in Southern heritage, carried easily, and she had no doubt his words reached downstairs to the entrance hall and beyond.

"We move out at noon, men! Less than two hours from now. To all the wounded: Those who are stable enough to travel, you're with your unit. General Bates's division is headed south to Murfreesboro. The rest of us are pushing on toward Nashville. General Hood's orders." The general shifted his weight, his hand gripping his scabbard-clad saber. "We lost sixty-nine field officers to casualties the other night, including fourteen generals. Of those, five were killed, as you know. Eight were wounded, and one was captured. Fifty-five regimental officers were either killed, wounded, captured, or are missing. So when we make camp, we'll reassemble troops. If you're not able to travel, then you will remain here. And when the Federal Army arrives . . . and they *will* arrive soon enough . . ." He stared hard across the gathering of men. "You will forthwith become prisoners of the Federal Army. But know this," he added quickly, "I give you my word that every appeal will be made to the honor of the United States government to allow you to remain here at Carnton until you're stable enough to be transported under Federal guard either to a hospital in Nashville or to prison for the duration of this conflict."

Lizzie heard finality in the general's tone, along with weariness and an undercurrent of regret. Silence, thick and heavy, seemed to blanket the house. The general's gaze moved steadily over the soldiers until it came to Captain Jones, where it lingered.

She saw a look pass between the two men, one that led her to believe they were familiar with each other beyond the simple chain of command. And that, perhaps, the two of them were privy to knowledge the others weren't. Looking back toward the hallway, she spotted Dr. Phillips, along with several corpsmen.

The general faced forward again. "May our gracious Lord strengthen you all and keep you in the days ahead." Then he saluted, his posture ramrod straight. "And may our great God be with the mighty Army of Tennessee!"

With one voice, the soldiers repeated the last declaration and saluted their commanding officer. Many were forced to salute with their left hand, Lizzie noted. Dr. Phillips entered the bedroom along with corpsmen who carried crutches. They began helping the men to stand, and her throat tightened as she watched the wounded soldiers hobbling out of the room and down the stairs. Most didn't seem well enough to be walking, much less traveling, but she guessed that whatever pain they would endure was preferable to being left behind to such an uncertain and unfavorable fate.

Winder hugged her legs tight. "The soldiers can stay if they want to. I don't mind sharin' my room."

She ran a hand through his hair. "It's all right, sweetheart. I'm sure they'll receive fine care wherever they're going." But even as she said it, she knew it wasn't true. Especially for the soldiers too seriously wounded to risk being moved.

She looked over at Captain Jones, who sat with his back against the wall watching other soldiers from the second floor make their way to the staircase. She could all but read his thoughts. She wondered if he'd sent word yet for his manservant. If George didn't arrive soon, who would assist the captain in leaving before the Federal Army arrived? And even if George did arrive in time, how would the man transport him? Would George bring a wagon? Or would he depend on a stretcher?

It hurt her to imagine the pain Captain Jones would endure while being jostled in a wagon over the rutted winter roads, much less being dragged over rough ground on a makeshift pallet for miles on end.

"Miss Clouston." Dr. Phillips's voice cut into her thoughts. "A word with you, please, ma'am."

"Certainly, Doctor." She motioned for him to give her a minute, then she gently coaxed Winder to loosen his hold on her legs.

From her peripheral vision she felt Captain Jones looking in her direction. And for reasons she couldn't define, his attention stirred her. Made her very much aware of being a woman. With that realization came an increased level of discomfort. Because he was a married man. He ought not be looking at her in that manner. *If* he was looking at her at all. She sneaked a glance at him. He wasn't. He was looking more through her, as though lost in thought.

She gave an internal shake of her head, feeling more than a little foolish now. Whatever it was about this man that attracted her to him, she was eager to see him returned to his wife. Even though part of her was already dreading his departure.

Lizzie knelt, placed the basket and pot of coffee on the floor, and looked Winder in the eye. "I need to speak with Dr. Phillips, Winder. But I have a very important task for you. Are you willing to help?"

The boy nodded, curiosity sparking his expression.

"The soldiers leaving here today have a long journey ahead of them, and I imagine they're going to grow quite hungry. So I want you to take this basket around to *every* soldier you see and ask him if he'd like to take a muffin with him. And when these muffins are gone—"

"I'll go get more from Mama in the kitchen?"

She nodded. "That's exactly right."

He grabbed the basket and raced first to Captain Jones, which she found telling.

"You want to take a muffin with you, Captain? To fight them dang Yankees?"

The captain smiled. "Thanks, Winder, but I've already got one." He held up his partially eaten muffin as evidence, then pointed to Winder's chest. "That's a mighty fine-looking medal you're wearing today."

Beaming, Winder peered down at his shirt. "Miss Clouston sewed it on for me this morning. She said Tempy had too much to do already. And since I don't like wearin' my coat, she sewed it on my shirt instead!"

"She did a fine job. Now head on out there and do your duty, young man!"

Winder returned the captain's salute and dashed into the hallway. Lizzie peered after him, making certain he was doing as told, before she gradually looked back at Captain Jones. He was definitely watching her now, and his expression held an uncertainty she hadn't seen from him before. Or perhaps he hadn't allowed her to see.

She joined the doctor by the far window.

"Miss Clouston," Dr. Phillips began in a quiet voice, his countenance somber, "I want you to know that it's only after much deliberation—and after having witnessed your strength of character under the most difficult of circumstances—that I am making this request of you."

Lizzie stared, not at all certain she wanted to hear whatever he was going to say next.

"From all calculations, ma'am, there are roughly three dozen men here at Carnton who are physically incapable of going with us when the army moves out. For them to travel now would, I believe, result in their certain demise. And I fear the only chance these men have of—"

"Doc, you might as well include me in this conversation, since I'm one of those men and I can hear every word you're saying."

Lizzie turned to see Captain Jones sitting alone by the hearth, his casual smile belying the tension in his gravelly voice. The number of wounded in the bedroom had thinned out considerably. Only four men remained, Second Lieutenant Shuler and two others—Second Lieutenant Taylor and Private Smith.

Dr. Phillips offered a conciliatory nod. "I'm sorry, Captain. It wasn't my intention to—"

"I know that, Dr. Phillips." The captain gave a single nod. "But it doesn't change the fact that sooner rather than later, Federal officers are going to be walking through that doorway with the aim of collecting prisoners. It appears as though I might be included in that number. So if there are decisions to be made, and I think there are, I believe I have a right to be part of that process."

Dr. Phillips grabbed a straight-backed chair from in front of the fireplace and set it beside the captain. He gestured for Lizzie to sit, but she opted for Winder's Poynor chair instead. As she sat, her gaze connected with the captain's, and in his gray eyes she saw courage mingled with dread. But she also glimpsed an acceptance—and even a peace—she couldn't begin to identify with.

"Captain Jones." The doctor settled into the chair. "There is no 'might be included' in your case, sir. If you leave this house, you'll not only never walk again, the effort will likely kill you. Your injuries are—"

"What if I were to say that I'd absolve you of any responsibility, Doc? That my death, should that occur, would not be laid at your feet."

The doctor shook his head. "I bent to your will once before, Captain Jones. And rightly so, as I've confessed to Miss Clouston here. Because though I do not believe I served you best by letting you keep that leg, I do think there's a fair chance you'll live through this. But to willfully allow you to be moved this soon would rip every suture from your wounds and would most assuredly dislocate the bone we've just set, which could puncture an artery. It's a miracle that didn't happen to begin with."

"And you think the men who inflicted this damage to his body are going to be more careful with him—and with these other soldiers— than their fellow soldiers would be?" The question was out of Lizzie's mouth before she could think to soften her tone and reframe it in a more genteel fashion, much less remember to whom she was speaking.

Both men stared. But it was the sly glint of admiration in Captain Jones's eyes that gave her the courage to continue.

"All I'm saying, Dr. Phillips, is that—"

"I know what you're saying, Miss Clouston." The surgeon leveled his gaze. "And I understand. And if you'll both give me half a chance, I'll lay out a plan that—while unconventional—I think has a fairly good chance of succeeding."

Lizzie promptly closed her mouth, then opened it again. "I'm sorry, Doctor, if I spoke out of turn. But it issues from honest concern. I simply want to see Captain Jones safely returned to his wife, and the rest of these soldiers returned to their families as well."

This time it was the doctor who stared, then looked from her to Captain Jones as though seeking assistance in knowing how to respond. But Captain Jones's attention was fixed on her, his expression one of question. Even confusion.

"Miss Clouston," the doctor began.

But the captain raised a hand even as a shadow passed across his face. "What I think the doctor was about to tell you, Miss Clouston . . . is that my dear wife, Susan, died from influenza last year. Along with our child. While I was away at war."

Chapter 16

"I-I'm so sorry for your loss, Captain," Miss Clouston said softly, myriad emotions chasing across her face.

Roland could all but see layers of misunderstanding falling away. He was certain he'd told her Susan was gone, along with Lena, when she'd read Weet's letter aloud to him. But he honestly couldn't remember now. His time at Carnton had largely been a blur of morphine, laudanum, and pain. What *was* clear to him, though, was that she'd not known until now.

"Thank you, Miss Clouston. I appreciate that." He met her gaze, wondering if he was imagining the flicker of relief he saw in her eyes.

"So," she continued, her tone uncertain, "you're alone."

"Yes, ma'am. I am now." Then another reason occurred to him as to *why* she might be relieved. Maybe she'd considered some of his actions toward her improper. And he had to admit, if he'd still been married, the overlong looks and even the brief times they'd touched would have been just that.

He was eager to set accounts straight, but he couldn't exactly do that with Dr. Phillips present. He'd have to broach that subject later, if he were ever alone with her.

He glanced over at Shuler, Taylor, and Smitty. He wasn't surprised they were among those staying behind, considering their injuries. Shuler had only lost an arm, but the young man, so slight of build, had been plagued with fever during the night and, as Dr. Phillips had shared, was of compromised health to begin with. As for Taylor and Smitty, they were amputees and thick as thieves, even in relation to their wounds. They'd both lost their left legs below the knee. But it was their gut wounds that had them staying behind, he felt certain.

Nevertheless, he was grateful to discover the three of them still jawing with some of the men who were departing, not having overheard the exchange.

Dr. Phillips cleared his throat. "Now, back to the plan I was about to share . . ."

Listening to what the surgeon had to say, Roland found the bulk of his own attention centered on the woman seated in the child's chair beside him. Compassionate, caring. And with a quiet beauty that drew a man's eye. How had she not been snapped up by some lucky fellow before now?

"So while I realize that what I'm suggesting is not how this process would customarily proceed, I believe that—"

"Wait." Roland blinked, the doctor's words registering. "You're not proposing that Miss Clouston take the lead in this, are you?"

The doctor looked between them. "That's precisely what I'm proposing, Captain. And furthermore, if you'll consider the reasons I shared, I believe this may be our best chance of—"

"It's out of the question." Roland shook his head. "I've seen how the Federal Army treats Southern women. It's not respectful, sir. Far from it. So I can't condone placing Miss Clouston in such a—"

"Captain Jones."

Roland looked over to see Miss Clouston staring at him, her expression claiming a slightly superior air. "If there are decisions to be made here, and I think there are . . ." Her voice held the sweetest measure of scolding. "I believe I have a right to be part of that process. Would you not agree?"

Dr. Phillips laughed softly. "Oh yes, Miss Clouston. You will do quite well."

Heart beating fast, Lizzie stood beside Colonel and Mrs. McGavock on the expansive rear porch of the house and watched regiments of the Federal Army march across the fields toward Carnton. For the past three days they'd kept watch, and what General Cheatham had said about the US Army returning soon enough was proving true. The soldiers were still some distance away, the formation in front astride horses. But as she watched wave after wave of blue coats appearing over the rise, a cold stone of fear settled in the pit of her stomach.

It wasn't that she'd never seen Federal soldiers, or was afraid of them. The US Army had occupied the town of Franklin for the better part of three years. But after witnessing the carnage on the battlefield, having seen with her own eyes the brutality left scattered across the Harpeth Valley by the hand of *both* armies, she felt a fear stir inside her seeing the two groups in such close proximity to each other and under such duress.

A bitter December wind swept across the fields and seemed to blow right through her. As the day stretched into afternoon, the more the gray skies portended rain. Or perhaps snow, if temperatures continued to drop through the night.

Struggling to focus on the task she'd been given, she found her own memory acting the traitor as it dredged up scenes from the battlefield—specifically those she'd seen just before she'd been warned away from the main breastworks. The Federal Army's few hundred losses paled in comparison to the over seven thousand Confederate dead and wounded. *Seven thousand* . . . When Colonel McGavock shared that figure with her, she'd had difficulty wrapping her mind around it. And still did. But each death was tragic. Both Confederate and Federal.

The closer the regiments came, the deeper the talons of doubt sank into her. As Dr. Phillips had laid out his proposal and the likelihood of its success, she'd seen the wisdom in his words. For obvious reasons, Federal officers held predisposed animus toward plantation owners, so having a more neutral party—and a woman—gently campaign for the wounded soldiers to be allowed to stay at Carnton to convalesce made sense. As did informing the Federal officers of the extent of each man's injuries, of which she was well versed. But now, thinking of what would happen if her persuasive efforts proved unconvincing, she wondered if Colonel or Mrs. McGavock might not be better candidates for the task. Yet when the colonel had agreed with the doctor's recommendation, Lizzie realized she had no choice, despite Captain Jones's adamant objections.

He's not married . . .

Even as nervous as she was now, the surprise of that discovery still felt fresh. And it *had* come as a surprise to her, followed swiftly by an inexplicable sense of relief. At the time, she'd told herself her relief was due to the fact that his not being married better explained the times when she had found him watching her. Not that his behavior had ever been inappropriate. But if she were married, she wouldn't want her husband looking at another woman the way that Captain Jones some-times seemed to be looking at her. And right or wrong, she liked the way he looked at her, and the way she felt when he did. Even though she knew she shouldn't.

She briefly bowed her head, shame warming her face. With no small effort, she narrowed her thoughts to the moment at hand. And now that the moment was here, what burdened her most was what would happen to him and the twenty-eight other soldiers inside the house if she failed.

Of the hundreds of men from the Southern army who'd been at Carnton, only these twenty-nine remained, all resituated among the four family bedrooms on the second floor. Before the soldiers had left Carnton, she'd searched the sea of beleaguered faces, looking for Towny, hoping he would stop in to say good-bye. He'd promised to come see her before he left. Yet she found it impossible to hold the unfulfilled promise against him, knowing why the army had to leave so quickly.

Word from the nuns who'd also been helping with the wounded in town was that every available house, school, church, and public build-ing in Franklin was being used as a hospital now. Forty-four in all.

Three of them for wounded Federals, the rest for Confederates. Each building, including Carnton, had been marked with a red flag.

Dr. Phillips and the other physicians had accompanied the army, but he'd sworn that he or another surgeon would be back at regular intervals to check on the men left behind. She'd heard soldiers talking amongst themselves before they'd left, saying that General Hood had plans to lay siege to Nashville in coming days, but she prayed that wouldn't be the case.

Because if the Rebels had been beaten so soundly here at Franklin, where General Schofield had only hours to entrench his army, how much more perilous would it be for General Hood's soldiers to face the enemy in a city the Federals had consistently held almost since the beginning of the war? And where they outnumbered the Southern army three to one?

A broad-chested Federal soldier astride a white stallion led the procession, and as he drew closer Lizzie could see his gaze—wary and appraising—sweep the surrounding area. She swallowed hard, then felt a hand close tightly around hers. She drew strength from Carrie McGavock's grip.

The Federal commander reined in and dismounted. Before his second boot even touched the ground, a young private stepped forward and took the reins. Never looking at the younger soldier, the general crossed the distance with minimum strides and stopped just shy of the bottom step. Gleaming stars denoting his rank accentuated his pristine blue uniform, and his leather boots were polished to a sheen.

"Colonel John McGavock?" The general's hand rested on the hilt of his scabbard-clad sword. He ascended the porch steps, his footfalls heavy. "General Folsom, United States Army."

"Welcome to Carnton, General Folsom. Allow me to make introductions."

General Folsom waited as Colonel McGavock introduced his

wife, then Lizzie. The general's expression, polite, mildly aloof, never changed. No question in Lizzie's mind—the man was formidable.

He gave a single nod. "Nice to make your acquaintance, Colonel. And that of your wife. And governess." He gave Lizzie a cursory glance. "In accordance with US Army regulations, we've come to Franklin, and to your estate, to collect Confederate prisoners and escort them to Nashville."

His accent was thick. Boston, perhaps? Or New York. Lizzie couldn't tell. The man was taller than she'd first estimated too, and despite knowing that both armies were guilty of atrocities, she couldn't help but wonder . . . Was he the one who had shot Towny? Or Captain Jones? Or had he killed Captain Hope and Colonel Nelson? Her gaze slowly moved over the dozens of soldiers behind him. She'd learned that on the night of the battle, Federals had marched dozens of wounded Confederate prisoners with them to Nashville, then had put them on flatbed railcars and shipped them to Federal prisons. Yet it was no less, she knew, than what the Confederates would have done had the tables been turned. She'd heard stories of Andersonville in Georgia, after all. She hadn't wanted to believe them, but—

Suddenly aware of the silence, Lizzie felt an invisible hand push her forward. "General Folsom." She curtsied, Dr. Phillips's guidance returning in a rush. "Welcome to Carnton, sir. You and your men must be parched after traveling such a distance. Should you desire, please help yourself to water at the well."

"Thank you, miss. But we drank from the river as we crossed."

Reading determination and the slightest impatience in his demeanor, she continued. "In the interest of time, then, allow me to escort you to the Confederate wounded inside, sir."

"I believe you mean Confederate *prisoners*, Miss Clouston."

She dipped her head. "Yes, of course, General. If you'll follow me."

She turned and walked to the door, hearing him behind her. She could feel his eyes on her, but she didn't turn. Without hesitation, he reached for the door handle.

"After you, miss."

Lizzie nodded her thanks and preceded him into the entrance hall.

"Cox!" the general called behind him.

Lizzie glanced back to see a group of soldiers respond with rifles at the ready. The troop followed them into the house. She spotted Tempy's backside as the woman shooed Hattie and Winder back into the farm office and away from the door. The neighbors who'd come to help in recent days had left, including the colonel's sister-in-law Louisa McGavock. But the nuns, currently tucked away in the kitchen, had volunteered to stay and assist. So the house was oddly still.

"The men are upstairs on the second floor, General." Lizzie moved toward the stairs when, without warning, the familiarity of her surroundings shifted. She'd been living in this house for eight years. Yet over the course of the last few days, all that was familiar was gone. She'd been so busy caring for the wounded, helping to cook and clean, that she hadn't fully taken in the enormity of the transformation.

Bloody handprints and streaks marred the wallpaper and door-frames. Deep crimson stains soaked every upholstered settee, chair, and footstool. She'd worked with the nuns to remove the piles of soaked bandages and the pots into which the soldiers had emptied their stomachs, or worse. But the lingering splatters and spills remained. As did the smells. And the floorcloth . . .

She glanced down at her own boots, which she'd given up salvaging long ago, then at the boots of General Folsom behind her. Not quite so pristine now. She couldn't imagine a person seeing this—and the condition of the men upstairs—and not being moved to compassion. Yet the general's expression revealed not a trace of the horror she continually felt when considering what humanity could do to its own.

She ascended the stairs, her heart racing as though she'd already climbed six flights. And with every breath, she prayed. Only her prayers had no words. Only silent, heartrending pleas.

CHAPTER 17

Lizzie paused at the top of the second-story landing and waited for General Folsom and the other soldiers. Hands clasped at her waist, she hoped she put forth a demeanor of calm collectedness. Never mind the knots twisting her stomach.

"General Folsom, there are twenty-nine men who were deemed by the surgeons to be too seriously injured to leave Carnton when the Army of Tennessee departed. Or to be moved at all at present. These men understand that they are now prisoners of—"

He held up a hand. "No fanfare is required, Miss Clouston." General Folsom shifted his weight and stared down at her. "While I appreciate from a tactical standpoint what you're attempting to do, it won't change the outcome. We're here to take prisoners to Nashville, where they will either be admitted to a hospital or sent to prison. And that based upon *our* doctor's recommendation. So please stand aside and allow us to carry on."

His tone, genteel enough, left little margin for negotiation. But what little margin was left she grabbed hold of.

"If you will allow me, General, the injuries of these men are so severe that—"

"Their injuries were sustained while assaulting the Federal Army of the United States of America, Miss Clouston. And just as the Confederate Army has taken prisoners, so will we. It's a necessary part of war." He turned to the men behind him. "Sweep the rooms. Check up there too." He motioned to the staircase leading to the attic.

The soldiers scattered, two of them heading upstairs.

"General . . ." Lizzie took a step toward him. "That's the attic. There's only storage up there. No one is—"

"I appreciate the hospitality that has been shown to me and my men thus far, miss, but I will not allow you to interfere with this prisoner transfer. We'll search the house same as we're currently searching the barn and other outbuildings. Dr. Nichols!"

One of the remaining soldiers stepped forward. In his early thirties, Lizzie guessed, he had a studious air about him. But in lieu of a rifle, he carried a leather satchel.

"Yes, sir, General?"

"Examine the prisoners, Doctor. Then make ready for travel."

Dr. Nichols nodded and entered Colonel and Mrs. McGavock's bedroom. The general followed. Lizzie went as far as the door, feeling the fragile threads of hope inside her being ripped apart stitch by stitch.

Dr. Nichols knelt before Private Cumming. "What's the nature of your wound, soldier?"

The pale young private—eighteen years old—looked down, then back up again, as though the question were absurd. "Cannonball took my legs right out from under me, sir. I's runnin' one minute, then felt a flash of fire and looked down, and they was gone. Then I was tryin' to crawl back to my unit when grapeshot bit my arm all up." He nodded to the bandaged stump on his left side.

Lizzie's throat tightened. *Jesus, you are the Great Physician. Intervene for these men. Please intervene . . .*

The doctor nodded. "Yes, I clearly see your injuries, Private. My question is, why weren't you evacuated with the others?"

The private looked at him, his brow furrowing. "Doc said something 'bout me bleedin' bad if I's to move. So I just been lyin' here still as a church mouse, sir."

Lizzie stepped inside the room. "Dr. Phillips sutured the femoral artery in Private Cumming's upper right thigh. The private nearly bled out on the table. To move him now would mean—"

"Thank you, Miss Clouston." The general looked back, his tone not at all appreciative. "That's twice I've warned you, miss."

The doctor moved on to Second Lieutenant Meeks. "And you, soldier?"

"Minié ball slammed into my right thigh. Cracked the big bone, the doc said. But what kept me behind was this." He lifted his shirt to reveal a twelve-inch gash, red and swollen, on the right side of his abdomen. "A bluecoat got me with his bayonet. Doc Phillips said I shoulda died then and there, but I didn't. He sewed me up best he could and said that my gut was all—"

He paused, then looked at Lizzie. As did the doctor. And finally, the general.

Lizzie met the general's gaze straight on, yet said nothing.

Finally General Folsom sighed. "Speak, Miss Clouston."

"The bayonet perforated the second lieutenant's colon and stomach. It also nicked his lung. Fluid has been collecting in the lower left lobe, and pneumonia is—"

General Folsom raised his hand, then turned back. "Continue, Doctor."

Lizzie briefly bowed her head. So much for a dose of femininity helping to ease the tension. And also contrary to what Dr. Phillips had thought, providing an explanation about each soldier's injuries only seemed to be further frustrating the situation.

The next few soldiers answered the doctor's questions at surprising length. Contrary to what she would've guessed—that these men wouldn't wish to speak about the frightful experience they'd endured— she discovered that most of them were, in fact, eager to share at least some of what they'd been through. Perhaps with the unconscious hope that the retelling would somehow dilute the strength of the memory.

Dr. Nichols finished his inquiries, and they moved next to Winder's room. Several of the soldiers who'd searched other parts of the house returned and followed them, shadowing their path. Seven soldiers occupied Winder's room now. But Lizzie couldn't bring herself to look at Captain Jones, who was seated on the floor by the hearth. Not because she thought she would see *I told you so* in his eyes, but because she knew she wouldn't. She would see only compassion and understanding, not a trace of blame for what was going to happen to him and the rest of these men who had already given so much. And she feared that seeing that tender measure of undeserved mercy would lay her battered defenses to waste.

Dr. Nichols began his line of inquiry with First Lieutenant Conrad, whom Lizzie had found to be a kind, humble sort of man, a cobbler from Alabama, a widower with no children who mostly kept to himself. Although she wondered if that had always been the case, or if his reticence was due, at least in part, to his recent injuries.

"I lost my arm to grapeshot, Doc," Conrad began, touching his bandaged head. "And a blue coat sabered me in the head. Cut me near clean to the skull, Doc Phillips said. He patched me up, though. Said I got me some sort of—"

The first lieutenant's mouth moved but no words came. After a moment, he looked over at Lizzie. Confusion and entreaty riddled his eyes, yet as much as she wanted to respond, she knew that doing so would not help Conrad's plight. So she said nothing.

General Folsom stepped into Conrad's line of sight, blocking his view of her. "Say it, soldier. Say what's wrong with you."

"M-Miss Clouston?" came the first lieutenant's shaky whisper. "C-can you help me, please, ma'am?"

Lizzie bit her lower lip, her chest aching with restraint.

"Well . . ." The general looked back at her. "I underestimated you, Miss Clouston. You've certainly done your homework. You've tutored every one of these men to parrot back what you believe will lead to a—"

"She hasn't 'tutored' any of us, General Folsom."

The air in the room evaporated, and Lizzie hiccuped a breath. She looked at Captain Jones and gave an almost imperceptible shake of her head, even though she knew it was too late.

General Folsom turned. "What did you say to me, soldier?"

Captain Jones didn't blink. "I said, sir, that she hasn't *tutored* any of us. Miss Clouston was there. She assisted Dr. Phillips in surgery for nearly thirty-six hours straight. So almost every absent arm and leg among us, every stitched-up hole and gash, she saw it all. Miss Clouston is simply continuing her effort to keep us alive. After you Federals did all you could to put us in the grave." A slow smile turned his mouth. "Which is only fair, sir. We were trying to do the same to you. Only you did it better this time."

Lizzie was certain her heart had stopped a few seconds back and her body simply hadn't gotten word yet. What was Captain Jones thinking, speaking to a Federal officer in that manner? A man hardened by war who would likely think nothing of the captain, and every other wounded soldier here, dying on their way to Nashville.

General Folsom strode to where Captain Jones sat on the floor. "Name and rank, soldier."

"Captain Roland Ward Jones, sir. First Battalion, Mississippi Sharpshooters, Adams' Brigade."

"A sharpshooter?" The general eyed his bandaged right hand. "Were you any good?"

"He was one of the best, sir," Lieutenant Shuler offered from across the room, his tone unapologetic. Even faintly proud.

"Is that so, Captain?" General Folsom stared, awaiting a response.

Finally Captain Jones shrugged. "I managed to do all right, I guess."

Again Lizzie held her breath. But then . . .

The general gave a soft laugh, not caustic like earlier, but one of a more humored nature. Then he turned to face her, his humor quickly fading.

"Was it as Captain Jones said, miss? You assisted the doctor?"

Lizzie nodded. "Yes, General."

His eyes narrowed. "And had you done that before, Miss Clouston? Assisted a surgeon?"

For some reason, the question took her back to the night of the battle, to the moment when Dr. Phillips first sought her out and asked her much the same thing. Emotion tightened her throat as she realized how swiftly life could come unhinged. How fragile and fleeting it really was. How many lives had been changed—and lost—since that night? Since the war started? And even now, how many women and children were praying for loved ones who would never be returning home?

Aware of the general's continuing stare, Lizzie shook her head. "No, sir." Her voice was meeker than she would have liked. "I had not."

"And you've never seen war so close up before now, have you?"

It wasn't a question. "No, I have not." A burning sensation flooded her eyes, and she clenched her hands to keep them from shaking.

"And the hard truth, miss, is that even with all you've witnessed here in this house, you still haven't. You've only seen the outskirts of war. And even that from a distance. You may have assisted a doctor with the wounded in this home, which is a commendable contribution. For either army. But a woman knows nothing of real war or the cost it exacts from a man. Or the glory that comes with fighting for your country." He took a step closer. "So while I do not doubt that you care about what happens to these men, the fact remains, they're prisoners of the Federal Army, and they're going to Nashville." His gaze never left hers. "Doc, get these men ready for transfer."

"Yes, sir, General!"

General Folsom strode toward the door, and the shaking within Lizzie worsened.

She swallowed past the constriction in her throat. "You're mistaken, General Folsom."

Her voice came out barely above a whisper, but the commander stopped dead in his tracks. And when their eyes met, Lizzie was certain she felt the wood planks beneath her feet partially give way. But whatever restraint had held her tongue in check moments earlier suddenly let loose.

"I've seen more than the outskirts of war, sir." She tried to mask the tremor in her voice. "I went to the battlefield the next morning. I saw what both armies did to each other. Thousands lay dead or dying on the field."

He stared at her, his expression inscrutable. But he didn't tell her to stop.

"So while you're right in one sense, General . . . I have not been to war. I did not charge headlong up that battlefield in full view of my enemy entrenched behind breastworks. And I cannot begin to comprehend the courage it took to do such a thing. But I do know what it's like to walk among the mangled and lifeless bodies of thousands of men who did. Men in gray. *And* men in blue. I walked the ground drenched with their blood. I saw the agony—and even hatred—captured in their expressions when they died. I've sat with too many men in their final moments as they've breathed their last, their bodies torn apart by shot and shell. And, to a man, none of them spoke of the *glory* of war in those final moments, sir. None of them bragged about how many Federals they'd killed. And I believe it would've been the same if I'd sat with your men. The dying speak about what's most important to them. These men spoke of their wives and children, and how they wished to return home to see them one last time." Her eyes brimmed with unshed tears. She took a steadying breath. "So for you to tell me that because I am a woman, I know nothing of war . . . That simply isn't true, sir. You know one facet of war." She lifted her chin. "But I know another."

He stared, his gaze appraising. "Are you quite finished, Miss Clouston?"

Resisting the inclination to look away, she nodded. "Yes, sir. I am."

"Good. Now if you'll be so kind as to help these men pack up and—"

"General Folsom!"

Attention turned to Dr. Nichols, who was examining Captain Jones. The physician wore a stricken look. "Sir . . . I think it's the measles."

Disbelief swept the general's face, and he uttered a curse. The rest of the Federal soldiers took a hasty step back, some going as far as the hallway. But Lizzie could only stare at the captain, sharing his obvious surprise. *Measles.* She needed to get him quarantined from the other soldiers. And the children! Winder had been in the captain's company that very morning!

The general hesitated, clearly torn. "You're certain, Doc?"

"Certain enough that I wouldn't advise risking the spread of the illness to our men. Especially since it's doubtful most of these men will recover from their injuries, sir."

Lizzie winced at the doctor's choice of wording, but knew from what Dr. Phillips had said that his estimation wasn't far off.

General Folsom blew out a breath. Resignation etched his features. "Well, Miss Clouston, looks like you'll be keeping these men after all. Although I very much doubt you'll be as eager to tend them now. Move out, men!"

The general strode from the room and down the stairs, his soldiers trailing closely behind.

Lizzie could scarcely believe it. First, that the army was leaving. And second, that after all the captain and these other men had endured . . . now this. Measles had swept through town years earlier, killing dozens. Scarcely a family had remained untouched. It simply wasn't fair.

The last to leave, Dr. Nichols hesitated in the doorway, satchel in hand. "Miss Clouston, I trust you've had experience with this illness before and will know what to watch for. How to treat it."

"Yes, sir. I have."

"Good." He glanced toward the now empty staircase, then back at her, his voice lowering. "I also trust you're aware that measles can be misdiagnosed on occasion. Certain rashes and skin irritations often masquerade as this disease." He gave a gentle shrug. "A misdiagnosis can happen to any doctor. No matter his experience—or which army he serves. Does that make sense to you, ma'am?"

An oddness in his tone led her to look at him more closely, and she read something in his expression she couldn't quite interpret. Yet instinct told her not to question it.

"Yes, sir. Of course."

"Good. Because I wouldn't want there to be any misunderstanding between us about this." He glanced back at the soldiers still watching him from the bedroom, the subtlest smile turning his mouth. "You were right, Miss Clouston."

She stared, not following.

"For a moment the other afternoon, when the Confederates marched onto that field . . ." His eyes narrowed as though seeing something in the distance. "We were all spellbound as we watched them from the breastworks. The sunlight was hazy, the day near spent, and in their yellowish-brown uniforms the Rebels in the front seemed to be magnified in size. One could almost imagine them to be phantoms sweeping along in the air. On they came . . . And in the center, their lines seemed to be many deep and unbroken, their red-and-white tattered flags with the emblem of St. Andrew's cross as numerous as though every company bore them, flaring brilliantly in the sun's fading rays."

He shook his head as though the clouds of memory were thick before his face. "Never, Miss Clouston, have I witnessed such a grand display of military precision as I did when the Army of Tennessee took the field that day. How those men marched forward in the face of such overwhelming adversity. We all watched in amazement. Some of us, even admiration. Despite their being the enemy." He gave a gentle nod. "Take good care of these men, ma'am. They are among the finest."

He bid her a quiet good day and descended the staircase.

Lizzie stood absolutely still for a moment, drinking in what he'd said, what had just happened. Then she looked across the room at Captain Jones and knew the expression on his face reflected her own numb disbelief. And overwhelming gratitude. Both to a Federal doctor and to the Great Physician.

CHAPTER 18

Later that afternoon, Roland replayed the scene in his mind and still had trouble believing it. The Federal Army had left without taking him and the other prisoners. In his mind, as General Folsom and the regiment had waited for the doctor to finish his examinations, he'd found himself already making peace with death, something he'd done many times over the past three years. But making peace with death was a tricky thing, because death wasn't something one merely acknowledged once and then it was done. Death was stealthy, shadowed. And above all, unreliable. Just when you were certain you were done for— that death had tapped you on the shoulder and your last breath was only a breath away—death would slip right past you. Much like what had happened with him the other night on the battlefield, before he'd spotted that big autumn moon.

But today, right here in this bedroom, he'd watched death be outwitted. And he still couldn't quite reason how Miss Clouston had done it. He'd give most anything to go back and listen to her again, to have the words she'd spoken to the general—so bold, yet with a decidedly feminine strength—captured so he could hear them again.

He smiled, thinking about it. Thinking about her. She'd been trembling like a leaf. Yet how much he and the rest of these men owed her. Because even though he wasn't eager to admit it to himself, he knew Dr. Phillips was right. If he'd tried to leave here with his regiment, the effort would have met with a bad end. And the trip to Nashville in company of the Federal Army almost certainly would have killed him.

Even shifting the slightest bit caused his legs to throb with pain that shot all the way up his back. As long as he stayed still—either lying or sitting—the pain was manageable. But when he moved his legs . . .

As if his thoughts had summoned her, Miss Clouston appeared in the doorway of the bedroom with a large stew pot, and Tempy beside her with a basket. He spotted the nuns beyond them in the hallway, along with Colonel and Mrs. McGavock and their children carrying similar containers.

"Is anyone hungry?"

Miss Clouston's smile—and the aroma of whatever was in the pot she carried—filled every corner of the room, and his mouth watered even as something else deep inside him responded to her kindness. To her wit and compassion. To *her*.

She carefully situated the pot on the brick hearth beside him and looked over. "Captain Jones, would you care for some of Tempy's famous chicken and dumplings?"

"Oh, they ain't my dumplin's, Captain Jones." Tempy gestured. "Miss Clouston, she done made these."

Miss Clouston pursed her lips. "But it's *your* special receipt, Tempy."

"Ain't no special receiptin' 'bout it, ma'am. You just throw together some flour and eggs, toss in a bit of sour milk and maybe some salt, if you got it. Then drop 'em on top of the chicken simmerin' in the pot."

"Which proves my point!" Miss Clouston eyed her. "That while I made them, it's you who showed me how."

Tempy grinned and shook her head. "For a woman with so much learnin', ma'am, you can be right stubborn-headed."

Miss Clouston laughed, and Roland was drawn to the lightness of it. Like parched ground in the deep of summer, he drank it in. He enjoyed seeing the two women so cheerful, especially after recent days. He ran a hand over his full beard, looking forward to that cleanup and shave Sister Catherine Margaret had promised him.

Miss Clouston handed him a steaming bowl of chicken and dumplings and a spoon. "Here you go, Captain."

He nodded. "Thank you kindly, ma'am. And thank you, again, for what you did this afternoon. For all of us." His gaze swept the room.

"Hear, hear!" Shuler added from a few feet away, and Conrad and the other soldiers echoed their thanks. Even Taylor and Smitty.

"You're all most welcome, gentlemen. But it wasn't because of me or anything I said. It was Dr. Nichols—and the Lord—who saved you all."

"Mmm-hmm. That's right." Tempy nodded and began serving cornbread to the other soldiers. "But sometimes the good Lord, he chooses to work through human hands and feet!"

Miss Clouston only smiled and shook her head, then ladled the creamy stew into bowls and served the others. Roland couldn't help but notice the way the other soldiers watched her. But it was only Taylor's overlong stare that bothered him. The man's attention held a good deal more than kindly meant appreciation. Taylor happened to look in his direction then and, as if sensing his displeasure, gave Miss Clouston—whose back was to him—a once-over that made Roland eager to walk again so he could cross the room and knock that leer right off the man's face.

Being in the same regiment, he and Second Lieutenant Taylor had had their share of run-ins before. But being cooped up with the man—and his coadjutor, Private Smitty—for what could be weeks on end didn't bode well. Taylor had an arrogance about him that often accompanied newly appointed junior officers. That, combined with an overinflated opinion of himself, made for a volatile mixture.

Miss Clouston returned and claimed the diminutive chair beside him, and Roland found himself thinking, again, about her reaction at discovering that he wasn't married. Recalling her look of relief made him wonder if perhaps she viewed him a tad differently than she did the others. Yet even if she did, which would be farfetched, it didn't change the fact that he wasn't the man he used to be. He aimed to get better, to walk again. But there was no guarantee of that. The only guarantee he had was that of likely losing his estate in the very near future, along with any way of earning a livelihood. He could scarcely provide for all the people depending on him now; how could he provide for a wife and children? The thought brought reality to the forefront.

He needed to focus on finding a way to keep his plantation. How he was going to accomplish that here at Carnton, near flat on his back and almost three hundred miles from Yalobusha, Mississippi, he didn't know. But at least he had some time to figure it out.

"Measles," she said. "Of all the things that Federal doctor could have said. That about scared me to death."

"It didn't do my heart much good either. Although . . ." He scratched his chest and grimaced. "I did notice the start of a rash earlier."

Her brow furrowed, then just as swiftly her eyes narrowed, and she smiled. Truly smiled. "Nice attempt, Captain."

He laughed. "Roland, please. If you're comfortable with that," he added, reading hesitance in her eyes. "It just seems that with all we've been through, we could at least be on a first-name basis."

She held his gaze for a moment, then finally nodded. "Elizabeth. But friends and family call me Lizzie."

"Seeing as how I already consider us to be friends, I think I'll choose Lizzie."

She nodded again, and Roland knew, even as he'd said it, that while being Elizabeth Clouston's friend was a privilege and an honor, friendship wasn't all he would have wanted with this woman. *If* they'd met at a different time and place in life. Then again, she might not have even considered him, due to their differing views on the Confederacy. And namely, slavery. Either way, it was a moot point.

Movement at the door drew his attention, and Colonel McGavock entered the bedroom, his wife beside him. The couple spoke to the men as they passed, then the colonel acknowledged Roland with a tilt of his head. "Captain, it's good to see you sitting up."

"It's good to be sitting, sir."

The colonel glanced at his wife. "My dear, Captain Jones here is quite the chess player, I hear."

"Is that so?" A hint of mischief lit Mrs. McGavock's expression, similar to what Roland had witnessed in her young son's. "My husband enjoys a rousing game of chess, Captain. But I'll give you forewarning: he does not like to lose."

"I've never met a man worth his salt who did, ma'am."

A glint shone in the colonel's expression. "Let me know when you're ready for a match, Captain."

"Will do, sir. And thank you."

He'd met Colonel McGavock over the course of recent days and had been impressed with the man. McGavock's generosity in opening his home to the wounded of Loring's Division constituted an enormous sacrifice. Not only in a financial sense—damage to the home had to be extensive, and feeding and caring for so many soldiers had no doubt cut into the family's food stores—but in an emotional sense as well. What mental and physical toll it had taken on the man's household, he could only imagine. Especially on young Winder and Hattie. Although each time he'd seen the children, they seemed to be weathering the storm well. He'd always heard that children were stronger than they appeared, but since Lena had died at scarcely a year old, he hadn't had the opportunity to learn that as a parent.

"Gentlemen . . ." The colonel turned to address the room. "As I relayed to the soldiers in the other bedrooms moments ago, before General Folsom departed, he charged me with administering an oath to each of you. This oath places every soldier here under a parole of honor. You will be granted certain liberties and freedoms in exchange for your solemn pledge that you will not attempt to escape—either to return to the Confederate Army or to return to your homes—and you will not participate in espionage of any nature against the Federal Army or the United States government. When you are well enough, you will either be sent to prison for the duration of the war or you could be used as collateral in a prisoner exchange. I gave General Folsom my word that I would personally administer this oath to each of you, and if any man did not agree to these terms, I would contact the Federal Army immediately. In that event, the soldier will forthwith be transferred under escort to a Federal prison in Nashville—no matter the extent of his injuries. Furthermore, if even one prisoner violates his parole, his violation will negate every freedom and privilege for every other soldier here, and you will *all* be sent to prison without delay. Are there any questions about the oath? Or any violation of it?"

Silence blanketed the room.

Colonel McGavock unfolded a piece of paper. "When you hear your name, please respond with either aye or nay."

"First Lieutenant Harold Conrad."

Roland looked at Conrad, who first looked at Miss Clouston, then at him. Roland mouthed, *Aye,* to the man even as regret over Conrad's injuries knifed him. Ever humble and kind, Conrad was now a ghost of the man and exemplary officer he'd once been.

"Aye, sir," Conrad said softly, then looked back.

Roland nodded and mouthed, *Well done.*

Conrad smiled and saluted him.

"Second Lieutenant James Shuler."

"Aye, sir. And thank you, sir, to you and your family for givin' us quarter."

Colonel McGavock gave a single nod, then continued. "Captain John P. Hampton."

"Aye, sir, Colonel McGavock."

"Second Lieutenant George E. Estes."

"Aye, Colonel."

"Second Lieutenant Hiram Taylor."

"Aye." Taylor stared up at McGavock, a flat note of belligerence underscoring his response.

McGavock paused and gave Taylor a look that to some might have appeared innocuous. But Roland, even having known the colonel so briefly, read clear warning. As should have Taylor, if the man had a lick of sense.

Roland knew then that he had to outpace the young second lieutenant in healing, if only so he could take Taylor down when the man tried to escape—which he would, Roland felt sure. It was only a matter of time. He had no intention of going back to prison, and certainly not because of something Taylor did. He wanted to live, and had been given a second chance from the Almighty to do just that.

"Captain Jones."

Roland nodded. "Aye, Colonel McGavock."

"Private Clement Smith," Colonel McGavock continued.

"Aye." Smitty glanced at Taylor and cocked that crooked little grin of his, and Roland made it a goal to take his first step by Christmas. No matter the pain it took.

LATE THE NEXT evening Roland spotted Sister Catherine Margaret and two other nuns in the hallway making their rounds, oil lamps in hand. With the soft glow of golden light on her face, Sister Catherine Margaret appeared almost angelic, which seemed only fitting.

She stepped quietly into Winder's bedroom, where a single oil lamp had been left burning on the table by the hearth. Its illumination mingled with the flicker of the white-and-orange flames to give the room a warm, homey feel. He'd been lying there on the floor, flat on his back, quietly appreciating the ambience for the past couple of hours—along with the blessing of not being in a Federal prison.

"Evening, Sister," he whispered from his pallet, mindful of the other men in the room already asleep, thanks in large part to Colonel McGavock breaking out those bottles of celebratory wine. The man's generosity stood up to its reputation, and more. It had been good wine too. In fact, the colonel had left a partially full bottle beside his pallet.

"You're still awake, Captain Jones?"

"I couldn't very well go to sleep without bidding you good night, Sister."

She grinned and shook her head. "You, my dear captain, are what young nuns fear most. A handsome—*and* good-hearted—man." She made a show of casting the lantern's light onto his face. "At least I think there are marks of handsomeness beneath all that dark hair and beard."

Roland laughed beneath his breath.

"But alas . . ." She settled in the Windsor chair by the hearth. "The passing years have served to remove that temptation from me."

"You were tempted, Sister?" he asked, at the same time wondering if he should. But his curiosity wouldn't let him not.

"Oh my, yes." She nodded. "Just because a woman becomes a nun doesn't mean she ceases to be a woman, Captain Jones. No more than you becoming a captain has made you forget what it was like to be a private, or a second or first lieutenant." She leaned her head back. "I can remember the days before I took my vows . . ." She sighed, her voice barely above a whisper. "And sometimes, in remembering, I catch glimpses of who I was then and can see myself more truthfully than I did at the time. Which, in turn, sheds light on who I have become, and how far I still have to go to become who I hope to be in Christ before I die, if that makes any sense."

Roland widened his eyes. "That's a mite too deep for me, Sister." That earned him the laugh he'd been aiming for. "Actually, what you said makes perfect sense. What I don't quite understand is how, when you're young and so eager to get on with life, the years seem to crawl by. Nothing ever comes quickly enough. Then suddenly, one day you look back and—just like that—you're the age of that person you used to think of as knocking on death's door." He laughed softly and stared into the flames in the hearth. "Yet somehow, despite time's passing and all that's happened to me—and all that didn't happen that I hoped would—there's a part of me that still feels the same inside. That still feels like I did when I was first starting out."

"Why, Captain Jones, I didn't realize you were a romantic."

He laughed. "I'm not. I'm just old."

Her smile deepened. "You feel old right now, Captain. But you're a man in the prime of his life. The best years are ahead of you, I'm certain of it."

"And how do you know that, Sister?"

"Do you know the Lord Jesus, Captain?"

While he didn't find her question particularly surprising, he did ponder the ease with which she asked it. "Yes, Sister. I do. And I'm most grateful for it."

Her sigh held contentment. "For those who are in Christ Jesus, the best is *always* yet to come. Believe that."

"I do," he answered after a moment. "I just wish I believed it more."

Her chuckle surprised him. "Welcome to faith, Captain Jones."

A comfortable silence settled between them, the fire in the hearth crackling and popping as the flame devoured the wood.

"How is it that you're still awake, Captain, while the rest of your companions slumber?"

He pointed to the bottle of wine beside him and smiled. "I only had a glass or two, while they might have had a bit more. But that's all right. None of them drank to excess. And after what they've been through, they deserve a good night's rest and the chance to forget about their troubles, at least for a while."

"And what about you? Do you not deserve those things?"

He rearranged Sir Horace beneath his neck, the bear's stuffing having flattened considerably from use. "There was a time I drank to try to forget. But in my experience, Sister, dulling a memory doesn't empty it of its power. Or its pain. It just pushes it off to the side for a while. But it always returns."

A moment passed.

"What painful memories have you pushed to the side, Captain Jones? With or without benefit of wine?"

He looked over at her, wondering at the twists and turns his life had taken to deliver him here—in Franklin, Tennessee, philosophizing with a nun late into the evening. "My wife and child died last year while I was away fighting. Influenza. I didn't even know about it until nearly a month later, when the letter from my mother finally caught up with me." He still had that letter, same as every letter he'd received from his family since he'd left for the war. But that was one he didn't care to reread. "Even though I know they're both safe and contented with the Lord, that doesn't stop me from wishing they were still here. Which is selfish, I know. Wanting to steal them from heaven." He gave a soft laugh to cover the emotion in his voice.

The silence lengthened, a soft wind whistling around a corner of the house.

"I'm so very sorry, Captain . . . for such a painful, terrible loss."

The tenderness in Sister Catherine Margaret's tone brought a lump to his throat.

"Sometimes," she continued, staring into the fire, "life on this side of the veil is far more difficult than I think it should be. Especially for those of us who belong to God. But then again, his promises do not eliminate suffering."

"No, they do not," he said softly.

"And yet, with all my heart," she continued, "I trust that God knows best." A slow, almost sad smile turned her mouth. "Even in those moments when I'm fairly certain I might know better."

"It does me good to hear you say that, Sister."

"Why? Because it shows my lack of faith?"

"Because it shows that one can have great faith and yet still question. At least on occasion. Which is heartening to someone like me."

They sat in comfortable silence until a shadow in the hallway drew his attention. When he saw who it was, he felt a distinct stirring in his chest. *Lizzie,* he almost whispered, then thought better of it, considering present company. "Miss Clouston. Join us, please."

Lizzie tiptoed across the room. "I promised Second Lieutenant Shuler I'd bring him an extra blanket." She looked at Shuler, who lay sleeping in the bed only feet away, then paused and looked back at Roland. "You gave him yours, Captain."

Roland shrugged. "He was cold. Said he couldn't get warm, so I tossed him mine. Besides, I'm closer to the fire, and Tempy brought me a sheet earlier."

Lizzie knelt and spread the thicker blanket over his legs and chest, then gently tucked it close. He caught a whiff of lilac soap and wished he could finger the brown curl teasing her temple. He told himself it wasn't wise to allow his thoughts to take this trail, but his thoughts didn't listen. He'd seen her earlier in the day, but they'd only exchanged pleasantries. Living in such close proximity to the other soldiers, combined with being immobile, made privacy nearly impossible.

Her pale complexion looked like a rendering from an artist's brush in the fire's glow, and when her eyes met his, he was both sorry—and grateful—that Sister Catherine Margaret was in their company.

"Thank you, Miss Clouston," he said softly.

Her eyes glimmered as though she shared a secret with him, and he couldn't help but smile.

"You're welcome, Captain Jones."

"Sister Catherine Margaret," came a whisper, and they looked to see one of the other nuns gesturing from the doorway. "It's time for vespers."

Sister Catherine Margaret rose. "Here, Miss Clouston. Take my place. The captain and I were waxing not so eloquently about life and time. And I'm certain, though you are considerably younger than I, that you will have much to contribute."

Lizzie shook her head. "And I'm certain I will only disappoint on both counts."

The nun only smiled and patted the chair. "While I am not a prophet, Miss Clouston, I do feel quite certain that, in this instance, disappointment is not a possibility."

Even in the dim light, Roland saw the blush creep into Lizzie's cheeks as she looked down and away. Watching her, he wondered again if she might look differently at him than she did the other soldiers. But even if she did, he already knew that didn't matter. Because despite the subtle wink Sister Catherine discreetly slipped him as she left the room, he had nothing to offer Elizabeth Clouston except friendship. And if friendship was all he could have with her, he would take every moment she gave him, and try not to dream of something more.

The seconds stretched, and Lizzie still seemed hesitant to meet his gaze.

Finally he cleared his throat, determined to set her at ease, while also not waking the others. "Why don't you go first. Share one of the most meaningful things you've learned about time . . . in ten words or fewer."

The start of a smile touched her lips, then swiftly vanished. She sat up straighter in the chair, folded her hands in her lap, and looked like she was about to deliver a formal recitation. She briefly narrowed her eyes, and he imagined she was silently counting the words to make sure her response fit into the parameters.

"One of the most meaningful things I've learned about time, in ten words or fewer: The older a person gets, the more swiftly time passes."

Triumph lit her expression even as Roland held up a hand.

"Lizzie Clouston!" he whispered. "You little eavesdropper. You were out in the hallway listening to what I said earlier!"

"I most certainly was not, Roland Jones!"

He enjoyed the defiant jut of her chin. And how she said his name.

"Wait!" She stilled. "Truly? That's what you said too?"

"Absolutely. Though you said it far more succinctly."

A single eyebrow rose. "I wasn't given much choice."

They laughed softly together.

"But it's true, isn't it?" She leaned forward in the chair. "Don't the years seem to be moving more swiftly than they once did?"

"Without question. Even though, as Sister Catherine and I were just discussing, I can't really say why that is."

The fire burned low, and she retrieved another log from the wood box to the right of the hearth and laid it on top. Knowing he should be the one doing that, Roland could only watch silently.

"Perhaps . . ."

Her voice was so soft he had to watch her lips to make sure he didn't miss anything. Not too unpleasant a task.

"Perhaps it's because once you reach a certain age, as we have, you're most likely closer to the end of your life than to the beginning."

He considered that. "Sort of like it takes a lot longer to push a cart up a hill than to push it down the other side once you've reached the top?"

Her serious expression turned decidedly less so. "If I'm not mistaken, Roland, I believe you just said I was . . . over the hill."

Reacting to the spark of playfulness in her features, he laughed. "If you're over the hill, Lizzie, then I've already got one foot in the grave." He looked down at his legs. "Oh wait . . ."

He laughed. But she only smiled and eyed him.

"I'm so very grateful you lived." Her eyes lit with a sparkle that precious stones would envy. "And that you got to keep your leg."

"And that, my dear Lizzie—" On impulse, Roland reached out his hand, much as he might have done if he were attempting to stroke a skittish doe. And to his surprise, she met him halfway. "That is completely due to you keeping your promise. For which I will forever be grateful."

He gently tightened his hand around hers, and the light in her eyes deepened. But too quickly for him, she pulled her hand away. And he reminded himself again, *Friendship. Only friendship.*

She reached into her pocket and pulled something out. A thin bundle of letters, he saw upon closer inspection, tied with string.

"I'd like to show you something," she said. "And get your opinion, if I could."

"Letters from a secret admirer?" he asked, forcing humor into his voice.

"No," she whispered, not looking up. "These belonged to a soldier who was here at Carnton. A boy. He was no more than thirteen or fourteen years old." She handed them to him.

Sobered, he turned the thin bundle in his hand. "There's no address."

"I know. So I have no idea where to send them. Or if Thaddeus wrote them. Or if they were written to him."

"Thaddeus?"

"I found the name written on a page torn from a Bible. It was with the envelopes in his pocket. But there was no last name. I asked Colonel McGavock this morning if he would check with the War Department to see if they could look up his first name to learn his last. He said he would contact them for me. But look at the string, Roland. It's tied in a knot. Who knots a stack of letters they intend to read again? And for some reason, I can't bring myself to cut it. It feels wrong somehow. Like I'm trespassing. Or maybe there's something in there I shouldn't be privy to."

He smiled at her. "Now you sound like a character from a mystery novel. I seriously doubt there's anything a boy that age would commit to paper, much less carry around with him, that would be too unseemly."

She leaned forward. "There's something else. It's what he said to me at the very last, right before he died."

"Now you really are sounding mysterious."

She briefly closed her eyes. "He said, 'Mama' . . . I think he must've thought he was speaking to her. He said he'd grieved over how he'd left things between them, but that he didn't take it with him like he'd apparently told her he had."

"He didn't take what?"

She shrugged. "That's just it. I don't know. He didn't say. But whatever it is, or was, he said he left it there, buried beneath 'the old willow tree.' And then, right before he died, he whispered, 'Somehow it makes dying easier, knowing you'll have it.'"

Roland said nothing for a moment, then sighed. "Well, that certainly sheds an interesting light on things, doesn't it?"

She nodded, staring at the bundle in his hands. "I think that's why I haven't been able to read these. I feel such a . . ."

"Burden?" he supplied.

"Yes. And also a responsibility. But the fact that the string is knotted tight . . ." She eyed it as though it were a living thing. "It doesn't make sense, I know."

"Do you think maybe one of the doctors gave the boy some medication that caused him to become delusional? Maybe he was speaking nonsense."

She shook her head. "The doctors weren't administering medicine to anyone who didn't stand a good chance of living. And he did not."

What she said about medication not being administered haphazardly was true. They hadn't even offered him any, until Dr. Phillips ordered it.

She looked down at her hands in her lap. "All I know, Roland, is that I can't cut the string. But . . ." She slowly lifted her gaze. "Maybe you could."

He raised his brows. "So let me get this straight. You want me to cut the string and open the envelopes so that whatever curse you apparently believe is going to befall the poor, unsuspecting soul who does such will settle on me instead of you. Is that what I'm to understand?"

The tiniest smile crept over her face, and she nodded. "Yes. That's pretty much the gist of it."

He eyed her for a moment, then gestured. "Hand me that knife on the table over there."

CHAPTER 19

Roland sliced through the knotted string binding the stack of envelopes, sensing Lizzie's trepidation. But being a soldier himself, and carrying his own bundle of letters, he felt at ease with what he was doing. He withdrew the contents of the first of three envelopes and began to read. The handwriting was rather slapdash, so the words were difficult to decipher.

"What?" Lizzie whispered, leaning closer. "You're frowning. What is it?"

Hearing her increased concern, he couldn't resist egging her on a bit. "Mmmm . . . Lizzie, this is bad."

She reached out. "What does it say?"

Her hand on his bare arm sent a small thunderbolt through him. It took concentration to continue reading. "It says . . . 'Hayrides. Walks by the creek. Warm biscuits on Sunday mornings. The smell of snow. Melvin, when he burrows down deep beneath the covers with me.'" He lifted his gaze and caught her droll look. "It's some sort of list."

Smiling, he scanned the wrinkled, stained piece of paper, then turned it over. The handwriting filled both front and back. He handed it to her, and she read silently, her lips moving. Softness swept her face.

"I think it's a list of things he loved." She fingered a dog-eared corner, her tone almost reverent.

"Sunsets painted orangey red. A fresh ticked bed and a warm blanket. The feel of mud between your toes come summer. Rain as it sluices off the metal roofing. Mist as it hangs over the hills."

Roland loved watching her. She possessed a kind of beauty that only seemed to deepen the more he got to know her. Features he'd thought comely upon first glance—her full lips, the slight up-tilt of her pretty nose, the womanly curves that not even the simplest blue day dress could mask—he now found intoxicating. She finally folded the letter, and he held up the other two envelopes.

"Should we?" he asked.

She nodded, but made no move to take them.

"Since I'm the one already cursed . . . ," he said beneath his breath, satisfied when the comment drew a soft laugh.

He opened the second envelope and withdrew a piece of paper similar in appearance to the first, with the same scrawled handwriting. "This one says . . ." Tempted to tease her again, he read the first few lines and all humor fell away. He cleared his throat.

> "You were right, Mama. This undertaking of mine is far more egregious than my thoughts ever could have conjured. I am not as brave as I once thought myself to be. Before battle commences, in those eternally fleeting moments before the first shot is fired, my bones all but shake free from their joints, and I do not know how my body holds together. I am thoroughly run through with fear. And I am ashamed of being afraid. But I am not the only one. I have seen grown men . . ."

He stopped reading aloud. Not that Lizzie would have been offended by the boy's description. He'd witnessed firsthand all she'd been through since the battle that night, and he was convinced there was nothing this woman couldn't endure with grace and dignity. Rather, he'd witnessed the same things the boy was describing and it had moved him just as deeply.

She gently tugged the pages from his hand. "'I have seen grown men,'" she continued, her voice a whisper, "'lose the contents of their stomachs, and worse, as the first blast of a Napoleon gun sends a cannonball screaming for the front line. Some men are very shaky. Often they take off running the other way. I have seen more than one officer use his revolver on his own men as they seek to retreat before the battle is fully begun.'"

She drew in a slow, painstaking breath, and Roland reached for the pages. But she shook her head.

"'Blessed quiet has fallen over the night,'" she read on. "'We are all tired to the bone. Sometimes I lie here and think of home and of all the things I miss about being there.'"

She looked up at him, and Roland could see she was thinking the same thing he was. About the list they'd just read.

"Then other times I do anything I can to chase those images from my rememberings. Because with their sweetness comes a pain, like how the sun sometimes breaks through the clouds and you shield your eyes lest its rays blind you. A thought came to me the other day that if both sides could but lay down our guns and meet in the middle of the field to converse instead of kill each other, we might could find a way to bargain. To work all this out. I said as much to my commanding officer, to which he laughed and called me a half-wit. I did not say my next thought aloud to him, lest he clap me a good one to the head like I have seen him do some others. But I pondered . . . He calls me a half-wit, yet I am not the one sending sea after sea of men to their bloody deaths."

Roland watched as Lizzie sifted through the rest of the pages. She didn't seem to be reading them so much as cherishing them, running her fingertips over the words.

"It's signed . . . Your loving son." She looked up. "He was so young, Roland. Too young."

He'd had much the same thought as she'd read aloud. He opened the third envelope and pulled out a single sheet of paper. But this time he handed it to her. She carefully smoothed the crinkled paper on her lap, then held it closer to the lamplight.

"It's another list," she whispered, her gaze moving across the page. "'Braver. More honest. Less selfish. Complain less. Give more.'" Her chin trembled. She blew out a soft breath, but tears still rose to her eyes. She blinked and handed him the piece of paper. "I can't see to read any longer."

He found where she'd left off and continued. "'Try harder. Forgive faster. Remember more good things. Be kind.'" He smiled at that one, thinking of how few boys at that age had gained this depth of wisdom. He knew he certainly hadn't. "'Think of others more. Go fishing more often. And take Bekah along. Pray more. Listen better. Love others. Build Jenny a house.'" He paused, a little surprised at that one. But even more surprising was how difficult it was to say the next one aloud. "'Ask Jenny to marry me,'" he whispered, keeping his eyes on the page. "'Be a good husband.'" Then his throat threatened to close. "'Be a . . . good father.'"

The words blurred on the page, and for a long moment he just stared at the watery image, thinking of Susan, of their precious Lena, and of a young boy sitting by a campfire at night, staring into the flames and missing home. When he finally looked back, he saw Lizzie's cheeks damp with tears.

"A list of things he wanted to do?" she asked.

"Or maybe a list of things he wanted to be, if he'd been given a second chance."

He looked into her eyes, and the quiet moved in around them, filling their silence. But still she didn't look away. His body warmed. What he wouldn't give to take her into his arms and kiss her, slow and long. Show her how he truly felt about her. But on the heels of that desire came a sharp reminder. Even if by some unexplained occurrence Lizzie were to begin to care for him, he had nothing to offer her. Nothing to make a life for her. And even though he was no longer bound to Weet in marriage, the vows they'd exchanged were still bound up within him. Death had torn that relationship asunder, but his heart was still tethered to her somehow. As evidenced by the guilt he felt over the desire coursing through him.

Roland forced himself to look away first, and he concentrated on what Lizzie had told him the boy had said there at the last. "Somehow it makes dying easier knowing you'll have it," he repeated softly. "Whatever *it* is. What would so young a boy have that he would consider so important?"

"I don't know. But one thing I am certain about, Roland. In those final moments, when a man lies dying, he speaks of what matters most to him. And whatever is buried beneath that willow tree, it mattered a great deal to Thaddeus. Enough that he wanted his mother to have it, even after all that had apparently gone wrong between them."

Roland stared into her eyes. "Which I firmly believe decides the course we are to take, Lizzie."

The hint of a smile touched her mouth. "We need to find his family."

"And if Colonel McGavock's lead doesn't pan out, I may have another idea."

The way she looked at him made him grateful that Loring's Division had been assigned to Carnton. If he had to be convalescing somewhere, he wanted to be near her.

A distant pounding rose from the front entrance hall, followed by an indistinguishable blur of voices. But it was the heavy footfalls advancing up the staircase that drew Roland's attention most. Dread filled him, and he prayed General Folsom hadn't changed his mind and returned, determined to make good on his threat of prison.

CHAPTER 20

To Roland's great relief, the man who appeared in the doorway, rifle in hand, was not General Folsom or any other Federal officer.

"Lizzie!" the man whispered, a smile near splitting his face. He crossed the room, took hold of her hands, and drew her to her feet, then hugged her tight.

Roland felt a stab of jealousy. He wanted to believe this was Lizzie's brother, but instinct—and the way the man drew back and looked into her eyes—told him that would be mighty wishful thinking on his part.

"Towny!" Lizzie blinked, as though not believing what she was seeing. "I thought you'd left! But . . . what are you doing here? This isn't safe! The Federal Army could still be in the area and—"

"Oh, it's safe enough, Lizzie. My company bivouacked a few miles from here. We're joining the rest of the army in Nashville soon. Some of us from here got permission to come back. Wanted to make sure the men left behind were all right. Besides, I didn't get the chance to say a proper good-bye like I promised. And I always keep my promises. Especially to you."

"Yes, you do," she whispered, a slight dissonance in her tone. She glanced down at Roland and hesitated. "Forgive my manners, Captain. Allow me to introduce Second Lieutenant Blake Townsend. Towny and I grew up together. Here, in Franklin."

Roland sensed there was meaning woven in and around that sentence that he couldn't quite discern. But whatever it was, his gut told him he didn't want to.

"Towny," she continued, "this is Captain Roland Jones from Mississippi."

Townsend bent down and extended his left hand. "It's an honor to meet you, Captain. I've heard your name, sir. You're a sharpshooter. And a mighty good one, from what I've been told."

Appreciating the man's awareness of his injured right hand, Roland accepted, wishing he could stand for this particular introduction. "I am a sharpshooter, Lieutenant, but don't believe everything you hear. Rumors tend to grow the truth. Especially after battles."

Townsend smiled as he straightened. "Even if I were only to believe half of it, sir, I'd still be impressed. It's an honor. But"—the man's gaze swept his body—"I'm sure sorry, Captain, about what happened to you."

"Thank you. I aim to be back on my feet soon enough."

"That's good to hear, sir. I just hope my Lizzie here is taking good care of you."

Townsend slipped a possessive arm around Lizzie's waist, and that gut-sinking feeling Roland had experienced moments earlier suddenly developed claws.

"Oh yes, she is. Miss Clouston is a fine nurse."

Roland tried to catch her eye, but she looked anywhere but at him.

"Lizzie can do just about anything she sets her mind to, Captain." Townsend kissed the crown of her head. "Now, if you'll excuse us, sir, I'm going to borrow her for a minute so I can say a proper good-bye to my fiancée."

The words landed a blow, but Roland did his best not to show any reaction. "Permission granted, Lieutenant." He forced a smile and finally managed to capture Lizzie's gaze. "Miss Clouston, thank you for the company this evening."

Her smile trembled. "Thank *you*, Captain."

In her eyes he read an entire exchange waiting to be had. But it was an exchange he didn't mind putting off. Indefinitely. "Good night to you both. And, Lieutenant, God be with you."

Lizzie walked hand in hand with Towny out the front door and down the front brick walkway into the bitter cold and dark. Moonlight shone through the bare tree limbs and fell across the front lawn, painting the night, and Towny's familiar features, in dappled silver shadows. But all she could think about was Roland.

Why hadn't she told him she was engaged to be married before now? The look on his face when Towny had called her his fiancée . . . She squeezed her eyes tight. She felt so traitorous. So false. And for good reason. But in her defense, at least at the outset, she'd assumed Roland was married, so the attraction she'd felt for him had been safe, in a way. She never would have acted on those feelings, much less revealed them to him, otherwise. And she'd never intended for them to be revealed at all. But she'd done a poor job at masking her surprise when learning he was a widower, and that was putting it mildly.

She needed to apologize to him. And would. Once she thought of the right words to say, and could say them without that telling flutter that nearly took her breath away every time he looked at her.

Towny led her as far as the front gate, then paused and leaned his rifle against the fence.

"Lizzie, I just had to see you again. Especially after the battle the other night. The more I've thought about it, about what could have happened to me . . ." He swallowed hard, his expression pained. "The more I've realized how lucky we are to have each other. Well, not lucky, exactly. But you know what I mean."

"Yes, I know what you mean," she whispered.

He cradled her face in his hands, and the way he looked down at her with such love brought tears to her eyes. But not for the reasons it should have.

"As I said, we're headed to Nashville soon, and we're going to pay back those Federals for what they did to us here. General Hood aims to end this thing once and for all." He looked toward the battlefield. "I just wish the men I've fought with for the past three years, the ones I buried in that field the other day, I wish they could see us. I wish they could see that their honor is being upheld."

She covered his hands on her face, his words striking a bitter chord. "Do you know what I wish, Towny? I wish we could stop talking about honor and death. I wish this war would end. I wish all the fighting and stabbing and killing and shooting would cease. And that somehow we could find a way to live peaceably together. As I've watched what's happened here at Carnton over the past few days— and I know that what I've seen is so small a slice compared to what you've witnessed—I've asked myself, *Is this really worth it?* Thousands of men dying in such horrid ways, some of them right in my arms. All the children who will grow up never knowing their fathers, brothers, or uncles. As I've watched doctors remove limb after limb, the piles growing as high as the table, I—"

"Don't talk that way, Lizzie. It *is* all worth it. Because once the Southern army takes back Nashville, which Hood says we will, we'll have the supply lines we need and it'll just be a matter of time before victory is ours. Then you'll be able to forget all this and put it behind you, and we'll get on with living our lives the way we were doing before the war started."

"But I don't want to go back to that life, Towny. And I don't want to forget. Not that I want to keep reliving the images from the battlefield every time I close my eyes. But far too much blood has been spilled to simply forget and move on. Instead, we need to learn from this. We need to make changes." She briefly considered telling him about teaching Tempy, then quickly decided against it. He would only try to change her mind. "You know how I feel about slavery. I believe we have an obligation to—"

"Lizzie, we don't have to decide this now." He wrapped her hands in his. "I came here tonight to see you. Not to talk about all this. I came to ask you to marry me."

She stared. "I've already told you I'll marry you, Towny. We're betrothed."

"No. I mean now. Marry me tonight."

"Tonight?"

"You've got your dress all sewn and ready. You said so in one of your letters. And it doesn't matter what I wear, just as long as I'm standing beside you when I say 'I do.' I've already stopped by Preacher Higgins's house in town. He's happy to do the honors. He said he's watched us grow up and that it's only fitting that he be the one to tie the knot."

Seeing his boyish grin spreading from ear to ear, Lizzie fought for something to say. "Towny, I—"

"I know it's not the wedding you dreamed of as a little girl, Lizzie. Getting married out in a field of flowers, birdsong all around you, the sun shining down."

Her heart warmed despite the slow panic mounting inside her. "You remember that? After all these years?"

"I remember everything about you, Lizzie." He winked. "So why don't you go get your dress and we'll go see Preacher Higgins. We can be husband and wife before the clock strikes midnight."

She looked up at him, everything within her screaming *No!* even as she saw Towny for the fine man he was, for the faithful friend he'd always been, and for the promise that he held. The promise of children. But this . . .

"I'm sorry, Towny, but I can't. It's too quick. After all, our families aren't here. And you know Hattie and Winder would never forgive me. She's excited about being the flower girl, and Winder has already started practicing carrying the ring. And . . ." She winced. "I don't have the dress anymore."

Confusion etched his features, and she rushed to explain. "The night of the battle we ran out of bandages. Mrs. McGavock offered up her finest dresses, even her undergarments. I offered my other two day dresses and a blanket. Then I imagined you lying somewhere wounded and bleeding, needing to be tended, and I knew I had to give the dress too."

He loosened his grip on her. "You cut up your wedding dress?"

She squeezed his hands tight. "I can make another one just like it. It only took me a couple of months, which isn't that long. And from what I've heard in recent days, the war could be over soon. Maybe by this summer. And we can be married then. So that will give me plenty of time."

He bent so his gaze was level with hers, like he used to do when they were children and he would study her eyes, trying to ferret out whether she was jesting or telling the truth. Only now he brought his face much closer to hers, and Lizzie was grateful for the shadows.

"You haven't had a change of heart, have you, Lizzie? About marrying me?"

It took everything within her to hold his gaze. How could she answer him honestly? If she said yes, she'd be sending him back to war brokenhearted. She couldn't do that. She'd given him her pledge. "No," she whispered. "I haven't had a change of heart." But that was the problem. Ever since she'd said yes to him, she kept praying her heart *would* change toward him.

He slipped his arms around her waist and pulled her to him, and she sensed a difference in the way he held her. An earnestness that hadn't been there before. He moved closer, his body pressing against hers, and she felt a wall go up inside her.

"I know it's been horrible for you," he whispered, stroking her back. "With everything that's happened here. But trust me when I say that it's been worth it. Or it will have been, once we win the war."

She looked up at him and took the opportunity to step back a little. "How are you so certain we're going to win? And even if we do, it's not worth it if it takes you, Towny. And Johnny. And the rest of the boys we grew up with."

"I'm not going to die. And your brother's smart. He's tough too. Like his older sister. After the war is over and I come home, I'm going to marry you, Lizzie. And as the years pass, we'll look back on this time as a distant memory, and we'll be grateful that the South rose up to defend itself. That we didn't tuck tail and run like the Federals did the other night."

Tuck tail and run . . .

The phrase reminded her of what Roland had said. *There's no way the Federals tucked tail and ran. They were ready for us.* Roland had a different opinion about the outcome of this war. He no longer believed the Confederacy would win. It was a view that more closely aligned with what she'd seen on the battlefield, evidence that pointed to—

Towny's kiss caught her so off guard, she didn't know how to react. Especially since the man kissing her wasn't the man occupying her thoughts. His arms tightened around her, his mouth full on hers, his lips urgent, and she instinctively pressed a hand against his chest. He broke the kiss and stared down, his breath puffing white in the moonlight. Confusion colored his expression, and she knew her reaction had injured him. Something she never wanted to do.

"I'm sorry." She bowed her head. "I simply wasn't expecting—"

He gently squeezed her arm. "Something's wrong, Lizzie. What is it?"

She wanted to tell him everything was fine. That they were fine. But she couldn't. She shook her head. "I don't know."

He stepped back. "Look at me."

She hesitated, then did as he asked.

"Do you love me, Lizzie?"

"Yes, I do," she whispered, tears filling her eyes. Yet she couldn't maintain his gaze.

"Look at me," he whispered again.

She did.

"Do you love me . . . in *that* way?"

Her lips trembled. Tears spilled over.

He sighed and nodded, then stared off into the night. A long, painful moment passed before he spoke again. "So why, then? Why did you say yes to me?"

She pressed a hand to her stomach, the truth roiling inside her. "I would never do anything to hurt you, Towny."

"I know that. But I still want you to answer my question."

"Because . . . we're good together. As you said before, we already know each other's good and bad sides. Our families get along well, and—"

"Just say it, Lizzie Beth. You never were good at beating around the bush."

She stared up at him, her own selfishness condemning her before she even said the words. "I want to be married because I want children," she finally whispered, then lifted a shoulder and let it fall.

"Children," he repeated, his voice hushed. "You always have loved children."

She nodded, waiting.

"I guess that's better than marrying me for my money."

The edges of his mouth tipped in a smile and lured one from her too.

He took hold of her hand. "Before Mama died, she told me I should marry you. She said that best friends made the best husbands and wives."

Lizzie squeezed his hand tight. "She and your father were a wonderful example of that."

He nodded and looked away.

"I'm sorry, Towny. I should have been honest with you from the very beginning."

When he looked back, emotion glistened in his eyes. "I love you, Lizzie. You're my best friend. And I think I'm yours."

He waited. She nodded.

"And I believe that, with time," he continued, "that kind of love will grow between us. I already feel it for you." He smiled down. "I'll spend my life trying to make you happy. And you know I want children too. Lots of children." His smile faded. "So, if you're still willing . . ." He reached into his pocket. "I would be honored for you to be my wife."

He opened his palm, and even in the darkness, Lizzie knew what he held.

"Mama wanted you to have it. Papa's been keeping it, but I figured you could keep it until the wedding. That is, if you haven't changed your mind."

As clearly as if a crossroads lay before her, Lizzie felt the weight of this choice. But she'd already given him her pledge. And he hadn't changed *his* mind. Maybe his mother was right. Marlene and Towny's father had shared a very loving relationship, and they'd started out as childhood friends. And now that she'd been honest with him, there was no reason for her to feel guilty anymore. Maybe that's what had been getting in her way of moving forward with her feelings.

Roland. Just thinking about him made her warm on the inside. What was it about him that did that? That made her heart beat a little faster even now. But was that enough to throw away a relationship with Towny? That would be foolish. She'd known Roland Jones a matter of days. She'd known Towny for well over half of her life. And in the end, she'd given her word. And a pledge was a pledge.

Lizzie took the ring from his hand and looked up. "I'll keep it safe. Until we're married."

His breath left him in a rush. He pressed a kiss to her forehead. "You've made me so happy. All over again. You won't be sorry, I promise." He grabbed his rifle and opened the gate. "Write me?"

She nodded. "I will." Then something within her shifted, and she wondered if this might be the last time she'd ever see him. The very thought brought her to tears, and she hugged him tight one last time. "You're so dear to me, Towny."

He laughed and embraced her again. But this time it felt more like she was accustomed to, before they were betrothed. More the way of friends. She watched his shadowy figure until he reached the edge of the woods, then disappeared into the thick stand of pine, swallowed up by night.

Holding the ring tightly in her palm, she returned to the house, only then noticing how cold she was. Shivering, she closed the door behind her. The lamp in the entrance hall had been dimmed, and it appeared as if everyone was already abed, including the nuns who were asleep on pallets in the best parlor. All except for the two sisters whose turn it was to keep watch over the men tonight. The nuns rotated that duty, and Lizzie didn't know how the household would have functioned without their help—and their surprising wit. Who knew nuns could be so amusing?

She walked to the lamp and held Marlene Townsend's ring up to the light. A simple gold band, one side more worn than the other, but still beautiful. And so precious. She tucked it into her skirt pocket.

Rubbing her arms to ward off the cold, she glanced up the staircase leading to the second-floor landing and recalled how she'd responded to Roland when he'd taken hold of her hand earlier. Why had she reached out to accept his hand in the first place? It felt as if her hand had moved of its own volition. The memory sent warmth coursing through her again. How could one man's slightest touch stir such desire within her, while another's kiss left her unmoved?

Regardless of how or why, she owed Roland an apology. She should have told him early on that she was engaged. She would apologize to him, and she had no reason to think he wouldn't accept that apology and be understanding. With that decision firmly made, she retraced her steps to the front door and set the lock.

She passed through the farm office on her way to her bedroom, deep crimson stains still marring the carpet and upholstery, same as in the other rooms. With everyone pitching in to help, they'd wiped down the doors and wooden casings and wallpaper in the house as best they could. They'd also soaked up what they could from the carpet. She'd overhead Colonel and Mrs. McGavock discussing the need to replace the wallpaper and carpet throughout. Yet in the same breath Mrs. McGavock, ever practical, had commented how trivial all those niceties seemed at present.

Lizzie agreed. Yet it had to be done. Much as she needed to return to teaching the children. But how did one return to normalcy after something like this?

She opened the door to her bedroom and was relieved to discover Hattie and Winder already asleep. She smiled, seeing the book that lay open on the covers. Apparently they'd waited for her, but sleep had won out. She closed the novel and laid it aside on the table.

She fetched her sewing box from the wardrobe and carefully tucked Towny's mother's ring into the corner for safekeeping. She'd expected to feel lighter inside somehow, having told him the truth about why she'd agreed to marry him. And she did, in a way. But still an unexplained heaviness remained.

She changed into her gown and slipped into bed—nudging Winder over a bit—then turned down the light. Roland had said *we. The course we are to take, Lizzie.* He was going to help her find Thaddeus. When she'd seen the emotion welling in his eyes as he'd read the boy's thoughts aloud, she'd been deeply moved. Especially knowing all he'd lost in his life. He'd been very much in love with his late wife, that much was clear from his reaction when she'd read Susan's letter aloud. His wife had signed the letter *Weet.* A unique name. Perhaps a pet name he'd called her.

Thinking of Susan's letter turned her thoughts to the letter Captain Pleasant Hope had written. She'd wrestled to pen some words to Captain Hope's widow that would offer comfort and hope, then included the note in an envelope along with the captain's tender message to their child. Mrs. McGavock had posted the missive in town yesterday after calling for a second time upon the Carter family with condolences on Tod's passing. Carrie McGavock knew the heartache that came with losing a child. She and the colonel had lost three of the five children born to them.

Lizzie had been at Carnton serving as governess for only two years when sweet little Mary passed at the age of seven, the same age Winder was now. Mary had been such a gentle-natured girl. And it had scarcely been two years since twelve-year-old Martha died. Martha, so bright, so inquisitive and eager to learn. John Randal, the McGavocks' firstborn son, had died several years before Lizzie arrived at Carnton, and had lived only a matter of months. Burying the McGavocks' older girls had torn Lizzie's heart in two.

Carrie had once confided that every loss was different. *Because each loss hurts and carves a hole inside you so deep you think it could never mend. And in truth it never does. Not really. But God promises that if you draw close to him, he'll draw close to you. He'll soothe that wound with his peace, comfort, and assurance. And with the firm hope of being with that beloved one again.*

Lizzie still couldn't begin to imagine what that kind of loss felt like as a parent. And hoped she never would.

Exhausted, she turned over, trying just as easily to turn off her thoughts. Sleep finally claimed her, and she dreamed she and Towny were children again, running through the fields, going hunting with Johnny, sitting by the creek plunking rocks. Then the dream shifted. She was older. She spotted someone in the distance. All she knew was that she had to get to him. She ran until her side ached and her lungs burned. But no matter how far she ran, or how fast, she couldn't get any closer.

Then she realized her feet were mired in mud thick as clay. She couldn't move. And somehow the distance between them kept increasing. She tried to call out, but her voice wouldn't carry. Until she awakened to earsplitting screams.

CHAPTER 21

Her heart pounding, Lizzie shot straight up in bed, then reached across Winder for Hattie. The girl's high-pitched screams fragmented the darkness. Lizzie pulled her close. "Hattie! Wake up, dearest. Wake up!"

The girl struggled against her. "Get it off me! *Get it off!*"

"It's Miss Clouston, Hattie. You're safe. You're here with me and Winder. In bed." Lizzie shot a look at Winder, who stirred beside them but slept on. The boy could sleep through anything. "I've got you, dearest. Open your eyes."

Hattie finally stilled, her breath coming hard.

A knock sounded at the door. "Miss Clouston! Is everything all right?"

"Colonel—" Lizzie quickly arranged the bedcovers over her legs. "Yes, sir. Come in, please."

The door opened and Colonel McGavock stepped inside, oil lamp in hand.

"It's all over me, Miss Clouston." Hattie ran her hands over her arms. "I can't get it off."

The colonel moved closer. "Get what off, Hattie?"

"The blood." The girl hiccupped a sob. "It's all over me."

"Oh, sweetheart . . ." Lizzie cradled her closer and exchanged a look with the colonel. "I know it must feel that way, but there's no blood on you. It was all a bad dream."

Lizzie heard the words come from her mouth and truly wished that were the case for everything that had happened in the past few days. Well, almost everything.

The colonel knelt beside the bed. "Hattie, would you like to sleep with Papa and Mama for the rest of the night?"

Hattie looked up at her father, then at Lizzie. Lizzie smiled and nodded, a bit surprised herself at the invitation. The McGavocks were excellent and loving parents, but rarely did they indulge their children in such ways.

Hattie finally nodded, and the colonel held out his arms. "It's going to be all right," he whispered against her hair.

Watching them, Lizzie remembered the safety of her own father's arms when she was younger. What a weighty treasure parenthood was. To have the ability to whisper to a child, "Everything will be all right," and have them believe you without question. Even though it really wasn't within your power to make that promise.

"Thank you, Miss Clouston," the colonel whispered and closed the door behind them.

Lizzie lay back down and pulled up the covers, but quickly realized that sleep was done with her. She turned up the lamp and dressed quickly, then glanced back before she closed the bedroom door behind her. Winder was now sprawled in the center of the bed, still fast asleep. She had no doubt that he, too, would carry scars from what had happened here, but how those scars would manifest themselves remained to be seen. For everyone, she guessed.

Downstairs, she stoked the flickering embers in the kitchen hearth and added more wood, then filled the coffee kettle with water and set it to boil over the flame. Dawn was only a couple of hours away, which meant Tempy would be down soon enough to start her day's work.

Waiting for the water to boil, Lizzie ran a hand over the rustic mantel, appreciating the history of this part of the home. Besides the second-story back porch, this kitchen was her favorite place in the house. She sometimes thought of this part of the home as the east wing, but it was actually the original farmhouse the colonel's parents had built. Constructed of red brick, the farmhouse abutted the larger, more spacious addition to the home that had been added later. The kitchen boasted three windows on both the north and south walls, which allowed ample sunlight, as well as a way for Lizzie to keep watch of Winder when he tried to sneak off to the barn or head toward the fields to play.

Lizzie added coffee grounds to the roiling water and gave it a stir. Minutes later, she poured herself a cup of the warm brew and had just sat down at the table when the stairs leading to the bedrooms creaked behind her.

"Well, ain't this a nice surprise." Tempy paused for a moment, still wrapping her hair in one of the colorful tignons she wore.

"You can do that without even looking in a mirror?"

Tempy smiled. "I do it way better not lookin'. Seein' this ole face starin' back at me, 'specially so early in the mornin', gives me a fright!"

Lizzie laughed. "That one is especially pretty. The blues and greens suit your coloring."

"The missus always picks out the cloth. She does a good job at it."

Lizzie heard the compliment in the statement, but could only think about how Tempy didn't even have the right to choose the material she wore. Lizzie took a long drink of coffee. *Lord, whatever changes are coming, let them come quickly. And let them last.*

"Tempy . . ."

Tempy turned from where she stood cracking eggs into a bowl.

Lizzie kept her voice soft. "I was thinking that either early mornings or late evenings would be the best times for our lessons."

Tempy glanced over to the stairs leading to the bedrooms above them, and Lizzie halfway expected her to say she'd changed her mind.

"I reckon you right, ma'am. But whatever we do, it's got to be us alone knowin' about it."

"We'll be careful, I promise." So many questions came to mind that she wanted to ask. But one stood out above the rest. "Have you ever heard from the slaves who were sent away from here at the start of the war?"

Tempy turned. "How long you been wantin' to ask me that, ma'am?"

Lizzie fingered the grip of her coffee mug. "A long time."

Tempy returned to her work. "I used to get word every now and then when I's at the market in town or someone brought somethin' to the house. But a lotta time done passed since I heard anything. I remember that mornin' so well . . ." She paused, cracked eggshell in hand. "I had everythin' that was mine all wrapped and tied up to go, but when I walked outside to get on the wagon, Colonel told me I'd be stayin'. Didn't make sense at first. We'd all heard that if the Federals came here to the farm, they'd be takin' us with 'em. Settin' us free. That's why the colonel was sendin' us all away." A sad smile turned her mouth. "But every soldier I's seen in a blue coat, he just looks straight through me like I ain't even there. I guess the settin' free part only counts if you ain't mostly dried up and old like me." She shot a look back at Lizzie. "But the colonel and the missus," she said quickly, "they been right good to me, ma'am. I got more than most slaves. A lot more."

Lizzie shook her head. "You don't have to say that to me, Tempy. I know the McGavocks are kind and generous people. But it doesn't change the fact that you're not free. Not yet, anyway."

Tempy gave her a look that held only the faintest glimmer of hope. But Lizzie couldn't blame her for feeling as though her station in life was never going to change. Slavery was all the woman had ever known. And while Lizzie couldn't change that, she could help her in other ways, and was eager to begin.

Tempy went to fetch some supplies from the larder, and Lizzie rose and stirred the pot of grits she'd placed over the fire, watching the butter melt and swirl. She turned in order to warm her backside and looked out the front window into the darkness. She stilled and squinted.

She would've sworn she saw movement outside by the front gate. Likely a deer. But—she crossed to the window—no, it was too large to be a deer. Her breath fogged the pane, and she wiped the ghosted glass with her palm. It was a man. He looked toward the house, then back down the road as though debating, then sat down on the ground by the front gate.

Her first inclination was to alert Colonel McGavock. But a man sitting by the front gate wasn't exactly a threat. And it was brutally cold outside. Lizzie grabbed her shawl from the hook and opened the kitchen door. "Who goes there?" she called out.

The man looked back, then slowly rose to his feet. He was wearing a pack of some sort. "Be this the Carnton place, ma'am?" His voice was deep, and the stillness before the dawn only amplified it.

"It is. And who might you be?"

"Name be George, ma'am. I come to be with Cap'n Jones."

Roland lay on the wood plank floor, his back aching with a pain that went bone deep, but he didn't dare try to sit up on his own. He wanted more morphine, but he'd seen what that medicine could do to a man once he began leaning on it too heavily. He already had enough obstacles to overcome.

He guessed the nuns on duty had fallen asleep in the hallway. Couldn't blame them. It had been a long night, the clock in one of the rooms downstairs chiming each hour and quarter hour. The symphony of snoring hadn't helped either. Although he knew that wasn't the real cause of his sleeplessness. Why was it that the night hours seemed to pass so much more slowly than those during the day? So much for time passing swiftly, as he and Sister Catherine Margaret had been discussing last evening.

The older a person gets, the more swiftly time passes.

Remembering Lizzie's smartish expression when she'd responded to his challenge last night tempted him to smile. Thinking of what had happened shortly after didn't. *Betrothed.* He hadn't been expecting that.

And what had he been thinking, taking her hand that way? Certainly nothing levelheaded when it came to Elizabeth Clouston.

The combination of his injuries and too much idle time had caused him to read something into her behavior that clearly wasn't there. He felt foolish. Even a little embarrassed. He sighed and situated the bear's head beneath his own. "Well, Sir Horace," he whispered, "it's just you and me, friend. What do you think we ought to do? Try to sit up? Or just lie here like the aging invalids we are?" The statement felt truer than he cared to admit. He didn't like not being in control.

Surely dawn couldn't be far off now. Peering through the window, he watched the night sky as it turned from black to deep purple, then gave way to violet with hints of pink, and he wondered again where heaven really was. Preacher E. M. Bounds—who'd traveled with the Army of Tennessee for the last few months, and with whom he'd enjoyed many an evening conversing by the campfire—had told him heaven was up there, beyond the clouds.

Roland knew his Bible well enough to know it spoke of Jesus being taken up into the clouds, so he figured the preacher's counsel was right enough. What treasures that place must hold, including the two he already knew were there waiting for him. He squinted, wishing he could see beyond the veil. He figured even a second or two of witnessing that splendor would last him for the rest of his life here.

A deep yearning filled him, along with a homesickness. *Weet, Lena . . . I sure do love you two gals. Always will.* He swallowed. *Take care of each other . . . until I get there and can do that for you both.*

He hoped Preacher Bounds had made it through the battle the other night unscathed. The last time he'd seen the scrappy little man of God, Bounds had been marching with them into the thick of it, as was his custom. Standing barely five feet tall and thin as a reed, the preacher was so burdened down by his backpack and equipment that the soldiers had taken to calling him "the walking bundle."

The man had an uncanny ability to remember names. Whenever

Roland saw him greeting a soldier, it was always by name. And unlike the other ministers who stayed back at camp, Bounds always marched right alongside them into the fray, his Bible raised and scripture pouring forth from him along with shouts of encouragement, exhorting the soldiers that if they hadn't yet bowed the knee to Jesus, right then would be an opportune time to do so.

Roland had long ago bowed that particular knee, but about a year ago he'd found himself surrendering yet again. They'd been on the outskirts of Chattanooga under heavy fire from a group of Federals who outnumbered them three to one. With bullets screaming past him, cannon fire exploding, shaking the ground beneath his feet, he'd thought for sure that his time had come. Then somehow, over the thunder of war, he'd heard that familiar voice calling out.

"'The LORD is my light and my salvation; whom shall I fear? the LORD is the strength of my life; of whom shall I be afraid?' God knows the precise moment he will call you home, my dear brothers. You will not stay on this earth one second longer than God ordains! Nor will you be swept up to heaven's peace a moment too soon. You are in his hands. So travel this life with that confidence tucked close against your heart!"

Every morning Bounds rose at four o'clock and prayed until seven, and encouraged others to pray too. "Prayers are deathless, Captain Jones. They outlive the lives of those who utter them."

Roland liked that thought. And while he'd never even come close to developing the discipline Preacher Bounds possessed in that regard, his communication with the Almighty had taken a definite downturn in recent months. If only he knew what the Almighty had planned for his life, and for the Confederacy, then maybe he'd be able to pray better.

"Come this way. He's right up here."

Roland recognized Lizzie's voice and the soft footfalls on the stairs. A heavier tread followed hers, and he turned in the direction of the door in time to see her enter, along with—

"George!" Roland's voice came out louder than intended, which earned him grumbles from those still trying to sleep.

"Cap'n Jones!" George said in his version of a whisper.

George crossed the room in minimum strides, joy and uncertainty taking turns dominating the man's features. Roland held out his left hand, and George took firm hold.

"It's sure good to see you, Cap'n."

"It's good to see you too. I wasn't certain the telegram I sent would even arrive."

"Took a mite longer for me to get here than I counted on, but I made it. And I come right away too. Some of the train tracks was busted up pretty bad. One of the army's doin's, I guess. That slowed me down." George settled beside him on the floor. "Miss Lizzie here, and Miss Tempy, they done fed me breakfast downstairs, sir. It was mighty good and plenty of it."

"Well, that was nice of them. I hope you left some for the rest of us."

Seeing George's wide-toothed grin again was like getting a glimpse of home.

"Yes, sir, I did. How bad has you been shot, Cap'n?"

"My legs got the worst of it." Roland lifted his bandaged right hand. "But the doctor says that with some work I should be able to walk again. Now that you're here, I'm hoping we'll get that started soon enough."

"Whatever you need, sir, you let me know and I do my best to get it."

"But you must take things slowly," Lizzie interjected. "At least that's what Dr. Phillips instructed."

Only then did Roland allow himself to look over at her, uncertain how he should address her now, since learning of her betrothal. But considering he could be at Carnton for what might be many more weeks, retreating to the more formal address could make things even more awkward between them.

"Good morning, Lizzie. And yes, I'll be certain to take measured steps, so to speak."

She nodded, her smile fleeting. "I hope you rested well last night."

"Not particularly." He gave a humored grimace to soften his response.

She shook her head. "I didn't sleep much either."

A quiet undertone in her voice told him that a conversation between them was inevitable, and he reined in a sigh.

"Speaking of breakfast . . ." Lizzie gestured, then knotted her hands at her waist as if she didn't know what to do with them. "If you'll both excuse me, I need to get back to the kitchen to help Tempy. We'll return shortly with eggs and bacon and some bread for everyone."

Roland nodded. "That sounds good. Thank you."

She dipped her head. "You're most welcome, Roland."

He watched her walk away. So much for not retreating to the formal. But if it was this renewed formality or not seeing her at all, he'd take this. But he knew he'd best be careful. Because like morphine, the woman had an addictive quality. Something he'd do well to remember.

"Mind if I see your legs, sir? See what we's up against?"

Roland lifted the sheet and blanket covering the lower half of his body, and winced at the pain reflected in George's expression. "The doctor wanted to take this one." He indicated his right leg. "But I told him no before I went under. Miss Lizzie was there during the surgery to make sure he stuck to my wishes. If not for her, this leg would be long gone."

George shook his head. "I ain't never had the gift of healin' like a real doctor, sir, but that leg sure does look tore up." As though suddenly realizing what he'd said, George forced a smile. "'Course, if we work at it together, Cap'n, I'm thinkin' we can get you walkin' again."

"That's the aim, George. And the sooner the better."

CHAPTER 22

"Sister, I can't tell you how good this feels. Almost makes me forget about my legs. Who needs morphine when they could be freshly shaved and shorn?"

Sister Catherine Margaret smiled down at him as she poured warm water over his head. "I believe I'll hang a shingle out in front of the convent."

Roland laughed, relishing the warm water and the opportunity to clean up, even if having a porcelain basin under his neck was beginning to cause an ache.

"I'm just sorry it took me so long to get to it, Captain. The sisters and I are helping at other places in town in recent days. So many are hurting still."

"I'm just grateful to you for doing it. And it's certainly been worth the wait."

He never imagined he would so enjoy being freshly shaven. He ran a hand over his smooth jawline and thought of Susan. Last time he'd seen her and Lena, he'd looked much as he had moments earlier. Hair nearly down to his shoulders and beard all wild and woolly. Susan had insisted on shaving off his beard before they'd gone to bed together that night. The memory brought a smile, and a pang of regret. This was his first shave since.

Sister Catherine Margaret helped him to a sitting position and handed him a fresh towel to dry his hair, then made a show of studying him. "I was right, Captain. There *were* marks of handsomeness beneath all that dark hair and beard. But only a wee bit." She chuckled.

Roland laughed too, then lowered his voice. "Don't you go and start being tempted over me now, Sister. You'll have to do more than a few Hail Marys to get out of that one."

He'd never heard a nun laugh so heartily or so long. The other men in the room just looked at her.

A moment passed, and she gave Roland a motherly pat on the shoulder. "Oh, Captain . . . If ever I'd had a son, I'd like to think he would've been like you."

Roland swiftly sobered, and for a beat words escaped him. He watched her gather the dirty linens and basin of sudsy water. "Sister," he finally managed, "that's most kind of you. And more than a little generous. The fact that you would even think such a thing gives me something to aspire to."

She shook her head and made a tsking sound. "There you go again, Captain. Handsome *and* good-hearted. Rest assured, we'll be sending no young nuns to help at Carnton while you're here!"

She walked out the door, still chuckling to herself, and Roland had to smile. He ran a hand over his smooth jaw, the sensation unfamiliar, to say the least. But a good kind of unfamiliar.

Someone passed in the hallway outside, and he looked back in time to see it was Lizzie. She didn't even look inside Winder's bedroom. The few times she'd come into the room over the past couple of days, she'd been cordial. But he didn't have to guess why she'd made herself scarce. He'd made her uncomfortable, and he didn't blame her for putting distance between them. It was best, he knew. Even if it wasn't what he really wanted.

"I wouldn't mind having me a young nun or two, Smitty. 'Cept I'd have them girls do more than just shave me!"

Taylor's high-pitched laughter followed the comment, trailed by something Smitty said beneath his breath that Roland couldn't hear and didn't wish to. As always, he chose to ignore them.

Not long after, George entered the bedroom carrying a steaming bowl.

"What you got there?" Roland eyed the concoction, able to guess its origin. The smell wasn't completely off-putting, but enough to make him wary.

"Me and Miss Tempy made a poultice for you, sir. Same as we did for the other men who got bad cuts. This'll help the healin'."

Roland looked up at him. "What's in it?"

A glint slid into George's eyes. "Pig guts and snake bellies, Cap'n."

Roland grinned, his memory swiftly turning back the pages of time. "I still remember that afternoon your grandmother came to the house with something like this. I took one look at it, and those were the first two things that came to mind. My mother didn't know whether to rub it on my chest or scrub the floors with it."

"Probably was good enough for both, sir."

They laughed together.

"Your grandmother sure had some healing ways about her, didn't she."

"Yes, Cap'n, she did. She was a good woman."

"How old were the two of us back then?" Roland said, counting back. "The day she brought that poultice. Eight years old, you think?"

"I reckon that's right, sir. 'Cuz my granny had just took sick about then, and she died the day you turned nine."

"And a week before you did," Roland added and saw surprise register on George's face. As though George didn't think he remembered that their birthdays were so close.

George had been a gift to him when Roland was younger. Roland hadn't understood the significance of his father's actions back then. But as the years passed and Roland came into his own and eventually took over the management of the plantation after his father died, he'd seen the importance of having someone like George to help him. They'd grown up together. George knew him as well as anyone did and could anticipate a need often before Roland even realized something was wanting.

"You being here is going to help me heal much faster, you know."

George nodded. "But only if we get this poultice on you while it's still fresh from the stove, sir. Like Granny always said, part of the healin' lies in the heat."

Roland pulled up the sheet and blanket covering his legs, and George began slathering the warm concoction onto his wounds. The sutured skin was still tender and puffy red, and more than once Roland had to grit his teeth. As if knowing he needed a distraction, George began recounting incidents from their youth, which soon had Roland laughing. He realized he hadn't laughed that much since before Weet and Lena died. It felt good. A little wrong still, but good.

"Hey, *boy*!"

Their laughter suddenly died.

Roland looked over at Taylor and saw the ugly sneer on his face, and the white-hot tip of something akin to hatred about burned a hole in his chest. The past few days of being cooped up with Taylor and Smitty had rubbed his last nerve raw.

"I said"—Taylor raised his voice—"get over here, boy, and put some of that stuff on my wounds." Taylor lifted his shirt to show his belly wound.

Roland leveled a stare. "You'll get your wounds tended when it's time, Taylor. And the nuns will help you. There's plenty of poultice to go around."

Taylor spat out a curse. "So you're the only one who gets to have his own personal darky waitin' on him hand and foot? That don't seem quite fair now, does it, Smitty?"

"No, it don't. 'Specially seein' as you and me each done lost part of a leg for the cause. Jones over there just lost a few digits."

"I agree, Smitty," Taylor continued. "I'm thinkin' that big black . . ."

Roland hoped the nuns weren't close enough to hear the contemptuous term Taylor used, one filled with hatred, and followed by language so foul Roland felt a scalding in his chest. Taylor was a good ten years younger, and lean muscled, so he had that going for him. But he was also an arrogant hothead, traits Roland used to be plagued with himself. But life—and Weet's love—had tempered those from his character through the years. Still, he itched to put the man in his place.

"George," Roland said calmly, "go on back downstairs and help Tempy with whatever she needs."

"Yes, sir, Cap'n." George retrieved the bowl and turned to leave.

Taylor cursed. "Boy, you heard what I said to you. You best get yourself over here right now and do as I say. If you don't, I'm gonna take the strap to you. And that's not all I'll do. I'll . . ."

The vileness that spewed from Taylor's mouth made Roland's blood boil.

"*What* is going on in here!"

Roland looked over to see Sister Catherine Margaret standing in the doorway, hands on hips, staring Taylor down.

"Lieutenant Taylor, I have not heard that kind of filth uttered since before I married my Lord and Savior, Jesus Christ. And then I only heard it from ignorant, spiteful hatemongers who could scarcely lace up their boots, much less understand their own dull-wittedness and idiocy. And I will certainly not tolerate that kind of talk in the house of a Christian man to whom you are indebted for your entire sustenance and physical well-being."

Taylor opened his mouth to respond, but the nun beat him to the punch.

"If you persist in this, Lieutenant, I will personally remove you from this house and let you fend for yourself out in the cold. Do you understand me?"

Roland worked to curb a grin. Especially when Taylor's neck went crimson.

"But you weren't here, Sister. You don't know what happened. It ain't fair that Jones has his own personal—"

Taylor had barely uttered the word again when Sister Catherine Margaret was on him. She reached under Taylor's armpits and dragged the man toward the bedroom door as though Taylor were nothing but a youth.

"Let go of me, you fat—"

Sister Catherine did precisely that and Taylor fell backward, smacking his head on the floor. She bent low over him, how close, Roland couldn't exactly see. All his perspective provided was a view of her backside, which he tried to peer around, sorely wanting to see Taylor's expression.

"You will listen to me very carefully, Lieutenant Taylor." The sister's voice sounded surprisingly calm. Even kind. "I serve my blessed Lord, whom I love with all my heart. But if you think that will prevent me from disciplining you in the manner in which you deserve, you are sorely mistaken. You are acting like an ignorant youth, so I will treat you as such. If I hear one more unseemly word come from your mouth, you'll be tasting lye soap until Easter. Have I made myself clear?"

"I'm tellin' you, Sister. It's Jones's fault. He's a no-good—"

Whatever Sister Catherine said next, Roland couldn't hear. But Taylor got real quiet real quick. Wanting to see what was happening, Roland leaned over as far as he could. But still . . . nothing but backside.

"Have you and I reached an accord, Lieutenant Taylor?" she finally asked, her voice as soft and sweet as a spring breeze.

Seconds passed.

"Yeah," came a rough whisper.

"Let's try that again," she said cheerfully.

"Yes . . . Sister."

"Very good, Lieutenant." She straightened. "Now, I'll go fetch a fresh bandage and some warm poultice, and we'll see to your wounds. And those of Private Smith as well."

Taylor's face was still flushed with anger, but Roland thought he detected a glimmer of fear too.

Sister Catherine Margaret straightened. But instead of leaving the room, she marched right toward Roland, and a feeling came over him that he hadn't experienced since that day years ago when he'd misbehaved in pretty Miss Putnam's class.

The nun knelt, her smile radiant as always. "Captain Jones . . ."

She kept her voice to a whisper, and from his peripheral vision Roland spotted Taylor leaning to one side trying to see, just as he'd done a moment earlier.

Her eyes held a merry sparkle. "I am well aware of how soldiers can often provoke each other, especially when days grow long and patience grows thin. So for the duration of your time here at Carnton, I am asking that you not do anything to intentionally provoke the lieutenant. As difficult as that will be at times, considering the fodder he is certain to provide."

Roland had difficulty holding back a smile. But knowing she wouldn't appreciate it supplied proper motivation.

"And since we both know," she continued, "that the lieutenant will likely, one day soon, when he gets the opportunity, attempt to assault you in retribution for this, I will advise the sisters to keep close watch on this room. I would move him to another room, but I fear he might begin to antagonize another soldier who does not possess your maturity and patience."

Roland stared. How did she do it? How did she speak with such kindness while, in no uncertain terms, laying down the law in regard to her expectations?

"Still . . ." She leaned closer. "I'd sleep with one eye open, if I were you. Now wipe the hint of a smile from your face so the lieutenant will at least wonder if you got a scolding as well."

Roland did as she asked. And she winked.

As soon as she left the room, Taylor looked across at him. "When

I'm better, Jones," he whispered, anger contorting his features, "I'm gonna teach you a lesson you'll never forget."

Reminded of his pledge to Sister Catherine Margaret, Roland showed not a hint of the pleasure that such a prospect held. "I'm looking forward to it."

CHAPTER 23

Her stomach in knots, Lizzie paused at the top of the staircase wishing she hadn't put this off. The sooner she apologized to Roland, explained why she'd not mentioned being betrothed earlier, the sooner they could get on with being friends. *Friends*. The word she'd once used to describe Towny. Yet no matter what word she used for Roland, her feelings for him were definitely something more than friendship. Thankfully, he didn't know that.

And even more important than their getting back on an even footing with one another was the fact that they needed to begin working in earnest together to find Thaddeus's family. Colonel McGavock had yet to hear back from his contact in the War Department. And with every day that passed, Lizzie grew more eager to receive word.

She'd heard about what had happened earlier that afternoon with Lieutenant Taylor and what he'd said to George. It turned her stomach just thinking about it. Everyone in the house seemed to be more on edge these days. The air in some of the bedrooms fairly crackled with tension. And this with Christmas scarcely two weeks away. It certainly didn't feel much like Christmas this year. Not with everyone waiting for news about the Army of Tennessee and what would happen next.

Around this time last year, the Women's Relief Society had sponsored an auction here at Carnton, and the event had raised an enormous amount of money to benefit the wounded soldiers. From start to finish, women had organized and carried out the event—something heretofore unheard of. Lizzie had been so proud. Change was happening. It simply wasn't happening fast enough for her.

She forced one foot in front of the other and crossed the

second-floor hallway, the hollow ring of her new heeled boots echoing on the bare wooden planks. The boots, an extravagance during such lean times, were still a bit tight but would loosen with wear. She was grateful for them. They'd been waiting for her in her room one afternoon, along with a homespun shirtwaist and skirt. She'd noticed new clothing and boots in Tempy's bedroom too. Mrs. McGavock's doing.

Lizzie stopped just short of Winder's room. Maybe Roland would be asleep. Or reading. Or maybe he and one of the other soldiers would be deep in conversation, so she wouldn't be able to—

Shoving aside the excuses, she peered inside the room and saw him. Or saw his lower half, the blanket covering his legs. He lay on the floor to the left of the hearth, on the far side of the bed. The other soldiers were either napping or reading, and she nodded at them as she passed, thankful that Taylor and Smitty were among the former.

The clock on the mantel chimed, drawing her attention. Four o'clock. It would be dark soon. How she longed for the warmer, longer days of summer that—

She rounded the bed and stopped short, scarcely able to believe her eyes. Roland was asleep, but that wasn't what brought her up short. He was . . . changed. He scarcely looked like the same man. He'd shaved his beard, and his hair looked freshly washed and cut. She took a step closer, wanting to get a better look. And the floorboard creaked.

He opened his eyes, then briefly squeezed them tight again. "Lizzie?"

His voice was groggy with sleep. He yawned and stretched and gave a sigh that was distinctly male, and Lizzie felt herself react to it. Then he tossed her a sleepy smile that kicked her pulse up another two notches. She'd found him attractive before, but now . . . The features of his face, strong and angular, were more pronounced. And his eyes. They looked an even deeper gray than she remembered.

He ran a hand over his jaw. "Sister Catherine Margaret did the honors. I'm still getting used to it. Right now my face is just plain cold."

He smiled, and Lizzie swallowed. Nothing about *her* was cold at the moment.

"It . . . looks nice, Roland."

His smile faded and it felt as though he could read every thought in her head, which offered no comfort. She fidgeted, and despite having come here to apologize, all she wanted to do right now was flee.

"I came up here to tell you—to tell everyone"—she included the rest of the soldiers in her nod as she backed from the room—"that dinner is almost ready. We'll be bringing it up shortly." She didn't wait for a response, but hurried downstairs to the kitchen and grabbed an apron from the hook.

"Heavenly days, ma'am, you's all flushed." Tempy reached up and felt her forehead. "You comin' down with somethin'?"

"No, I'm fine. I feel fine." Lizzie reached for a knife and started peeling potatoes alongside her, grateful when Tempy didn't force the subject.

But when they served dinner to the soldiers later, Lizzie made certain Tempy was the one to serve the soldiers in Winder's room.

Sitting against the wall, a pillow at his back, Roland studied Dr. Phillips's expression. He tried to parse the doctor's thoughts as the man scrutinized the incisions on his right leg. Another doctor had come by two days ago but had quickly deferred to Phillips's counsel.

"Captain, I want you to tell me if this hurts."

"Why is it that whenever a doctor leads with that, it almost always does?"

Phillips smiled, and Roland braced himself.

The doctor gently pressed on his upper right thigh, and Roland sucked in a breath.

"I'll take that as a yes, Captain."

Roland felt sweat breaking out on his forehead. "Does that mean anything, Doc? That it still hurts this much?"

"It means you've got a severe leg wound that needs time to heal. And by time, I mean weeks, not days. You also need to be on a bed. Or a cot. Not the hard floor." The doctor glanced down. "I see they had the carpet removed up here, same as they've done downstairs. I'm sorry they had to do it, but there was no choice."

Roland nodded. "Some of the neighbors came over to help with the undertaking a couple of days ago. I overhead Miss Clouston say that the McGavocks will replace it, but it could be a while."

Roland looked at the wooden boards stretching across Winder's bedroom floor, especially those over by the window where the surgical table had been. Although Tempy and the nuns had scrubbed and cleaned, the boards still bore the bloodstains, and he guessed they always would. From where he sat, he thought he even saw the outline of Dr. Phillips's shoes where he'd stood performing surgery throughout the long night.

"I'll speak to Miss Clouston about getting you a bed of some sort," the doctor continued, tugging Roland's thoughts back.

"I'd appreciate that, Doc. But you said it takes weeks, not days, for a wound like mine to heal. What do you mean by weeks? My manservant arrived a few days back, and I figured we could get started on some healing rituals of some sort soon."

Phillips rose. "You're bound and determined to undo the work I've done, aren't you?"

"No, sir. But I *am* bound and determined to walk again. And from what I've heard of late, some say that being up and around sooner rather than later is good for mending a bone." He decided not to add that George was the one who'd shared that information with him.

"So you're a physician now too, is that right, Captain Jones?"

"I'm a man who wants to walk again, Doc. That's it. Plain and simple."

"I want that for you too, Captain. I honestly do." Phillips's gaze sobered. "But remember that the sooner you walk, the sooner you go to prison."

The doctor paused as though wanting to let the words settle in, and settle they did. Not that Roland had forgotten about the prison sentence hanging over his head. Prison was something that, once experienced, a man didn't forget. But since George's arrival, the prospect of walking again had eclipsed nearly every other thought. Especially when he thought of Taylor, and what Taylor and Smitty might be planning for him.

"And even once you are able to move about in what, hopefully, will be the near future, complete healing for your legs will still be a good ways off. So please take your time. Rest up. And no crutches. I brought those for the other men." The doctor's sternness eased a mite. "From our previous conversations, I know you enjoy reading. Colonel McGavock has an extensive library that I'm certain he'd be more than willing to share with you. Because if you end up in a Federal prison too soon, you won't get the care you require. And I guarantee you, a Federal doctor won't think twice about either cutting off that leg or letting it go to gangrene."

Laughter erupted behind them, and they turned to see Second Lieutenant Shuler playing "war" with Winder, who had proudly displayed to the room a box of painted toy soldiers he'd received the previous Christmas.

Phillips looked back. "As we've discussed, Captain, gangrene at this stage would be most grave indeed."

Roland nodded. "I understand, Doc. And I give you my word, I'll do as you say. Hard as that will be."

Phillips returned his stethoscope to his satchel. "I will say, though, the skin is healing very nicely. It's farther along than I would've expected after such deep wounds."

"That's thanks to George, my manservant, and Tempy. They've been faithful in applying warm poultices."

Lizzie entered the bedroom carrying a tray laden with food, her footsteps more pronounced on the bare wooden floor, and Roland tugged the blanket back over his legs. Despite the healing taking place, he wanted to spare her the bright red scars. Or maybe it was that he wished not to appear so much of an invalid in her eyes.

Dr. Phillips glanced in Lizzie's direction and smiled. "For what it's worth, Captain, I can think of worse places to be than here at Carnton. And for sure, worse company."

Having no trouble reading the man's thoughts now, Roland started to respond when Lizzie turned in their direction.

"Here you are, Captain Jones. Lunch today is ham and lentil soup, and angel biscuits."

She bent down and handed him a bowl and a cloth napkin containing the bread. Her gaze barely brushed his before she looked at the doctor. Roland didn't like the stiff politeness that had developed between them, but he figured it was for the best. She was betrothed to another man, after all. Still, he missed her company and her smile. And their conversations.

The other day, when he'd awakened from a nap to find her standing there, he'd glimpsed a softness in her eyes that had given him hope. Hope for what, he couldn't say. But as quickly as it had come, the softness vanished and she'd left.

"Dr. Phillips," she continued, "I'd be happy to bring you some lunch too, if you have the time."

"Thank you, but I've already eaten. Tempy insisted on feeding me as soon as I arrived. I need to finish up my rounds here, then move on into town. Everyone in Franklin opened up their homes to the wounded. Same for the churches and the businesses. We need to see all of those soldiers before we rejoin Loring's Division. Or what remains of it," he added quietly.

"What's the final count after the battle here?" Roland asked.

"Loring's had thirty-five hundred men, as you know. And we left nearly a thousand of them buried on the battlefield."

Roland bowed his head. So many.

"Has the Army of Tennessee advanced on Nashville yet?"

Roland heard the concern in Lizzie's voice and thought of her young Lieutenant Townsend. A fine man, by all counts, and one thoroughly besotted with her. Which he certainly couldn't fault him for.

"No, Miss Clouston, but word is they will any day now. Hood's made no secret of his wish to even the score. Which, to that end . . ." Phillips picked up his satchel. "I need to be on my way. Captain Jones, I'll see you again in two weeks, if not before then. Miss Clouston, a pleasure as always, ma'am."

Roland set the bowl and napkin on the floor beside him, wishing the doctor would have lingered a little longer. He read determination in Lizzie's expression and sensed what was coming. The other soldiers staying in that bedroom had begun to hobble about on crutches in recent days and were out in the hallway. Only Shuler and Winder remained in the room, which meant he and Lizzie were effectively alone. Something he would've welcomed earlier on. But not at the moment.

"Roland . . ." Her gaze met his, then flashed away again. "I want to tell you how sorry I am that I wasn't more forthcoming about being betrothed to Lieutenant Townsend. I feel as though I owe you an apology and—"

"There's no need for you to apologize, Lizzie. You did nothing wrong." What could he say to allay her guilt without revealing more than he wanted to? Or than was proper, under the circumstances? "Any misunderstanding about our friendship was solely on my part. And I truly wish you and Lieutenant Townsend only the very best. He's a most fortunate man."

Empty tray in hand, she stared at him for several seconds, as if caught off balance, then she finally nodded. "Thank you. For being so understanding."

"It's no problem. And thank you for lunch." He pointed to the bowl.

With what looked to be a pieced-together smile, she turned to leave, and relief filtered through him that this particular hurdle was behind them. It hadn't been as bad as he'd anticipated. Hungry, he unwrapped the napkin and popped the entire angel biscuit into his mouth. Delicious . . .

"Roland." She turned back unexpectedly. "You're so kind to say there's no need for an apology, but I disagree."

Dangerously close to choking, Roland looked around for something to drink. But all he had was the soup, and taking a swig of that in front of her right now just seemed rude. Besides, she'd already positioned Winder's little chair beside him and taken a seat.

She took a deep breath. "Frankly, I won't be able to move past this if I don't tell you why I wasn't more forthcoming. In fact, the reason is actually a tad humorous." Her laughter came off a bit flat.

Roland managed to swallow the bread. He should have known that a woman so bent on keeping her word wouldn't be put off so easily. Which only increased his admiration of her. *Not* her intent, he knew.

"Lieutenant Townsend—Towny, everyone calls him—has been my dearest friend for as far back as I can remember. He and I grew up together."

She looked at him wide-eyed, and Roland sensed she needed some encouragement to continue. So, somewhat begrudgingly, he nodded.

CHAPTER 24

Lizzie chose her words carefully, wanting to offer an explanation that made sense and was truthful. She'd learned as a child that if you always told the truth, you never had to remember the web of lies and half-truths you'd spun. But sometimes, as she'd learned since becoming an adult, it was best to share only a portion of the truth. Like now. Because to share the whole truth would only deepen the hole she'd dug for herself.

Now if only she could remember the thoughts she'd laid out on paper earlier that morning—which wasn't easy considering how closely Roland was watching her.

She sat up a little straighter, determined to get this done quickly and to look at him as little as possible. Those smoky gray eyes would only make this more difficult. He'd said no explanation was needed, but of course a man of such integrity would want to know. She couldn't very well blurt out, *The reason I didn't say anything to you about being betrothed is because I feel a closeness to you I can't explain, and I'm attracted to you in a way that no promised woman should be—except to the man she's going to marry.*

But since she couldn't say that . . .

"Towny asked me to marry him in January, before he left to rejoin his regiment. He'd been home for a couple of days, and we'd spent time together at his father's house. His mother passed several years ago. Marlene was such a lovely woman." Speaking faster than she needed to, she smoothed a nonexistent wrinkle from her sleeve. "She and I used to cook together on Sunday afternoons. She made the most delicious corn chowder. But I'm close to Towny's father, John, as well. Mr. Townsend is a very fine man, and Towny is just like him."

She was rambling. This wasn't the speech she'd written down, edited, rehearsed, and edited again. And now she'd completely forgotten her line of thought. She sneaked a look at Roland, who seemed to be watching her even more closely than before.

Warmth rose to her face. "I'm sorry, I forgot where I was . . ."

"Lieutenant Townsend's father is a fine man, and Towny is just like him."

"Ah, yes. Thank you." She brushed back a bothersome curl. "What I'm trying to say is that Towny and I have been betrothed for a while now."

"Since January," Roland offered, his voice quiet.

"That's right. And I think what the problem is . . . is that it's still all so new to me. Being betrothed." She forced a smile. "I believe I'm still growing accustomed to the idea."

"Growing accustomed to it?" he repeated softly.

She chanced a look back and found his eyes slightly narrowed.

"Yes, that's right." She averted her gaze again, realizing how the words sounded. "No, I-I don't mean to say that—" What did she mean to say? *Don't look at his eyes. Don't look at his eyes.* "It's not my intention to reflect negatively on Towny in any way. I would never do that."

"No, you wouldn't."

"So what I'm attempting to say—although I'm doing a very poor job of it—is that it's the *idea* of being betrothed that's still new."

"That's taking you some adjustment."

She exhaled. "Precisely."

Relieved to have that out and done with, she intentionally loosened her white-knuckled grip on the tray in her lap. The silence lengthened, and she finally looked back at him, surprised to see such warmth and understanding in his gaze, as well as a smile tipping one side of his mouth. Which only made hers go dry. She licked her lips.

"I understand, Lizzie," he whispered, holding her gaze. "And I believe Lieutenant Townsend is a most fortunate man."

Emotion rose to her eyes. If anyone else was in the room, she wasn't aware of them. She saw only Roland. And felt only desire for him. An invisible cord seemed to draw her closer, and she knew she needed to leave. She rose, tray in hand.

"Thank you, Roland. For being so understanding." She offered a smile, then rushed from the room.

She descended the staircase and heard the nuns chatting in the family parlor, so she ducked into the dining room, grateful to find it empty. She closed the door behind her, heart racing, and let the tears come. How was it that now, after she'd said yes to Towny—after waiting for so many years, especially compared to all of her friends who'd been married for nearly a decade now—a man would come into her life who made her feel things she'd never felt before? Things she should feel for Towny. But didn't.

She inhaled, then slowly let out her breath. She wiped away the tears. Feelings, in themselves, couldn't be trusted. She knew that. The heart was a deceitful thing, the Bible said. Marriage, on the other hand, was a lifelong commitment based on mutual love and trust. And love could have many faces. And she *did* love Towny. And prayed she would grow to love him more and more over time.

She straightened. She'd met Roland Jones under the most extreme of circumstances. That's what had to be coloring her emotions right now. The past few days had been trying, and that was putting it mildly. She simply needed to rest, to get back into the routine of life. She'd already begun conducting morning sessions with the children again, and would soon move to the afternoon as well. And she and Tempy were set to have their first session soon. She loved teaching. Hence the reason she'd become a governess.

That, and because she'd never met a man she'd truly wanted to marry. Until now.

THE NEXT MORNING Lizzie awakened early, feeling a spark of excitement she hadn't felt in ages. She dressed and checked the time on her chatelaine watch as she pinned it to her shirtwaist. She gathered the books she'd laid out last night and smiled as she hurried past Tempy's closed bedroom door, thinking about how she was going to scold her newest student for being late to class on their first morning.

But halfway down the stairs the smell of coffee told her she was the one who needed the scolding. She stepped into the kitchen to find Tempy sitting at the table, cups of coffee poured and both of their breakfasts plated and ready.

Lizzie claimed her seat and placed the books on the table. "What time did you get up?"

"Get up?" Tempy shook her head. "I's barely able to get to sleep for thinkin' of what we gonna be doin' this mornin'." She blew out a breath. "I done thought of somethin' too. Look'a here." She scooted a crate out from under the table. "If we hear a squeak on them stairs, we toss all of that teachin' stuff of yours into here and shove it under the table."

Lizzie was tempted to smile, but the seriousness in Tempy's expression kept her from it. The woman truly was frightened of what might happen if someone caught them. Perhaps *she* should be more frightened than she was. But at the moment all she felt was the thrill of anticipation.

In between bites, Lizzie turned the pages of the primer and explained how she would conduct their lessons. Tempy nodded, her gaze never leaving the lesson book, her breakfast untouched.

"So the first thing we'll do"—Lizzie sipped her coffee—"is learn the letters of the alphabet and which sound—or *sounds* in some cases—go with each." She opened to the page with the letters, and Tempy leaned forward. "These are the letters in *upper*case, meaning the capital or big letters. Letters that are used for the beginning of sentences or people's names or places like Franklin, Tennessee. And these are each of the corresponding letters in *lower*case, or small letters."

Tempy frowned.

"Think of the big letters as wearing a fancy coat." Lizzie pointed to the capital letter *T* and tugged on the collar of her shirtwaist, as though she were adjusting the collar of a fancy cloak. And this"—she pointed to the lowercase letter *t*—"is the very same letter, only with the fancy coat taken off."

Tempy didn't say anything for a moment. "So . . . it's like them two letters is the same person, only with a different coverin'. Same smile, same good and bad about 'em."

"Yes! Precisely. And they share the very same sound. And this letter here"—Lizzie tapped the capital *T* again, then pulled the slate and chalk closer—"is the first letter of your name. *T-e-m-p-y*," she said, writing each letter as she sounded it out.

Tempy leaned close. "That's my name, Miss Clouston?"

Lizzie nodded. "But please, call me Lizzie. At least when we're alone."

"I like the looks of my name . . . *Miss* Lizzie."

Tempy laughed, and Lizzie shook her head at the woman's obstinance.

"All right, next, let's go letter by letter and I'll—"

"Good mornin' to you both."

Lizzie nearly jumped out of her skin, and Tempy began grabbing the books and shoving them into the crate. Lizzie turned to see George looking from them to the books and then back again.

Lizzie rose, feeling a little queasy. "Good morning, George. We . . . didn't hear you come in."

He nodded slowly. "I can see that, ma'am."

The excitement she'd felt moments earlier was gone, replaced by a sourness in the pit of her stomach. Would George tell Roland? If he did, would Roland feel obligated to tell Colonel McGavock?

George looked pointedly at Tempy. "What you doin' in here, Miss Tempy?"

Tempy stood. "You can see with them eyes o' yours what I'm doin'."

"Yes, ma'am, I can. But can you see how full of danger this is?"

Lizzie stepped forward. "George, I take full—"

"I'm sorry, Miss Lizzie." George shook his head. "From all the cap'n says about you, you're a fine woman. But you ought not be doin' this, ma'am. I reckon you see it as a kindness. But Miss Tempy here would be in a world o' hurt right now if it was someone else walked through that door instead of me. So I'll thank you kindly to—"

"You listen to me right now!" Tempy whispered in a harsh tone, walking straight up to him. She barely reached his chest. "You ain't gonna tell me or Miss Clouston what we gonna be doin'. You a young fella, George. You got time for the world to change. I ain't got no time." Her voice caught. She looked up at him and stretched to her full height, which still seemed petite next to George. "You ever heard of a place called *Pal-es-tine?*"

George stared at her. Then gave a little shake of his head.

"That's where the Lord hisself was birthed. That's where he walked and where he lived while he's down here. And I ain't never gonna see that place with my own eyes." She took a shuddering breath. "But I aim to read about it from people who been there. I been wantin' to know things far back as my memories can take me. And my mama, God rest her, told me the same thing you just did. *Tempy, you gotta stop askin' them questions, girl,* she'd say. *You know we can't have no book learnin'.* But, George . . . the world is changin', son. Right here. Today. In front of our eyes."

Lizzie's heart squeezed tight. With emotion, with pride. Then she heard it. A creak coming from overhead. Tempy must have heard it too, because she quickly turned to the worktable and started cracking more eggs into the bowl. Lizzie grabbed the books and slate from the crate and placed them where she usually did on the table by the stairs leading to the main house. Then she turned to George.

"Are you going to say anything to Captain Jones?" she whispered.

George looked from her to Tempy and back again. "He wouldn't like what you're doin', ma'am. If that matters to you any."

"It does," she acknowledged. "It matters a great deal." She searched his gaze. "But not as much as teaching Tempy does."

He shifted his weight, clearly not pleased. Then he sighed. "I won't tell him, ma'am. But only if you do one thing."

Taken slightly aback, Lizzie stared up at him, aware of Tempy watching too. "And what would that one thing be?"

"You gotta teach me too."

"Be careful, Captain Jones. Your next move could be your last."

Roland smiled at the warning in Colonel McGavock's voice, but only because he had yet to learn the man's tell—that subconscious gesture that revealed what a person was thinking without their realizing they were giving away their thoughts. Some people blinked more often, or shifted in their seats, pursed their lips, or rubbed their jaws. He knew his own tell. Had become aware of it while playing poker behind the mercantile as a lad. Correction: while losing numerous hands of poker as a lad. He'd asked the fellow who'd beaten him so soundly at the game what his secret to winning was. The older boy had simply narrowed his eyes and stared.

Roland maintained the colonel's gaze, acutely aware of his own facial features and of all the soldiers gathered around them watching.

"No problem, Colonel. You don't have me in check yet, sir."

It was McGavock's turn to smile.

Roland studied the few remaining pieces on the wooden chess set and board that sat balanced on a footstool between them. And the colonel, seated in the Windsor chair by the hearth, seemed to be doing the same. This was their third game in two days—with one win chalked up for each of them—and the gatherings had quickly become an event.

After mentally moving every piece on the board—twice—Roland looked up. "I believe we have a stalemate, Colonel."

"You're certain about that, Captain?"

Not nearly as certain now, Roland looked back and tried for a third time to envision the possible moves remaining to him—and again found none. Then he gradually became aware of the colonel's grin and shook his head.

"Correction, Colonel. I *know* we have a stalemate, sir."

McGavock held out his left hand. "Well played, Captain Jones."

Roland accepted the praise as a couple of the fellows behind him patted him on the back. "Excellent game to you too, sir. Thank you for the pleasure."

McGavock rose. "Tomorrow? Same time?"

"Thursdays are busy for me, sir, but I think I can fit you in. I'll check my social calendar and let you know."

McGavock laughed, as did others.

"Bring it right through here, Winder! But be careful. You too, Hattie!"

All attention shifted to Mrs. McGavock, who stood in the doorway of the bedroom, then to Winder, who walked in beaming—and carrying a little potted cedar tree all decorated with strung popcorn kernels and red ribbon. And bells, if the tinkling sound was any indication.

"Merry Christmas!" the boy shouted. "Even though it's not Christmas yet!"

Mrs. McGavock waved Hattie on in. "The children have decorated a tree for every bedroom. Under Miss Clouston's creative tutelage, of course."

Lizzie and Tempy each entered, carrying decorated trees as well, the nuns following closely behind them, smiles wide. Lizzie's gaze swept the room but only touched Roland's briefly, which he'd come to expect since she'd delivered her apology—which he'd found most revealing. They'd spoken on several occasions since, though not at any length.

George entered last, bearing trays of something delicious smelling. Roland acknowledged him with a tilt of his head, grateful to have the man here, even though, per Dr. Phillips's orders, they couldn't begin a physical regimen yet. George's presence made him feel less homesick somehow, especially with Christmas approaching. But the letters George had brought from his mother and sisters had only increased his burden. According to them, the estate had suffered greatly in recent months, possibly beyond repair. Food was growing increasingly scarce both for the family and relatives and for the remaining slaves who hadn't fled.

So Roland had sent two wires. The first to his mother, instructing her to sell or barter the mahogany wardrobe and dresser along with the mahogany table and chairs—all the heirloom pieces, if necessary—in order to garner the staples they needed. The second wire he'd sent to Harvard Davis, the banker in Yalobusha County. He informed Davis that while he'd been wounded at the battle in Franklin, he was very much alive and would return home after convalescing. Roland chose to omit the part about the prison sentence that awaited. In his experience, men with whom one had financial dealings didn't respond favorably when learning you were on your way to prison.

Thinking of home and of who was waiting there for him—as well as who was not—brought a stab of longing. Was it any wonder he had trouble sleeping at night?

"Captain Jones!"

Roland turned and spotted Winder coming straight for him, the boy's small tree bouncing up and down in his arms as ribbons and bells liberated themselves from its branches.

"*My* tree's for in here, Captain! I decorated it all by myself. Well, mostly anyway."

"You did a fine job too, Winder. That's a right handsome tree."

Winder looked over his shoulder, then leaned close, mischief in his eyes. "Mama's making you all somethin' for Christmas, but I'm not supposed to say what it—"

"Winder!"

The boy looked back at his mother, whose expression said she knew her son only too well.

Mrs. McGavock's eyebrows rose. "Do not share the secret, Winder. It's for Christmas."

"I wasn't tellin' him what it is, Mama. I was only tellin' him somethin's comin'."

Winder turned back to him. "I wouldn't like it much myself, but y'all might."

Roland smiled. "Whatever it is, I'm sure we'll all enjoy it. What are you hoping to get for Christmas this year?"

A smile stretched the boy's face. "Some new marbles and a clockwork train. One that really moves all by itself!"

"That's a fairly tall order."

"I've been pretty good though." Winder nodded. "'Cept for the other day when I broke Miss Clouston's special hair comb." The boy glanced back in Lizzie's direction, then bowed his head. "I thought those little things that stick out would bend. But they don't."

Roland curbed a grin. "Well, maybe the next time you're in town, you can buy her a new one."

"That's what Mama said." A frown formed. "But I ain't got no money, so I'm havin' to do extra chores in the barn with Papa."

Roland knew Lizzie would correct the boy's grammar if she overheard him, but he didn't have the heart. He remembered what extra chores in the barn in the dead of winter were like for a young boy.

"Want some of these, Captain Jones? Master Winder?" George bent down, tray of food in hand. "Miss Tempy calls 'em sausage and cheese and biscuits in a ball. But . . ." His voice dropped to a whisper. "They just look like balls o' sausage to me, sir."

Winder grabbed two and stuffed both of them into his mouth. Roland helped himself to a couple. And true enough, the little morsels tasted like a sausage and biscuit with cheese, only all rolled up together.

As Winder engaged George in conversation, Roland's focus moved to the frosted windowpanes and the world beyond. As George had told him earlier, it was still bone-chillingly cold outside, the ground covered with a perfect sheet of ice while heavy fog blanketed the hills and valleys. Even now the wind moaned and howled, lonely and forlorn sounding, and Roland thought of his Confederate brothers hunkered down in trenches, likely hungry and near frozen to the bone somewhere outside Nashville. And before he could even form the words within himself, he felt a silent plea rising heavenward on their behalf. Little good it would do them, coming from him—he and the Almighty not being on the closest of terms. But he figured they needed all the prayers they could get.

According to what Colonel McGavock had heard earlier in the week, General Hood still aimed to take back the city, even with a third of his army dead or wounded.

Ever aware of Lizzie's presence, Roland watched her as she conversed with Colonel McGavock and the soldiers. After a moment she looked in his direction. He caught her eye and smiled. She returned the same.

I believe I'm still growing accustomed to the idea.

Her words played over and over in his mind. Since when did a bride-to-be have to become "accustomed" to the idea of marrying the man she loved? And how many times had she referred to the second lieutenant as a "fine man"? Not that there was anything wrong with a bride believing her groom to be a fine man. One would hope that would always be the case. But it was the way Lizzie said it that made him question her feelings for the lieutenant. No, more than question. Made him doubt. Which was a dangerous combination for a man with only time on his hands and a fair amount of his heart already invested.

He'd never intentionally do anything to come between Lizzie and Lieutenant Townsend. But that didn't mean that *if* the woman were to waver in her choice somewhere down the way—and *if* he learned to walk again and could save his family estate—he wouldn't be there to take advantage of her change of heart. Then again, that possibility was flush with *ifs*, and he wasn't too sure she would even consider someone like him.

She'd not said a word to him aloud about slavery, yet she'd made her stance on it resoundingly clear. And he was a slave owner. Of course, if the North won the war, slavery wouldn't be a divisive factor for the two of them anymore. Slavery would be abolished—and he would become a pauper with nothing left to offer her. Only with a Confederate victory did he stand a chance of keeping his estate and a means of providing for a wife and family. So either way, he stood little to no chance of ever winning Lizzie's affections. The truth of the realization barbed him.

"She reads it to us every night. The story has a *mean* man in it. And ghosts too!"

Roland looked beside him to see Winder perched on Lieutenant Shuler's bedside.

Shuler, still practically a boy himself, looked across the room at Lizzie. "My mother used to read to us when we were kids. I miss that," he added quietly.

Winder's eyes went wide. "I bet Miss Clouston would read to you too!"

The hint of a smile shaded Shuler's expression as he eyed the boy. "Do you think?"

Needing no further prodding, Winder darted back across the room toward Lizzie. Roland sat back and watched, already able to guess what was coming.

Winder yanked on Lizzie's skirt, which immediately earned him a scolding look, then Lizzie knelt, eye level with him. Roland could well imagine the lesson the boy was getting on how to properly engage someone's attention. Seconds later, as anticipated, Lizzie glanced beyond her young charge to Shuler, who sat in the bed looking decidedly more forlorn than a moment earlier, which was all part of the ploy.

Roland smiled to himself. Elizabeth Clouston didn't stand a chance.

She crossed the room. A smile played at the corners of her mouth, saying she knew she was being set up, which only increased Roland's enjoyment as the scene unfolded.

"So, Lieutenant Shuler, Master Winder tells me that you, too, enjoy being read to at night."

"Yes, ma'am, I do. It's long been one of my favorite pastimes. My mama used to read to me and my brothers and sisters."

"Is that so?"

"Yes, ma'am." Shuler nodded, a mischievous gleam lighting his eyes.

Roland was impressed. Young Shuler had missed his calling. He should've chosen the stage.

"And what is your favorite genre, Lieutenant?"

Roland waited, seeing the question on Shuler's face.

"Your favorite kind of story, Lieutenant," Lizzie added, not a hint of judgment in her tone.

"Oh, that." A blush crept into his cheeks. "I'm mighty partial to stories about . . . mean men and ghosts."

Lizzie's smile went full bloom, and the blush on Shuler's face fanned out.

"I'd be most happy to read that story to you, Lieutenant. And to all the other soldiers, if they'd be interested in hearing it."

A chorus of enthusiastic "Yes, ma'ams" rose up, Roland's among them.

As everyone returned to their conversations and their various rooms, Lizzie gradually looked Roland's way. "Did you put Lieutenant Shuler up to this?" she whispered.

He shook his head. "No, ma'am. But I've always loved a good bedtime story."

Her eyes sparkled, and he knew in that moment that even if the door to her heart never opened to him, he wanted her as his friend. He would accept that and make it enough. And he would determinedly set aside his feelings for her and move forward with his life. Something he'd had a lot of practice doing in recent months.

"Excuse me, gentlemen. And ladies."

Roland heard Colonel McGavock's voice in the hallway, and everyone fell silent.

"I've just received word that General Hood is expected to launch an attack on Nashville at any hour."

CHAPTER 25

A smattering of enthusiastic whoops and hollers rose from a handful of soldiers following Colonel McGavock's announcement, but the majority of the gathering remained silent. While Lizzie wasn't shocked at the reactions from the four men—particularly Second Lieutenant Taylor and Private Smith, who seemed a rougher type—she certainly didn't appreciate the outburst. From where she was standing, she could see Colonel McGavock in the hallway, and judging by his somber expression, neither did he. Nor Roland, close beside her, whose features were like stone.

"Let us be in prayer for the Army of Tennessee," the colonel continued, "and for the Confederacy. But ultimately, let us petition God Almighty for his will to be done. Whatever that may be."

Lizzie stared, hearing the solemnity in the colonel's voice. She'd heard him pray for God's will to be done many times through the years, but never in relation to the outcome of this war. Until this moment. Perhaps he, too, sensed the end was near and would not be the one he'd anticipated.

A deep-throated chortle sounded from the corner of Winder's bedroom. "I'm prayin' for God's will, all right. But I already know it's for the Federals to go straight to Hades. And I'm glad General Hood's about to send them there."

The silence that filled the house a moment earlier was nothing compared to the vacuum following Lieutenant Taylor's comment. The air itself seemed to flee as Colonel McGavock's expression hardened. Lizzie felt a shudder as he strode into Winder's bedroom, his gaze appraising.

"Who made that comment?"

Taylor raised a forefinger, a smile curving his mouth. "That would be me . . . sir."

Colonel McGavock crossed the room to stand before him. "Second Lieutenant Taylor, isn't it?"

Taylor nodded. "That's right, Colonel."

"You're remarkably offhanded, Lieutenant, in sharing your opinions."

"As a soldier in the great Confederate Army, I figured I'm still allowed to have my own opinions."

"As a soldier in the Confederate Army, you may hold whatever opinions you like. But while you are in my home, Lieutenant Taylor, you will refrain from using language like that in front of members of my household. You will also refrain from speaking in a manner that disparages and cheapens the deity of God Almighty. Have I made myself clear?"

Taylor glanced beside him at Smitty, another member of the unruly cohort whose countenance had gone noticeably paler. Same for the other men who'd cheered over the imminent attack on Nashville.

"Have I made myself *clear*, Lieutenant Taylor," the colonel repeated.

Taylor's smirk lost a degree of confidence. "Yes, sir. You have."

"Good. Because the next time I hear such words issuing from your mouth, I will personally deliver you to the Federal prison in Nashville. Same for any other soldier here who speaks in such a manner. I can tolerate a great many things, but lack of respect for our Creator and his hand in our lives is not one of them. Especially from someone who is enjoying the bounty from my table and finding shelter in my family's bedchambers."

Defiance sharpened Taylor's gaze, yet he said nothing.

Colonel McGavock didn't move. Simply continued to stare down at the man before him.

"Yes, *sir*," Taylor finally responded, and it felt as though a tiny trickle of air had been let back into the room.

Colonel McGavock turned. "Gentlemen, my family and I will bid you a good evening. I hope you all rest well tonight."

He gestured for Mrs. McGavock and the children to precede him, and Lizzie caught the furtive look Carrie McGavock sent her as she passed.

The sisters, who'd been silent yet watchful during the exchange, commenced helping the soldiers back to their respective rooms. George pitched in too, his strength alone a boon when it came to lifting the men who were still immobile. It had only been three days since he'd found her and Tempy in the kitchen having their first lesson, and Lizzie hadn't seen him alone since. But his request still surprised her. It also worried her.

It was one thing to teach Tempy, with just the two of them knowing. But if word about what she was doing ever got back to Roland—and he learned she was teaching one of *his* slaves—she honestly didn't know what he would do. But sooner or later, assuming that General Hood would be thwarted in his attempt to take back Nashville, Roland was going to have to come to grips with changes in his life. If she could aid him in any way in doing that, she wanted to. Not that he would welcome her help once he learned of her Northern-leaning opinions . . .

"Miss Clouston . . ."

Lizzie met the colonel on his way out.

"In light of the news we received tonight," he said, "I believe it would be best to wait until another evening to begin the reading."

"I agree completely, Colonel. I'll come straightaway and see the children to bed."

He shook his head. "There's no rush. Mrs. McGavock and I are enjoying this time with them." He glanced toward his family descending the staircase. "Even from the most horrible events, we know that 'all things work together for good to them that love God, to them who are called according to his purpose.'"

Lizzie recognized the verse from the Bible, though she couldn't recall exactly where it was found. Unwavering conviction filled the colonel's eyes, and though she was still struggling to reconcile what had happened here in this home and on that battlefield, she nodded, wishing she had a deeper faith in that regard.

"Also, Miss Clouston, along with the telegram tonight came a response from my contact at the War Department."

Lizzie's spirits brightened, until he shook his head.

"I wish I had more hopeful news. I'm afraid he has no record of a Thaddeus having served in Loring's Division."

"But . . ." She frowned. "That was the name I found on one of the belongings in the boy's pocket. Perhaps he was in a division other than Loring's but was brought here to Carnton by mistake?"

"My contact had that same thought, so he checked the military rosters of every other division here at Franklin that day. He found six Thaddeuses listed. Two of them died last year near Chattanooga, three died in Atlanta earlier this fall, and the other Thaddeus—in his twenties—is at the front in Nashville right now. I'm so sorry, Miss Clouston. I wish the inquiry had turned up something helpful to you. It's a good thing, what you intended to do."

A heaviness settled in Lizzie's chest. "Thank you, Colonel McGavock. I appreciate your checking for me, and am grateful for your colleague's thoroughness."

Disheartened, she helped collect the empty trays and soiled napkins throughout the bedrooms. How could the boy not be listed anywhere? Didn't the army keep better records than that? Yet she wasn't willing to give up. Roland had said he might have another idea. She only hoped he did.

As she helped Tempy clean up in the McGavocks' bedroom, she prayed. For Thaddeus's mother, whoever and wherever she was. For Towny. For the Confederate—and Federal—armies. She even prayed for General Hood. But despite her prayers, she ached inside, imagining Towny and the thousands of other soldiers hunkered down somewhere on the outskirts of Nashville in the freezing cold. But it was envision-ing the carnage that would soon engulf the men once the battle started that weighed on her the heaviest.

"Miss Clouston, would you help me, please?"

Lizzie looked up to see Sister Catherine Margaret in the doorway. "Of course, Sister." She set aside her stack of trays and soiled nap-kins and followed her to Winder's bedroom, surprised to find Roland already asleep. She knelt beside him.

"I gave him some laudanum a few moments ago to help him rest," the nun whispered, opposite her. "He's not been sleeping well, he said. But it seems the laudanum is already doing its work. So with your help, we'll remove the bandages George applied along with a poultice earlier today, then we'll gently wash the incisions. We won't bandage them again, though. We'll let them air for the night."

Sister Catherine pulled back the blanket and sheet, and Lizzie realized she'd not seen Roland's leg wounds recently. Remembering how Dr. Phillips had painstakingly sutured the ribbons of flesh cut to pieces from grapeshot, she was surprised at the extent of healing that had taken place in such a short time. The process had to have been so painful for him. Yet he never complained.

"If you'll gently lift the captain's right leg, Miss Clouston."

"Yes, of course." As carefully as she could, she lifted his leg enough for Sister Catherine to remove the bandages. They did the same with the left, then took turns wiping the incisions clean with warm water. Lizzie watched his face. If doing this caused him pain, his expression didn't show it.

She'd intentionally put some distance between them in recent days, but she missed his company. His quick wit. Their conversations. *Any misunderstanding about our friendship was solely on my part*, he'd said the afternoon she'd told him about Towny.

It had taken a moment for his meaning to sink in, but when it had, she'd felt her world go slightly off-kilter. He admitted he'd misunderstood their friendship. That he'd thought it was leading to something more. Or at least that was how she interpreted his comment. It would explain why he'd reached for her hand the night they'd sat by the hearth talking. The night Towny had shown up.

She looked into his face, grateful for the chance to watch him while he slept. Had Weet ever lain awake and watched him like this? Surely she had. Judging by the letter Roland had asked her to read, Weet—or Susan—had loved him very much. And they'd had a child together. A little girl. Who was gone now too.

Roland shifted a little and sighed, and Lizzie and Sister Catherine paused momentarily. But when he didn't wake up, they continued. Lizzie liked the way Sister Catherine had cut his hair. Shorter but not too short. Still touching his collar. The stubble shadowing the sides of his face made her wish she could run a hand along his jawline. Towny's face was naturally smoother. He'd only grown a beard once and it had come in thin in places, so he'd shaved it off. She'd told him she liked him better without it anyway. And she still did.

Roland was well muscled through his shoulders, chest, and arms, which would help him greatly, she thought, once he began the regimen that would get him walking again. Looking at him, she wondered how it would feel to be held close in those arms, to be kissed by him, to feel the roughness of his face on her cheek. His lips on hers. To stare close up into those steel-gray eyes. The thoughts felt traitorous, and with good reason. But the next felt even more so. What might her future have held, had she not been betrothed to Towny when she'd met Roland? That was something she would never know.

Then again, perhaps her accepting Towny's proposal when she did was part of the "all things working together for good" in her life, as the colonel had said earlier. She'd simply have to trust that that was the case, regardless of what her heart told her.

Sister Catherine gestured. "All done, Miss Clouston," she whispered. "Now on to my next patient."

Lizzie eased Roland's leg to the floor, then pulled the sheet and blanket back into place. She rose and hadn't gone three steps when she heard his deep voice.

"Lizzie?"

She turned back to find him watching her.

"I'm praying tonight," he whispered. "For your Lieutenant Townsend."

She smiled down at him, able to hear the laudanum in his voice. "Thank you, Roland. I've been praying that General Hood would change his mind."

"I'll pray for that too." He yawned and rubbed his eyes. "But it's not likely. The man was bested here in Franklin, and I think he's determined to get revenge. Hood's like a wounded animal. There's no reasoning with him."

What he said made sense. Colonel McGavock held much the same opinion. Thinking of the colonel jogged her memory. "We received an answer back about Thaddeus."

Roland blinked and came a little more awake.

"But it wasn't good news, I'm afraid. They couldn't find any record of his being here at the battle."

"But that's impossible. He *was* here."

"I know. So I'm hoping that whatever idea you were referring to the other night might still be an option."

He nodded and yawned again. "I'll do the best I can."

She smiled. "I wouldn't have expected any less. Oh, and per Dr. Phillips's instructions, Colonel McGavock ordered several cots from the quartermaster earlier this week, so you should be off the floor very soon."

"That's good," he whispered. "That's real good."

A handful of seconds passed, and she figured he'd fallen back to sleep. She turned to go.

"Lizzie?"

She paused, realizing the laudanum was definitely having an influence.

"I'm grateful we're friends again," he said softly, his eyes slipping closed.

"Me too," she whispered, doubting he heard her. "Far more than you know."

CHAPTER 26

The next morning tension filled every corner of the house. The air pulsed with it. Roland shifted on his pallet on the floor, ready for that cot Lizzie had told him was ordered last night. The men, including him, were sullen and moody, snapping at each other and even at Tempy and the nuns as they'd cleared the breakfast dishes earlier. No one had eaten much, same as no one had slept much all night. Everyone's thoughts were centered on Nashville and Hood's attack.

All Roland could think about were the remaining men in his regiment and how they were likely fighting right this minute. While part of him wished he were beside them, he also knew that if he were there, he wouldn't be fighting with the same fervor he'd fought with before. Because he'd glimpsed the ending on the battlefield the other night. And like someone who was reading a novel but skipped to the back and read the last page out of turn, he felt as though he already knew how this story was going to end.

He looked at the clock on the mantel—nearly half past eleven—then outside the window, where another night of ice and snow had coated the trees and hills and everything else he could see in its frozen grip. He studied the sketch on the pad of paper in his lap and ran the tip of the pencil over the wide curve that represented the Confederate troops entrenched around Nashville. No matter how many times he worked the scenario in his mind, he always came to the same conclusion.

Footsteps on the second-story landing drew his attention. Sister Catherine entered the bedroom, carrying a basket of medicinal supplies. Lizzie followed with fresh cloths and a basin of water. Time to change bandages for those who needed it. Lizzie's gaze eventually moved to him, but Roland sensed she might have wanted to look sooner. Or maybe that was just wishful thinking on his part.

The women tended to Conrad first, and the once-strong, now much-too-feeble first lieutenant rambled on about how to fix the heel of a man's boot. Conrad seemed to lapse back into his former life whenever he got nervous or the memories became too dark. Lieutenant Shuler was still sleeping. The young man had had a rough night of it, a lot of pain, he'd said. Roland hoped the morphine they'd given him earlier would help. Captain Hampton and Lieutenant Estes, the quietest in the bunch, had taken advantage of the colonel's offer to borrow from his library and were both reading.

In the corner of the room, Taylor and Smitty argued over a game of checkers, Taylor occasionally punching Smitty in the arm. At least Taylor wasn't still going on about what a great military leader Hood was.

Finally Lizzie came and knelt beside him. "Afternoon," she said quietly and reached for his right hand.

"Afternoon." He gave a nod. "And thank you."

With a fleeting smile, she gently began removing the old bandage. She looked tired. Beautiful, but tired, the fine lines at the corners of her eyes more pronounced. No doubt she was thinking of Lieutenant Townsend, wondering where he was and worrying for him, hoping he was all right. But she also had to be heartened, at least to some measure, thinking that the North was going to be victorious.

He watched her as she cleaned his hand wound, working gently yet methodically. If she'd been born a man, she would have made a fine doctor. She was certainly smart enough and had a compassionate nature people responded to. She leaned closer, inspecting the stitches on his palm, and he caught a whiff of lilac and a sweetness that was distinctly feminine.

She glanced down at the sketch he'd drawn. "What's that?"

Grateful for the distraction, he forced himself to refocus. "Just me, thinking on paper."

Her expression encouraged him to continue.

"I've been going over different scenarios of what might be taking place in Nashville. What strategies each side might be employing. It helps me occupy the time."

She finished wrapping his hand in a fresh bandage, then pulled Winder's chair closer. She took a seat. "You said 'scenarios.' Is there one that rises above the others in your mind?"

"It's only my opinion, mind you, but yes. With what I've seen of the tactics of both the Southern army and the Northern, I believe General Thomas—commander of the Federal troops in Nashville—will try to turn the Confederate left flank." He ghosted the tip of the pencil along the same curve from a moment earlier. "This represents our troops. And this . . . farther north up by Nashville . . . is the Federal line." He traced a path with his forefinger along the dark line at the top of the page. "Sherman did the same thing to break Hood's final hold on Atlanta, and it worked. It's the same strategy the Union's employed since the war started." He sighed. "Turn the Confederate left flank."

Lizzie leaned forward, looking closely at the drawing. She pointed. "You've made marks along the Confederate front."

He nodded. "For the different brigades."

"Do you know which brigade is stationed along each portion of the line?"

He looked at her and knew what she was really asking. "What brigade is Lieutenant Townsend in?"

She stared for a moment, then softly answered, "Tucker's."

He looked back at the paper and pictured from memory the over-lay of assignments from the battle at Franklin. "For Franklin, Tucker's Brigade was stationed here." He pointed to the far left and north-westernmost edge of the curve. "But Hood could well have adjusted the positions according to what spies told him or to movement he observed on the ground."

For the longest time she stared at the pencil drawing. Finally she looked up. "Do you think this could be the end?" she whispered. "Of the war, I mean."

He studied her gaze—her eyes a robin's egg blue, maybe a shade darker. He couldn't quite remember when it was that he'd first realized what a jewel this woman was. Was it that first night when he'd looked up, not knowing if he was dead or alive, and thought her an angel? Or in the days following, when he'd realized she truly *was* one?

"I think, Lizzie, that what happened here in Franklin"—he lowered his voice, not only so others wouldn't hear, but because he wasn't sure his own voice would hold beneath the weight of truth—"has determined the outcome of the war. And I believe that what will happen in Nashville . . . will be the nail in the Confederacy's coffin."

She firmed her lips, and her chin trembled the slightest bit. But she nodded. And he glimpsed the internal struggle going on inside her that he'd imagined moments earlier.

"I'm praying for him," he whispered. "For your Towny."

Her eyes filled with emotion. "Thank you, Roland."

The way she looked at him threatened to plant a seed of hope within him. *Don't go there,* he told himself. *She's a promised woman.*

"He's a good man," she added softly.

He struggled not to reach out and cradle the side of her face. "You wouldn't be with him if he were not."

"Hood's the best leader this war has ever seen!" Taylor pronounced from across the room. "Them Federals will be hightailin' it back north when he's done with 'em."

Smitty let out a whoop, and Roland took a deep breath.

"I've had to sit here and listen to those two jawing on about Hood all morning."

Lizzie opened her mouth to respond, then apparently thought better of it.

"What?" he pried gently.

She narrowed her eyes. "It's about General Hood. I saw him that day, Roland. On the battlefield here in Franklin. The morning after."

"You saw Hood?"

She nodded. "He was sitting astride his horse, not too far from the Federal breastworks. Full-bearded, with a long tawny mustache, and absent a leg."

"That's Hood, all right. He lost that leg at Chickamauga." Though he knew she'd gone to the battlefield that day, it still hurt him to think of all she'd witnessed. Things a woman should never have to see. Of course, she'd seen almost as bad right here at Carnton.

"I didn't know who he was at first." She kept her voice low. "But I asked one of the soldiers, and he told me. General Hood was staring out across the fields. The closer I came to him, the more I expected him to look my way, but he didn't. It was as though I weren't even there. And . . ." She paused. "I'm almost certain he was crying, Roland. And though someone else might have felt sorry for the man"—she stared at the fire crackling in the hearth—"I couldn't. Because as I looked back across that field, all I felt was fury. And injustice."

Roland watched her, her gaze transfixed. For the longest time, neither of them spoke.

"Miss Clouston?"

They looked back to see Tempy standing in the doorway, an envelope in hand.

"Letter come for you just now, miss. I figured you'd want to see it straightaway. I think it's from your Lieutenant Townsend."

The older woman crossed the room and handed Lizzie the envelope. Conversations around them fell silent.

"Thank you, Tempy. I appreciate you bringing it up to me."

She fingered the envelope, and Roland couldn't decide whether she was eager to read the letter but didn't know how to excuse herself to do so—or if, for whatever reason, she wasn't eager to read it, yet didn't want to convey that feeling either.

"I hope it holds good news," Sister Catherine offered, changing the bandage on Smitty's leg.

"Me too, Miss Clouston," Shuler said from the bed, and Roland looked over, only now aware that the young man had awakened.

"Who's Lieutenant Townsend?" Conrad asked from across the room.

The question, draped in such innocence coming from Conrad, seemed to grow overloud in the quiet. Even Taylor and Smitty looked up from their game of checkers. And Hampton and Estes from their books.

Lizzie finally lifted her gaze. "Lieutenant Townsend is . . . my fiancé."

"You're betrothed?" Surprise colored Shuler's tone.

Lizzie looked over at him and nodded.

"Well, I'll be . . ." Shuler sighed. "Somebody asked you before I could."

The young lieutenant's smile hinted at his intended humor. But it was the quick look Sister Catherine shot in Roland's direction that made Roland feel most uncomfortable.

Lizzie opened the envelope, withdrew the letter, read it briefly, then looked up. "It's about Nashville. Not what's happening now, of course, but from earlier this week." Her gaze scanned the room. "I can read it aloud, if you like."

Everyone nodded, eager for the least bit of news. Roland nodded too when she looked his way.

"'Dear Lizzie Beth,'" she started, then peered up. "That's what Lieutenant Townsend has called me since we were children."

"You've known each other that long?" Sister Catherine claimed a seat in the Windsor chair near Roland.

Lizzie nodded, her gaze returning to the page. "'I hope this finds you and everyone at Carnton faring well. The wounded who were treated there have spoken often about the hospitality afforded them by Colonel and Mrs. McGavock, and they consider themselves most indebted to the family's generosity.'"

She paused briefly, and Roland was certain she was skipping a line or two. Probably personal references meant for her eyes only. His gut twisted as he imagined her with the lieutenant.

> "I promised to keep you abreast of what was happening, if the opportunity allowed. And since I learned moments ago of a courier leaving for Franklin within the hour, I am hastily penning a few lines with the hope that they reach you. Customarily, I might not share the details of our situation here so freely. But in the earnestness of time, I will write the words that come to me without any doctoring. We are encamped on the outskirts of Nashville, as we have been for nearly two weeks. There is vicious skirmishing and sharpshooting day and night. Federals have been killed so close to Confederate lines they could not be carried back, so they remain where they fell, frozen as hard as a log."

Laughter rose from the corner, but the slightest look from Sister Catherine silenced Taylor and Smitty stone-cold.

"'Federal batteries daily shell the Confederate trenches,'" she continued. "'But we must take it without reply because General Hood has ordered no return of fire in order to save ammunition.'"

Her grip noticeably tightened on the page.

> "The Federals have been busy these last three years constructing defensive works around Nashville. They've built forts along that curved front. The largest of them is called Fort Negley, and it looks particularly formidable. I saw it from a distance the other day. From where I stood, I could not help but think what a fool's errand it would be to try to scale that defense. We have been told that additional Northern troops arrived by river yesterday, escorted

by a fleet of iron-clad gunboats. So the river barrier is also well defended."

Lizzie's eyes narrowed.

"The bloody tracks of our men can be plainly seen on the ice and snow. I had read of such things occurring during the Revolutionary War, and we have certainly borne our share of suffering thus far. But here, as was in Franklin, are scenes eclipsing in suffering all that I had ever imagined."

Her lips formed a thin line, and Roland didn't have to close his eyes to visualize what Lieutenant Townsend was referring to.

"The Federals have taken charge of Belmont Mansion—Mrs. Adelicia Acklen's home—and word is she and her family have sought shelter at Mrs. Polk's house in the city."

Roland felt a touch of home at the mention of Mrs. Polk. The late President Polk's estate bordered his own in Yalobusha, so he'd known President and Mrs. Polk the majority of his life.

"'The Federals are using Mrs. Acklen's home as their headquarters,'" Lizzie continued. "'And her water tower as an outpost by which they can see for miles. It seems there is nowhere we can move that their eyes are not upon us. In many ways, it feels like we are destined to relive what happened in Franklin. Though I earnestly pray not.'"

Lizzie wiped the corner of her eye before continuing. "'But it is a freeing thing, in a way, to be ready and willing to die.'" She stopped again, clenching her jaw tight.

"To have accepted that your death could come at any time. If war has taught me one thing, Lizzie, and it has taught me many, it's that living with the knowledge that death is imminent frees you to embrace life in a way you didn't before. Because you realize the precious fleetingness of it, and of how very little time we all have here. Which is all the more reason not to delay once you find what you want with all your heart."

She sucked in a breath, then let it out slowly. "'I must close for now,'" she finally continued, her voice scarcely above a whisper.

"Time is short. A pea-soup fog is settling in, swallowing the whole of the city. Swallowing us all. Please convey my best to the household there at Carnton, to my fellow soldiers convalescing within its walls, and give my earnest love to my father, when next you see him. Remember us all in your prayers, for they are the foundation upon which we stand. In closing, I . . ."

Her voice trailed off, tears slipping down her cheeks. Silence hung heavy in the room as she folded the paper and slid it back inside the envelope. Heavy footfalls sounded on the staircase, distant at first, but growing louder the closer they came. Indistinct conversations from the other bedrooms fell away.

"Gentlemen . . . and ladies."

Although Roland couldn't see him, he recognized the colonel's voice.

"I have received a telegram."

The silence seemed to stretch forever.

"The Federal Army attacked this morning. The fog was still so thick, they were able to get their entire corps in place before our men even knew they were there."

Lizzie looked over at him, and Roland discreetly took hold of her hand. She clung to him.

"When the fog lifted, twenty thousand bluecoats were already bearing down hard on our men."

Though she made no sound, Lizzie bowed her head, her shoulders gently shuddering.

Roland tightened his hold, and as he watched her, he felt two undeniable confirmations within him. First, though the battle at Nashville was likely still being waged, the war was over. And second, he was in love with Elizabeth Clouston.

CHAPTER 27

The rest of that day and into the next, they waited. That evening, Lizzie sat in the kitchen with Tempy and George, cups of lukewarm tea before them. No one drinking. Was Towny dead or alive? Lizzie kept seeing his face, his smile, the way he'd bend down and make his eyes even with hers, trying to read her expression. And the letter he'd written. She swallowed hard.

Not knowing whether he'd made it through the battle was even worse this time, because she'd seen the many ways he could have been killed. Or if he was alive, she'd seen the aftermath of the horror he'd lived through. How much of that could someone endure before something broke inside them? *We weren't made to do this to each other, Lord.*

She'd finally gotten Hattie and Winder to sleep upstairs in her room, but only after reading another portion of the Scrooge story to them, as Hattie called it. She'd promised Lieutenant Shuler she'd begin reading the story to him and the other soldiers, and felt bad that she hadn't. The same way she felt about not yet beginning the lessons for Tempy and George. But considering the circumstances, she knew they understood. And she knew better than to think the soldiers would be interested in being read to at the moment.

George scooted his chair back, then leaned forward and rested his muscular forearms on his thighs. "How'd you come to believe the way you do, ma'am?" His dark eyes seemed fathomless in the flicker of the oil lamp. "'Bout us, I mean. Is your family like you?"

"No, they're not. I was raised in a household with slaves." Lizzie felt Tempy's attention as heavily as she felt his. "My father is a druggist, and people used to come to him for doctoring on occasion. I liked the idea of helping to make people better. So I decided I would become a druggist like him. Either that, or maybe a doctor."

George's mouth tipped on one side.

"But as you well know," Lizzie continued, "that could not happen, because I am a woman. So you might say that the doors that were closed to me due to my gender are what first opened my mind to what injustice was. Even though I had no idea what that word meant as a child."

An almost imperceptible frown crossed his face.

"Then I began to see other instances of unfairness around me." She glanced at Tempy. "I'm ashamed that it's taken me this long to actually step out and act on what I believe. And I'm sorry we have to do it in secret."

George shook his head. "No, ma'am, don't you be shamed by that. What you're gonna do for me and Tempy, it's a brave thing. Even if we gotta meet behind closed doors."

Lizzie thanked him with a look. Then, having answered his question, she felt entitled to ask one in return. "How long have you known Captain Jones?"

He leaned back in the kitchen chair, the legs creaking. "I was given to the cap'n when I was a boy. Cap'n was just a boy hisself. We's 'bout the same age, him and me."

Lizzie felt surprise register in her expression. She'd not expected that longevity between the two men.

"Mr. Jones, the cap'n's father," George continued, "he bought my whole family. He told my papa years later that he only come to market to get two slaves that day. But when he bought my father and another man, he learnt my father had a family, so he went back and bought us all. My mama, me, my sisters. Even my granny." He smiled. "Brought us to his big ol' place in Yalobusha, Mississippi, and we been there ever since."

"Is all of your family still there?"

"Papa and Mama done passed on. Granny too, o' course, years back now. My two sisters lived with they's families in cabins just over the ridge. But they all left three years back. Took off after the cap'n went to war. They headed north." His voice gained a flat edge, and he briefly looked away. "The rest of the slaves run off a few months back."

Lizzie remembered Roland telling her that several of his slaves had left. "Did you ever consider leaving too?"

He held her gaze for what felt like a very long time before answering. "Yes, ma'am. I give it a lotta thought. The cap'n's mother and his sisters, they ain't the cap'n, but they think like him. They take care of what they own. And if a slave's on a plantation, then he's mostly safe. But if he's caught runnin' . . ." Muscles corded in his jaw. "They string him up. And if he got his family with him, they hang his children first, one by one. Then his wife, after they take turns defilin' her right in front of him. The last hangin' would be mine, so I could see what my choice to run done cost me. And those I love."

Lizzie's eyes filled. She'd read newspaper accounts about runaway slaves for years. She'd seen the ads taken out for slave auctions. Had passed slave pens in town. None of it was new to her, and sometimes she regretted having the memory she did. But to hear George describe it, to see the anguish in his face, made the evil he described far more real. And vile.

He sniffed, his eyes glistening. "So, yes, ma'am. I thought about leavin'. Many times. But each time I did, I thought of my sweet Sophia and our five children. And I couldn't. I just couldn't." He looked down at his hands clasped between his knees, then gradually lifted his gaze. "The life we got there with the cap'n ain't the life I'd choose. But it's a life I can live with. For now, at least. Until a better life comes."

Lizzie couldn't speak for a moment. Emotion stifled the words. "Five children," she finally managed, thinking about what a blessing those children were, while also thinking of Roland losing his wife and the only child they had. And now, likely all he'd fought for.

"There's Little Frank," Tempy piped up. "Oscar, Susanna, Jack, and little Patsy. They sound cute as little bugs in a rug."

George sighed, a hint of pleasure returning to his features. "We call him Little Frank, but he ain't so little no more. He's nine years and growin' every day. The rest of 'em are too."

Lizzie loved the way his eyes lit. A father's love. "I bet you miss them. And they you."

"They're my life, ma'am. And I'm grateful to the cap'n for lettin' us stay together. But from what I been hearin', the South's army's been beat down pretty bad and the North is still strong. So I got to be ready." He lowered his voice. "I know the cap'n won't like it, if he knew. But I got to learn. I heard somethin' a while back from a man who was speakin' in the town square. Tall man with a voice as deep as a river. Said his name was George White. I 'member 'cause his front name is like mine. And I 'member his back name 'cause he's a white man." He laughed, and Lizzie and Tempy did too. "Bunch of other white folks run him off. But before they did, he said somethin' that'll stay with me all my days. How I say it won't be as good as he did, but he said that anybody who treats books as dear to him is on the road to freedom, but anybody who ain't readin', who ain't treatin' 'em like they's gold, is on his way back to slavery. And me and my family, Miss Lizzie . . . we on our way to freedom."

Lizzie had trouble finding her voice again, and George's smile deepened as if he understood.

"I will do everything I can, George, to prepare you and Tempy for—"

She heard the colonel's voice, followed by Mrs. McGavock's, as they descended the stone steps from the main house to the kitchen wing. George and Tempy immediately rose. Tempy walked to the stove, and George slipped out the back door and headed toward one of the slave houses a short distance away. Suddenly feeling guilty and like she needed to do something too, Lizzie grabbed their teacups and took them to the washbasin.

Mrs. McGavock rounded the corner and lightly touched Lizzie on the shoulder as they passed. "The colonel and I are retiring for the night."

Her eyes were red-rimmed, just as Lizzie figured her own were. "I hope you're both able to get some rest."

The colonel nodded, looking as tired or more so than Carrie. "We wish the same for both of you."

"Good night, Colonel," Tempy said, wiping down the cast iron stove. "Rest well, Missus."

As they ascended the creaky wooden staircase, Lizzie and Tempy exchanged a look, and Lizzie couldn't shake the feeling that she was somehow behind enemy lines now. But the McGavocks were not her enemies. They were like family. She loved them. They loved her. They were an important part of the people who made up her world, and she didn't wish to hurt them or dishonor them in any way. She simply couldn't live the way she'd been living. Not anymore.

"I think I'll head to bed now too, Tempy."

"Ma'am?"

Lizzie paused at the bottom of the stairs.

"Just so you know . . ." Tempy looked away briefly. When she looked back, her lips formed a thin line and tears flooded her eyes. "What George told you 'bout a man runnin' with his family—"

The sudden sharpness of Tempy's breathing made Lizzie go absolutely still inside.

"That weren't just a story. He was tellin' you 'bout one of his sisters and her family. And what happened to 'em on the way north."

Lizzie reached out for the worktable and gripped it hard.

"I just figured you oughta know the truth. George, he's a good man. Real good. But he's got a whole bushel of hurt inside him. Anger too."

"With reason," Lizzie whispered.

"What you doin' for me is good, ma'am, and I'm much obliged

for that. But what you doin' for him—" Her tears spilled over. "You changin' a *whole* bunch of lives. For a whole lotta years."

Lizzie managed a smile, her eyes burning. "Good night, Tempy." Lizzie reached out and gave her arm a gentle squeeze.

Tempy patted her hand. "Good night, Miss Lizzie."

LIZZIE AWAKENED DURING the night to knocking on her bedroom door.

"Lizzie? Lizzie, do you hear me?"

She blinked, still a little fuzzy. "Mrs. McGavock?" She grabbed her dressing robe and hurried to open the door.

Carrie held an oil lamp aloft, her face ashen despite the flame's glow. "I need you to come with me, please."

Lizzie stared for a beat. The somber note in the woman's voice, mirrored in her expression, caused her to question whether she truly wanted to go along or not. After checking the children, Lizzie trailed Mrs. McGavock downstairs to the kitchen, then back upstairs to the farm office, buttoning the front of her robe as she went. Mrs. McGavock continued to the entrance hall. The clock in the family parlor struck three chimes as they walked onto the front portico.

Tempy stood outside, along with Sister Catherine Margaret and Sister Mary Grace, peering into the night. Lizzie thought she heard gunfire in the distance, but the thud of a horse's hooves drowned it out. She spotted a rider coming up the drive.

"It's the colonel," Carrie whispered. "He couldn't sleep. He was out on the back porch when he heard the gunfire and commotion."

"From what?" Lizzie whispered, but the words were lost as Colonel McGavock reined in the stallion by the porch steps.

"It's our men." His breath came hard. "The Army of Tennessee, or what's left of it, is in a full and apparently uncontrollable retreat. Men told me the blue coats are in pursuit and are shooting men in the back."

"Oh, John!" Mrs. McGavock grabbed Lizzie's hand, and Lizzie held on tight.

"Our boys are cutting through the woods and fields. Some are coming down Granny White Pike and Franklin Pike. Their only hopes of escape."

"Have you seen anyone we know?" Lizzie asked, hoping he would say yes. That he'd seen Towny.

He shook his head. "A captain told me the main Confederate line broke so suddenly they had to abandon the artillery. They didn't even have time to get the horses harnessed to move it with them as they retreated. They lost close to sixty guns, which is more than half of the army's artillery. Gone now. To the Federals." The stallion pranced nervously, as though somehow aware that their world was crumbling down around them. "Men told me they were being shot at from all sides. Somehow the Federals managed to turn the Confederate left flank. It was all the boys could do to escape."

A cold wind whipped around the southeast corner of the house, and Lizzie pulled the collar of her robe up tighter about her neck. Roland had been right.

"Where is the Army of Tennessee headed now?" Sister Catherine asked.

Colonel McGavock gestured. "Down south to Spring Hill, then on to Columbia. The streams are still swollen from the rains, so it's making the going a little rougher."

Mrs. McGavock shook her head. "I only pray it's making it rougher for the Federals too. Which may give our boys something of a lead."

Only then did Lizzie notice how quiet Tempy was beside her. Lizzie looked over. She couldn't make out the precise definition of Tempy's features in the shadows, but somehow she knew that Tempy felt much as she did. Glad to hear this news, because it meant a step toward freedom for so many. Yet heartbroken at all the needless, senseless death.

Lizzie turned back toward the colonel when she felt Tempy take hold of her hand. Lizzie squeezed tight.

Sister Mary Grace stepped forward. "What can we do, Colonel?"

"Pray," he said simply. "That God will see us all through this to whatever waits on the other side."

Both sisters immediately returned to the house. Lizzie stared out into the night, the sound of rifle fire echoing across the valley once again. She squeezed the hands of the women on either side of her, feeling as though they were on a precipice about to take a plunge. And whatever came of it, good or bad, they were destined to take it together.

Roland awakened to distant gunfire and to the sound of horses and wagons. At first he thought he was dreaming, then as he listened more closely, deep in his bones, he knew the truth. His eyes felt hot and gritty. A punishing fist squeezed his heart tight. Grateful for the dark, he didn't bother to wipe away the tears. His chest ached with regret and loss, disappointment and dread, but he didn't make a sound. He lay still in the darkness and listened, somehow knowing he needed to memorize this moment. Needed to take it in. Needed to remember what the Confederacy sounded like in its final moments.

Chapter 28

"Are there any more questions, men?" Colonel McGavock asked, the strength of his voice belying the lines of weariness on his face.

Conrad slowly raised his hand.

"Yes, First Lieutenant Conrad."

"Can we . . . stay here, Colonel?"

The colonel's expression gentled. "First Lieutenant Conrad, you and every other soldier here will continue to remain at Carnton until you're deemed well enough to leave. And as I stated before, at that point you will either go to a Federal hospital or to prison."

Roland listened even as his attention was drawn beyond the windows in Winder's bedroom, where all the soldiers had gathered, to the first light of dawn edging up over the distant hills. It seemed too beautiful a morning to follow so tragic a night. Shortly after five o'clock that morning, Colonel McGavock had awakened the men who'd somehow managed to sleep through the night and had delivered news of the Confederate retreat.

Seeing tears in some of the men's eyes even now, Roland was grateful he'd had the opportunity to work through that privately. He wondered if Lizzie had heard from Lieutenant Townsend. Roland hoped he was all right, for both the lieutenant's and Lizzie's sake.

"A warning as well, men," the colonel continued. "Since there are currently more Federal troops in this area, there's a higher chance a patrol will stop by to check the roster of soldiers convalescing here. So unless you have spoken to me and I have personally cleared you to leave Carnton for a certain task—at which time I'll provide you with a written order stating such—you are bound by the oath you took to remain here.

And if any one of you tries to leave or rejoin the Confederate Army, every one of you will be immediately taken into custody and sent to prison. Any other questions?"

"Where's the Army of Tennessee headed after they meet up in Columbia?"

Roland bristled at Taylor's query. Not only due to the lack of respect Taylor showed by not using Colonel McGavock's honorary title, but because the question also prodded his suspicions. He had a feeling Taylor and Smitty were up to something.

"I don't have that information, Lieutenant Taylor," the colonel answered. "And I doubt the men I spoke with during the night even knew themselves. Those orders will likely come down from General Hood today."

Frazier, a private from Alabama, huffed. "*If* Hood's even still in charge after the catastrophe that his leadership has—"

"You shut your trap, Frazier!" Taylor yelled, then lunged for the private who sat on the floor in front of him.

"Gentlemen!" Colonel McGavock shouted. *"Gentlemen!"*

Taylor managed to get in the first punch before Frazier even knew what was coming. But Frazier, a good deal heavier with a layer of muscle beneath his bulk, swiftly delivered a solid right hook to Taylor's jaw. Taylor went down, but not for long. Smitty, along with another of their contingent, helped push Taylor back up, and the melee continued, with several other soldiers taking sides.

A shrill whistle cut through the shouting and name-calling, and Roland turned to see Sister Catherine Margaret standing in the doorway with Sister Mary Grace, Sister Angelica, and the rest of the nuns shoulder to shoulder behind her. He couldn't have been more pleased to see the women if he'd been Catholic. Both Taylor and Frazier paused in their fighting, as did the rest of the men, and the sisters quickly took advantage of the moment. They separated the men and, with George's help, began taking them back to their rooms. Roland looked over at

Colonel McGavock and read the same relief—and grief—on his face that Roland felt.

It still wasn't quite real to him. The defeat. Even though he'd told Lizzie last night that a defeat was what he expected. And though Colonel McGavock never said the war was over, he had painted a bleak future for the Confederate States. Until the night of the battle here in Franklin, Roland had honestly thought the Confederacy stood a good chance of coming out on top. That everything that he and so many others had fought for would lead to victory. All the blood that had been spilled. All the lives lost. For what?

"Captain Jones . . ."

He looked up. "Sister Catherine."

She took his left hand in hers. "How does this new and most challenging day find you, Captain?"

The sincerity in her tone, in her question, had a greater impact on him than Roland would have imagined. He thought for a moment, remembered back to that night they'd sat talking only a few feet away, and met her gaze once again. "Sometimes life on this side of the veil is far more difficult than I think it should be. But then, God's promises do not eliminate suffering, do they, Sister."

She leaned down and kissed his forehead. "Well spoken, my son." Her eyes shone with a light from within. "The Lord dwells with us in this present moment as surely as he already inhabits those in the future. He sees every step and will guide each one too, if we ask him." She leaned closer. "So *do* ask him, Captain."

Roland nodded, not quite trusting his voice. If only the Lord knew how to save a twenty-five-hundred-acre estate that had been in the Jones family for three generations but had fallen into ruin on his watch. How would he provide for his mother and sisters? And George and his family and the rest. George had been so faithful to stay while so many others had left. But now. Roland looked down at his legs. He couldn't even stand up, much less take a step and walk.

He hadn't spoken to the Lord in a long time, not like he used to before the Lord took Susan and Lena from him. And he didn't really feel like it now. But the wordless plea working its way up from somewhere deep inside him seemed to rise of its own accord. And if what Preacher Bounds said was right—*When faith ceases to pray, it ceases to live*—Roland knew his faith was living on borrowed time.

His back against the wall, he carefully scooted forward and leaned back on his pallet. Moving still hurt, but not nearly as much as it had at first. Grateful to see that the bedroom had all but cleared out—Shuler was still dozing in bed, the morphine doing its work, and Conrad was reading—Roland stared up at the ceiling and searched for the right words. Words that would persuade. That would open heavenly doors, so to speak. A moment or two passed, and he came up blank. So he decided that simple words were better than nothing. He took a deep breath.

Sister Catherine says you see every step, and that you'll guide each one too—if I ask. So, Lord, this is me . . . asking. He paused, not fool enough to think that the Almighty would answer him that quickly. But still, he waited. He studied the ceiling as seconds ticked by, then he sighed. *I don't rightly know what's coming next in life, what to expect now that things have worked out this way. Which wasn't the way I anticipated, based on how I thought you were leading me. What I mean is, you didn't exactly work things out like I thought you would.*

Roland felt a stab of bitterness, but knew enough to know that the Almighty wasn't keen on being blamed, even though he was the one in charge. *And you already know this, Lord, but I can't walk. I can't even stand right now. And I need to. Sorely, I need to. I have people depending on me. A lot of people. So if you could see fit to help me heal quickly, that'd be much appreciated. More quickly than Taylor and Smitty, for sure.*

He had no desire to be transferred to prison anytime soon. But neither did he want to end up there due to some hoople-headed stunt Taylor pulled. Because, as Dr. Phillips had said, going to prison in his current condition would guarantee his death.

Roland shifted on the pallet, his back beginning to ache. He wasn't really sure how prayer worked, and he wished Preacher Bounds were there so he could ask him. He'd always thought of prayer as something you did when you got to the end of your rope. That God expected you to run on your own strength and get the job done. But that if you needed more, he was there to help. Roland had made it a priority years ago to run the race God set before him, and he'd attempted to do that the best he could.

He scoffed beneath his breath. Little good that had done him.

He'd asked the Lord to watch over Susan and Lena while he was away fighting for his home and family. And the Almighty hadn't come through on that one either. And what about the war? He'd sought God's wisdom on that as well, about whether or not to take up arms and fight. He thought he'd heard a resounding yes on that count. Yet there again, it hadn't panned out. *You're not quite keeping up your end of the bargain, are you, Lord?*

The longer he lay there, the more his mind and gut churned, and the angrier he became. His emotions spiraled until they hit rock bottom, all the guilt, shame, regret, and fear balling up tight. *Preacher Bounds says that a believer is in your hands and there's nothing we should fear. But I got to tell you, God, I'm not feeling too secure in your hands at present. If this is what it means to be safe in you, then I might be better off on my own.* The words were coming now. He no longer had to search for what he wanted to say. He thought about the autumn moon he'd seen on the battlefield.

Why did you save me that night, make me think you had a reason for me to still draw breath, when I've been shown time and again that I've got nothing? I've lost my family. My home. I'm a cripple. A man "in my prime"—he recalled what Sister Catherine had said—*trapped in an old man's body. I can't move. I can't do anything myself. I have control of nothing! And after I thought I'd never love again, I meet Lizzie, and she's got more of my heart than she'll ever know. But she's pledged to someone else. But you knew that when you sent me here.*

A sharp pain in his side caused him to suck in a breath, and only then did he realize how hard his chest was heaving, his teeth gritted tight, fists clenched at his sides. Bitter emotion burned his eyes. *You say you're the strength of my life. Is this what you call making me strong, Lord?* He raised his head and looked down at his legs. *Because if this is your idea of strength, then I think I can do better on my own.*

"You're certain they would be receptive to that, Colonel? Considering all that's happened in the last couple of days?" Lizzie didn't like to question him, especially in front of Mrs. McGavock, but what he was proposing seemed a little untimely to her. And no offense to Charles Dickens, but the bulk of her thoughts were centered on Towny and on what would happen next to the Confederacy.

"I think *because* of all that's occurred, Miss Clouston, along with the uncertainty we're facing, this would be a great boon to their spirits."

"Tempers are running high among the soldiers, Lizzie." Carrie sighed. "Especially this afternoon. Yesterday's defeat has been hard on all of us. The men are restless, wanting to know more when there's no more to share."

The colonel's look turned sheepish. "I already took the liberty of telling them you'd be willing to start tonight. And that anyone who wanted to participate should let George know and he'd make sure they were ready."

"I think a story is exactly what they need," Carrie added gently. "Tempy has plenty of tea cakes made, and hot chocolate is warming on the stove."

Catching a spark of their hopefulness, Lizzie nodded. "I'll get the children ready for bed, then we'll make our way upstairs."

"Very good." The colonel nodded his approval, and Carrie smiled.

As Hattie and Winder changed into their bedclothes, Lizzie shared the plan with them. When they discovered they'd be starting the novel from the very beginning, they both grabbed their pillows and raced upstairs. Lizzie retrieved the book and followed, hoping that at least a handful of the men would be interested. She would have one, at least. She knew she could count on Lieutenant Shuler.

When she gained the top stair, she found the second-floor hallway full. Soldiers and nuns sat packed closely together on the landing and overflowed into the thresholds of the bedrooms. Every soldier was present. Some sat on chairs; others lay on pallets on the bare wooden floor. A few sat on the stairs leading up to the attic. Roland, she noticed, was on one of the cots that had arrived earlier that morning—but still looked no more rested than he had yesterday. George was beside him, sitting on the floor. Tempy was there too, having already served everyone tea cakes and hot chocolate.

Lizzie felt the weight of their expectation and hoped she wouldn't disappoint.

CHAPTER 29

"Good evening, gentlemen. Sisters. And children." Lizzie took her seat. Staring out at her audience, she felt far more "onstage" than she'd imagined when first agreeing to read.

"Are you going to do the voices?" Lieutenant Shuler asked from a cot near the front.

"She *always* does the voices," Winder countered, grinning back at him.

Lizzie simply smiled and opened the book. "*A Christmas Carol* by Charles Dickens. Or the title that Master Winder likes best . . . *A Ghost Story of Christmas.*"

"I like that one better too!" Shuler piped up, and several other soldiers agreed.

"'Stave One,'" she read and held up the book, wanting everyone to have a chance to see the decorative chapter title. "'Marley's Ghost.'"

Winder grinned and scooted a little closer, as did Hattie. Lizzie waited until everyone was absolutely quiet before she began.

"'Marley was dead: to begin with. There is no doubt whatever about that. The register of his burial was signed by the clergyman, the clerk, the undertaker, and the chief mourner. Scrooge signed it: and Scrooge's name was good upon 'Change, for anything he chose to put his hand to. Old Marley was as dead as a door-nail.'"

Soft chuckles rippled through the soldiers, while the nuns sat wide-eyed, staring.

As Lizzie read aloud, knowing most of the opening paragraphs by heart, she sneaked occasional looks around the entrance hall, including in Roland's direction. He didn't seem nearly as engaged as the others, and she wondered if perhaps he'd read the book before.

"'The door of Scrooge's counting-house was open that he might keep his eye upon his clerk, who in a dismal little cell beyond, a sort of tank, was copying letters. Scrooge had a very small fire, but the clerk's fire was so very much smaller that it looked like one coal. But he couldn't replenish it, for Scrooge kept the coal-box in his own room.'"

"Selfish," whispered Sister Mary Grace, then she clapped her hand over her mouth. The reaction drew a smattering of laughter.

As Lizzie read, she delighted in catching the subtle changes in expressions from her audience.

"'"A merry Christmas, uncle! God save you!" cried a cheerful voice. It was the voice of Scrooge's nephew, who came upon him so quickly that this was the first intimation he had of his approach.'"

"'"Bah!" said Scrooge'"—Lizzie lowered her voice—"'"Humbug!"'"

She picked out Shuler's laughter among the crowd, finding it interesting to see which lines drew laughter from some yet not from others. But it was Roland's laughter she was listening for. She glanced over at him and found him looking at her. Intently. But he wasn't smiling. She turned the page and continued.

A moment later her gaze fell to a section of dialogue between Scrooge and his nephew—the nephew insistent to know the reason behind his uncle's refusal to attend Christmas dinner at his home—and her cadence slowed.

"'"Why did you get married?" said Scrooge.'" Lizzie stared at the question on the page, the nephew's oh-so-candid and honest reply already resonating inside her. "'"Because I fell in love."'"

Her throat tightened. So simple and easy a response from the nephew. Why had she never noticed it before? And why did her thoughts immediately go to Roland?

Aware of the sudden silence in the room, and of her placement of a pause in the story where Dickens had intended none, she continued, careful not to look in Roland's direction. She added a touch more drama to her voice in hopes of covering her blunder.

"'"Because you fell in *love!*" growled Scrooge, as if that were the only one thing in the world more ridiculous than a merry Christmas . . .'"

Lizzie quickly found her rhythm again and read with a flourish, pausing on occasion to hold up the book and show the pencil-drawn illustrations. Since Christmas was only a week away, she'd planned to read only a portion of the first chapter, having divided the story accordingly. But after Scrooge soundly rebuffed the two portly gentlemen who called on him to request donations for the poor, Lieutenant Shuler insisted she read on.

At Sister Catherine Margaret's hearty "Amen," Lizzie complied, clearing her throat. She wished she'd had the foresight to bring a glass of water with her. And there were no more cups of hot chocolate that she could see.

"'Scrooge took his melancholy dinner in his usual melancholy tavern; and having read all the newspapers, and beguiled the rest of the evening with his banker's-book, went home to bed. He lived in chambers which had once belonged to his deceased partner, [old Jacob Marley]. They were a gloomy suite of rooms . . .'"

From the corner of her eye, she saw Roland lean down and whisper something to George, who ducked into the bedroom and appeared moments later with a glass of water.

"Thank you, George," she whispered and took a sip.

She shot a look of gratitude at Roland too, and he offered a tiny salute with his bandaged hand. But still no smile.

Parched throat refreshed, she found her place in the story again and made note to pay close attention to the nuns. "'The yard was so dark that even Scrooge, who knew its every stone, was fain to grope with his hands.'" She softened her voice, and everyone seemed to instinctively lean forward.

"'The fog and frost so hung about the black old gateway of the house, that it seemed as if the Genius of the Weather sat in mournful meditation on the threshold.

"'And then let any man explain to me, if he can, how it happened that Scrooge, having his key in the lock of the door, saw in the knocker, without its undergoing any intermediate process of change—not a knocker, but Marley's face.'"

The nuns took a collective breath.

"'It was not angry or ferocious,'" Lizzie continued, delighted to find even the soldiers spellbound, including Lieutenant Taylor and Private Smith. Even Roland seemed to be enjoying it now. "'As Scrooge looked fixedly at this phenomenon . . . it was a knocker again.'" She widened her eyes.

"Lord help us all," Sister Angelica whispered, then made the sign of the cross and kissed her rosary.

Lizzie couldn't help but smile, as did others. But knowing what part of the story lay ahead, she dissolved her smile quickly. She read to them about Marley's ghostly visitation upon Ebenezer Scrooge and of the purpose of Marley's coming. "'"I am here to-night to warn you, that you have yet a chance and hope of escaping my fate."'"

She turned the page. "'"You will be haunted . . . by Three Spirits . . . Without their visits," said the Ghost, "you cannot hope to shun the path I tread. Expect the first visit to-morrow, when the bell . . . tolls . . . One."'" As if someone downstairs were in cahoots, the clock in the family parlor chimed the hour.

Lizzie could almost feel the cumulative rise of gooseflesh. Eyes widened. And she swiftly took advantage of the moment. "And that, my dear listeners, is where we will pause in the story for this evening."

A resounding chorus of noes rose up, but she assured them she would read more the following night. As she closed the book, something slipped from the pages and fell to the floor. Thaddeus's letters that she'd slid between the back pages for safekeeping. She reached down to pick them up, but George beat her to it.

"Here you go, Miss Lizzie."

"Thank you, George." As she took the letters, she felt Roland's attention and looked over.

We need to talk about those, he mouthed silently, and she nodded. She slipped the bundle into her skirt pocket.

"You read mighty fine, ma'am," George offered. "Your voice is somethin' akin to music. It's easy to listen to."

"That's very kind of you to say. Thank you. And I'm not sure if Tempy told you yet, but I have some things that need to be moved in the morning. If you'll check with her, she'll give you the details."

Without a blink, George nodded, seeming to understand. "Yes, ma'am." He turned back to Roland. "You ready, sir?"

Roland sighed, his expression resigned. "Do I have a choice?"

Puzzled by his reaction, Lizzie watched as George lifted the foot of the cot and started pulling the bed toward the bedroom. Only then did she notice—the cot had wheels on the other end.

"Can I ride with you, Captain?" Winder asked.

"*May* I ride with you," Lizzie corrected.

"May I?" Winder repeated.

Roland nodded and gestured for the boy to climb aboard up by his head, but he didn't seem his usual self. Little wonder, considering what had happened yesterday. He had to be thinking about how drastically his life was going to change if the Confederacy fell. And she already knew he was itching to walk again.

"Dr. Phillips should be by tomorrow or Wednesday," she said, following as George pulled the cot back into the bedroom. "Maybe he'll allow you to begin doing some exercises."

"I hope so. If not, I'm beginning to wonder if I'll ever walk again."

George situated the cot by the hearth, then gave Lizzie a discreet look before he left to help the others.

She leaned down and straightened Roland's blanket. "So how do you like your cot thus far?"

"I'm grateful for it." He grimaced as he pulled himself to a sitting position. "It's a far sight better than the floor."

Giving him the space she sensed he wanted, Lizzie crossed to the bedside to help Sister Catherine assist Lieutenant Shuler into bed. It was then that she caught a whiff of something unpleasant. The nun's furtive look said she smelled it too. Several of the soldiers weren't as mindful of hygiene as they should be, but she hadn't noticed that with Shuler before. And this smelled . . . different.

"Lieutenant, Miss Clouston and I are going to check your wound, if you don't mind."

"I don't mind at all, Sister. It's taken to hurtin' in the last day or so. Kept me up some of the night too."

Sister Catherine removed the bandage from his arm, and Lizzie schooled her features not to show a reaction. A black spot, no larger than a dime, had formed on the incision near the drainage hole, and the skin around it was red and swollen. She'd checked the wound herself yesterday, and while it had been swollen and sensitive when she cleaned it, there'd been no blackened flesh.

She exchanged a look with Sister Catherine, who gave an almost imperceptible shake of her head. Lizzie laid a gentle hand on the lieutenant's arm.

"I believe we need a fresh bandage on this, Lieutenant Shuler. I'll fetch some water while Sister Catherine Margaret gets some clean cloths. We'll be back shortly."

Lizzie reached the hallway first and turned. "Gangrene," she whispered.

Sister Catherine nodded. "If Dr. Phillips doesn't come within the next two to three days, we'll need to send for someone."

"Agreed. And if it spreads, they'll likely need to take more of his arm." She winced at the prospect. "But for now, we'll clean it as best we can. I'll give him a small amount of morphine for the pain." Lizzie glanced back toward the room. "He's so young."

"And he may yet live, Miss Clouston. If God chooses," the nun added quietly.

Together they cleaned the lieutenant's wound and dressed it with a fresh bandage. After which Sister Catherine offered a prayer on his behalf and excused herself to help another soldier. Lizzie administered the morphine, then set the bottle on the bedside table.

She pulled a chair up beside the bed, ever mindful of Roland on his cot only feet away, watching her every move.

Roland couldn't explain it, but being around Lizzie tonight, watching her as she read, listening to her voice, studying the soft curves of her face, only made him feel more alone. And desperate. Like a man parched with thirst with the fountain of life lying just beyond his reach.

Lizzie scooted her chair closer to Shuler's bedside, and the young lieutenant's countenance brightened. Shuler hadn't felt too well lately, so it was good to see that reaction from him.

"Lieutenant . . ." Lizzie leaned forward. "You said your mother used to read to you when you were younger."

"Yes, ma'am, she did. She read good too. But maybe not as good as you."

Gratitude lit her eyes. "Since you love reading so much, I'll bring you a couple of my favorite books. Then you can choose which one you'd like best to read."

A shadow flitted across the boy's face, as though he couldn't believe she'd made such an offer. Or maybe, Roland wondered, there was another reason behind that look.

"Thank you, Miss Clouston," Shuler said softly. "That's real kind of you."

"Do you know, Lieutenant, that yours was the very first surgery I ever assisted Dr. Phillips with?"

"I wondered about it that night, ma'am. But you had such kindness in your face, I figured what you didn't know, the doc could walk you through. And that somehow all his learnin' would make up for how affrighted you looked. But kindness . . ." He exhaled slowly. "Kindness is a harder thing to be taught."

Her expression softened. "That's very true about kindness, Lieutenant. And also very gracious of you to say. Thank you."

Shuler nodded, his eyes briefly slipping closed.

"What's also true is that I certainly *was* affrighted that night." She made a face that drew a grin from the young lieutenant and encouraged a similar reaction from Roland.

Shuler laughed, then a shyness seemed to come over him. "I'd be obliged, Miss Clouston, if you'd call me James."

"James it is." Lizzie narrowed her eyes. "James . . . Campbell . . . Shuler, I believe."

"You remembered!"

"How could I ever forget you, James? Now—" She rose, a glistening in her eyes. "You let that morphine relax you, and you get some rest."

"Yes, ma'am. I already feel it tuggin' on me. Like one of those apple-brandy hot toddies my mama used to make." He yawned. "They sure were good."

She leaned down and kissed the young man's forehead. "I'm sure they were. And I'm sure your mother misses you very much and looks forward to you coming home."

Shuler went quiet. "My mama's in heaven, Miss Clouston. She died last year, while I was away fightin'. I hate it that . . . that I wasn't there for her in her last days."

Lizzie brushed the hair back from his forehead, and Roland could all but feel the softness of her touch on his own skin. Shuler closed his eyes, and soon his breathing came steady and even. Same as that from the rest of the other soldiers in the room, if their gentle, morphine-induced snores were any indication. She rose as if to leave, but Roland didn't want her to. Not yet.

"He's right, you know," he whispered.

She looked over.

"About your kindness. It's the second thing I noticed about you."

Brow rising, she stepped closer. "What was the first?"

Liking her response, he didn't answer immediately, and a blush slowly crept into her cheeks.

"That you're a woman of honor. A woman who keeps her word."

He'd meant it as a compliment, but even he had heard the regret in his voice. And judging by her expression, so had she. The clock from somewhere downstairs struck the eleventh hour, and the chimes reverberated in the silence. He held her attention, wondering if she had any idea what effect she had on him. His gaze lowered to her mouth and lingered, and he would've sworn her breath quickened. Even without touching her, which he wanted to do, she sent his pulse and thoughts racing. The last chime faded and she looked away, fingering the collar of her shirtwaist.

"Thank you, Roland," she whispered. "That means a great deal to me, coming from you. Now, was there something you wanted to tell me?"

Hearing the definite closing of a door between them, he begrudgingly followed her lead. "I sent George to town yesterday to look for a man, a preacher, who was with us the night of the battle. I hadn't heard what happened to him, if he'd made it through. But George said a lieutenant told him the preacher had been wounded but was very much alive. George left word with the officer to ask him to come to Carnton as soon as he can. If that man ever met Thaddeus, he'll remember him. I'm sure of it."

"Thank you for doing that."

He could tell from her tone that it wasn't as promising of a prospect as she'd hoped it would be.

"Don't lose heart, Lizzie. There's got to be record of that boy somewhere. We'll find it."

She nodded. Seconds passed, and she turned to go.

"I wasn't there either, you know. For Weet and Lena when they got sick. I was away fighting, like Shuler. Fighting for home and family. While my wife and daughter died." The wind howled beyond the windows, and a downdraft caused the fire in the hearth to dance and sputter. "Influenza took Weet first. Lena followed three days later. I didn't even know about their deaths until they'd already been gone nearly a month. My mother wrote to tell me, but the mail hadn't caught up with our regiment."

"I'm so sorry, Roland."

The compassion in her expression moved him, which only fed his frustration over the fact that she could never be his. "I've wondered this for a long time, but especially over the last couple of days . . . Was all of this worth it? And now, looking where we've come to, I don't think it was. Because maybe if I'd been there, they wouldn't have died. Susan asked me to come home so many times in her letters. But I was so busy fighting to keep our land, our home, our future." He gave a rueful smile. "Ironic, isn't it?"

"Roland, there was no way you could have known they would get sick and die. And with influenza, there was likely little, if anything, you could have done to prevent the outcome."

"But I could've been there for them, couldn't I? If I hadn't been away fighting. Surely you've thought that of me."

She stared, an injured look moving over her face. "No, I've never thought that about you."

"Really? Even with how you feel about this war?"

She froze. Then swallowed hard. "I-I don't know what you mean."

"Don't you? Don't you feel about the Confederacy the same way you feel about men who own slaves?"

The instant he said it, Roland saw the shock—and fear—on her face and wished he could take back the words. But the guilt gnawing at him over not having been there for Susan and Lena, coupled with his growing desire for the woman standing before him—so beautiful, so close he could touch her, yet so unattainable—had him surly and itching for a fight.

CHAPTER 30

Lizzie's heart pounded in her ears. She wanted to believe she'd misheard him, but knew she hadn't. "H-how do you know—"

"I'm sorry, Lizzie. I shouldn't have said that. Or at least, I shouldn't have said it in that manner."

"But how do you know?" If the McGavocks found out, if he were to tell them . . .

He sighed. "It was the day you gave me Sir Horace here." He gestured to the bear wedged behind his head.

She looked at the bear, then back at him, not following.

"You were surprised to discover George was a slave. Then you asked me how many slaves I owned. Your disapproval was fairly tangible."

She didn't like it that she could be so easily read. But even more frustrating, she realized that he'd been waiting to bring this up. "It's true." She kept her voice low and quickly surveyed the room to make certain everyone was still asleep. "I've long believed that slavery is immoral."

His expression darkened. "So you're saying that *I* am immoral?"

His voice came out a harsh whisper, and she gestured for him to keep his voice down.

"No, I—" She firmed her lips. "I don't think you're an immoral man. At least, not in a general sense. But I do believe that . . ."

"That I'm immoral in the sense that I own slaves?"

She squeezed her eyes tight, the toll of recent days catching up with her. "Roland, I don't think that now is the appropriate time for this conversation. Why don't we wait until we're both more—"

"I'd like an answer to my question," he whispered. "Do you believe I am an immoral man because I own slaves?"

She'd sensed earlier in the evening that something was troubling him, but she never would have suspected this. She saw the anger and hurt in his eyes and wanted to believe that his lashing out stemmed from the Confederate defeat and his mourning his wife and child, and that she had just happened to get in the way. But she wasn't so sure. She took a breath, then gave it slow release. "I believe that it is immoral for one human being to own another."

He laughed beneath his breath. "Even though slavery has existed throughout history and it's the natural state of mankind? You're an educated woman, Lizzie. Surely you know that the Greeks had slaves, the Romans had slaves, and the English had slavery until very recently. Even Abraham, in the Bible, had slaves."

"Yes, but just because something has always been a certain way doesn't mean it's right."

"Saint Paul returned a runaway slave, Philemon, to his master." He continued unabated, as though he'd faced this argument before. "And slavery was widespread in Jesus' time, yet he never condemned it."

"You know your Bible. Good. But the Word of God also says that he created man in his own image, both male and female. So we are *all* made in the image of God. Would you agree with that?"

"Most certainly. But we are not all equal in our abilities and our roles. God has gifted us differently, both individually and according to our gender. And also in varying groups of people."

She eyed him. "So you're saying that God created some groups of people specifically to be slaves?"

He held up a hand. "I do not share the belief that Negroes are biologically inferior to whites. I've encountered that argument numerous times in both social and scientific circles and find it a baseless premise."

"Well, at least that's something we can agree on. Except that I find that specific argument not only baseless but demoralizing and wrong-headed." Knowing she was dancing close to a line best not crossed, she wanted to help him see where he was wrong. "So tell me, if you don't believe Negroes are inferior to whites, have you allowed your slaves to be educated? To learn to read and write?"

His face flushed red. "Firstly, to have taught my slaves to write would've been against the law of the land, and you know that. Secondly, learning to write isn't a skill that's required in their daily lives. So to have taught them to write would have been for naught."

Heat rose in her chest, yet she kept her voice low. "Actually, it isn't the 'law of the land.' If it were, that would mean it was applicable to the entire country. Anti-literacy laws were passed by individual states." She knew she sounded like a teacher addressing an unruly child, but she didn't care. "As for what's required in a person's daily life, I believe each person should be given the right to decide that for himself. I doubt either of us would take kindly to someone else deciding for us what we can and cannot do, or where we can and cannot go. Or whether we are allowed to learn to read and write. Or even how we should be treated. Is that the life you would want to live if you had the power to change it?"

"I have always treated my slaves with decency and respect, Lizzie. I've never lifted a harsh hand to any of them."

"I'm not insinuating that you have."

"I care for George and his family. And for Ezra and Rachel, our house slaves. George and I grew up together. He and his family mean almost as much to me as my own blood relations."

"I don't doubt that for a second." And she didn't. She'd observed his behavior toward George. She heard the earnestness in his voice even now, and the look in his eyes was nothing short of sincere.

"Have you considered, Lizzie, the profound effect that abolishing slavery will have on our economy? The cotton market will collapse. Tobacco crops will dry in the fields. Rice will no longer be a profitable crop to raise. Tens of thousands stand to lose their jobs. Uprisings and chaos are sure to ensue."

She shook her head, hearing what he'd said but wondering if *he* had. "I'm not saying adjustments won't need to be made. Difficult and widespread adjustments. But if something is morally wrong, Roland, we have a sacred obligation to make it right. After all, as someone wise once said"—she offered a smile to soften the words, praying he would receive them as she intended—"real heroes are the ones who do what's right even when no one's looking, and who give up something for someone else even when it costs them dearly."

He winced but didn't look away. And neither did she.

"You feel most strongly about this, don't you?" he finally whispered, his voice surprisingly calm.

She nodded, hopeful that some of what she was saying was getting through. "I do. Very much so."

He nodded. "So I'm curious . . . What do the McGavocks think about your beliefs on slavery? And your feelings about their being slave owners?"

She blinked, knowing he already knew the answer. "Colonel and Mrs. McGavock are not aware of my beliefs. I am their children's governess. They hired me to teach them, not to impose my personal views on the family. Besides, I'm not a landowner, nor do I hold influence in that realm. And as a woman, I don't even have the right to vote."

"I see." He studied her. "So what you said a moment ago, that when something is morally wrong and we have a sacred obligation to make it right—that only applies if it falls within our purview. Or what we believe our purview to be. If not, then we can turn a blind eye and do nothing. Are you saying that's the scope of our 'sacred obligation'?"

An anvil to the gut would have been less painful. Lizzie put a hand to her midsection, her breath shallow and uneven. She wanted to respond but couldn't. Not with the weight of her own culpability pressing down hard.

"You know," he continued, "perhaps you were right. Now may not be the appropriate time for this conversation. Allow me to bid you a good night."

"Good night," she said and managed to hold back the tears until she reached the stairs leading down to the kitchen. There she sank down on the cold, hard stone, face in her hands, and wept.

She'd wondered before what might have happened between her and Roland if she were not already betrothed to Towny. The one thing that certainly would have kept them apart—slavery—had been dealt a near deathblow yesterday. Yet as kind a man as Roland Jones was, as much as his first wife had obviously loved him, and even as well as he seemed to treat George, he was still a man who considered it morally acceptable to own another human being. And being married to a man who held that belief was something she could never abide.

Not that he'd given her any indication that his personal interest in her ran along so deep a line.

But what cut her to the quick was the lie she'd believed for so long. She'd been raised in a world where slavery was accepted, even celebrated, and for years she'd lived beneath the facade of being powerless and unable to bring about change. When in reality, she'd had the power all along. Not to change the world. That wasn't her "purview," as Roland had so plainly put it just now. But to change her corner of the world . . . here at Carnton. And she was more determined now than ever before to do just that.

But what if Roland chose to tell Colonel and Mrs. McGavock? She honestly didn't know what they would do, how they would react upon learning about her opinions. She wished now that she'd had the presence of mind to ask him. But if he did choose to tell them, she would simply have to deal with the repercussions. The thought of which turned her stomach.

Minutes later, as she eased into bed beside Winder and Hattie, she curled onto her side, wondering if Roland had realized yet what he'd said when he'd listed the effects that abolishing slavery would have on the economy. He hadn't used the word *if* or *might*. He'd said *will*, as in will happen. And that gave her a sliver of fresh hope. Because that told her that not only did he, too, believe the end of slavery was coming, but he was already thinking about what his life would be like without it. And that meant change was coming for George and his family.

Roland slept fitfully and awakened before dawn, his body slicked in sweat despite the chill in the room. He wished he could go right now, find Lizzie, and apologize to her. Tell her he didn't know what had gotten into him but he was sorry. Yet he *did* know what had gotten into him, why he'd taken his anger out on her. At least in part. She'd held a mirror up to him, and he hadn't liked what he'd seen.

I doubt either of us would take kindly to someone else deciding for us what we can and cannot do, or where we can and cannot go.

He raked a hand over his face. How many hundreds of times had he lain here in recent days feeling helpless? Unable to go anywhere or do anything. Having no control over his destiny.

But it wasn't that way for George and the other slaves on his estate, he told himself. He had always prided himself on running an efficient, humane estate. He took care of his slaves. But teaching them, even if it were not against the law, wouldn't have been a good use of time or energy for either party. Slaves had no need of book learning. And though what he'd said to Lizzie was true, that he didn't consider Negroes inferior to whites, they *were* different. He'd learned that from his father and grandfather. Slaves didn't take well to schooling. They found the various subjects frustrating and needless, and forcing them to take part would soon become a source of contention. Lizzie didn't understand that because she'd never owned slaves.

Thirsty, he looked out toward the hallway, wishing George were within earshot instead of staying in one of the slave houses near the barn, so he could have better attended to his needs.

Is that the life you would want to live if you had the power to change it? Even now in the early morning silence, Lizzie's question dogged him.

She'd spoken to him last night like he was some recalcitrant youth. At the time it had sent the heat in his chest to a steady simmer. But in reflection, and as streaks of purple began coloring the horizon beyond the windows, the questions she'd asked began to seep deep inside. He still didn't agree with her, but at least he understood better now how she'd arrived at her conclusions. While Lizzie Clouston wasn't what some would consider young anymore, she still had an innocence about her. She simply didn't understand what it took to keep the wheels of progress—the economy in this instance—maintained and moving forward. It was larger than any one person or group of people.

If he'd broached the conversation differently last night, which he wished he had, he could've told her how vile he considered the all-too-common mistreatment of slaves. He in no way condoned that. But there *was* a natural order to things. There always had been. For all her book learning, she simply didn't understand that.

His lower right calf began to itch. He slowly pushed to sitting and reached down as far as he could. George had said that as the poultices did their work and the wounds continued to heal, they'd itch something fierce. And they did. Roland looked around for something to use to reach the itch, but he couldn't find anything nearly long enough. So carefully, very carefully, he bent his right knee as far as he could. He carefully ran his fingertips over the wounds and sighed in relief. Drawing up his leg hadn't hurt as badly as he'd anticipated. Again recalling what George had said about how movement went hand in hand with healing, he decided to try it again. And then a third time. He switched to his left leg and discovered he could move that one even more easily. Which made sense, it being less damaged.

He lay back, grateful again to be off the floor, and gripped the sides of the wooden cot. He tried lifting his right leg straight up and made it about halfway before the pain said enough. He slowly lowered it and switched back to the left.

By the time the sun came up and others in the room were awakening, he was bathed in sweat again and his strength was all but depleted. But he felt better than he had since the moment that stand of grapeshot had exploded right in front of him. Surely that portended something good.

CHAPTER 31

Lizzie slipped in through the back door off the gallery porch and quietly closed the door behind her. It was still early yet. The sun wasn't up, and the house was quiet. Her first teaching session with Tempy and George had gone fairly well, and already she could see that Tempy was going to be a quick learner. But George, like a parched sponge ready to soak up water, was almost too eager to learn. While patient with others, he did not extend the same grace to himself, and he'd left their lesson frustrated and dejected looking. She felt for him. But having taught many pupils to read thus far—granted, all of them children—she firmly believed that once he loosened the grip on the reins, things would fall into place. But where to meet for their lessons had proven to be a challenge.

After George managed to surprise her and Tempy in the kitchen days earlier, they agreed that somewhere outside the house would be best. After discussing it, they'd settled on the barn. Since sending the slaves away three years earlier, the colonel had hired hands who helped with the farm, and Lizzie knew their schedules. The barn was a hefty stone's throw from the slave house where George was staying, so he could slip over through the trees with little chance of being seen. Plus, no one would question his entering the barn so early.

As for her and Tempy's excuse should they be seen coming and going, Tempy had come up with a believable alibi. With the soldiers convalescing at Carnton, Lizzie spent more time helping in the kitchen and sometimes gathered eggs from the coop behind the barn. Hence, the slightly heavier than usual basket on her arm. A thick cloth nesting fresh eggs hid her teaching materials on the bottom. Tempy carried a basket with something she'd retrieved from the springhouse. They had everything covered. Still, Lizzie wished they didn't have to resort to subterfuge.

Adjusting the basket, Lizzie crossed the entrance hall toward the dining room.

"Miss Clouston. A word with you, please."

She jumped at the voice, then spotted Dr. Phillips descending the staircase. "Good morning, Doctor." She set the basket on the floor inside the dining room, then met him at the base of the stairs.

Voices drifted down from above, and she was certain one of them was Roland's. Her first order of business that morning was to ask him if he intended to tell the McGavocks what he'd confirmed about her last night.

"Miss Clouston, good day to you, ma'am."

"Good day. You're certainly here early. I'd heard you might come this morning. I hope you're well." The tiny lines around the surgeon's eyes were more pronounced than she remembered, and he wore a beleaguered look she'd seen on too many faces in recent days.

"I am, Miss Clouston, for the most part. And hope you're the same. But you're up before the sun. When exactly do you sleep, ma'am?"

Lizzie waved away the comment. "I manage. And as you say, I'm well too, for the most part. Ready for this war to be over."

His sigh seemed to carry the weight of the world. "As am I. And as I am coming to believe it soon will be."

She frowned. "Do you come with news?"

He nodded. "Though not good news, I'm afraid. At present Hood's army is scattered and desperately trying to escape wholesale destruction. He's issued marching orders. The troops are to meet in Tupelo, Mississippi, where they'll set up winter camp. But the men are worn down, hungry, and half frozen. What they've endured is simply too much for weary, mortal men to stand. Many see an inevitable end in sight and are deserting."

Even as the softest brush of hope swept through her, so did a sense of dread. "I don't expect you to remember him specifically, Doctor, but by chance have you come across a Lieutenant Blake Townsend? The soldier you were treating when I met you both on the battlefield that day. I have yet to hear from him after Nashville."

"I'm sorry, ma'am, I haven't. But I've mainly been with Loring's Division."

She nodded. She knew it had been a long shot. *Please, Towny, be alive and well somewhere.* The thought swept heavenward, and she made a mental note to relay the doctor's update to Towny's father at the first opportunity.

Breaking with decorum, Dr. Phillips took a seat on the second to last stair, and she joined him. A warm sun shone through the arched fanlight window above the front doors, and though the temperatures were still chilly, the ice and snow that had held the land in their frozen grip had finally begun to melt, as evidenced by the runoff from the roof and upper porches.

She listened as he spoke of what had happened during the battle in Nashville and in the days following. With every word, Lizzie felt the end drawing steadily closer.

"I'm sorry, Miss Clouston. Perhaps I speak more freely than I should."

"Not at all, Doctor. I appreciate your candor. Although this news doesn't inspire optimism for the Confederacy."

His smile held a sad quality. "If one desires optimism, one should not seek it amidst war."

Knowing he was right, she found her gaze drawn to a particularly dark stain on the bare wooden floor. "I'm weary of death," she whispered.

"And I'm weary of men devising new ways of killing one another." He opened his palms and stared at them. "These hands have become far too proficient at suturing holes in men's bodies and at removing limbs, Miss Clouston." He looked over at her. "And I hesitate to tell you, but I have yet another to amputate."

She didn't have to guess. "Lieutenant Shuler."

He nodded. "I told the young lieutenant just now. It's his only hope against the gangrene that's set in. He's frightened, understandably, and he asked if you would be there to assist me. However, if you're busy, there's another doctor in town making rounds. I could send for him and—"

"No." Lizzie forced a reassuring look. She was not at all eager to repeat the experience, but how could she say no, considering? "If Lieutenant Shuler wants me there, I'll be there. When do you prefer to do the procedure?" Reading the answer in his expression, she nodded. "All right then. Give me a few moments to tell Mrs. McGavock and to see the children settled in the kitchen with Tempy. I'll fetch an apron and join you. Upstairs, I presume?"

"Yes. Thank you, Miss Clouston. I'll see you shortly." He started back up the stairs.

"Doctor . . ."

He paused.

"Do you believe this will work? That it will save young James?"

"I believe that taking that arm will give him the best possible chance. But as I learned long ago, Miss Clouston, there's a reason we physicians still use the term *practicing* medicine."

LIZZIE CLIMBED THE stairs to the second-floor landing, her stomach in knots as details of the surgical procedure returned with all-too-vivid clarity. Why she would be struck with such nerves after already assisting and observing the surgery so many times, she wasn't sure. Until she walked into the bedroom and saw James lying atop the freshly painted bedroom door that had once again been removed from its hinges. This time she knew the patient.

Before, these men had simply been unknown wounded soldiers to her. Now she knew their names and details about their lives, their wives, their families. They'd become friends. Some of them *dear* friends. Her gaze reluctantly moved to Roland who, she discovered with caution, was already looking her way.

To her surprise, his expression held only warmth and understanding, and she could all but read his thoughts—*You can do this, Lizzie. I know you don't want to, but you can do this.*

A rush of gratitude poured through her, covering every trace of lingering frustration from their conversation last night. His confidence in her inspired her own, and she mouthed a soundless, *Thank you*, thankful they'd laid aside their differences in opinion, at least for the moment.

"You're lookin' right nice this mornin', Miss Clouston."

Lizzie turned toward Lieutenant Taylor, whose flirtatious smile had the exact opposite effect of his intention, she felt certain. Not to mention, the way the man sometimes looked at her made her skin crawl. Only two days ago he'd complained most of the day about his amputated leg hurting "somethin' awful." But today that was apparently no longer the case.

"Lieutenant Taylor, you appear to be feeling considerably better today. You must have rested well last night."

"Oh, I did, ma'am. Had me some real sweet dreams. But I, ah . . ." He ran a hand over the several days' growth on his jaw. "I'd sure enjoy me a nice hot shave this afternoon."

Lizzie smiled, two steps ahead of him. "Of course you would. One of the sisters will be free soon enough, and I'm certain she'll be happy to assist you."

His gaze leisurely trailed her up and down. "I was hopin' you'd do the honors, ma'am."

She cocked her head to one side. "I assure you, Lieutenant Taylor, the last thing you want is me holding a razor to your throat."

Smitty snickered softly, and Taylor punched him hard in the arm. Lizzie chose to ignore it. "But again, one of the sisters will be happy to oblige, I'm sure."

To her surprise, Taylor's smile only broadened, and he tipped an invisible hat to her. "Some other time then, Miss Clouston."

If she didn't know better, she might've guessed he'd been into Colonel McGavock's brandy, but that was impossible. Not only because the brandy was locked in a cabinet in the colonel's farm office, but because Lieutenant Taylor wasn't mobile enough to get down the stairs yet. Granted, he did have a pair of crutches, but he wasn't too steady on them. Nor had he, or any of the other amputees, received their artificial limbs yet. Those should be coming soon enough, according to her recent conversation with Jake Winston.

Jake and his wife, Aletta—a woman Lizzie had come to deeply respect and admire, and felt blessed to call a friend—had become quite adept in recent months at designing and fitting artificial limbs for the wounded. They'd visited Carnton in recent days and had fitted all the soldiers for artificial arms and legs. The increasing demand for their work was keeping the couple far too busy.

Focusing her thoughts, Lizzie approached James as he lay waiting, and she felt an unwelcome sense of déjà vu. Only this time, a blanket covered the makeshift surgical table and a tarp had been spread out beneath.

"Good morning, James." She smiled down at him, his face upside down to hers. And even more than the first time they'd met here in this very spot, she saw the fear in his eyes and wished she could say something to relieve it. But everything she thought of seemed so weak and inconsequential compared to the strength he needed in this moment.

Dr. Phillips joined them and placed a gentle hand on the young man's shoulder. "All right, soldier. You know the routine."

"Yes, sir. I-I do." Shuler swallowed hard, the sound audible in the quiet.

Lizzie picked up the cloth and bottle of chloroform. "I'll be right here when you wake up, James."

"*If* he wakes up," came a coarse whisper from the corner.

The lieutenant's breath caught. "Wh-what did Taylor say? Did he say 'if'?"

Lizzie exchanged a look with Dr. Phillips, then leaned closer. "Listen to me, James. You're in very good hands. Dr. Phillips knows exactly what he's doing. And I'm here for you. I won't leave your side for a minute."

"I'm here for you too, Shuler," Roland volunteered from across the room.

"Me too, Shuler," Lieutenant Conrad said, his timid voice sounding rather emboldened.

Emotion pooled in James's eyes and he nodded. A tear slipped down his temple. Lizzie gently wiped it away, then tented the cloth over his nose and tipped the bottle ever so—

"Wait!" Shuler whispered.

Lizzie held the bottle in check.

"Miss Clouston . . ." He blinked. "Would you speak somethin' over me as you put me under? Anything. I don't care what. I just want to hear your voice. The sound of it does me good."

His request brought tears to her eyes. "Of course," she whispered. Then as she reached for what to recite, her mind went blank. She couldn't think of anything. Not a paragraph from a book, not the beginning of a story. Not even—

Then it came to her, and she smiled down at him. "'The LORD is my shepherd,'" she said softly. "'I shall not want. He maketh me to lie down in green pastures: he leadeth me beside the still waters. He restoreth my soul.'" She tented the cloth over his nose, aware of him watching her. "'He leadeth me in the paths of righteousness for his name's sake.'" She tipped the bottle ever so slightly, until it dripped . . . dripped . . . dripped. "'Yea, though I walk through the valley of the shadow of death, I will fear no evil: for thou art with me; thy rod and thy staff they comfort me.'"

His eyes fluttered closed, but his hands remained fisted at his sides.

"'Thou preparest a table before me in the presence of mine enemies: thou anointest my head with oil.'"

Gradually, his fists went lax on the table.

"'My cup runneth over.'"

His body went limp. And Dr. Phillips, scalpel in hand, began.

"'Surely goodness and mercy shall follow me all the days of my life,'" Lizzie continued, leaning close to James's ear. "'And I will dwell in the house of the LORD for ever.'"

"Lieutenant Shuler . . ." Dr. Phillips leaned over the bed. "Can you hear me, soldier?"

Roland raised up on his cot to see the young lieutenant's face better. It had been a good two hours since the doc completed the surgery, and Shuler should have awakened by now.

Perched on the bedside, Lizzie brushed the hair back from the man's forehead, and Roland had no trouble whatsoever picturing her as a mother with children of her own. How blessed those children would be to have her in their corner. He had yet to talk to her about their conversation last night, but he'd felt a sense of peace between them when she'd walked into the room. But knowing her as he did, she'd make sure that conversation was continued at the first possible moment. And he was counting on it.

He only hoped she'd given his perspective some thought, as he'd given hers. In his experience, abolitionists often didn't think the issue through on a thorough enough level. Which, he was certain, was the case with her. She had a kind and caring heart, no doubt about that.

She simply needed to be shown a broader perspective. Then she would understand.

The doc placed the bulb-shaped end of the stethoscope against Shuler's chest. "His heart sounds fine."

Lizzie peered up, worry in her eyes. "You don't think I administered too much chloroform?"

The doctor shook his head. "No. You performed excellently, Miss Clouston. As good as any attendant who's ever assisted me. Better, in fact. Those young boys don't possess near the bedside manner you do. But neither do I, for that matter." He smiled, then looked back at Shuler. "I've seen this on occasion, this resistance to awaken following surgery. Though, granted, it usually occurs in older patients. But there's no need to be alarmed yet."

"I told you he wouldn't wake up."

Roland glared across the room, looking forward to the day he could put Taylor in his place. "Taylor, I—" But before he could finish his sentence, Lizzie was up off the bed and marching toward the second lieutenant.

"Lieutenant Taylor, you are a hair's breadth away from being carried from this house and placed in one of the outbuildings, without benefit of care, until the Federal Army can be contacted to come and escort you to prison. Do you understand me?"

Taylor grinned up at her. "You're not in charge around here, missy. Your threats mean nothin'. If I have to, I'll take up my case with Colonel McGavock."

Lizzie stared. "Whose idea do you think this was to begin with?"

Taylor's grin faded. "Well, it's not my fault that—"

Lizzie held up a forefinger, looking every bit the schoolmarm. Or school*master*. "Not. One. More. Word."

Taylor's face went beet red, and Roland wondered if the man's head would explode from keeping all that bull and guff bottled up inside him. One could only hope.

Lizzie strode back to the bedside, took Shuler's hand in hers, and bent close to his face. "James Campbell Shuler," she whispered, her tone tight with emotion, "if you can hear my voice, I want you to squeeze my hand." She waited, her attention glued to his features, her own growing more desperate. "James, I said . . . *squeeze my hand*."

She sucked in a breath and looked down at the lieutenant's hand clasped in hers, then over at the doctor—and smiled. Roland felt a stirring in his chest as the young soldier's eyes flickered open. Lizzie pressed a quick kiss to the lieutenant's forehead, and Shuler grinned like a young boy.

"I'm still here," he whispered, his voice hoarse.

"Of course you're still here, James." Lizzie beamed. "And everything with the surgery went perfectly."

Dr. Phillips briefly examined him, then reached into his leather satchel and withdrew a bottle. "Miss Clouston, let's give him two grains of morphine to help ease the pain. Slightly more if he needs it. He can have this up to three times a day."

"Actually, I have a bottle right here on the—" She paused and searched the bedside table. "Oh, I must have taken it back downstairs." Then she turned and looked back across the room. Her eyes narrowed. She strode to where Taylor sat, reached down, and grabbed his dingy knapsack.

"What are you doin'? That's mine!" He reached for the pack.

It was all Roland could do not to come off the cot. Or at least try. But he had a good mind about how that would end up.

Lizzie easily evaded Taylor's efforts and rifled through the contents. "Yes, the pack is yours, Lieutenant Taylor. But this"—she held up a bottle of morphine—"is the property of the Confederate Army."

Taylor shook his head. "I don't know how that got in there." He looked around. "Smitty probably did it."

Private Smith gawked. "It weren't me. You told me—"

Taylor socked him in the jaw, then pointed at Roland. "It musta been that no-good darky that belongs to Captain Jones. I seen that boy in here rootin' around everybody's stuff."

Before Roland could respond, Lizzie threw the pack back at Taylor's chest.

"We both know it wasn't George, Lieutenant." She held up the bottle. "I've a good mind not to give you any more of this at all."

Taylor's face blanched. "That ain't your call! I'm a soldier of the—"

"It might not be her call, Taylor. But it *is* mine." Dr. Phillips stood over him. "And you just lost one dose a day."

"But, Doc, I'm hurtin'—"

"Try anything like this again and you're on your way to Nashville. I'll load you onto the flatcar myself. Now shut your mouth and be grateful I'm not taking you to the station right now."

Taylor did as Phillips said until the doctor left a few minutes later. Then he grabbed his crutches, managed to stand after a couple of tries, and hobbled to the bedroom across the hall, glaring at Roland and Lizzie as he did.

"That man," she said beneath her breath, feeling Shuler's forehead.

Roland eyed her. "Remind me not to play baseball with you, Miss Clouston."

She shook her head, then a smile tipped her mouth. "I do have a pretty strong throw."

Roland laughed softly. "As evidenced. But can you skip rocks?"

"With the best of them."

He felt a definite truce between them, especially when she came over and sat in the chair by the hearth.

"About what we were discussing last night," she said in low tones.

He already knew where she was headed. "Say no more. It won't go any further."

Her eyes widened. She seemed surprised. "Thank you. I *will* tell them. I simply want to tell them in my own time."

He nodded. "Understood. It's not my business to share anyway.

And I'm sorry that I broached the subject the way I did. It was rude of me."

She held his gaze for a beat, then smiled. "Yes, it was."

He laughed, knowing more than ever how lucky a man Lieutenant Townsend really was. Last he'd asked her, Lizzie hadn't received word from him following the battle in Nashville. But he knew she would tell him when she did.

She rose to leave, then paused. "Have you received any word from the preacher? About when he might be coming to see us?"

"Not yet. But we will. If there's one thing he is, it's dependable." Yet with every day that passed since George had gone into town looking for him, Roland wondered if Bounds had ever gotten his note. Perhaps he had moved on south with the army, per the doc's latest update. Whatever the case, Lizzie's fading hope was evident in her wistful expression, and Roland knew how much this meant to her. Whatever he needed to do, he was going to help her find that boy's mother.

CHAPTER 32

Lizzie headed toward the kitchen to get the children's midmorning snack. Customarily she didn't hold class on Saturday mornings, but since she and the children had missed so many lessons earlier this month, they were making up for lost time—with Mrs. McGavock's blessing. But even with the Christmas tree adorning the table in the front entrance hall and candles lit and set in the windows, it simply didn't feel like Christmas Eve. Not with all that had transpired in the past month.

Thus far, the definite highlight of recent days had been her lessons with Tempy and George. She looked forward to their time together and was impressed with the questions they asked and the progress they were making. George remained impatient to begin reading. But as she'd told him more than once, he had to learn to walk before he could run. She'd also visited Mr. Townsend earlier that week when she'd gone into town to see her parents and to order teaching supplies. Seeing Towny's father had done her heart good. She relayed the news Dr. Phillips had shared about the army wintering in Tupelo. Mr. Townsend hadn't received any word from Towny either, but was clinging to the hope that his only son was still alive. She was doing the same.

The nightly readings from *A Christmas Carol* had also been a bright spot. But tonight would be their last, following a dinner of beef stew and Tempy's fried dried peach pies.

As Lizzie entered the kitchen, she smelled the buttery aroma of piecrust frying in the pan. She inhaled deeply. "It wouldn't be Christmas Eve, Tempy, without your fried pies. The soldiers are in for a treat!"

Tempy smiled. "I always like makin' 'em. Makes me feel closer to my mama somehow. Even though she been gone now for more years than I can recollect."

Lizzie moved closer so she could watch how Tempy was cooking them. "Do you have any family left? That you know of," she amended, knowing how slave families were often separated.

"My sister and brother may still be out there somewhere, but I got no way of knowin'. I always think, though, come this time of year, how fine it would be for one of 'em to walk through that door and surprise me."

Lizzy wished that could happen, even while knowing the likelihood was slim. Since she and Tempy had started their lessons together, their conversations were fuller and richer. They were becoming friends instead of two women who worked in the same house. And Lizzie liked the change.

"You ain't heard from your Lieutenant Townsend yet?"

"Not yet. I keep hoping to." Lizzie saw the tray for the children mostly ready. All except for the glasses of milk.

"Last time he came by, did y'all have a chance to talk 'bout your weddin' plans?"

Lizzie retrieved glasses from the cupboard, then paused. "That night he was here, he asked me to marry him. Right then. He'd already stopped by the preacher's house in town to arrange it. He even gave me his mother's ring for safekeeping."

Tempy turned and looked back, her gaze appraising. "I had me a feelin' somethin' was goin' on when he raced up them stairs that night. I guess from the looks o' things, Miss Lizzie, you told him no."

"I simply couldn't do it. It felt too quick. And . . . not right."

Tempy paused from turning the pies, spatula in hand. "Why not right?"

Lizzie debated whether or not to share her and Towny's last conversation. Specifically the part about how she'd been honest with him about why she'd said yes. She told herself her hesitation was due to her not wanting to disparage Towny in any way—but really, she didn't want to risk Tempy thinking any less of her. So she told her.

Tempy said nothing at first, just stared. "You told your Lieutenant Towny that? Just straight out, that you was marryin' him in order to have children?"

"Well, no. Not as candidly as I just told you, but I did finally manage to get the words out. I felt like I had to be honest with him."

Tempy blew out a breath. "You's sure one brave woman, Miss Lizzie."

Lizzie didn't know quite how to react to that.

"What did he say, once you told him?"

"He said he loved me and that he thought our friendship love would grow into more of a married love over time. And I *am* very fond of Towny. I've known him forever. And as you've said, he's going to make a wonderful husband. I simply wish that I—"

"Loved him like you think a wife ought to love her husband."

"Yes," Lizzie whispered. "And I wonder if those feelings are ever going to grow between us."

Tempy carefully flipped the peach pies. "What kind of feelin's you think you was gonna have, ma'am?"

Lizzie struggled to put it into words. If she could've said, *What I feel when I'm with Captain Jones*, that would have been easiest. But she didn't dare.

"You talkin' 'bout them feelin's that make you go all squishy inside."

It wasn't a question, and Lizzie couldn't help but laugh. "Yes, those feelings. Shouldn't a wife feel those for her husband?"

"Yes. And also no."

Lizzie frowned, waiting for more. Tempy pulled the skillet off the stove and waved her over to sit at the table, then joined her.

"You never got to meet my Isum. He was already dead and laid to rest by the time you come to Carnton. He and I was together almost forty years. Not married proper like, of course. Colored folk ain't got that choice. But we was sure married in God's sight. And all the angels too!" Tempy smiled, and a glimpse of the younger woman she'd been flickered in her eyes. "I's just a girl, and Isum, he was a growed man. I sure didn't feel no warm, squishy feelin's for him either. I's scared to the bone. But he was right patient and kind with me. He give me time. And that seed of love you talkin' 'bout, it grew real slow like. And with gettin' to know each other."

"So you were glad you chose him?"

"*Chose* him?" Tempy looked at her as though she'd grown a third eye. "There weren't no choosin' for me, Miss Clouston. I was told who I'd be with. Slaves don't get to make them kind of choices, ma'am." Tempy laid a gentle hand on her arm. "What I'm sayin' to you is that it ain't so much who you marry as it is your thinkin' on marriage. Me and Isum, we both knew we hadn't got no other choice, so we worked 'til we built somethin' fine and strong. But you, you got choices, ma'am. Though not as many as you mighta once had, with all the marryin' men dyin' in the war. The only thing worse than havin' no choice is havin' it and throwin' it away."

Tempy's eyes filled with earnestness. "So whatever way you go with your Lieutenant Townsend, you make sure it's of your own choosin'. Not somebody else choosin' for you. 'Cause when it's done, it's done. There ain't no turnin' back. Not for women like you anyway. And while I'm sure it's a fine thing to walk this life with a man who can make your heart go all soft and buttery, there's a heap of pleasure found in walkin' life with a good man who will cherish and care for you. Who'll give you a home and a safe place to grow old. And who'll be a good father to your children."

Tempy gave her hand a pat, then rose and returned to the stove. After filling the glasses with milk, Lizzie retrieved the tray and headed upstairs, Tempy's counsel settling inside her and more than confirming the decision she'd made. And it wasn't lost on her that such wisdom was coming from, and very graciously so, a woman who'd never been given the right to make such a choice for herself. Or even to be legally married.

BALANCING THE TRAY in one hand, Lizzie opened the door to the best parlor, where she'd left Hattie and Winder working their lessons. Mrs. McGavock and two other ladies from the community were busy in the schoolroom upstairs putting finishing touches on "the soldiers' Christmas," as they'd called it. Lizzie had gotten a glimpse of what Carrie had done for them. No wonder the men loved her as they did.

"Thank you, children, for waiting patiently for your—"

Hattie was seated in a chair, still intent on her primer. Winder was nowhere to be seen.

"I told him not to leave, Miss Clouston. I *told* him he'd receive a discipline."

Lizzie deposited the tray on a side table. "I appreciate you staying faithful to your studies, Hattie."

A much-too-angelic smile tipped the girl's mouth. "May I have his cookies?"

"No, you may not."

Hattie's face fell.

"But you *may* have your cookies and twenty minutes of leisure time to read whatever you would like."

Her countenance lit. "Thank you, Miss Clouston!"

Lizzie didn't have to ask where Winder had gone. She already knew and headed for the staircase.

"Oh, Miss Clouston?"

Lizzie paused at the door.

"Are we still having the reading tonight? Upstairs, with the nuns and soldiers?"

"Yes. It's our last one."

Hattie grabbed a lady finger from the plate. "It's been fun hearing the story again, knowing what's coming."

Lizzie nodded. "That's the mark of a good story. And a good writer. There are certain books I've read countless times. Each time is a pleasure. And each time I find something new."

Lizzie closed the door, thinking of the novels she'd loaned to Lieutenant Shuler earlier in the week. She'd chosen *Ivanhoe* by Sir Walter Scott and *The Three Musketeers* by Alexandre Dumas. And simply for fun she'd also included her favorite—*Sense and Sensibility* by Jane Austen—only to see his reaction.

She prayed as she climbed the stairs that the gangrene wouldn't return. He was such a dear boy and had already endured so much. She'd only learned that week that he'd lost his brother, one year younger than him, to the war last year.

In a flash, Thaddeus's face came to mind, and she prayed the inquiry Roland had made would turn up something. But recently it had felt as though her prayers fell flat. At times her heart was so heavy, she couldn't seem to get the words to come. She'd heard a preacher say once that he didn't think it mattered so much what words you chose. That it was the person's faith in the One to whom the request was being made that gave the prayer wings, not fancy words. She hoped that was true. Because even in the moments when she questioned what God was doing and wondered if he still heard her—like now—she chose to believe he did.

Before she even reached the second-floor landing, she heard Winder's laughter and peered around the corner. She saw the little urchin perched atop Lieutenant Shuler's bed, the two of them huddled over something and laughing.

CHAPTER 33

"This is one of my favorites!" Winder pointed. "You ready?"

Lizzie paused in the doorway as Winder began speaking again. Or more rightly, began to read.

"'I . . . see . . . a . . . pig. How . . . fat . . . it . . . is! Can . . . the . . . pig . . . run? It . . . can . . . not . . . run. It . . . is . . . too *fat*!'" Winder giggled, and Shuler did too. "You wanna try one this time, Lieutenant?"

Shuler shook his head. "I don't think so."

"Oh, come on, I read wrong all the time. You won't never learn to read it right unless you let yourself read it wrong."

Lizzie's mouth nearly dropped open. No matter that Winder hadn't remembered her words precisely *or* that he'd used a double negative—a pet peeve she found most irksome—the fact that he remembered her counsel at all was something. But even more shocking . . . Lieutenant Shuler couldn't read?

Movement beyond the bed drew her focus, and she saw Roland watching her—and holding a forefinger to his lips. She nodded and stayed hidden around the corner, watching.

Winder scooted closer and held the book out to Shuler. "This is a good one too. I'll start you out. 'See . . . the . . . old . . . rat.'"

Eyes down, Shuler shook his head. But Winder nudged him and smiled. "You read it, and then after dinner I'll go get my soldiers and we can play."

Shuler eyed him. "You'll go get your soldiers after dinner anyway."

Winder grinned, then pointed back to the page.

Lizzie felt a catch in her throat. That was exactly what she did to Winder when he got off topic. She would smile and gently direct him back to the page. She sighed. She'd been teaching since the age of twelve, and it wasn't often a teacher got to see moments like this. Moments when progress could actually be witnessed. And what she found especially humorous . . . Winder was reading the primer from which she'd instructed him to read earlier. So, in a sense, he *was* doing what she'd told him to do, the little rascal.

"'See . . . the . . . old . . . rat,'" Winder started again.

Shuler exhaled, then squinted as he looked at the page. "'C-can . . . the . . .'" He shook his head again. "I can't do this. I only learned a bit, and it seems even that's gone from me."

"'Can . . . the . . . ,'" Winder said and pointed to the page.

Lizzie was familiar enough with the McGuffey Reader to know there was a picture of the rat above the reading exercise.

"'Rat,'" Shuler said, then stared at the page as though trying to memorize the word.

"Very good!" Winder grinned.

Again Lizzie saw trademarks of her own teaching in the boy's reaction, and her heart warmed.

"'Can . . . the . . . rat . . .'" Shuler's mouth twisted to one side. "'Run!'"

Winder and the lieutenant laughed and nudged each other.

Lizzie spotted Sister Catherine Margaret and Sister Mary Grace exiting Hattie's bedroom. When the nuns looked her way, their expressions grew curious. Lizzie just smiled and indicated for them to wait with her and listen.

Finally, after Lieutenant Shuler finished reading, she winked at the nuns, backed up a few steps, and retraced her path. She made certain her heeled boots well announced her entry this time.

She might have been tempted to laugh at the look of guilt on Winder's face, if not for the surprise—and shame—on Lieutenant Shuler's.

"Hello, Master Winder. I wondered where you were."

"I . . . I . . ." The boy cast about the room as though looking for a convenient tale to grab hold of.

Wanting to spare him the temptation to lie, Lizzie quickly jumped in, also eager to salvage the lieutenant's gentle pride. "Lieutenant Shuler, I appreciate you allowing Winder to read through his lessons with you today. That was most kind of you. But in the future, Winder, I would appreciate you asking permission before you leave the lesson room. Do you understand?"

Relief flooded the boy's face. "Yes, ma'am, Miss Clouston. I won't do it again. Ever."

Lizzie knew better than to believe that. Yet she also appreciated his not attempting to share the blame with Lieutenant Shuler, but taking it fully upon his own slender shoulders. "I appreciate your reassurance, Winder. Now, if you'll take your primer and return to the parlor, your cookies and milk are waiting."

"I still get cookies?"

"*This* time," she said, giving him a stare she'd mastered over the years.

He sobered further. "Thank you, Miss Clouston. Thank you a lot!"

"You're most welcome, Winder. I'll see you downstairs."

The boy crawled off the bed and shot from the room. Lizzie dared a quick look at Roland, whose handsome face was the perfect definition of composure, all but the faint glimmer of awareness in his eyes. Lieutenant Conrad, on the other hand, was as wide-eyed as Winder had been. Same for Private Lowe and Lieutenant Baker. And Lieutenant Taylor and Private Smith—she discovered thankfully—weren't in the room.

But despite her having done her best to give the lieutenant an out, young Shuler looked up at her, eyes filled with remorse.

"Miss Clouston, the fault don't lie with him, ma'am. Leastwise, not all of it. You see . . ."

He glanced at the three books on his bedside table, and Lizzie wished she could think of something else to say to spare him embarrassment.

"I don't read that good, ma'am. I never did. My mama didn't only read to us when we were young'uns. She read to us all through our home years. I think that's why I like listenin' to you." He smiled, then shrugged. "Makes me feel close to her somehow. Like she's not fully gone. You know what I mean?"

Lizzie nodded, struggling to find her voice. "Yes, James. I know what you mean. And as soon as we finish *A Christmas Carol* tonight, we'll start reading whichever book you'd like next."

He smiled. "Really?"

"Really."

"Can I listen in too?" Conrad asked, still wide-eyed, but with excitement now.

"Of course. We'll meet like we've done thus far and—"

All attention in the room moved past her, and Lizzie turned to see a Federal soldier standing in the second-floor hallway.

Roland recognized the officer; he'd been with General Folsom the day the Federal regiments showed up to take him and the rest of the wounded to prison. The captain had a memorable air about him, much as Folsom did. And it wasn't difficult for Roland to imagine that he could be downright cruel with very little effort.

Lizzie whispered something to Sister Catherine Margaret, who did an immediate about-face and left the room, cutting a path straight through the contingent of Federal soldiers, who parted like the Red Sea. That nun certainly had spunk. And God on her side too, Roland figured, which didn't hurt.

The captain pulled a list from his pocket. "We're here to escort the following Confederate prisoners to Nashville." His voice carried in the sudden quiet.

"Excuse me, Captain." Lizzie stepped as far as the doorway. "I believe there's been some mistake. These men aren't—"

"There's been no mistake, miss. This is an affair of the United States military, and interference of any kind will not be tolerated."

Roland willed Lizzie to look at him, but she didn't. She merely stared at the captain, who continued reading.

"These are the prisoners who are leaving with us immediately. Captain John Hampton. Second Lieutenant George Estes. Brigadier General William Quarles. Captain Joseph Bond. And Second Lieutenant Conrad."

Lizzie looked back at Lowe and Baker, then at Conrad, and her gaze snagged on Roland's. Roland gave the slightest shake of his head, clearly seeing she was searching for a way to intervene. With a look he tried to tell her no. Because whatever attempt she made to delay or derail what these soldiers came to do, the prisoners they took with them were the ones who would pay. And pay dearly.

Bridled anger showed in both Lowe's and Baker's features, but Conrad wore a baffled expression.

"I'm not supposed to go yet, Captain Jones," Conrad said in a loud whisper, as if the entire room couldn't hear him. "The doc didn't give his say. That was the rule. Doc says go first, and then we go." Lieutenant Conrad turned to Lizzie. "Miss Clouston, can you tell them for me?"

"Conrad." Roland managed to respond before Lizzie could. "You're going to need to go with these soldiers. They'll take you to a hospital in Nashville."

"No, no, no . . ." Conrad clutched his bandaged head. "I'm supposed to stay here. I want to stay *here*!"

Lizzie stepped forward. "Please, Captain. If you'll only—"

The captain gave a sharp whistle, and two soldiers stepped into the bedroom and took hold of Lizzie by her upper arms. Roland bolted from the cot but scarcely made it to his feet before his legs gave way. Pain scuttled his strength, and he fell back. His shoulder hit the edge of the cot, and he went down hard. A million jagged needles shoved themselves deep into his legs, straight to the bone. He bit back a moan, and his head swam. But it was the boot that came down on his right arm that jerked him back to the surface—and to a world thrumming with pain.

"No!"

A scream sounded from a long way off, and Roland groaned, gritting his teeth to keep from crying out. "Let her go," he managed. "She won't interfere."

"Oh, I know she won't interfere, Captain Jones. That is your name, isn't it?"

Roland looked over at Lizzie, who was still flanked by soldiers, then up at the captain. The pressure on his arm increased.

"Yes," Roland answered, swallowing the bile rising at the back of his throat. "Captain . . . Roland Ward Jones."

"A decorated Rebel sharpshooter."

Roland couldn't tell if the caustic smile he felt in the moment reached his face or not. "What is it about sharpshooters that you fellows don't like?"

"Always have a witty response, don't you? Just like last time."

"Not always." Roland squeezed his eyes tight. It took concentration just to breathe. "I've just found that . . . when you're near death . . . it helps to keep your sense of humor."

"Then you should be laughing your head off, Captain. Because when I come next time, I'm coming for you. And we'll see how well you do without that Enfield rifle of yours."

Roland searched the man's face for recognition beyond the memory of having seen him here at Carnton. But nothing came.

"Does the name Lieutenant Riley Birch mean anything to you, Captain Jones?"

Roland reached past the pain and sifted through memories, trying to find one with that name attached to it. "No," he finally said. "It doesn't."

"Riley Birch was my best friend since we were kids. He was standing right next to me at Chickamauga before the battle started, when a Rebel sharpshooter took him out. Right there beside me. One minute he was talking, the next he was lying in a pool of blood, a hole torn open in his chest."

"I wasn't even at Chickamauga."

"I don't care," he said slowly. "You're a Johnny Reb sharpshooter and that's all that matters. You're all the same. Bunch of backwoods yokels who think you have a prayer of winning this war. While I may never know who killed my best friend . . ." His eyes darkened, and his voice dropped to a whisper. "At least I'll know who killed you."

A scuffle sounded from the hallway, and Roland spotted Colonel McGavock pushing his way through.

The colonel strode forward. "Who's in charge here?"

The captain rose, pressing his boot down on Roland's arm as he did. Roland sucked in a breath.

"I am, sir."

"And you are?" the colonel asked.

"Captain Robert Moore of the United States Army."

"Well, Captain Moore, I'm Colonel John McGavock, the owner of Carnton. And I want to know why you've barged into my home and are demanding to take these wounded soldiers without benefit of a doctor's examination and release, which is the agreement General Folsom made with me when he was here."

"You may own Carnton, Colonel McGavock. But may I remind you that every one of these men is a prisoner of the United States Army, and hence answers to that authority. Any grace given them can be rescinded at any time. So step aside and let us do our duty."

"Would you at least be willing, Captain Moore, to allow me to write General Folsom and remind him of our agreement that—"

"Folsom's the one who wrote the order, Colonel."

Moore pulled a document from his breast pocket and handed it to Colonel McGavock. The resignation in the colonel's expression stripped away what little hope Roland had remaining. The colonel handed the order back.

Moore gave Roland a last look of warning, then strode from the room toward the hall. "If your name was called, you have five minutes to get to the wagon out back. Or we'll come back for you and *escort* you down."

Lizzie pulled free of the soldiers holding her and raced to Roland's side. She touched his face, his arms, then his face again. "Are you hurt?"

He gently pushed her away. "I'm fine."

She shook her head. "No, you're not, you're—"

"See to Conrad, Lizzie! He needs you to help him or he won't be able to do this. And things will go bad very fast." He spotted George entering the room with Sister Catherine Margaret and Sister Mary Grace.

Colonel McGavock knelt beside them. "Captain Jones, may I help you up?"

"Yes, sir. I'd appreciate that." Roland looked at Lizzie. "*Go.* And watch the clock. You don't want them coming back up here."

CHAPTER 34

"Lieutenant Conrad, you must look at me." Lizzie gently turned the man's face toward hers. "I'm truly sorry this is working out this way, but we are still at war. And you *are* a prisoner of the Federal Army. Now . . ."

"But, Miss Clouston, we haven't finished reading that book yet. The one with the ghosts."

Lizzie steeled herself against the tears rising in the man's eyes. And in her own.

"I know. But you know what? I'll send the book to you once you're all settled in at the hospital there. All right?"

"It won't be the same without you reading it."

She forced a quick smile, feeling the seconds ticking by. "Sister Catherine Margaret is gathering your personal belongings for you. And George here"—Lizzie glanced beside her—"is going to carry you down to the wagon."

Conrad looked up at him. "You belong to Captain Jones. Isn't that right?"

George didn't answer immediately, and Lizzie looked up to find his expression inscrutable.

"Yes, sir. I do," he finally answered.

"So that means you're a good Negro." Conrad nodded. "Seeing as you belong to him."

Lizzie cringed inwardly. She knew Conrad no longer had full use of his faculties following his injuries, but still . . . She sneaked a look in George's direction as he knelt beside them.

George placed a large hand on the lieutenant's arm. "It matters who we belong to, don't it, sir? Says somethin' 'bout who we are."

"It does." Conrad sniffed. "It matters a lot."

A smile dawned on George's face. "I'm a good man, sir. Least, I tries to be. Now, come on and let me tote you outside. I'll take good care goin' down all them big windin' stairs."

As George lifted the lieutenant in his arms, Lizzie caught George's attention and whispered, "Bless you."

Lizzie followed them from the bedroom, sneaking a look back at Roland, who was watching her from his cot. She understood why he'd pushed her away, but she also knew he had to be hurting. She gave him a quick nod, then checked the clock on the mantel.

Only one minute remained . . .

She hurried to catch up with George and the lieutenant, who trailed behind Colonel and Mrs. McGavock and the nuns, who were all helping the other four soldiers to descend the staircase.

"Miss Clouston!" Sister Catherine came alongside. "If you'll permit me to speak with Lieutenant Conrad before we reach the wagon, I have an idea that I believe may be of help."

"Yes, Sister, please. But do it quickly!"

Lizzie managed to get George's attention before they reached the back door. "Sister Catherine has an idea."

Sister Catherine took hold of Lieutenant Conrad's hand. "Lieutenant, I need for you to be Catholic. Only for a day or so."

Conrad's eyes widened. "But I'm *not* a Catholic, Sister. I'm a good Baptist."

The nun smiled. "Yes, I know. But if you *could* be Catholic, only for a little while, then I would be allowed to go with you in the wagon. And I can make certain that you—and your other fellow soldiers—are all safely delivered to the hospital in Nashville."

"But wouldn't that be lyin', ma'am? To say I'm Catholic when I'm not?"

Sister Catherine spoke quickly. "Do you remember the story of Rahab the harlot, in the Old Testament? How she hid the two spies when the king came looking for them? She told the king's messengers that the spies were not in her home, even though they were. Because she knew the king had sent his men to do them harm. So she protected them."

Lizzie peered out the front door and spotted Captain Moore headed back to the house, a detail of soldiers with him. The other wounded men were already being loaded into the wagon. "*Hurry*, Sister!" she whispered.

"Much like Rahab, Lieutenant, I can protect you. And the other four wounded men. But only if one of you is Catholic. Do you understand?"

Conrad slowly nodded, his features somber. "Catholics do believe in God. Right, ma'am?"

Sister Catherine laughed. "Oh yes, Lieutenant. We do very much believe in him. Now I simply need you to . . ."

Lizzie heard footsteps on the front portico and hastened outside. "Captain Moore! Lieutenant Conrad is coming right now. It simply took us a little longer to—"

"Out of my way, miss."

Hearing George's footsteps behind her, Lizzie acquiesced and stepped to one side.

George met the captain at the door. "Ready for me to put him in the wagon, sir?"

From Lizzie's perspective, the captain looked almost disappointed that they'd made it in time.

"Yes. Put him in the back with the others."

George moved down the portico steps with the lieutenant—and with Sister Catherine Margaret right on their heels.

Captain Moore followed. "Where do you think *you're* going, Sister?"

Sister Catherine paused in the yard, as did George.

Still on the portico, Lizzie moved slightly to the left for a better view. And when she saw the rosary Lieutenant Conrad clutched in his hand—and heard his whispered, "Hail, Mary, full of praise. The Lord is with me"—she felt a sinking feeling inside her. She wasn't Catholic either, but one of her best friends growing up was, and she'd heard Christina pray the rosary many times. But never quite like this. If Captain Moore knew the rosary . . .

Sister Catherine laid a gentle hand over Lieutenant Conrad's, and Lizzie noticed the nun squeeze his hand ever so slightly until he halted midprayer.

"I am merely doing my duty, Captain Moore. I will accompany Lieutenant Conrad to Nashville, as allowed in the guidelines published in 1861. They state, 'Any prisoner of war who is facing the uncertainty of death, may beseech his captors for a source of spiritual guidance by which his faith shall be instructed to greater—'"

"You're not going, Sister. This man is not near death. But he might be, if you interfere further." He motioned to George. "Get him on the wagon. Now."

With a gentle hand to George's arm, Sister Catherine belayed the order. "Captain Moore, may I assume you're familiar with General William Rosecrans?"

A muscle twitched at the corner of the captain's eye. "Sister, everybody in the Federal Army is familiar with General Rosecrans."

"And have you had the opportunity to be in his company, Captain?"

Captain Moore eyed her, then shifted his weight. "No, Sister. I have not."

Sister Catherine smiled. "You may not be aware then, Captain, that General Rosecrans is Catholic. He has great esteem for sisters of the faith. He is himself, in fact, a great advocate of assuring that every man—Federal or Confederate—is granted the opportunity for spiritual guidance and encouragement that—"

"There's no room for you in the wagon, Sister. And we don't have any extra horses."

"I can walk, Captain."

"It's over twenty miles to Nashville."

Sister Catherine briefly bowed her head. "God will provide me the strength."

Grave-faced, the captain glared at the nun, then looked over at the wagon, then back again, and Lizzie prayed with everything in her that God would somehow provide a way.

"Hanson!" Captain Moore shouted, spittle flying from his lips.

A young soldier stepped forward, boyishly handsome, with an innocence about him that reminded Lizzie of Lieutenant Shuler.

"Yes, sir?" the soldier responded.

"The nun rides with you!"

"Yes, Captain!"

The weight in Lizzie's chest lifted by half.

The captain and his soldiers headed for their horses, and George strode toward the wagon near which the McGavocks and the other nuns stood. But Sister Catherine hurried back up the portico steps.

She grabbed Lizzie's hands, her eyes twinkling. "I need you to pray for two things. First, that Captain Moore does not develop a sudden hankering to brush up on his military guidelines." She leaned in. "I was quoting from a book of service issued by the Holy Sisters of Charity."

Feeling her mouth slip open, Lizzie shook her head.

"And second, that he does not ask me further about General Rosecrans . . . whom I have never met."

Lizzie hugged her tight. "Thank you for doing this, Sister. And please take care of yourself."

A light slipped into Sister Catherine Margaret's eyes. "Psalm 27, Miss Clouston. Do you know it?"

Lizzie hesitated. "I know I've read it before, but—"

"Well, read it again. Soon. And be encouraged! Now . . ." The sister glanced over her shoulder. "The other nuns are going to be so jealous. I get to ride all the way to Nashville with a handsome young soldier! And who knows, he may even be Catholic!"

Lizzie's smile faded as the wagon rumbled down the long graveled drive. She saw Conrad begin to wave, and she waved in return until the wagon disappeared around the bend at the far end of the road.

"Thank you, Mrs. McGavock. This is a right handsome muffler." Seated in a chair by the fireplace in Winder's room—his first attempt at such—Roland draped the knitted scarf around his neck, wishing they all felt more jovial today. Especially since the women had worked so hard to make everything so nice. Though he continued to be on uneasy speaking terms with the Lord, he still thought Christmas Day should be a time to celebrate, not to mourn. "It's most kind of you and the colonel, ma'am. I hope he helped you knit all of these if he's taking some of the credit."

Mrs. McGavock smiled. "He helped by staying out of my way."

Roland laughed softly. That sounded like something Weet would've said. Oh, how he missed her today. Lena too. What was it about Christmas that made the heart turn home? The festive decorations, the comforting food and drink, and, of course, the memories that crowded in. Even the violinist in the corner playing Christmas carols—"Hark! the Herald Angels Sing," "O Come, All Ye Faithful," "Joy to the World," "It Came upon a Midnight Clear"—while expert at his craft and filling the house with music near fit for heaven, only contributed to Roland's melancholy mood.

The colonel looked him over. "Are you sure you're faring well after the incident yesterday with the soldier? It appeared as though he got pretty rough with you."

Roland shrugged off the comment. "I'm fine, sir. He's a young officer. Newly appointed, I'd bet. Seems they always have something to prove."

Mrs. McGavock gestured. "Would you like something else from the buffet, Captain? I'll be happy to get it for you."

Roland put a hand to his belly. "I couldn't eat another bite. Well, except maybe for another one of Tempy's fried pies."

"It would be my pleasure!"

"Thank you, ma'am."

Roland felt honored when the colonel claimed the ladderback chair beside him.

"It would seem, sir, that the artificial limbs are a definite win with the soldiers." He smiled and nodded toward Lieutenant Shuler, who was walking around encouraging people to shake his wooden hand, only to pull it back real quick at the last second. But the men with artificial legs . . . Roland had grown so accustomed to seeing the amputees absent their limbs that now to see them *walking* around normal-like was a tad unnerving. Some wore trousers that hid the makeshift legs, which really played with the mind. Most of the men with artificial legs were getting the hang of them, but some were still holding on to walls or using crutches to navigate their way. Twenty-four men remained at Carnton, and each one of them, Roland included, hoped the Federal Army took their time in coming back.

He'd been continuing his exercises. He did them three times a day. Early in the morning before sunrise, and shortly following lunch when the soldiers in his room either slept or met in other rooms to play cards or checkers. Then he went through the repetition again at night after everyone was asleep. Not that anyone would tattle on him to Dr. Phillips. But the doc had harped on and on to them about the importance of waiting to walk or exercise until they'd healed properly, so Roland wasn't taking any chances. And he was being smart about it. When he grew light-headed, he rested for a minute. When he started hurting, he stopped. He knew Dr. Phillips still wouldn't approve, but he had to do something to contribute to his healing and regaining his strength. He'd added push-ups as well. And he did it all from his cot, which he now considered a lifeline.

Colonel McGavock fingered his beard, a glass of punch in his hand. "Captain Jake Winston and his wife, Aletta, do a fine job making them."

His thoughts having trailed, Roland backtracked to what they'd been talking about. *Artificial limbs.* "Yes, sir, they do."

"They've taken an old warehouse in downtown Franklin," the colonel continued. "They've done quite a bit of work to it and are helping wounded soldiers to recuperate there. They're an extraordinary couple."

Roland spotted Jake and his wife out in the hallway speaking to Lizzie and Tempy, who was serving. Jake was a fellow sharpshooter, but he'd lost a portion of his vision due to an injury. It was especially troubling to learn, because Jake Winston had been one of the best.

Conversation came easily between Roland and the colonel, and they covered a variety of topics before Colonel McGavock dropped his voice by a degree.

"So, Captain Jones, I see you routinely reading the newspaper from front to back and every page in between. What is your view of what awaits us?"

Roland weighed his response before answering. From what he'd witnessed firsthand, John McGavock was as fine a man as they came, and far more generous with his wealth than most. His wife was cut from the same cloth. Some of the men had taken to calling Carrie McGavock the Angel of Carnton, a title the woman had more than earned through her nurturing compassion and near constant attention to the soldiers. Although, at least for him, another woman already held that rank. The McGavocks lived in a beautiful home with nice furnishings, but nothing ostentatious that he'd seen thus far. A well-grounded second-generation Scotch-Irish family from Cairn, Ireland. But he wasn't certain where the colonel's thinking was in relation to the Confederacy. Did McGavock consider it a lost cause, as he did? Or was he one of those still clinging to the weary dream?

"Well, Colonel," Roland began, choosing his words carefully. "First, sir, I appreciate you making the newspapers available to us. And second, I don't think we can trust the newspapers much. Especially the ones from Nashville." He gave a soft laugh. "Not that we can't glean information here and there. But the Federal Army currently holds sway over most every publication in that city, so I don't think you'll get much of a fair reading from any of those."

"Hear, hear," the colonel said, downing his punch as he watched his wife from across the room.

Roland had noticed that about the McGavocks before. They still sought each other out in a crowd, which said a lot about them as a couple. He wondered what it said about him that he knew exactly where Lizzie was right now, and had ever since the Christmas celebration had started. She looked especially pretty tonight. She'd done something different with her hair. He liked it. Although he'd prefer to see it loose and down around her shoulders.

"Continue, Captain. Please."

Roland obliged, sensing the colonel desired bluntness. "To cut to the heart of the matter, sir, I believe the future of the Confederacy is bleak." He felt John McGavock's attention turn to him, but kept his gaze on the flames in the hearth. Staring at a fire was comforting; there was something fascinating about watching a force of nature that, when contained, could help keep a man alive, but if unleashed would destroy with merciless ferocity.

"From what I gathered from senior officers in the weeks leading up to the battle here," he went on, "the Confederate Treasury is cranking out millions of dollars in notes unbacked by gold. And the Confederate States as a whole are nearly bankrupt. As we both know, sir, wars are expensive. Our last army in the field took a severe beating here, both physically and in the morale of the men. Then in Nashville, we were beaten again. But that time we were sent running. And it does something to a man on the inside when he turns his back on his enemy and runs. There's something innately wrong about it. So if General Lee can't find his way out of Virginia past Grant, which, from all reports, seems doubtful . . ." Roland looked over at him. "I believe we're done for, sir."

McGavock's stare turned appraising. "Remind me never to solicit your opinion if I do not earnestly wish to hear it, Captain."

At first Roland thought he might've offended his gracious host. But John McGavock's slow nod, coupled with the sad resignation in his eyes, said he was in full and complete agreement. They sat in a silence Roland might have considered comfortable if not for the shared sense of impending doom and dread of the unknown.

He saw Lizzie out in the hallway again. But this time she was alone. The cheery countenance he'd glimpsed earlier when she was in the company of guests was gone. She looked like he felt on the inside—weary, worried, and uncertain. Which he found interesting since, based on the current tide, she was on the winning side of the war.

They'd originally planned to have the final reading of *A Christmas Carol* last night, but the Federal patrol's unannounced visit changed that. It simply hadn't seemed right, so they'd all voted to wait. That had suited him fine. While he enjoyed listening to Lizzie's voice as she read, the story itself had taken a darker turn with the second ghost's visit. And though he knew it was only a story, he found himself thinking about it at odd moments—like now—and seeing himself through Scrooge's experiences. The similarities were disturbing. So as he did every time this happened, he purposefully turned his thoughts elsewhere.

He hoped the men who'd been taken were holding up well.

Especially Conrad. Knowing Sister Catherine Margaret was with them helped ease his mind. The woman was a force of nature all her own.

Roland shifted in the chair, his back muscles beginning to ache. He'd appreciated the evening, but was ready to put this Christmas and this year—this war—behind him.

"Here you are, Captain Jones." Mrs. McGavock returned, china plate in hand. "There are plenty more where that came from."

"Thank you, ma'am."

The colonel rose and offered his left hand. Roland shook it.

"Captain, it's always a pleasure. I'm sorry you've suffered such wounds, but I'm grateful God saw fit to bring you to our home."

"It's I who am grateful, sir. Your hospitality and generous hearts are helping us all to heal—far more, I might add, than Dr. Phillips's snake oil ministrations."

"Do I hear my name being taken in vain?"

Roland laughed along with the McGavocks, already having spotted the good doctor working his way toward them. After a brief exchange, the couple resumed their circulation among their guests, and Dr. Phillips claimed the now vacant chair.

The doctor exhaled through his teeth. "Captain, I believe I am ready for this Christmas to come to a close."

"Although I'm grateful for everything our host and hostess have done for us, I could not agree more. Do you bring any more news since you last visited?" Roland took a bite of the fried pie.

"None that's good, I'm afraid. The army is still scattered. Regiments in disarray. They're supposed to be making their way toward winter camp in Tupelo, but the army's in ruinous condition. A shell of what it was even six months ago. Also, there's rumor"—the doc's voice lowered—"that Hood is going to resign."

Roland stopped chewing midbite.

"Word is," Phillips continued, his gaze forward, "that he's humiliated, utterly crushed by what happened here and in Nashville."

"And with good reason."

Phillips nodded but said nothing else.

Roland let the news settle within him. If the rumor proved true, General Hood would take leave of commanding the Army of Tennessee scarcely six months after being appointed to lead it. Roland set aside his plate, no longer hungry.

"So . . . how're you feeling this week, Captain?"

"All right. Better than all right, actually. Except for my back. I'd really appreciate a lie-down about now."

When Phillips didn't respond, Roland glanced over—and found the man looking at him. "What?"

"Anything you want to tell me?"

Hearing a tone in the man's voice, Roland didn't know how Phillips had found out about his exercising. He only knew that he had. Roland reached for innocence he'd lost long ago. "No. Nothing I can think of."

"You're sure."

Roland nodded, then Phillips glanced down at the blanket covering Roland's legs.

"I'm a doctor, Jones. I'm trained to notice things."

"Trained to notice," Roland scoffed. "Through a blanket?" He shook his head, letting his smile show. "Who squealed on me?"

"You have to ask?"

He thought for a minute. "Taylor!"

Phillips's laughter said he'd guessed correctly.

"I give you my word, Doc. I haven't put any weight on my legs yet. I'm just lifting them up and down. And bending them a little."

"Even though I told you not to until I gave you the go-ahead."

"Pretty much." Roland feigned a grimace.

"How did you get into that chair?"

"George helped me. Sitting in a chair seemed more befitting for a party than lying on the cot the whole time."

"After everyone leaves, I want to check your legs."

"Fine by me. You're the doctor, after all."

Phillips gave him a droll look.

A minute later, Lizzie happened to glance their way and smile. Roland returned the gesture.

"Miss Clouston's a fine young woman."

Roland nodded. "She is that."

"Is she still betrothed to that young lieutenant?"

Roland looked over.

Phillips shrugged. "Word travels."

"Yes. She's still betrothed."

"Does she know how you feel about her?"

Roland resisted the urge to look beside him again, not all that surprised that the doctor had noticed. As he'd said, he was an observant man. "I'm pretty sure she has some idea of my feelings."

"But?"

"As you said, Doc, she's betrothed. She's given her pledge, and she's a woman of her word."

Phillips seemed content to let it go at that, and Roland was grateful. He wasn't in the mood to discuss it.

Lizzie had told him she hadn't heard from Lieutenant Townsend yet following the battle of Nashville. And there had come a moment, late one night, when he'd allowed himself to consider what might happen if Townsend had been killed. If Lizzie were no longer pledged to another man. As soon as the thought had come, he'd banished it, ashamed. Any man who would think such a thing wasn't worthy of Elizabeth Clouston. He gave a rueful sigh.

Almost an hour later, everyone seemed to have had their fill of both delicacies and conversation, and what guests there were from town took their leave. The nuns began helping the men get ready for bed.

George moved Roland from the chair to the cot, and Roland

was careful not to meet his gaze. As much time as he and George had spent together in their lives, Roland had quickly realized they'd never had much physical contact. Being carried by your manservant was not something any man relished, but there was something about being dependent on George in this way that Roland found especially uncomfortable.

As promised, Phillips returned a few minutes later. Lizzie was with him.

"All right, Captain, let's have a look at those legs." Already the doc's tone held a hint of disapproval.

Roland stretched out on the cot, his feet slightly hanging over. Lizzie held an oil lamp aloft as Phillips examined him. Roland caught her attention, shot a look at the doc, and rolled his eyes. She tried unsuccessfully to curb a smile. Roland realized something then. When he'd first met her, he would've sworn the woman could scarcely hold a smile. Now the reaction seemed to come far more naturally and more often. And it suited her.

"More light, please, Miss Clouston."

Lizzie moved closer to the bed. So close Roland caught the sweetness of whatever scent she was wearing. They'd talked some earlier in the evening, but they had yet to continue their conversation from several nights ago. Part of his eagerness to heal, to be able to at least move again on his own, had to do with her. They were friends. He'd accepted that, for the most part. But he wanted time to talk to her. Alone on occasion. Get to know her better. For whatever time he had left here at Carnton. Yet it was a fine balance, he knew. Because the sooner he walked without aid, the sooner he went to prison.

Dr. Phillips straightened, and Roland could tell by his frustrated expression that he wasn't pleased.

Phillips gave him a look. "The healing in your legs simply isn't coming along as quickly as I'd hoped it would, Captain."

Roland stared. "But that can't be right, Doc. I—"

"And I believe the reason is——"

Frustrated, Roland held his tongue.

"——that you need to get your lazy buttocks off that cot and get to exercising."

Phillips laughed. But it was Lizzie's reaction—she grinned and gave his forearm a quick squeeze—that felt like a rush of morphine and coffee shot straight into his veins.

Roland smiled. "As soon as I'm able to kick again, Doc, I'm comin' for you."

Phillips gripped his left hand and gave it a firm shake. "I've never been more pleased to have been wrong, Captain. Both tonight . . . and that other night." Phillips glanced beside him at Lizzie, whose features softened with pleasure.

Roland swallowed. "I owe you both a lot."

Phillips looked over at George, who stood off to the side. "I need to find out what you're putting into those poultices, George. And how you're applying them. I think those have greatly accelerated the captain's healing."

"I be happy to tell you, sir."

The silence lengthened, and Roland felt Lizzie looking at him. He clearly read in her eyes what she was thinking. *Aren't you going to thank George too?*

Feeling that twinge of unease again, Roland shifted his gaze. "And . . . George. Thank you as well."

George lifted his head and met Roland's stare. "You welcome, Cap'n Jones."

BY THE TIME breakfast was served the next morning, Roland was famished. His appetite had definitely increased since he'd started his daily exercise, and Tempy had noticed. She'd begun giving him extra servings of hoecakes, eggs, and bacon. And he ate every bite.

As he finished his second cup of coffee, Dr. Phillips walked into the bedroom.

"Morning, Doc. I thought you'd be long gone by now."

"You know me. I couldn't leave without having one more of Tempy's breakfasts."

Hands in his pockets, Phillips crossed to the window and stared out. Roland looked over at him, then realized the room had emptied out. Even Shuler, who stuck pretty close to his bed these days, was gone. Roland set his empty coffee cup on the floor beside the cot.

"Whatever you've come to say, Doc, I think you need to say it."

Phillips slowly turned to face him. "You always have been a bottom line sort of man."

"I thought you were too, Doc. That's something I've always liked about you." Roland narrowed his eyes. "I think that may be the only thing."

Phillips smiled, then leveled his gaze. "I want you to know before I tell you this, Jones, that this may not apply to you."

Roland forced a laugh. "Why am I not reassured by that?"

Phillips closed the door, grabbed a chair from the corner, and sat down across from him. Roland felt a slight shudder.

"Despite the medical advances that have been made in recent years, there are still so many things about the human body we don't—"

"Just say it, Doc, all right? For both our sakes."

Time slowed to a crawl, and Phillips's gaze turned rock steady. Roland felt his pulse kick up a notch.

"For men with extensive injuries such as yours, where the blood supply has been compromised to certain parts of the body for a lengthy period of time, there can be notable increases in the inability of the patient to procreate. This doesn't mean you cannot still enjoy the act of marriage, and that—"

Roland held up a hand, his attention stuck on one word passed over far too quickly. He swallowed. "Are you saying I can no longer father a child?"

"I'm saying that due to your injuries, there is a *chance* you may not be able to."

Roland blinked, and all he could see was the fading image of Lena's sweet face. "What . . . are the odds?"

"Shooting from the hip? Sixty to seventy percent."

"That I'll be able to?"

Phillips's silence answered before he did. "That you won't," he said softly.

Roland's chest tightened, and he let out a held breath. "I appreciate you telling me, Doc."

"But just remember, Jones, this may not apply to—"

"I understand. I may be fine or . . . I might not." His eyes burned. He turned away, eager for Phillips to leave. "You best be on your way, or Loring's Division may up and move on without you."

For a moment Phillips didn't respond. Then he rose, returned the chair to its place, and reached to open the bedroom door.

"Hey, Doc?"

Phillips looked back.

"Why are you telling me this now?" Roland asked, then attempted a cavalier tone. "Is it because of the way you've seen me looking at Miss Clouston?"

"No. It's because of the way I've seen her looking at you."

Roland felt a stab of pleasure mixed with pain. "Last thing, Phillips." He struggled to keep his voice even. "If I had let you take my leg when you wanted to that night, would that have made any—"

"No. That would have made no difference."

Roland nodded. "Good to know."

CHAPTER 35

Lizzie dressed in the dark, doing her best to be quiet, not wanting to awaken Hattie and Winder. Especially after the night they'd had. She grabbed her Bible from the bedside table and tiptoed softly down to the kitchen, mindful of the worst offenders among the creaky stairs. The kitchen was dark and still, and she walked to a window and stood for a moment in the quiet, staring out the window into the night. The sun, still tucked in slumber, wouldn't rouse for a while yet, and she watched transfixed as grayish tufts of clouds wafted across a thumbnail moon. *Towny, are you still alive?*

Images of the battlefield at Franklin rose in her mind, but she shut them out, refusing to believe he'd met with that end. During the past week she'd intentionally reached back into her memory, recalling the years they'd grown up together. Towny had always watched out for her, championed her. When they'd shared lunches he'd always given her the best portion of whatever his mother had packed for him. He *was* a good man. Patient and unselfish. And it was growing easier for her to imagine building a life with him. And the catalyst for that, at least in part—which she wasn't proud of—was Roland's reticence in recent days.

Though they'd spoken on several occasions, it felt different between them. He was distant, preoccupied. She knew he was struggling, both with wondering if he'd ever walk again and with what his own future held if he did. She heard the other soldiers conjecturing about what-ifs, but Roland kept his thoughts to himself. As she'd been reading *The Three Musketeers* to James—the book the young man had chosen of those she'd given him—she'd tried to engage Roland as well, but to no avail. She'd noticed how difficult it had been for him to thank George the other night. He was wrestling with hanging on to the past order of things even as he knew in his heart—because he had admitted as much to her—that their world was changing.

Sunday services at most local churches had been temporarily suspended due to the entire town caring for the dying and wounded. But services were set to resume this next week, and the McGavocks were planning to attend with their children. Lizzie had already volunteered to stay and help the nuns with services for the soldiers, wanting to give Colonel and Mrs. McGavock and Hattie and Winder time to be a family together.

She heard a creak from overhead and paused, listening, hoping it wasn't Winder. The boy had awakened during the night, as he had twice in the past week, kicking and thrashing, his little body covered in sweat. Unlike Hattie, he hadn't screamed. Lizzie had held him as he'd clung to her, burying his face in the crook of her neck as though trying to burrow to somewhere another world away. He, too, was struggling to make sense of what had happened here. Much as they all were. And, perhaps, much as they always would.

Her eyes watered. She loved these children so much. She wished she could reach into their little hearts and restore their innocence. Erase all they'd seen and heard in the past weeks and months. Despite the current trajectory of the war, she feared the days ahead and all the conflict yet before them.

She'd read in the newspaper earlier that week about General Sherman's plan to redistribute roughly four hundred thousand acres of fertile plantation land along the strip of coastline stretching from Charleston, South Carolina, to the St. John's River in Florida, including Georgia's Sea Islands as well as a portion of the mainland. Sherman proposed to give the land to newly freed black families, some of whom had been following his army as his soldiers had marched south "demonstrating the Union's might and destroying sources of food Southerners had saved for the winter," as the article stated. The journalist then reported that desertions were on the rise in Robert E. Lee's army in Virginia. Men who'd heard of what Sherman had done were abandoning the fight and returning to protect their families.

If what the newspaper printed were true, Sherman believed his campaign would help shorten the war. And while Lizzie prayed fervently for the war to end, she feared his tactics would have a devastating ripple effect. Although Carnton had food stores that, if managed frugally, should see them through the winter months, many families in Franklin and in the smaller communities beyond had so little. Only yesterday she'd helped Tempy and Mrs. McGavock box up food that Carrie, with George's help, had distributed to widows and orphans in Franklin. The Union wanted to break the backs of Southern plantation owners, that much was clear to her. And though it had taken her a long time to reach, then accept, this conclusion, she knew that negotiation between the two sides had never been possible. Not with owning human beings at the core of the conflict. One side and one side only would be left standing after this war was done. But how many tens of thousands of people—both white and black—would starve to death as this country struggled to regain its footing after the war? There had to be a different way to negotiate the land. To work together. To find common ground once slavery was abolished. And it *had* to be abolished before this country could move forward.

She laid her Bible on the kitchen table and replenished the fire in the hearth, then stoked the flames until the fresh wood caught. The firelight cast a warm umber glow around her. Tempy had left the coffee kettle filled with water and hanging from the pot crane in the hearth. Lizzie swung the kettle over the fire to start the water boiling. She prayed Conrad and the other men the Federals had taken one week ago were faring well. She could still see Conrad waving from the back of the wagon, his expression full of uncertainty and fear.

She'd promised the remaining soldiers she'd read the final

installment of *A Christmas Carol* tonight, and she and Tempy had a special surprise for James too. Then she planned on sending the book to Conrad and the other men, if that were possible. Sister Mary Grace told her yesterday that they had not yet received word from Sister Catherine Margaret. Only after Lizzie was in bed last night did she recall the nun's last instruction to her.

She sat down at the kitchen table, lit the oil lamp, and turned in the Old Testament to the book of Psalms. *Psalm 27, Miss Clouston. Do you know it?* Lizzie felt the touch of a smile recalling the ever-present hope in Sister Catherine's voice. *Well, read it again. Soon. And be encouraged!*

Lizzie pulled the oil lamp closer, and as she read the first verse, she felt the heaviness inside begin to lift. *The LORD is my light and my salvation; whom shall I fear? the LORD is the strength of my life; of whom shall I be afraid?*

Her eyes devoured the text. Her heart drank it in. Only once she finished reading did she hear the water boiling for the coffee. She added coffee grounds to the pot, gave it a quick stir, and began reading the psalm a second time. She knew she'd read these verses before, but the way they spoke to her now, the words so applicable to what the country was going through at the—

"I said good mornin', Miss Lizzie!"

Lizzie looked up to see Tempy standing there watching her, an inquisitive smile on her face.

Lizzie breathed a little laugh. "Good morning, Tempy. I'm sorry, I didn't hear you come in."

Tempy's gaze dropped to the open Bible. "What you reading there?" She claimed the chair beside Lizzie.

"Some verses Sister Catherine encouraged me to read before she left with the men last weekend."

Tempy looked back at the Bible, then up at her. "What's the good Lord say in them verses?"

Lizzie turned the Bible around so Tempy could see it too, and with her forefinger she traced a path beneath the words as she read. Tempy stared intently at the page. Lizzie looked up when she finished.

Tempy gestured. "Would you read the part again about waitin' on the Lord? That's my favorite of all."

Lizzie nodded. "That's the very last verse. 'Wait on the LORD: be of good courage, and he shall strengthen thine heart: wait, I say, on the LORD.'"

"Mmm-hmm," Tempy murmured as though tasting the words. "Be o' good courage. I like that too. And I got a feelin' we gonna be needin' a whole lot more of that in comin' days."

FOLLOWING DINNER THAT night, Lizzie stuck her head inside each of the bedrooms upstairs and let the soldiers know that the reading would commence soon for anyone interested. She forced a cheeriness to her voice, not feeling up to the theatrics of reading aloud tonight. But when she came to Winder's room and spotted Roland absorbed in a book— and not just any book—she found her humor encouraged.

Looking thoroughly engaged, he didn't seem to notice her approach.

"*You're* reading *Sense and Sensibility*?"

He didn't look up, but a roguish smile turned his mouth. "The way you say it makes it sound almost wrong."

"Not wrong." She grinned. "Just a little surprising."

He peered up. His gaze was a mixture of shyness and playful challenge, and some other emotion she couldn't define. "I heard from somebody that this was her favorite book. So"—he shrugged—"I thought I'd try it on for size."

"And how does the story fit, Captain Jones?"

He narrowed his eyes. "Fairly well, Miss Clouston. But right now I'm wishing I could throw that half brother's greedy little banty hen of a wife, Fanny, into the stockade."

Lizzie laughed, feeling a measure of ease returning between them. "I feel that way every time I read it. I'll be interested to know what you think of the novel once you're finished."

He gave a nod. "Then I'll be sure to tell you." He looked past her. "You getting ready to finish reading the Christmas story?"

She nodded.

"I take it we're going to see how things end up for old Scrooge."

She eyed him. "So you haven't read the book before? I wasn't certain."

"No, I haven't." He tucked a torn piece of paper into the pages of the novel and shut the book with a clap. "So I guess I'll just have to wait and find out later whether or not Miss Elinor bumps into Edward Farrars at the party."

She noticed he hadn't commented on *A Christmas Carol*. Perhaps the story wasn't to his liking.

"Count me in on hearing the rest of the Scrooge story, Miss Clouston!"

Lizzie turned to see James sitting up in bed, a big smile on his face.

"We've already met two of them ghosts," the young man continued. "I'm ready for the third!"

Lizzie laughed. "It's good to see you feeling better, James."

"I do feel good, ma'am. Real good."

Grateful to see such improvement in him, she heard the heavy tread of footsteps on the stairs and knew it had to be George helping Tempy with the surprise. It was a treat for all the men, but she'd gotten the idea from something James had shared with her.

A photograph on the table beside James's bed caught her eye. "What a nice picture," she said softly, guessing the identity of the person seated next to James.

"That's my younger brother, Thomas. Before we joined up to fight, he said he wanted to get an image of us in our uniforms for Mama. Said she'd be so proud." His smile faded a touch. "But she just cried when she saw it, Miss Clouston. I don't think it made her happy like Thomas thought it would."

"I'm sure your mother was very proud of you both, James. But I imagine it was very difficult for her to say good-bye to you and your brother."

He nodded, looking at the picture.

"You and Thomas favor each other a great deal."

"People were all the time gettin' us mixed up. Even Mama couldn't tell us apart from behind."

Lizzie smiled and glanced over at Roland to find him watching her, and something in his eyes, a yearning perhaps, stirred a desire within her. Or maybe it was her own yearning she was wishfully seeing mirrored in his eyes. She looked away, noting he did likewise at the very same time.

As Lizzie always did, Roland had observed, she waited until everyone was quiet and still before she began. As was her custom, she flipped back a page and read the final sentences of the previous section to remind them where they'd left off in the story.

"'The bell struck twelve.'" She read slowly, deliberately.

"'Scrooge looked about him for the Ghost, and saw it not. As the last stroke ceased to vibrate, he remembered the prediction of old Jacob Marley, and lifting up his eyes, beheld a solemn Phantom, draped and hooded, coming, like a mist along the ground, toward him.'"

Roland saw the nuns lean in as she turned the page. Young Lieutenant Shuler downed the rest of his apple-brandy hot toddy, a special refreshment Lizzie and Tempy had made for everyone in memory of the lieutenant's mother. Everyone except for Hattie and Winder, that is, who were enjoying warm apple cider.

"'Stave Four,'" Lizzie announced. "'The Last of the Spirits.'"

She was truly gifted at reading aloud. She rarely even had to look at the page; it was as though she already knew the words. And she captured the nuances of the people in the story and of the places. She quieted her voice at the right times, made it louder at others. Made him feel as if he was right there in the midst of it, instead of just reading along, or being read to. Charles Dickens would be proud.

She held up the book to show another drawing of Scrooge. And watching her, feeling himself respond to her not merely physically but deep within himself, Roland tasted again the bitter news Phillips had delivered to him. After Weet and Lena died, he'd accepted that there was no guarantee he'd marry again, much less have more children. And that was if he even lived through the war, which had been doubtful. Then he'd met Lizzie. And he'd felt that faint pulse of life begin to stir inside him again. And even without being conscious of it, he'd begun to hope. Which was a dangerous thing. But knowing now that the odds were stacked against him in regard to ever being a father again felt like yet another death. One he couldn't even properly mourn.

"'The Phantom slowly, gravely, silently, approached,'" Lizzie read.

"'When it came near him, Scrooge bent down upon his knee; for in the very air through which this Spirit moved it seemed to scatter gloom and mystery.'"

The words she read, or maybe it was the way she read them, tugged on Roland's attention. And he wondered what the third ghost in the story was going to be like. The first, the Ghost of Christmas Past, had been an odd sort of phantom, childlike in appearance with a glowing head. Not frightening, to him at least. Although the journey the child phantom had thrust upon Scrooge had been unsettling. But Roland had walked that particular road before. He was expert in revisiting past mistakes and wishing, hopelessly so, that he could make them right. Scrooge had come to learn what he knew only too well. That the past was written in stone.

The second phantom, the Ghost of Christmas Present, while

definitely distressing in what he'd shown Scrooge, seemed akin to a majestic giant clad in a green mantle bordered with white fur with a holly wreath on his head. Hardly an intimidating figure. Still, the lens through which the giant had led Scrooge to view the unfolding of his present circumstances had been disturbing. And even though Roland had tried not to, he'd drawn comparisons between Scrooge's life and his own. Few of them favorable. Especially the crutch without an owner, which portended the death of the child. Something Scrooge was wise to have dreaded.

"'It was shrouded in a deep black garment,'" Lizzie continued, her soft voice intense, "'which concealed its head, its face, its form, and left nothing of it visible save one outstretched hand. But for this it would have been difficult to detach its figure from the night, and separate it from the darkness by which it was surrounded. He felt that it was tall and stately when it came beside him, and that its mysterious presence filled him with a solemn dread. He knew no more, for the Spirit neither spoke nor moved.'"

Roland realized he'd guessed correctly. *This* ghost promised to be far more compelling than its two predecessors.

"'"I am in the presence of the Ghost of Christmas Yet to Come?" said Scrooge.

"'The Spirit answered not, but pointed onward with its hand.

"'"You are about to show me shadows of the things that have not happened, but will happen in the time before us," Scrooge pursued. "Is that so, Spirit?"'"

Lieutenant Shuler and Winder both bobbed their heads up and down as though answering Scrooge's question.

"'The upper portion of the garment was contracted for an instant in its folds, as if the Spirit had inclined its head. That was the only answer he received.'"

As Lizzie continued, Roland wondered what it would be like to see his future as it would be, given his life on its present course. There was something sinister in the silence of this phantom. It didn't speak. Only pointed. Roland closed his eyes as the words created images he could all but see.

The ghost stopped beside a group of businessmen, and Scrooge moved closer to listen, only to hear the men speaking of someone's death in a rather callous and offhanded manner. The men even laughed. And as it turned out, Scrooge knew the men. The ghost led Scrooge to another setting, then another. And as the story unfolded, Roland felt an impending sense of doom. But no matter how Scrooge pleaded for the spirit to answer his many questions, the ghost only pointed, its spectral finger extending beyond the sleeve of its garment. Until, finally, it led Scrooge to a cemetery, then to a grave overgrown with weeds and forgotten with time.

""'Men's courses will foreshadow certain ends, to which, if persevered in, they must lead," said Scrooge. "But if the courses be departed from, the ends will change. Say it is thus with what you show me!"''"

Roland's eyes came open, Scrooge's question resonating within him. If a person changed on the inside and therefore made different decisions than he would have before, could the course of his life be altered? Of course, that assumed the decisions he'd initially made were poor ones.

"'Scrooge crept toward it, trembling as he went,'" Lizzie read, her voice never faltering. "'And following the finger, read upon the stone of the neglected grave his own name . . . Ebenezer Scrooge.'"

One of the nuns gave a soft gasp, but Roland didn't laugh this time. Neither did anyone else.

""'Am *I* that man who lay upon the bed," Scrooge cried, upon his knees.

"'The finger pointed from the grave to him, and back again.'

""'No, Spirit! Oh no, no!"''"

Roland shifted on his cot, feeling a measure of discomfort similar to that he'd experienced the night Lizzie challenged him about owning slaves. When the day of his passing came, hopefully years from this one, who would mourn his death? But far more important, what difference would his life have made? And would his life have been well spent? He turned the questions over in his mind, feeling as though the answers he sought were just beyond his grasp. Hidden from him. Frustration swept through him, followed by a cold rush of fear.

From where he sat he could see the wash of emotion in Lizzie's eyes, and he felt the hint of it in his own. He heard the clock chime from somewhere downstairs, but paid it no mind. Neither did the others around him, as Scrooge clutched at the spirit's robe.

"'"Hear me! I am not the man I was. I will not be the man I must have been but for this intercourse. Why show me this, if I am past all hope!" For the first time,'" Lizzie whispered, her own voice thinning, "'the hand appeared to shake.

"'"Assure me that I yet may change these shadows you have shown me, by an altered life!"'"

Roland would have sworn he felt a brush of wind sweep across the hallway. Yet no one had moved. No window or door had opened. A prickle skittered up his spine.

"'"I will honour Christmas in my heart," cried Scrooge.'" Lizzie's expression grew earnest. "'"I will live in the Past, the Present, and the Future. The Spirits of all Three shall strive within me. I will not shut out the lessons that they teach."'"

"Oh, praise God!" Sister Mary Grace exclaimed, kissing the cross hanging from her neck.

Roland laughed along with everyone else as Sister Mary blushed and gestured for them to look elsewhere. As Lizzie read of Scrooge's transformation, an unmistakable lightness and joy replaced the former tension and despair in the room.

"'And it was always said of Scrooge, that he knew how to keep Christmas well . . . May that be truly said of us, and all of us! And so, as Tiny Tim observed'"—Lizzie paused and looked around the room, inviting everyone to repeat with her—"""God bless Us, Every One!"""

Lizzie closed the book, and applause broke out. Soldiers whistled in approval. At their encouragement, she stood and took a bow. It was the happiest Roland could remember having seen her. Same for his fellow soldiers.

"Well done," he whispered to her as George rolled his cot back into the bedroom.

"Why, thank you, Captain Jones."

"Yes, ma'am." George gave her a smile. "That sure was some mighty fine readin'."

Her eyes twinkled. "Thank you, George. I appreciate that compliment."

"You welcome, Miss Lizzie!"

Roland looked between the two of them, sensing a definite familiarity that hadn't been there before. And one he wasn't completely comfortable with. He realized that George helped Tempy in the kitchen and so did Lizzie, on occasion. No doubt, knowing Lizzie, she'd engaged George in conversation and they'd become better acquainted. But there was still such a thing as respecting social boundaries. For everyone. George, he knew how to approach. Lizzie was another matter. He saw his opportunity when George left to help the nuns move soldiers back to the other rooms.

"Lizzie," he whispered, and her quick glance said she'd be right there.

She finished helping Lieutenant Shuler to bed and gave him his medication. Judging by the young man's adoring expression, her nurturing demeanor was of great comfort to him. When she turned to Roland, she was all smiles.

"I'm so glad the reading went well. Between the two of us?" She leaned closer. "I wasn't all that excited about doing it tonight. But once I started reading and felt everyone beginning to—"

Roland held up a hand, needing to seize the moment while the rest of the room was engaged in conversation. "Yes, I'm glad it went well too. You did a wonderful job. But I need to ask something of you."

"Of course." Her brows rose.

He chose his tone carefully. "I gather that you and George have become fairly well acquainted while he's been here. And I know we feel differently about this, Lizzie. But it's simply not appropriate for someone of George's position to be so informal with someone of yours."

Her brows lowered.

"There are certain . . ." He searched for the right words, half expecting her to fill in the blank for him. She didn't.

"Rules of decorum," he continued, further gentling his tone, "that are applicable in such situations. I'm asking you to respect my wishes in this regard. That's all."

Her lips formed a flat line, her eyes now more stormy gray than blue. "That's 'all' you ask?" She shook her head. "Roland, did you learn nothing from—" She stopped, glanced around them, then looked back at him. "What are you so afraid of?" she whispered. "What is it that you think is going to happen if you begin treating George like a fellow human being instead of a—"

"I *do* treat him like a fellow human being. I've told you that. I've known him most of my life, and I've always treated him with respect. But as I said, we all have different roles to—"

Now she put up *her* hand. "I respect you, Roland. And I can respect that you see this differently than I do. But I will not treat him any less than the man he is. Nor will I treat Tempy any differently. Not anymore. And you only have yourself to blame."

Roland opened his mouth to respond, but she beat him to it.

"You were willing to lay down your life for what you believe. Same as every man who marched onto that field that afternoon. And while I don't know that I would have the courage to do that, I do know that God has given me the courage to say yes to what he has called *me* to do. So finally, after all these years, that's what I'm doing. And I hope you'll respect *my* wishes in that regard."

She turned and left the room, and he itched to follow after her, explain himself, make her listen. Instead, he clenched his jaw and bit back all the things he wanted to say and couldn't. Things he lay awake for the better part of the night turning over in his mind, while the question she'd asked him thrummed beneath it all with a belligerence that wouldn't let go. He tossed on the cot, trying in vain to get comfortable. Finally he heaved a sigh and turned onto his back, his mind and body spent.

What are *you afraid of, beloved?* Roland's eyes came fully open. He rose on one elbow and looked around the room, heart ricocheting off his ribs. All was quiet, dark. No one stirred. Pulse hammering, he lay back down. His breath came hard as the soft echo of the question filled every part of him. But it was the love he'd sensed wrapped around and within the question that caused his eyes—and conscience—to burn.

He took a shaky breath, suddenly, painfully aware of God's omnipresence, and of his own earnest desire not to be seen. Yet the very air trembled with God's nearness. Roland took a shuttering breath. He'd made it clear to the Lord that he didn't need his strength. Didn't want it. That he could do this on his own. But he'd been wrong. In a flash, all the things he'd said in anger to the Almighty came rushing back, and he was nearly crushed beneath the weight of his own pride and self-sufficiency. And fear. His chest constricted. *I-I'm sorry*, he whispered from a place deep inside him, wishing he could take it all back.

In the space of a heartbeat, the anvil of regret lifted from his chest, and he took a deep breath. The first deep breath he'd taken in nearly two years, it felt like. Certainly since before Weet and Lena had gone home. He lay on his back, staring up. *Oh, Jesus . . . I don't know what to do. It feels like the entire world is unraveling and there's nothing I can do about it.*

As soon as he said it, he heard the pride and self-sufficiency yet again. He sighed and slowly nodded, the sting of truth rising to his eyes. What *was* he afraid of? The question hovered patiently yet persistently around him, quietly demanding he give answer. And as the sun finally edged up over the horizon, he did.

CHAPTER 36

Lizzie slipped out the back door of the kitchen, sunrise still a ways off. She'd overslept, so was already a few minutes late. She picked a nondescript path toward the back of the barn and the chicken coop, keeping to the shadows and away from the moon's silvery cast. She glanced behind her to the second-story windows along the back of the house, wanting to make sure no one was watching. The heavy curtains lay undisturbed.

She breathed in the cold January air, the tang of winter sharp and clean. Every time she sneaked to the barn like this, she thought of all the people who wouldn't approve. Roland, for certain. Towny would think it too dangerous. And the McGavocks. She wasn't fully certain what they would think. But she knew she needed to tell them. It had been weighing on her conscience for nearly two weeks now, ever since Roland had told her that she and George were "too familiar" with each other. If Roland got angry over that, she could only imagine his anger when he learned about this. But she didn't plan on telling him anytime soon.

She looked across the field to the wooded line where Towny had disappeared that night. The last time she'd seen him. Almost a month had passed since the battle in Nashville. Had he survived it? And the retreat? Was he still alive? If he was, why hadn't he contacted her? Or his father?

If he had been killed, wounded, or was missing, his name should have appeared in the lists the War Department issued in the newspaper. She'd checked every day without fail. No Blake Rupert Townsend. Yet having walked the aftermath of the battle in the Harpeth Valley, she knew firsthand that some of the bodies had been mutilated beyond recognition. "'But it is a freeing thing, in a way, to be ready and willing to die.'" She spoke aloud to the night, his last letter as familiar to her now as her own mirror image. "'To have accepted that your death could come at any time.'"

She'd never had to come to grips with death as he had. Or Thaddeus. Or Roland and all the others. But it was what Towny had written after that about life that had deepened her determination to be a wife worthy of his affection. *Because you realize the precious fleetingness of it, and of how very little time we all have here. Which is all the more reason not to delay once you find what you want with all your heart.*

She gave a soft sigh. *Towny . . . Come home to us.*

She opened the barn door and breathed in the familiar scents of horse sweat, hay, and saddle oil. Over the whinny of horses she heard soft voices. She followed the soft glow of lamplight and found George and Tempy in an empty stall, each sitting on a barrel, their expressions earnest.

"Good morning," she whispered, her breath puffing white.

"Mornin', Miss Lizzie," they responded, voices overlapping.

Lizzie lifted the cloth from the top of the basket and removed the teaching materials. They'd agreed it was safer for her to keep the slates and primers in her possession. But she had a surprise for them today. She withdrew two brand-new notebooks with sharpened pencils. "You've both been working so diligently, I wanted to do something to encourage you in your studies. We can use these occasionally instead of the slates." She held out the gifts.

George and Tempy looked at each other first, then back at her before gingerly accepting. The way they held the notebooks and pencils, carefully, almost reverently, impressed upon Lizzie again how grateful she was that God had opened a door for her to share this time with them.

They set to work reviewing previous lessons, then took turns reading. Both of them knew their letters fairly well now, but sometimes they still confused the coordinating sounds. Which wasn't unusual.

"You can slow down, George," she said gently. "Take your time. We all must walk before we run."

"I ain't got time for walkin', ma'am. I got to learn this so I can take care of my family."

"You will learn it. You already are learning. See here." She turned in the primer. "Read this part for me."

He shook his head. "That's cheatin'. The drawin' on the page half tells me what the words are."

"Please, read this part for me," Lizzie said again, feeling Tempy watching them.

George clenched his jaw, his grip tightening on the book, and it struck her how very much alike he and Roland were. Impatient with their unknown futures, anxious about caring for their loved ones, and stubborn to the point of being prideful in some things. She wished she could have seen them together as young boys, before Roland had been taught that George was somehow less than he was—or had a "different role" in life—because of the color of his skin. People had to be taught those kinds of preconceptions. She knew that from experience. She'd been teaching for over sixteen years, and on more than one occasion when she'd been outside with her youngest pupils, either taking a walk or sitting beneath a tree studying, slave children would wander up and join them. And the children would talk and play together, without any thought of their color or their differences. It was only once her pupils were older, after they'd watched and learned from their parents and other adults, that the animosity and prejudgment took hold. And once that hideous seed had taken root, it seemed only Jesus himself could restore what had been ruined.

"'See . . . the . . . dog . . . c—'" He exhaled.

"Sound the word out," she encouraged.

"I know I'm gonna say it wrong."

She bit back a smile and pointed to the first two letters in the word. "When a *c* and an *h* are together at the beginning of a word, what sound do they make?"

Tempy sat a little straighter and Lizzie gave her a quick look, knowing she knew the answer. And so did George, if only he would be half as patient with himself as he was with others. Lizzie asked him the question again, and he rubbed the back of his neck.

"*Ch?*" he said simply, then shook his head as though waiting to be told he was wrong.

"Yes! That's exactly right." Lizzie smiled. "Now finish sounding out the word."

He brought the book a little closer to his face. "'Ch . . . aaa . . . sss . . .'" He squinted, then looked over at her. "I think that last little letter there ain't got no sound this time."

"If that's the case"—she cut her eyes at him—"and it is"—she saw the light inch back into his expression—"how would you pronounce the word?"

He eyed the word for a few seconds. "Chase! 'See the dog chase . . . the mouse.'"

"Excellent. And do you realize, George, that not quite a month ago, if I had handed you this book, you wouldn't have been able to read a single word. Much less that sentence."

He nodded. "Give me another one?"

Smiling, she turned the page. "One more and then it's Tempy's turn."

"It better be my turn soon, or I'm gonna die o' old age."

They all laughed, and the lesson time flew as it always did. Hearing the first warble of birdsong, Lizzie peered up through the cracks in the barn roof and saw the subtle change from darkness to dawn. Wishing they had more time, she packed her teaching materials into the basket when George and Tempy both held out their notebooks and pencils.

Lizzie shook her head. "I bought those for you."

"Comin' here and learnin' is one thing, ma'am." George's expression held warning. "But us bein' caught with these? There won't be any mistakin' what we doin' then. I know o' slaves who been horse-whipped for a lot less."

Knowing he was right, and feeling foolish for not considering that, Lizzie took the paper and pencils. "I'll keep them for you. For now. But hopefully one day very soon you'll be able to keep them for yourselves. For good."

"Oh Lord, for that day." Tempy's whisper sounded more like a prayer.

Lizzie followed them to the back door of the barn when she noticed it. The goings-on in the last stall. "What on earth?" It had been so dark when she entered, she hadn't seen it. She stepped closer and heard George's soft laughter behind her.

"It's somethin' for the cap'n, ma'am. And for the other men too, if they want it. I started on it a few days back, once the doc give the cap'n the okay to move on to walkin'. Colonel McGavock give me the lumber, the rope, and the bricks. Tempy give me some old dishcloths. It ain't much to look at, but it'll get the job done."

Lizzie's gaze trailed up to the top of the stall, where a rudimentary pulley-type system had been attached. Ropes hung down, one end tied in loops, the others tied around bricks wrapped in cloth. "Does Captain Jones know about this?"

"Not yet, ma'am. I ain't quite done with it. Soon, though. Then I'm gonna show it to him."

Lizzie looked back at him. "Please let me be here when you do."

As customary, they exited the barn separately. George to his cabin, Tempy to the springhouse, and she to the chicken coop. She ducked inside and managed to catch three roosts unoccupied. She grabbed the eggs, closed the door behind her, and hurried toward the house. She was halfway to the back door when the sound of a twig snapping heightened her senses. She glanced behind her, prickles of fear inching up her spine. She didn't see anyone, but couldn't shake the feeling she was being watched. She turned and bolted for the house when someone grabbed her from behind.

CHAPTER 37

Lizzie tried to scream, but a hand clamped hard over her mouth and the sound came out muffled, barely audible. But the man had taught her well. She dropped the basket, lowered her body, and spun, then brought her elbow up hard and fast to the—

"Lizzie!"

She froze, her breath coming hard. The hand fell away.

"Towny?" she whispered.

He gave a cautious laugh. "Yep. Or what's about to be left of me once you're done."

She threw her arms around his neck, and he hugged her close.

"You made it through the battle," she whispered, then pulled back to check his face, his arms, his legs.

"I did. And I'm all right." He kissed the top of her head, emotion in his voice. "I don't know how, though. I thought I was done for so many times I lost count. God just isn't finished with me, I guess."

She smiled. Hadn't Roland said much the same thing to her the first night they'd met? She pulled back. "It's dangerous for you to be here. Federal patrols are by here all hours of the day and night."

"I know. I saw a couple earlier. From the woods. There're a few of us who held back to get word to families."

Lizzie glanced around. "You're not alone?"

He shook his head. "We split up about a mile back. But don't worry about us. We know these woods far better than those Yanks ever could."

She tugged at his sleeve. "Come on inside. I'll get you some coffee and we can talk." She bent to pick up the basket, only now remembering the eggs. But knowing Towny was alive, she didn't care. "Tempy will want to see you, and so will the—"

"Lizzie Beth," he said softly, and something about his tone, the gravity of his voice, made her throat go dry.

She straightened.

"I don't have much time. Our commander's only given us a few hours, then we have to report back." He brushed the hair from her face. "Did you get my letter? The one I wrote you from Nashville?"

"Yes," she whispered, her throat beginning to tighten. "I've written you back, but I didn't know where to send it. I can go get it if you—"

He took both of her hands in his. And though he hadn't moved, his breath came quicker. "I have loved you all my life. And you will always be my first love."

Hearing a finality in his voice, she felt tears rise to her eyes.

"But life is so short," he whispered. "And so precious. We're here and then we're gone. And what we do with our lives matters. Not only in this life, but in the one to come. And, Lizzie, I want you to have the most wonderful life you can. You deserve that. I want you to marry, to have children, to grow old with the man you love. But—" His voice caught. "I'm not convinced I'll ever be that man for you. Will I?" he finished in a whisper, a desperation in his voice that pierced her heart.

Lizzie pressed her lips together. "Towny, I—"

He cradled her face. "Only the truth this time, all right? Not what you think you *should* say. Or what you think I want to hear. Or even what you hope to one day be able to say to me. I would marry you right now, this very minute, if I were certain you believed I'm that man for you. And I *will* marry you, Lizzie Beth, if you say that I am."

She nodded, her chest aching. She tried to speak, tried to force out the words. But nothing came.

The first hint of dawn revealed his sad smile. "I've given you my pledge, and I will stand by that promise all the days of my life. Because

357

I love you. But *because* I love you—" He struggled, his composure slipping. "I'm also willing to let you go. If that's what you want."

Lizzie hugged him tight, wishing they could go back to what they had been and feeling as though her heart was being torn in two. "I do love you, Towny. You're the dearest friend I've ever had."

A strangled noise rose in his throat. His arms came around her. Lizzie held on to him tighter, trying unsuccessfully to stifle her sobs. Finally he drew back, and with a trembling hand wiped the tears from her cheeks, his own wet with emotion.

"I release you from your pledge, Lizzie." He waited, a question in his reddened eyes.

She nodded, scarcely able to speak past the knot at the base of her throat. "I release you too."

He took a sharp breath, then cupped her chin. "I only wish the very best for you. Remember that."

"You too," she whispered. "I'm just sorry that—"

"Shhh . . ." He pressed a kiss to her forehead, hard and quick. "I love you, Lizzie Beth," he whispered.

"I love you too, Towny. And I always will."

Standing where he left her, she watched him until he disappeared back into the woods. She gathered the basket, not bothering about the broken eggs. Deep inside, she knew this was for the best, so why did it feel as though her heart had been ripped from her chest? She walked back into the kitchen by rote, unaware of her surroundings.

"Miss Lizzie, you all right?"

Lizzie shook her head. "It's Towny."

Tempy gasped. "Oh Lord, no . . ."

"No, he's not dead! I just saw him. Outside. He's very much alive." She tried to smile but couldn't. She drew in a breath, but her lungs wouldn't function as they should. "He said he released me from my pledge. That he only wishes the very best for me and—" Her voice broke.

Tempy drew her into her arms, and Lizzie held on tight. "You do deserve that, ma'am. And so does that Lieutenant Towny."

That Lieutenant Towny, Lizzie noticed. Not *her* lieutenant. Not anymore.

"And you both are gonna find it. Just wait and see."

"I never meant to hurt him. But I did."

Tempy smiled. "We all go through life not meanin' to hurt each other, Miss Lizzie. But we do. Seems like those we love best, we hurt the most. Don't make sense, I know, but it's the plain truth of it. Now you sit down right here." Tempy pulled out a chair. "And let me get you some hot coffee and breakfast."

Not hungry, Lizzie did as Tempy bade, thinking again about Towny's last letter and what he'd said about imminent death causing him to embrace life in a way he hadn't before. *Because you realize the precious fleetingness of it, and of how very little time we all have here. Which is all the more reason not to delay once you find what you want with all your heart.* She'd thought he had meant her by that last phrase. But he hadn't. He'd been talking about finding a woman who would love him as he deserved to be—

"Miss Clouston."

Lizzie looked up to see Sister Mary Grace standing at the base of the stairs leading to the main house.

"It's Lieutenant Shuler, Miss Clouston. You need to come quickly."

LIZZIE HURRIED UP the staircase, passing Sister Mary Grace. When she reached Winder's bedroom, she paused in the doorway to catch her breath, only to have it stolen away again. James looked so pale and small in the bed. So different from when she'd left him last night. She crossed to him, her gaze connecting with Roland's. And if she hadn't already known the truth, the sadness in his eyes would have confirmed it. Sisters Angelica, Elizabeth, and Faith stood teary-eyed at the foot of the bed, and even Taylor and Smitty had the decency to look somber.

Lizzie moved the straight-back chair aside and sat on the edge of the bed. She pressed a hand to James's forehead, the flush of his cheeks foretelling the heat of his skin.

His eyes fluttered open, then closed again, and his parched lips curved in a weak smile. "You're here . . ." His voice held a measure of surprise.

Lizzie swallowed. "Of course I'm here. And I won't leave your side for a minute."

"Just like you promised."

She nodded. "Just like I promised."

The moment stretched.

"Does it hurt much?" he whispered.

Lizzie looked over at Roland, but his expression said he didn't understand either. So she answered as she thought best. "No, it doesn't hurt. Not at all."

"Good . . ." Again his pale lips curved as he opened his eyes. His gaze found hers. "'Cause I'm tired of hurtin', Mama."

Lizzie held her breath to keep from sobbing. "I know you are, James," she finally managed. "And I'm sorry, sweetheart . . . that you've been through so much."

He lifted a shaky hand from the bedcovers, and she grasped it. To her surprise, he held on tight. Then his breathing changed. It grew thready and uneven. She recognized the moment for what it was, having been with Thaddeus at his death. She took a deep breath and leaned closer.

"It's time to come home, James." How she spoke in that moment, she didn't know. "Thomas and I . . . are waiting here for you."

And once again she felt the slender thread binding soul to body stretch until it gave way. James's hand gradually went lax in hers as he breathed his last. Behind her Lizzie heard the hushed prayers of the nuns, but she couldn't look away from James's face. If it hurt this badly to lose this precious young man, how much more did it hurt to lose one's own son or daughter?

Moments passed, and she tucked his hand back beneath the covers and rose. She met Roland's gaze, his eyes red-rimmed, and wondered if perhaps he was thinking about his sweet daughter. And maybe Weet too. And though he said nothing, he said everything she needed to hear. She wished she could walk straight into the comfort of his arms and feel his strength come around her. She turned to see Colonel and Mrs. McGavock in the doorway, and Carrie crossed the room and reached for her hands.

"Well done, my dear," Carrie said through tears.

Lizzie tightened her grip, fresh emotion rising. "How did you do this?" she said softly. "How did you go through this *three times*? He wasn't even my son and I—"

Carrie looked into her eyes. "I didn't go through it alone. The Lord was with me every step of the way. He was with both me and John."

Lizzie nodded as though she understood, then hurried from the room and down the stairs, eager to get somewhere by herself where she could give in to the grief building like a wave inside her. She opened the front door and ran down the steps and across the yard until she reached the shelter of the towering Osage orange tree. Hidden from view of the house, she sank onto the bench nestled by a hedge of hydrangea and wept.

CHAPTER 38

Balancing on crutches, Roland slowly shifted some of his weight to his right leg and braced himself for a conflagration of pain—which didn't come. Feeling the sweat on his brow, he looked over at Dr. Phillips, then at George, whose expressions both held anticipation—and cautious hope.

"Now's about the time, Captain, when you tell me what a stupendous surgeon I am."

Roland smiled. "I think I'll hold that accolade until I actually take a first step."

The doc shook his head. "Doubter."

Roland slowly lifted his left leg, placing a greater portion of his weight on his weaker side, and he winced at the discomfort that shot from his foot straight up into his back. "How is it I can lift both of my legs repeatedly on the cot, and I'm fine. Then I try to put weight on this right side and it's like needles running through my veins."

"One, you're using different muscles when you lie flat and lift that way. There's not as much pressure on your back. And two, you haven't been on your feet in over a month, Jones. Give it some time. It'll hurt at first, but that'll ease up the more you move. Your bones are still healing. But you're strong. You'll get there."

Phillips looked over at George. "You think he's ready for it?"

George smiled. "I reckon he is, sir."

"Ready for what?" Roland looked between them, not trusting the glimmer in their eyes.

George stepped forward. "I got somethin' to show you in the barn, sir."

"What is it?"

"I really don't wanna say, sir. I want you to come and see it."

Roland frowned. "But if you'd just tell me——"

"Jones." Phillips leveled a stare. "For once in your life, don't dissect something to death. Just trust him and get moving."

Roland knew the doc couldn't possibly know how timely his words were. But—he smiled to himself—he and God did. With the aid of his crutches, he reached back to his cot for one of Weet's letters he'd been rereading. He folded it and slid it beneath the thin mattress with the others. As he turned, he saw Winder's empty bed and could still imagine James Shuler lying there, that crooked little smile on his face. It had only been two days since Colonel McGavock, Dr. Phillips, George, and Lizzie had buried the young lieutenant with the others of their regiment who lay to rest in the Harpeth Valley. Roland planned on walking that field again as soon as he was able. He still had some formal good-byes to say.

Working to keep his balance, he made his way toward the open bedroom door.

"Goin' for a walk, Captain Jones?" Taylor asked, looking up at him.

Roland didn't trust the straightforward question, nor the look of forced interest on Taylor's face. "Going for a run, Lieutenant."

Taylor laughed and nodded. "That's a good one, sir."

Sir? Roland's grip tightened on the crutches. Taylor had been on his best behavior lately, which meant only one thing. Trouble was brewing.

Roland made it to the door without mishap. It felt good—and odd—to move on his own accord. Or mostly on his own. A little later than his goal of taking his first step by Christmas, but he'd finally made it. He started across the second-floor hallway toward the stairs when George came up alongside him. Phillips followed.

"I help you down, Cap'n."

"No, I think I'd rather try this on my——" Roland saw the steep set of stairs descending downward. And much as he didn't want to depend on George in this particular way, he knew that if he tried it on his own and fell, it would delay his recuperation by weeks. Or do even worse damage than before. He nodded and handed the doc his crutches. "All right then."

George picked him up—one arm supporting his back, the other beneath the bend in his legs—and carried him down. Roland kept his gaze forward but sensed that George could feel his discomfort. No matter his determination not to worry about the family estate or how he was going to care for his mother, sisters, and the female relatives from Georgia now staying with them, he still thought about the challenge before him constantly. He thought about George too, and wondered if he was planning on leaving with his family soon. If George did decide to leave, Roland knew that would mark the end for his estate. All would be lost. And it might well be anyway, for all he knew.

Feeling the burden of worry settling in again, he swiftly centered his thoughts. God knew what was coming down the pike, even if he didn't. The Almighty had made that much clear. And while Roland wished the Lord would be a little more openhanded with his plans, he determined to take one step at a time. And right now that meant learning to walk.

"You's a mite heavier, sir, than some of them other smaller fellas upstairs."

Phillips laughed behind them. "It's all that sitting around and eating he's been doing, George. We need to get this man moving."

"Yes, sir, Doc. We do."

At the bottom of the stairs, George set him down and assisted him with his crutches, and the act wasn't lost on Roland. The slave helping the slave owner to stand. Roland felt lesser inside because of it and was grateful his father and grandfather weren't alive to see him like this. To see what the world was becoming. But even as those thoughts took shape, Roland felt a nudge of shame, thinking about how Lizzie would react if she heard them. And what had she meant the other night when she'd said God had given her the courage to say yes to what he'd called her to do? What was that exactly? he wondered. And why did it worry him?

George helped him out the back door and down the porch steps and toward the barn. Roland paused for a minute and let the sunshine warm his face. The air was cool and crisp, and he felt a measure of gratitude simply for the chance to stand there and drink it in. He was thankful to Dr. Phillips, most certainly. But also to George. George didn't have to be here. Not anymore. Roland knew, when he'd sent that wire to his mother, that George could have refused to come. But he hadn't. And ever since he'd been here, he'd been nothing but helpful. Even if the familiarity between him and Lizzie was more than a little bothersome. Was that all part of how things would be changing as well? He was fairly sure he just heard his father and grandfather roll over in their graves. The sardonic thought brought a humorless smile, but beneath that was another layer of experience and memory Roland had yet to probe. And wasn't eager to.

Because if Lizzie was right—and that *if* still loomed large in his mind—and owning slaves as his family had done for years was immoral, that made his grandfather and father immoral men. And that struck against everything within him. Because he'd patterned his life after those two men. They'd not only shown him how to farm and run a plantation, but they'd sown the seeds that had become the foundation of his faith. How could they have done that if their actions in this regard had been so reprehensible? He stood on their shoulders and had the life he did due, at least in part, to the legacy they'd left behind. Both physical and spiritual. To admit his own guilt was one thing. But to assign such wide-sweeping wrongdoing to them was more than he could manage.

Almost to the barn, he heard the kitchen door open and saw Lizzie and Tempy hurry out to join them. "Why do I get the feeling you were both waiting and watching?" he said, giving them a wry smile.

They both ignored the comment and fell into step with the group. Roland caught a revived twinkle in Lizzie's eyes and was glad to see it. She'd taken young James's death especially hard. But what she'd done on that young man's deathbed . . . answering him as she had. Roland felt a stirring in his chest just remembering it. She would indeed make a fine mother to Towny's and her children someday.

Once inside in the barn, Roland stood for a second and let his eyes adjust to the dimmer light. The comforting scents of leather and horse-flesh surrounded him. It smelled like home. And childhood.

"Come on back here, Cap'n." George gestured.

Roland followed him, hearing the others' footsteps behind them, until George stopped in front of an empty stable. Roland peered inside and frowned. A pulley system of some sort hung from the back of the stable, complete with ropes looped and coming off with something tied to . . .

Roland looked from George to the doc. "What is all this?"

"This, Captain Jones"—Phillips stepped forward and picked up one looped end of a rope and pulled, lifting a weight that had been tied on the other end—"is you regaining your strength."

Roland watched as Phillips demonstrated and explained how the contraption worked. It was primitive in design. And simple. But also . . . genius. At the doc's urging, Roland tried it with his left hand. Then with what was left of his right, slipping his forearm through the loop in the rope.

Phillips picked up a separate rope. "Now try this one on your legs."

George retrieved something resembling a two-sided ladder with fewer rungs that was leaned up against the wall. "Settle back onto this, Cap'n. It'll help keep you upright when you doin' your legs. That is, 'til you can balance again on your own. Which'll come about soon enough, I know."

Roland did as they said. And though lifting the weight, light as it was, with his right leg brought a fair amount of discomfort, it wasn't the shooting pain he'd experienced before. He attempted it again with his left and lifted the weight even higher. He exhaled, more than pleased. "Doc, this is really something. You've outdone yourself."

Phillips shook his head. "It wasn't me, Captain." He nodded. "It was all George here. From start to finish."

Roland frowned but read confirmation in the doc's face. Roland looked over at George. "You did this? For me?"

George gave a single nod. "Yes, sir, Cap'n. We gotta get you back to healthy so you can get home. Back to your mother and sisters. And to the farm."

Roland's throat tightened. He looked from George to the contraption he'd built and back again, feeling Lizzie's attention on him. Tempy's too. Did this mean George wasn't planning on leaving as all the other slaves had done? Roland wasn't about to ask. But for the first time in a long time, he felt a trickle of hope. He cleared his throat, careful not to look in Lizzie's direction.

"You did well, George," he finally managed. "You did well."

Two days later, Lizzie peered inside Winder's bedroom. But Roland wasn't there. Her gaze trailed to the empty bed, and tears lodged in her throat. She pulled the photograph of James and his brother Thomas from her skirt pocket, along with the page from the book of Psalms. *You three precious boys . . . May you rest in his peace. And, Lord, would you please provide a way for me to get Thaddeus's message to his mother? Wherever she is.*

Winder was taking James's death especially hard, but Colonel and Mrs. McGavock were spending additional time with him, helping him cope. Even with a house still full of soldiers, it felt especially empty without James.

"You lookin' for the cap'n, Miss Lizzie?"

Lizzie turned to see George coming up the stairs, fresh linens in his arms. "Yes, I am." She returned the keepsakes to her pocket.

"He's sittin' out yonder on the back porch. Enjoyin' what's left of this fine day."

She glanced in that direction. "A letter came for him earlier this afternoon, so I thought I'd bring it up." She didn't need an excuse to see Roland, she knew. Especially now. She hadn't told him yet about Towny's recent homecoming. She simply hadn't found the right time. But that was an excuse, and she knew it. The real reason was curled cold and tight in the pit of her stomach.

George held out his hand. "Want me to take it out to him, ma'am?"

"Oh no. That's all right. I don't mind. But thank you."

He looked at her a little overlong before he walked on toward Hattie's room, and she wondered if her feelings were written as clearly on her face as she suspected they were. The jib window in the guest room stood partially open, and she found Roland sitting alone on the northwest corner of the porch overlooking the backyard and the battlefield beyond, his crutches leaning up against the railing.

It was good to see him sitting upright in a chair these days. Even better to briefly watch him yesterday morning working the weights and pulley system George had constructed. She'd seen Roland and George go back to the barn that afternoon, then again last evening. She didn't know if it was his finally being mobile again, but she'd noticed a subtle difference in Roland. His shock when discovering that George, and not Dr. Phillips, was responsible for constructing the mechanism had been telling as well. Was it George's ingenuity that had surprised him? Or the obvious care and concern behind the action that had touched him most?

Her footsteps announced her entrance, and he glanced back.

"Evening, Lizzie." He gestured to the chair to his right. "Please join me. But you might want to grab a blanket. It's been pleasant, but it'll get chillier once the sun goes down."

"I'll be fine." She claimed the rocker beside him, the simple act feeling as natural as if she'd done it a thousand times. "You received a letter today."

She glanced again at the initials on the return address as she handed the envelope to him, curious. It was written in a most feminine hand script. She'd thought about his mother or his unmarried sisters, but their last name wouldn't begin with the letter *P*.

Roland read the return address and smiled. "Well, this is certainly a surprise. Mind if I read it now?"

"Be my guest."

He tore open the envelope and scanned the brief missive.

"Good news, I hope?" she said after a moment.

He nodded, glanced inside the envelope, and pulled out another piece of paper, from which slipped several paper bills. Lizzie counted the money as he picked it up.

"Twenty-five dollars," she said, hearing the incredulity in her voice.

He looked over at her. "A gift. From a very kind and *older* woman." With a gleam in his eye, he handed her the letter, then pulled it back slightly. "But only if you read it aloud. I like hearing you read."

The playful gesture reminded her of James, and judging from the look in Roland's eyes, he was thinking of him too. She unfolded the letter—and felt her jaw slip open. "Mrs. James K. Polk? As in the former president of the United States?"

Roland laughed. "Well, actually she wasn't the president. Her husband was."

Lizzie swatted his arm.

"But yes, as in that Polk. My family's plantation in Yalobusha borders theirs. Our families have known one another for years."

"And she's sending you money?"

He gestured. "Read the letter."

"'To Captain R. W. Jones of Mississippi. Dear Sir . . .'" Lizzie gave him a look. "'I received a letter yesterday from Mr. I. M. Avent at my plantation in Mississippi informing me that you had been wounded in the battle at Franklin and perhaps needed some currency to suit this region. Dr. Brinton, the medical director at Nashville, has kindly offered to convey to you any communication I wish to send. I herewith enclose $25 and beg that you will write to me the amount you need.'" Lizzie paused, looked over the top of the letter, raised her eyebrows, and mouthed, *Beg?*

With a smile, Roland waved for her to continue.

"'I will take pleasure to remit to you the sum you require. I will be pleased to hear from you. And if I can serve you in any way, I hope that you will not hesitate to call on me. I am, very respectfully, Mrs. James K. Polk.'" She stared at the letter. "You know the wife of a former president of the United States."

"And *you* know someone who *knows* the wife of a former president of the United States."

They both laughed and then sighed at the same time.

Lizzie handed him the letter, their fingers brushing as she did. A shiver went through her. She'd come with a purpose other than delivering the letter. She'd come with a question. But just for a moment, she wanted to enjoy being in his company. Being a woman sitting with a man on a porch, watching the sun set. Far from any semblance of war or pain or anguish or death.

She turned ever so slightly and looked at his profile in the waning light of day. He was so handsome and kind. Far from perfect. But so was she. She had yet to broach the topic of slavery with him again, and wasn't eager to bring it up now. But she'd been praying about it, asking God to work in Roland's heart much as he had been working in hers. Yet beyond that chasm of a difference between them lay another one. And in some ways, this one was far more frightening to her.

She was certain that, at least at the first, Roland had been interested in her. But in the weeks that had passed and in all the life that had been lived within these walls since that horrible night, had his feelings for her changed? Maybe they had. She no longer caught him looking at her as she used to. Or maybe he'd just accepted, as she had until recent days, that they would only ever be friends.

"It's beautiful up here," he said, his tone reflective.

"It's one of my favorite places at Carnton."

Behind them in the house, she heard some of the soldiers returning to their rooms and knew she needed to forge ahead. "I finally heard from Towny," she said, and Roland turned toward her.

"He's alive." It wasn't a question.

She nodded, smiling. "And doing well. He says he doesn't know how he made it through."

Roland looked back across the battlefield in the distance. "I know that feeling."

"He came here to tell me that he was all right. But he also came to tell me something else. He and I are . . . no longer betrothed, Roland." She felt his attention again but didn't look at him. It would be easier to say this if she didn't. And impossible if she did.

"Towny and I have been friends forever. You already know that. When he asked me to marry him and I said yes, I wasn't completely honest with him. After the battle here, one of the nights when he came to see me, he could tell something was wrong. That I wasn't . . . responding the way a woman should to her future husband." Her face heated at the admission. Her throat went dry. And Roland's close attention wasn't helping. "When Towny pressed me for the truth," she continued. "I told him."

"Lizzie, you don't have to—"

"No, I want to. I want to be completely honest with you." She turned to look at him then, and the emotion in his eyes was nearly her undoing. She felt a rush of warmth and wondered if he did too. But when his gaze dropped to her mouth, she didn't have to wonder anymore. The desire she felt, she saw mirrored in his eyes. But she needed to finish. She looked away, struggling to focus.

"I don't want you to think ill of Towny. Or to think he simply decided to break his pledge. That's not what happened. You see, what he didn't know when I accepted his proposal—what I was too afraid to admit—was that the reason I said yes wasn't because I truly wanted to marry him." Her voice fell away. Emotion rose in her chest, and she took a quick breath. "I want children." She gave a gentle shrug. "And I knew Towny would be a good father. That's the reason I said yes. I'm twenty-eight years old, and the opportunity for me to become a mother won't always be here. I knew Towny and I weren't right for each other. In that way. And now he's realized it too."

She held Roland's gaze and felt a weight lift from her shoulders. She waited for him to respond, but he just stared. Then he faced forward again, the muscles working in his jaw.

"I'm sorry," he whispered, his graveled voice rough with emotion. "For you and Towny. You're both such . . . fine people."

Lizzie blinked. This wasn't the response she'd expected. Or had hoped for. Or the one she'd thought was coming, based on what she'd seen in his eyes just a moment—

"It's getting late. We'd better get back inside."

Hesitating, she touched his arm. "Roland . . ."

He stilled. Then shook his head. "Lizzie, I—" He covered her hand on his arm, his own warm and strong. He looked over at her, and she felt the distance between them lessening—and was certain it wasn't only of her doing. She caught the scent of mint on his breath. His gaze moved to her mouth and she swallowed, every imagining she'd ever had about him coming back with a force—and vividness—that took her breath away.

He rose. "We'd better go inside."

He reached for his crutches, and she felt as though she'd missed something. She wanted to ask him, but when he motioned for her to precede him into the house, she realized she'd gotten the answer to the question she'd brought. And his answer was no.

CHAPTER 39

For the umpteenth time Lizzie glanced at the clock on the table, counting the minutes until lunch. The children finished their reading assignments, and she escorted them toward the stairs. Winder didn't look into his bedroom when they passed, and Lizzie took that as a good sign. She gave his hair a quick tousle, and he looked up and smiled, then tucked his little hand into hers as Hattie chattered away about making cookies with Tempy. When they reached the entrance hall, Winder ran ahead through the dining room and down to the kitchen.

Hattie looped her arm through Lizzie's. "Tempy said she'll teach me how to make them all by myself."

"Well, if Tempy is teaching you, then those cookies will be the best—"

Three hard raps sounded on the front door.

Lizzie pressed a kiss to Hattie's forehead. "You go on down, dear. Please tell Tempy I'll be right there."

"Yes, ma'am."

As she turned, Lizzie spotted Roland and George through the dining room window. They were walking toward the barn. In the past month, Roland had made remarkable improvement. He still walked with the aid of crutches, but his legs were getting stronger. Soon he'd only need a cane. Yet the sooner that happened, the sooner he'd go to prison. So despite his apparent lack of romantic feelings for her, she selfishly hoped he wouldn't get too well too quickly. She would miss his company terribly, along with their conversations.

The knocking sounded again, and she crossed to answer the door. The McGavocks weren't expecting any company that she knew of, and as her hand closed around the knob, she had a sinking feeling. *Please, not another Federal patrol.* They'd received word two days ago of convalescing soldiers being taken from other Franklin homes, but the patrols hadn't returned to Carnton. Yet.

She opened the door and to her relief saw an older man standing on the threshold. He was a few inches shorter than she and thin as a reed, with a bandaged forehead and a large Bible in his hand.

He tilted his head in greeting. "Good day to you, miss. E. M. Bounds calling."

He said the name as though she should recognize it, but she didn't. "Good day, Mr. Bounds. Are you here to see Colonel McGavock?"

His eyes gained a sparkle, and he fingered his salt-and-pepper beard. "Actually, it's Preacher Bounds, ma'am, and I'm responding to a request sent from Captain Roland Jones. If he's still convalescing in this home."

At the mention of Roland's name, the pieces fell into place. "*You're* the preacher the captain wrote to! The one he said might be able to help us locate a boy's family." She gestured for him to enter. "It's been so long, we thought perhaps you'd moved on with the army."

The man stepped into the entrance hall, his smile encompassing his entire face. "My apologies for being so tardy in responding, but I didn't receive the good captain's message until recently. I was wounded during the battle here some time back, then was briefly incarcerated in one of the Federal prisons."

"Oh, I'm so sorry!"

"Don't be. The Lord has ordered my steps, and he opened many doors in prison for me to share his grace and love. Though none of them a cell door as he did for Saint Paul, I must add."

Lizzie smiled, appreciating the man's humor. "My name is Miss Clouston, and I'm the McGavocks' governess."

"A pleasure, Miss Clouston." He tipped his head. "The captain didn't go into detail as to what he wanted. All he said was that he required my help. But if there's anything I can do to aid Captain Jones, I'll move heaven and earth to make it happen." He leaned in. "In fact, as soon as I received his note, I began petitioning heaven on his account, so I have full confidence that God is already at work, whatever the need."

"A young boy, you say?" Preacher Bounds studied the pieces of paper in his hand. "By the name of Thaddeus. A fine name," he added thoughtfully.

"Yes, that's right." Lizzie leaned forward on the settee. "He was among the first of the wounded to be brought to the house that night. It was in this room, the best parlor, that he died."

Sitting beside her on the settee, Roland heard the hope in her voice and prayed that Bounds could be of help. He knew how much she wanted to find the boy's mother, and he wanted to be the one to help her see this through while he could. He wanted to be so much more to her in other ways as well, but he knew now that would never happen.

"He couldn't have been more than thirteen or fourteen years old," she continued. "And that brief note and those lists are among the items I found in his pockets, along with a knife, some scriptures, and a rock."

"As Captain Jones says, I do have a knack for remembering names, which comes in handy in my profession, as you might imagine." He glanced in Roland's direction. "I've met four soldiers by that name, but they're all older. None of them as youthful as you've described, and three of them are already with their Maker, God rest their souls. Are there any other distinguishing characteristics that you can remember about the boy, Miss Clouston?"

Lizzie shook her head. "None other than those I've told you about already."

Bounds stared a moment more at the pieces of paper, then sighed. "It hurts me more than you know to disappoint you, ma'am. Sadly, we have lost far too many of our young men in this war. While I've done my best to minister to every man and boy whom God has placed in my path, I fear I did not cross that of the dear lad you're describing. Or if I did, I simply don't have recollection of him. If I'd seen these lists or if he'd mentioned some of these things to me, I would most assuredly have memory of them, and of him." He glanced again at the lists Thaddeus had made. "What a remarkable young man he must have been."

Lizzie's shoulders drooped, and Roland felt responsible. After all, it had been his idea to contact Preacher Bounds. The preacher rose, and he and Lizzie did likewise.

Disappointment furrowed her brow. "I'm sorry to have wasted your time, Preacher Bounds. Thank you, sir, for coming out to see us."

"No time or effort is wasted that is spent in service to the Lord, Miss Clouston. And from what Captain Jones shared with me while you left to fetch the boy's belongings, you have most certainly been serving him here at Carnton." Bounds handed her the pieces of paper and picked up his Bible from the side table. "As sad as this is, and the boy's death is certainly to be mourned, I would also have you be encouraged. Because the God of all comfort knows who this boy's mother is and he has been comforting her, and will continue to do so, in ways you and I cannot begin to ask or imagine."

Lizzie nodded, her eyes growing moist.

Bounds took her hands in his. "Take heart, dear daughter. The Lord keeps track of all our sorrows and collects all our tears. For as David wrote in the Psalms, 'Thou tellest my wanderings: put thou my tears into thy bottle: are they not in thy book?'"

Lizzie stared. "That's one of the verses Thaddeus had with him. From the page of a Bible I found folded in his pocket."

This time it was Bounds who stared. "Would you happen to have that page with you, ma'am?"

"Of course. I have it right here." She pulled it from her skirt pocket. "I keep it with me to remind me to pray for his mother."

Bounds took the page from her and carefully unfolded it. He stared for a long moment, then with a slight tremor in his hand, he opened his own Bible to a point roughly halfway through. There he slipped the page into the opening, the page identical in size and print to those of the Bible he held. Bounds looked up at her with a watery smile. "I remember *this* boy quite well, Miss Clouston. Except his name was not Thaddeus. It was Levi. Thaddeus was the name of my own dear son . . . who died at birth. I penned his name here, very poorly I might add, late one night, only hours after my wife and I buried his little body." Bounds ran a hand over the name he'd written in the margin. "I wrote it alongside three verses that the Lord wrote, and continues to write, on my heart."

Bounds held out the Bible, and Roland took it. The three verses were underlined.

"'When I remember thee upon my bed,'" Roland read aloud. "'And meditate on thee in the night watches. Because thou hast been my help, therefore in the shadow of thy wings will I rejoice.'" He took a steadying breath, recalling the many nights he'd lain awake contemplating the Almighty and regretting how much he'd doubted the Lord's protection and guidance in recent months. And wanting to trust him for the future all the more. "'My soul followeth hard after thee: thy right hand upholdeth me.'" Roland looked down at his own crippled right hand, and felt a swell of gratitude for Scripture and for the Lord's generous strength.

Bounds swallowed. "I remember that night very clearly. Young Levi was frightened as he contemplated going into battle." A melancholy smile turned his mouth. "I shared these verses with him from memory, and afterward he said he wished he could remember them forever. So I tore out this page and gave it to him."

Roland looked at Lizzie, saw the hope shining in her eyes, and nodded.

"By chance, Preacher Bounds," she asked, "did you happen to learn where the boy was from?"

Bounds looked between the two of them and smiled.

CHAPTER 40

"Colonel, the boy was from Thompson's Station. Scarcely nine miles south of here."

Sitting across the mahogany dining room table from Colonel McGavock, Lizzie nudged the lists that Levi had written closer toward him—a little too forcibly so, in Roland's opinion. He read trepidation in John McGavock's expression and tried to signal Lizzie to stop pressing so hard.

"We could get there and back in one day," she continued. "And—"

"Actually, Colonel . . ." Roland leaned forward. "Considering the time it will take to canvas the community and to inquire about the boy, we would likely need to spend one night away. Though there is a slight possibility, if all goes well, that we'd be able to return within the time frame Miss Clouston has proposed."

Lizzie shot him a discreet look of displeasure.

"In my experience, Captain Jones, if there's a slight possibility that all could go well, it never does. And what lodgings, may I ask, would you procure for Miss Clouston and yourself?"

Roland heard no insinuation in the query, only concern. "My division was through that town last fall. Thompson's Station is a small community, but there's a boardinghouse and a tidy little inn. I'm sure I could find lodgings for Miss Clouston. As for myself, though Carnton has spoiled me, I'm accustomed to much less refined accommodations."

The colonel smiled briefly, then finally sighed and shook his head. "I can appreciate your desire to find this boy's mother, Miss Clouston.

Sincerely, I can. But I must weigh that well-meant desire against the importance of your personal safety, as well as that of the captain's. Federal patrols routinely scour the area looking for deserters."

"But, Colonel"—Lizzie's voice gained the slightest edge—"you said yourself that with your written permission, a soldier could leave Carnton for a certain amount of time without breaking the parole of honor or fear of Federal reprisal."

Roland nudged her arm ever so slightly with his elbow.

"But," she added, dismay shading her features, "if you deem the trip too risky at this time, then I'll understand. And we'll simply have to wait."

Roland detected a flicker of uncertainty in McGavock's features. Having played many a game of chess with the man, he knew his next move. He took Lizzie by the elbow and rose, using the table for support. "Miss Clouston, I believe we have our answer. Thank you, Colonel, for hearing us out."

She looked at him as though he'd sprouted horns. Either that or she wanted to tear into him right then. They got as far as the door when the colonel pushed his chair back from the table.

"Captain Jones."

Roland paused and tossed Lizzie a quick wink before turning. "Yes, sir, Colonel?"

"There's a family who lives in Thompson's Station. Dr. Elijah Thompson, the town's namesake. I'll write to him and request lodgings for Miss Clouston. And for you as well, room permitting. I would feel much more comfortable agreeing to this if I knew her needs were guaranteed to be cared for."

"I agree completely, sir. That's my utmost concern as well."

Roland felt her nudge his arm ever so slightly and curbed a grin.

McGavock came around the table. "I'll write a letter to Dr. Thompson immediately and ask for his reply posthaste."

Roland extended his left hand. "Thank you, sir."

Roland closed the door behind them, and Lizzie threw her arms around his neck.

"That was brilliant!" she whispered. "But how did you know he was wavering?"

Roland ran a hand down her arm, her nearness rousing desires he hadn't felt in a while. "I've played chess with him, remember?"

He stepped back, needing to put some distance between them, and saw the subtle hurt in her eyes. She briefly looked away, but when she looked back the hurt was gone.

"Thank you, Roland. We're close to finding Levi's mother. I can feel it!"

ROLAND AWAKENED DURING the night with a muscle cramp in his right calf. He'd been working that system of George's pretty hard. He straightened his leg, gritting his teeth until the knot in his calf gradually loosened. Dr. Phillips had said this would happen and that drinking a good amount of water might help.

Roland pushed from the cot and reached for his crutches. Another soldier had taken Winder's bed a couple of weeks back, which had been fine by him. Somebody should use it. He still saw James just about everywhere he looked, yet there was a comfort in knowing the young man was done with the struggles and strife of this world. That he was home.

Roland ran a hand over his face, still a little foggy. He crossed the room as quietly as he could, poured water from a pitcher into a tin cup, and downed it. Then drank a second cup. His thirst slaked, he made his way back to the cot and looked around. Something didn't feel right. Then it registered. *Taylor.* His knapsack and pallet were gone.

Roland checked the other bedrooms, but Taylor was nowhere to be found. Roland returned to Winder's room and gave Smitty a swift kick.

Smitty lifted his head. "What the—"

"Where's Taylor?" Roland whispered.

Smitty looked beside him and cursed. "I told him not to do this! If he gets me sent back to that prison, I'm gonna—"

Roland was already on his way to the staircase. He took the stairs as quickly as he could, knowing where Taylor would head first. And sure enough, when he peered out the back, he saw the barn door slightly ajar. Roland looked over at the cabin where George was staying. All was dark. If he took the time to wake up George, Taylor would be long gone.

Roland peered inside the barn. Silver slices of moonlight fingered their way through the cracks in the roof, and he spotted movement in a stall toward the back. He made his way there and found Taylor saddling up a horse. And not just any horse. The colonel's stallion. *Idiot.* The thoroughbred pranced and snorted nervously in the stall, giving Roland opportunity.

"Taylor!"

The man spun. Roland caught him in the jaw with a crutch, but Taylor didn't go down. He charged. Roland turned but couldn't escape Taylor's momentum. They both went sprawling.

Taylor punched and missed, his fist connecting with the ground. He spat out a curse. Roland managed to stand. And when Taylor came at him again, he got him with a left hook under the jaw. Taylor went down on all fours, but not for long. He grappled for something in the hay beside him, then stood.

"Now comes the time I teach you that lesson, Jones."

Roland saw what was in his grip and grabbed a wooden stool. He managed to block Taylor's first lash of the whip. But when Taylor brought it down again, the *crack* sliced the air and the strap caught Roland on the side of the neck. He felt the sting of flesh tearing and staggered back, dropping the stool. His right leg gave way, and he went down hard on his back. The stallion went wild, kicking the stall door. Taylor raised the whip a third time, and Roland braced himself for the lash.

"Get ready to die, you—"

But the whip didn't come down. The barn spinning, Roland struggled to stand, the side of his neck pulsing hot. He heard the distinct sound of bones crunching, and Taylor let out a scream. George had the man's fist in his hand. Taylor fell to his knees, screaming curses loud enough to wake the dead. George threw the whip across the barn and strode toward Roland as the barn door flew open. Soldiers filed through the doorway, moonlight glinting off their bayonets.

A Federal officer stepped forward. "Identify yourselves!"

His head fuzzy, Roland didn't recognize the soldier or any of the men with him. "Captain Roland Ward Jones," he managed, an arm coming around his shoulders to keep him upright. "First Battalion. Mississippi Sharpshooters. Adams' Brigade. And Federal prisoner here at Carnton."

Taylor continued to scream, clutching his hand, until the officer instructed in language Taylor could understand to shut up. Taylor gave his name and rank through clenched teeth.

"And you are?" The soldier walked closer.

"I'm George, sir."

"And which of you can tell me what's going on in here?"

"Cap'n Jones here was tryin' to stop that man from leavin', sir."

"You lyin' black son of a—"

Taylor didn't see the rifle butt coming. He fell face forward, stone-cold, on the ground.

"Is this true, Captain Jones?"

"Yes, sir." Roland nodded, holding his neck. "We all took an oath under the parole of honor. And if one of us leaves, then—"

"The rest of you go to prison," the officer finished. "Have you experienced one of our prisons before, Captain?" The officer glanced back at his comrades, and they laughed along with him.

"Actually, sir"—Roland blinked to clear his vision—"with all due respect, I have."

The officer's eyes narrowed. "Where were you?"

"Shiloh, sir."

"And how were the accommodations there?"

Already seeing where this was headed, Roland felt a wave of fatigue wash through him. Or maybe it was the loss of blood. Whichever, he found he couldn't quip about the war anymore. Or prison. Or soldiers killing each other. All he could see was Lizzie's face, and he wished again that they'd met in a different time and place. Wished he'd been a better man. "It was prison, sir," he finally answered. "And somewhere I never want to be again."

The officer stared, his demeanor appraising. "Butler!"

A soldier stepped forward. "Yes, sir."

"See to this captain's injuries. And, Stewart!"

"Yes, sir," a second man echoed.

"Clean up this piece of trash off the barn floor and get him ready to march."

Sitting against the stall, Roland grimaced as the attendant saw to his neck.

"He got you right along the collarbone, Captain," the young soldier said. "I'll bandage you up as best I can, but you'll need a few sutures."

"I appreciate your tending my wound, but I doubt a Federal doctor will be sparing any sutures on me."

"Who says you're going to prison, Captain Jones?"

Roland looked up at the officer in charge. "You're . . . not taking us all with you?"

The officer knelt beside him. "You look as dog-tired of this war as I am, Captain. If you and I were in command, I do believe we could find a way to put an end to all this. Right here, right now." He raised a brow.

Roland's throat tightened, only too aware of George listening beside him. "Yes, sir. I believe we could."

The officer rose. "Fall out!" But he didn't leave with the others. His gaze shifted to George. "You're a free man now. You do know that, don't you?"

George hesitated. "Yes, sir. I do."

"And yet you're still here."

"Yes, sir. But don't free mean that I get to choose?"

The slightest hint of admiration touched the man's eyes. "It does."

"So for now, sir, I'm choosin' to stay here. I might choose different down the line. Dependin' on what comes."

The officer looked between the two of them and nodded, then turned and left.

Roland heard what George wasn't saying and yet was. And though it struck a dissonant chord within him, he forced himself to look past that and to his own life through the lens of George's—through the lens of his own life over the past few weeks and months. He'd been powerless to change anything. Had no control over his future. Felt like a prisoner in his own body. And he would've done just about anything to be given the chance to change that. What man wouldn't?

Roland looked up and saw George's outstretched hand. And grasped it.

CHAPTER 41

"You're certain you still have the written order signed by the colonel?"

Roland eyed Lizzie seated beside him on the wagon bench. "How many times do you plan on asking me that?"

"I've only asked once since we left."

"And three times before that."

"But I haven't actually seen the order for myself since we've been in the wagon."

"But I have. So trust me, Lizzie."

With a slight tilt of her chin, she faced forward. But he saw the corner of her mouth tip. He also felt the curve of her thigh rubbing against his own with every jostle and jolt of the wagon. With a good five miles yet to be covered, he estimated he would combust in about half that.

He'd been none too certain that Colonel McGavock would give final approval to his request to accompany Lizzie. And without Dr. Thompson promising lodgings for her, the colonel likely would have said no. He reached up and felt his neck, the sutures healing well but starting to itch.

"Does it still hurt?"

"Not much."

"I'm so grateful they didn't take you. Or the others."

"Me too. I'm only sorry I held up our trip by a couple of weeks."

"Nonsense." She smiled. "You needed time to heal."

They rode in silence for the next mile, then she sighed.

"I think about James a lot. Do you?"

He nodded. "Every day."

"I can still see him with that artificial arm, pulling his hand back."

"I can still see how he looked at you that last morning."

She nodded. "Me too."

He looked down at her, and a blush crept into her cheeks. He faced forward again, already having had several conversations with the Lord about this trip and about her. She was young still—no matter what she said—and of child-bearing years. He'd seen her with Hattie and Winder, and with the younger soldiers in the house. She was born to be a mother. To rob her of that would be to rob her of one of life's greatest joys. And he couldn't—wouldn't—do that to her.

But he did need to discuss something with her. Wanted to get her perspective. He simply hadn't worked out all the details in his mind yet. But he was getting there.

A cold March wind nipped at their backs while a warm sun shone overhead. The wagon bumped and jarred along the rain-rutted road, and when Lizzie reached down and gripped the seat between them, he offered his arm as extra insurance. She tucked her hand into the crook of his arm and held on. Even when the road smoothed, she kept it there.

They arrived at Thompson's Station shortly before noon and went first to the school, figuring that held their best chance for finding someone who'd known Levi. School was in session, the classroom full, and Lizzie spoke with the teacher during lunch.

"His first name was Levi. He would've been thirteen or fourteen years old. Unfortunately, that's all we know."

The young teacher shook her head. "I've been teaching here for almost four years, and I've never had a student by that name. I'm sorry."

"If we wait," Lizzie said, never one to give up, "would you allow me to query your students? We've come all the way from Franklin, and I'd like to exhaust every possibility before we return."

The young woman agreed, but as Roland had feared, when the time came no child raised a hand.

He assisted Lizzie back into the wagon, then struggled to climb back in himself. He stowed his cane beneath the bench seat. Would he ever regain the strength he'd had before the battle at Franklin? He spotted a mercantile ahead and drew the wagon to a stop. "Let's get something to eat, then we'll canvas the businesses."

Using some of the money Mrs. Polk had sent him, he purchased meat, cheese, bread, and milk from the mercantile, and they ate in the wagon. He hoped the rest of the money, which he'd sent to his mother, had arrived safely. After they ate, he managed to get through the businesses on one side of the street while Lizzie visited the other. His right leg ached with fatigue, but he wasn't about to come this far only to give up.

"Here." Lizzie pointed to a bench outside a barbershop. "Could we sit for a few minutes?"

Knowing she was resting on his account, he complied.

He gauged the sun overhead and knew that if they were to get home today—which seemed likely, since they'd done everything short of combing the hillsides—they only had another hour or so before they needed to head back in order to reach Carnton before dark.

"Maybe we're not meant to find his family, Roland." Her voice was fragile. "Still, to have gotten this far . . ."

Sensing and sharing her frustration, Roland looked beside him to see her rubbing the smooth white stone. He gestured. "Why don't we get back in the wagon and I'll drive back through town. We'll go up and down every street. We'll knock on every door."

Her smile bloomed, and she nodded and stood.

"But first," he continued.

She sat back down.

"I want to talk to you about something. Get your opinion on a . . . business prospect."

She eyed him. "You want *my* opinion? On a business prospect?"

He tried to smile, appear more relaxed than he felt. And failed.

He leaned forward, forearms on his thighs, his stomach in knots, and covered his right hand with his left so that he almost appeared whole again. "I've been thinking about sharecropping. On my estate back in Mississippi. Maybe giving George and his family some of the land and working out a system where I'd get a share of the crops they raise. Either that, or I lease him the land for a set amount, and he gets to keep whatever profit he makes." He shrugged, unable to look over at her. "If that works out, I figure maybe some other sl—" He caught himself. "Some other freedmen might be interested in—"

She slipped her hand between his and squeezed tight. "Look at me, Roland."

He did and was rewarded with the sweetest smile he'd ever seen from her. And that was saying a lot. He held her hand between his, emotions warring within him. He saw not a trace of condemnation or *I told you so* in her eyes.

"I know the coming changes are going to be difficult for you. They won't be easy for any of us. No matter what side we *were* on, we all need to get on the same side." Her eyes watered. "Or none of us will make it through this."

He nodded, then looked away. "The one thing I have trouble getting past . . . is my grandfather, and my father. By acknowledging that I believe slavery was a mistake—" He grimaced. "No, not a mistake. That it's a sin." Her grip tightened on his. "I feel like I'm condemning the two men who most shaped my life. And my faith. It's like I'm saying they weren't good men after all. That their lives didn't measure up."

"No," she whispered. "You're not saying that at all."

He felt the gentlest touch on the side of his face and looked back.

"You're simply admitting that they were flawed men. That they did things that were wrong. And hurtful. And that they needed an *extraordinary* amount of grace to cover their sins. Which describes every single one of us."

He shook his head. "I was so certain I was right that night. The first time we had this conversation. I was bent on teaching you a lesson, you know."

She smiled. "Oh, I know. I could see it in your eyes."

He stood and pulled her up with him, tempted to pull her the rest of the way to him. But, with restraint, he released her hand and gestured. "How about we get back in the wagon and start knocking on those doors?"

He released the brake and snapped the reins. They drove for the better part of two hours, stopping and talking with everyone they saw. Leaving no stone—or front door—unturned. But nothing. No one had ever heard of Levi. Roland began to wonder if maybe Preacher Bounds had gotten it wrong. Maybe it wasn't Thompson's Station. Or maybe the man's memory had failed him. And yet, when Bounds had come by that day, the pieces of the puzzle had just seemed to fit.

"Okay, let's walk through this again." He looked down at her, keeping an eye on the washboard road. "It wasn't a coincidence that Preacher Bounds gave Levi that page of his Bible. And that Levi ended up at Carnton though he wasn't even part of Loring's Division. Right?"

She nodded.

"I tell you, somebody here has to have known that boy. We just haven't—"

The back of the wagon slid hard to the right, then dropped. Roland grabbed hold of Lizzie as she fell forward, and he pulled her back against him. The sudden weight of her body on his sent shock waves through him. Some pleasurable, some not. But feeling the fullness of her curves, he decided the former outweighed the latter.

"Are you all right?" he asked, her face inches from his.

Her breath came heavy. "Yes. Are you?"

He laughed. "I'm okay." *I could stay like this for quite a while, in fact,* he thought to himself.

"Need help with that wheel, traveler?"

Roland looked up to see an older man walking toward them.

"We have company," he whispered, then helped lower her safely to the ground. He climbed down behind her, grabbing his cane, the exertion taking a toll.

The older man held out his right hand, then saw Roland's and quickly shifted to his left. The old-timer had a strong grip. "You got yourself a busted wheel there, partner. But lucky for you, this town has the best wheelwright in all of Tennessee. 'Course he's closed on Wednesdays, seein' as that's his huntin' day."

"And where would his place be?"

"Not far. Just a few streets over."

Roland nodded. "And the wheelwright's name?"

The man grinned. "Virgil Owens, at your service."

Roland laughed, and heard Lizzie do the same. "I should've seen that coming, sir."

Roland arranged for the wheelwright to fix the wagon the next day. He and Lizzie thanked him for his help, unhitched the mares, and headed in the direction of Dr. Thompson's house.

On the way Roland suggested they stop back by the mercantile. "My mother always says it's part of Southern politeness to take something to the hostess when you visit a house."

Lizzie chose a pretty blue vase, and he asked the clerk to wrap it up. He saw an older woman enter the store. She came and waited right behind him, so he stepped to the side.

The clerk looked up from wrapping the vase. "Mrs. Gibbons, what are you doing back so soon?"

The woman gave a shy smile. "I got halfway home and realized I'd forgotten peppermint sticks. I always take those when I go. The children love them."

The clerk looked in Roland's direction, as if asking whether he minded if she assisted the lady, and he nodded his approval. He saw Lizzie looking through a stack of books and wished he could give her everything she ever wanted. Not just a book but a life, whole and full. She deserved that and so much more.

"Thank you, sir, for allowing me to help her."

"No problem." Then it occurred to him. "We didn't see you when we were in here before. We're from Franklin, ma'am, and we're trying to find anyone who might have known a boy by the name of Levi. We're trying to locate his family."

"Did you say Levi?"

Hearing a voice behind him, Roland turned and saw the woman, Mrs. Gibbons, paused by the door. She slowly walked toward him.

"Yes, ma'am, I did. Did . . . you know him?"

"*Did* I know him?" she repeated, her brow furrowing.

Despite the distress in her tone, the recognition in the woman's expression rekindled his hope. He looked over at Lizzie to see she was already making her way back toward him.

"Yes, ma'am." He nodded. "A young boy by the name of Levi was involved in the battle at Franklin at the end of November. He was brought to an estate called Carnton, where . . ."

He looked at Lizzie, and she picked up where he left off. And when Mrs. Gibbons grasped Lizzie's hands, tears filling her eyes, he was certain they'd found what they'd come looking for.

"My dear, sweet Levi . . ." Mrs. Gibbons struggled to speak. "My husband and I have been helping his family for a few years now. Levi's father died some time back and left a wife and six children. Levi is . . . was the oldest, and the only boy." She took a shaky breath. "I've taught the children for the past few years. My husband and I never were able to have children of our own, so God gave me those precious children to love and care for. At least that's the way I look at it." A tender, heartbreaking smile eclipsed her face. "And Levi was an especially bright boy. One of those students a teacher gets only once in a lifetime."

Lizzie smiled, and Roland knew she understood what the woman was saying. He also knew that he'd made the right decision about not pursuing something more with Lizzie. Despite how much he loved her, he couldn't abide the thought that one day she would reach this stage in her life, where Mrs. Gibbons was now, and look back with regret at what might have been if she hadn't been with him.

Mrs. Gibbons sighed, staring briefly at the sack of peppermint sticks in her hand. "When Levi went and joined that war, it broke his mother's heart. And so will this news. Although I wonder if, deep inside, Elsa already suspects her son is gone."

ROLAND LOCATED A livery, and after he explained their circumstances to the owner, the man generously loaned them a two-wheeled pony cart and agreed to keep the other mare until they returned.

Roland and Lizzie rode a good distance outside of town and into the hills, following Mrs. Gibbons's instructions, until they quickly ran out of road. They watered the horse in the stream they'd been following, then tied it securely and continued on foot, Roland leaning heavily on his cane. The surroundings were exactly as Mrs. Gibbons had described. The path, narrow but not too difficult to traverse, curved up ahead. And when they rounded the bend, the house came into view. Or shack, more like it. Run-down and ramshackle, the structure leaned to one side.

Lizzie's steps slowed. "She said they were poor, but I didn't expect this."

"I was thinking the same thing." Roland reached for her hand, and she slipped hers into his. "No matter what happens, please know that you did what Levi asked you to do."

Lizzie smiled up at him, but he knew she wouldn't be at peace until she talked to his mother and shared what the boy had written, and until they found whatever it was that he had left buried.

When they reached the shack, Roland paused. Lizzie nodded and he knocked on the door. A minute later, the door creaked open, and a little girl stood staring up, her dress ragged, her face smudged with dirt. A woman followed close behind her, her expression wary.

"Can I help you folks?"

"My name is Miss Elizabeth Clouston, and this is Captain Roland Ward Jones, First Battalion, Mississippi Sharpshooters, Adams' Brigade in the Army of Tennessee. We've traveled from Franklin and, with the help of Mrs. Gibbons, whose path crossed ours at the mercantile in town, we are here to—" Lizzie's voice faltered. She looked up at him.

"We're here," Roland continued, "to tell you what an extraordinary young man your son Levi was. And to give you a letter he wrote to you, along with his final belongings that Miss Clouston has kept for you."

Elsa's eyes filled. She reached out for the door as though needing support, and Lizzie stepped forward and wrapped her in an embrace. Lizzie held her as she wept and spoke to her in soft tones, assuring her that her son did not die alone, and that he died with dignity and with love of family foremost in his heart.

Roland marveled at the language women shared, sometimes without speaking a word. Elsa invited them inside and offered them tea. They sat at the table and answered all of her questions as best they could.

"And before I forget . . ." Lizzie pulled the wrapped package of peppermint sticks from the pocket of her cloak. "Before we left Mrs. Gibbons in town, she asked us to give you these for the girls. She said she'd be by within a day or two to check on you."

Elsa smiled. "Mrs. Gibbons has been a godsend." She handed the package to the oldest girl, who doled out the sugary treats to her sisters one by one.

"There's something else," Lizzie offered gently. "Levi gave me a message for you. He said he was sorry over how he left things with you. And he left something buried beneath an old willow tree. He said, 'It makes dying easier knowing you'll have it.'" Lizzie took the woman's hands in hers. "Do you know what he meant by that? Do you know which willow tree he's talking about?"

Closing her eyes, Elsa nodded. "I can show you."

A while later, shovel in hand, Roland dug at the base of the tree, Lizzie and Elsa with her five girls huddled around him. He hadn't gone a foot down when his shovel hit something hard. He pulled a metal box from the dirt, brushed it off, and held it out to Elsa, but she shook her head. So Roland sat down on a boulder and opened it. A piece of paper lay across the top, and when he read it and then saw what lay beneath, he had no doubt about what Levi's situation had been. But one look at Elsa told him she already knew.

"He was a substitute," he said softly.

Elsa nodded, her chin trembling.

"A substitute?" Lizzie repeated.

"We had a couple of them in our regiment. They take someone else's place and fight in their stead. From the looks of it, there's close to three thousand dollars or more in this box. A small fortune. What Levi was paid for taking another man's place."

"Money I would give away in a beat of my heart," Elsa said, her voice small, "if I could have my son back. I said as much that night when he told me what he'd done. I told him that he could take all that money with him. That I didn't want a cent of it." Her features contorted with grief. "Oh, my dear, sweet son . . ."

"There's a note for you in here, ma'am." He handed it to her. *For Mama* was written in Levi's familiar hand across the front.

CHAPTER 42

The next morning Lizzie rose early, eager to check on Elsa and the girls, so grateful to Dr. and Mrs. Thompson for welcoming not only her and Roland into their home last night, but Levi's family as well. She simply hadn't been able to leave them there yesterday afternoon, not after everything that had happened. Roland had only smiled and nodded when she'd told him she needed to see their journey through a little farther down the road before they returned to Franklin. "Why am I not surprised," he'd whispered.

She heard chatter coming from the kitchen, and when she opened the door the sight did her heart good. The Thompsons' cook was busy with breakfast at the stove, and Mrs. Thompson and her eighteen-year-old daughter, Alice, were already engaged with Elsa over cups of hot coffee. The five girls sat lined up on a bench, sipping milk from tin cups.

Mrs. Thompson looked up. "Good morning, Miss Clouston. Join us!"

Not ten minutes later, Roland entered. Alice Thompson perked up considerably, Lizzie noticed, not blaming the girl one bit. Lizzie was more in love with the man now than she'd ever been. And she sensed deep down that he felt the same way about her. Yet something was holding him back.

Following breakfast, Roland fetched the mares from the barn. Lizzie met him out front and they, along with Elsa and the two oldest girls, walked the short distance to town to get the wagon. As Roland suggested at breakfast, Elsa brought the metal box with her, and they deposited its contents with the bank they'd seen the day before. It had taken some encouragement, but he'd finally convinced Elsa to accept the gift from her son.

"Being a son myself," he'd told her, "I know how much I want to take care of my mother and my sisters. So please, let your son do the same for you."

As they approached the wheelwright's shop, Lizzie glanced over at the girls on either side of Elsa. Marianne and Martha held tightly to their mother's hands, their eyes wide as they took in the town around them. She wondered at how their lives were about to change. Over three thousand dollars. The going rate, apparently, for having someone fight in your stead. Only then did she think of Levi and James in the hereafter together. Not quite certain how eternity unfolded once a person died, she sent up a silent prayer that perhaps the two boys could meet up and share their stories.

"Well, who do y'all have with you today!" Virgil Owens met them as they walked through the open doors of the barn, wiping the grease from his hands onto an old cloth.

Roland tied the mares to the post and made quick introductions, and Lizzie noticed how the girls hid behind Elsa's skirts.

"Got your wagon all ready to go, Captain Jones. Went out and mended the wheel this mornin', then Miss Bessie right here"—he pointed to an old mule in one of the stalls—"she pulled it back to the shop. You had some boards comin' loose in the back bed too, but I won't charge you for that. Fixin' them was my own doin'."

Roland paid the man. More, Lizzie noticed, than Mr. Owens had charged.

Mr. Owens bent down to eye level with Marianne and Martha. "You little ones like critters from the woods?"

The girls looked up at their mother.

"I'm sorry, Mr. Owens," Elsa offered. "We don't get to town much, so they ain't used to swappin' names. Leastwise with strangers." She smiled. "This one's Marianne. And this one's Martha."

"Well, howdy-do. But I ain't no stranger, ma'am. Everybody in town knows ol' Mr. Owens. Been here all my life." He reached into a drawer and pulled out something, which he showed to Elsa. Her eyes softened with grateful approval. "This one here's for you, Miss Marianne," he said. "And this one, Miss Martha, he's all yours."

The girls stared at the carved wooden animals in their palms, their smiles growing wide. Mr. Owens beamed, his pleasure seeming to outdo theirs.

"We need to be heading back," Roland whispered.

Lizzie nodded and helped situate Elsa and the girls in the back of the wagon. She climbed up to the bench beside Roland.

Virgil Owens reached up and shook his hand. "Godspeed on your trip back to Franklin, Captain. You too, ma'am."

Lizzie smiled. "Thank you, Mr. Owens. It was a pleasure to meet you."

"Oh, the pleasure be all mine." He paused, his gaze moving toward the back of the wagon. "Them little critters belonged to my own two girls. They're gone now. Both of 'em passed on with their sweet mama some twenty years back. I been savin' them critters. Got more of 'em in the drawer. But it's high time I start givin' 'em away."

Lizzie reached for his hand and gave it a squeeze. "I wish you all the best, Mr. Owens. I'm grateful our paths crossed."

He sniffed. "Thank you, ma'am. And same to you."

Roland gestured. "Mrs. Colton and her five girls will be moving into town soon. They'll be needing a wagon. May I send them your way?"

"Yes, sir, you can. I'll be happy to help."

As Roland negotiated the turn, Lizzie heard Virgil speaking to Elsa.

"Y'all come on back, Mrs. Colton, and I'll help you with a wagon. I got more of them critters too, for the rest of your girls."

"Thank you!" Elsa called, waving as they pulled onto the street.

Lizzie sneaked a look at Roland. "Do you think that maybe he and—"

"What I think"—he kept his attention focused forward—"is that you helped Levi change his family's life in ways he never dreamed."

THEY TALKED MOST of the way back to Franklin, and Lizzie didn't want this time with Roland to end. But by that evening, when they reached the outskirts of town, he'd grown more reticent. And when he turned onto the road leading to Carnton, she felt that familiar distancing between them again.

She wrestled with how much of her heart to share with him, all while feeling the swing of a pendulum inside her. Tempy's counsel resonated above it all. *The only thing worse than havin' no choice is havin' it and throwin' it away.* Lizzie didn't want to lose this chance. Didn't want to lose him.

"Thank you, Lizzie—"

She looked over, surprised that he'd spoken, but even more so at the strained emotion in his voice.

"—for sharing all of this with me. For allowing me to be the one to take you."

"Allowing you?" She shook her head. "I was just sitting here thinking about how I can't imagine not having taken this trip with you." She studied his profile as she'd done for miles now. "Much as I can't imagine not having met you."

A muscle worked in his jaw. "I feel the same about you."

She tucked her hand into the crook of his arm, hoping to ease whatever was bothering him. He covered her hand with his, then brought it to his mouth and kissed her palm, his lips warm and tender. Her body heated, and with that heat came unexpected courage. She moved closer to him on the seat, and he exhaled.

"Lizzie, we need to talk."

"That's all we've been doing. Is talking."

He laughed, but it held no humor. He looked down at her, his gaze first on her eyes, then her mouth. He swallowed, then reined in the horses. "There are things I need to say to you. Now. While we still have time."

"I have things I want to say to you too. Because as we both know, there's no guarantee of—"

He set the brake and pulled her to him. He kissed her, not gently like the kisses on her palm a moment earlier, but with a hunger that stoked a fire inside her. He dug his hands into her hair, and when she parted her lips for a breath, he deepened the kiss. She had the sensation of falling, yet welcomed it, gave herself to it. Because with his arms around her, his mouth on hers, she felt a certainty she'd never felt before. But part of that certainty stemmed, she knew, from what he'd shared with her on the trip. Not only about sharecropping but about his struggle with reconciling the actions of two men he greatly esteemed. She'd had to do her own bit of reconciling in that regard.

"Lizzie," he whispered against her lips, then gave a soft groan. "I wish I could be the man you need. The man you deserve."

She cradled the side of his face, seeing the struggle in his eyes. "But you are that man. I see it in you." She saw it in the way he treated George now too. And Tempy. He was changing, whether he saw those changes or not.

Tentative and unsure, she brushed her lips against his, relishing the way his stubbled jaw felt against her skin, rough and distinctly male. He drew her closer and kissed her slowly this time, patiently, as though trying to memorize what they felt like together. He kissed her cheek, her jawline, then the curve of her throat, and she couldn't seem to catch her breath. Yet she didn't want him to stop. He pulled back and took hold of her hands, his own shaking. Or was it hers?

"The night you told me about you and Towny no longer being

betrothed . . ." He looked down at their hands. "You told me the reason you'd said yes to him was because you wanted children."

Lizzie felt the weight of that shame all over again. "It's true. I *do* want children, with all my heart. But it was wrong of me to say yes to him when really I was only—"

He pressed a finger to her lips. "There's a very good chance, Lizzie, that I *can't* father children anymore. Not after what happened to me on the battlefield. Dr. Phillips told me when he was here for Christmas."

As the words sank in, Lizzie felt her mouth moving, but nothing came. In a flash, their conversation from the night she'd told him about Towny returned. And filtering what she'd said then through what she knew now brought a fresh wave of guilt, and she winced. Especially when thinking of his already having lost his precious daughter. "Roland, I'm so sorry."

"I am too." He exhaled. "But . . . at least now you know."

He let go of her hands and reached for the reins.

"Wait." She grabbed his arm, what he'd told her still taking hold. The seconds seemed to slow to a crawl. With Towny, she'd had what felt like a guarantee of children, and yet she hadn't loved him the way she loved Roland. But now with Roland—without whom she couldn't imagine spending the rest of her life—she had the near guarantee of never bearing children. After all they'd been through, Roland especially, it didn't seem fair. Particularly when she took into account his willingness to humble himself, to admit he was wrong. To change. Granted, she knew those changes would not be easy, and the road to freedom would be fraught with still more challenges. And losses. Like Levi. James Shuler. Captain Pleasant Hope. All the soldiers whose blood still stained the hallways and rooms of Carnton. Martha, Mary, and John—the three precious children the McGavocks had buried far too young. And Roland's own Susan and Lena. Lizzie's eyes watered. Life was so uncertain. It came with no guarantees. Hadn't she learned that by now?

400

But as soon as that thought came, another countered it. And she heard Sister Catherine Margaret's voice. *The LORD is my light and my salvation; whom shall I fear? the LORD is the strength of my life; of whom shall I be afraid?* And deep inside, Lizzie began to smile.

"Lizzie, it's all right." Roland's voice held resignation. "Believe me . . . I, of all people, understand what it means to have a child. Children are gifts from God. And I could never rob you of that. So it's all right."

He snapped the reins, but she pulled them taut. He looked down.

"If you and I have learned anything, Roland, it's that while life itself holds no guarantees, we both trust in the One who holds our lives. So there's nothing to fear. When couples marry, they don't know what their life together will hold. Whether they'll have children or whether they won't. Like Mrs. Gibbons and her husband." She softened her voice. "Or whether a husband and wife will have a child only to lose that precious soul before the child can even grow up."

She detected a wavering in him, then he shook his head, and she could well imagine how this had been eating away at him. And here she'd thought he'd changed his mind about her. She turned on the bench seat, the question she needed to ask him making her heart thud a painful, uneven rhythm.

"Do you love me?" she whispered.

"It's not that easy, Lizzie. I simply can't—"

"Do . . . you . . . love me?" She could scarcely breathe for watching his face, trying to read the contents of his heart.

"More than my own life," he finally said. "But to think that I might prevent you from enjoying as full and meaningful a life as you deserve is—"

"There are children enough in this world who have no parents. Especially with the war. So if we—" She couldn't bring herself to say the words. But his slow smile said he was going to.

"If we marry and try to have children"—the look he gave her sent her pulse racing—"but can't . . ."

She touched his face. "Then we'll love the children God brings into our lives through other ways. But we'll always have each other."

He brought his face closer, his gray eyes searching hers. "You're certain."

"I've never been more certain of anything in my life."

His smile reached all the way inside her. He kissed her again, but with a possessiveness that hadn't been there before, and she responded to it. To him. After a moment he broke the kiss, as breathless as she was.

"Would you marry me, Elizabeth Clouston?"

She pursed her lips. "I thought you'd never ask."

He laughed and gathered the reins. "Is there anyone's permission I should ask first? Your father's, perhaps?"

She smiled. "I'm sure he would like that. But I think Winder's will be more important."

As they drove around the bend and up the drive, Carnton came into view, and the wash of color in the night sky looked like a backdrop God had painted especially for them.

Roland pulled the wagon around to the back of the house, and Lizzie froze. A unit of Federal soldiers was escorting the men from the house. She felt Roland tense beside her.

"No." She heard the word come from her lips, but it sounded so far away.

"Stay here, Lizzie."

She reached for his arm.

"Stay in the wagon. And whatever happens, do not interfere. Do you understand me?"

She shook her head.

"I love you," he whispered. "Now promise me you will not interfere."

She hesitated.

"Promise me."

"I-I promise."

He climbed down, grabbed his cane, and walked toward them.

But it was the officer approaching him—the one she recognized—that siphoned the air from her lungs.

"Captain Jones, how nice of you to join us." Captain Moore punched Roland hard in the gut, and Roland went down on one knee.

Lizzie jumped down from the wagon, then saw Roland look back at her. She stood where she was and didn't move. Not when the captain grabbed Roland's cane and threw it aside. Not when they bound his hands behind his back. Not when they marched him away.

CHAPTER 43

She hadn't told him she loved him that day—the afternoon the Federal patrol took Roland and the rest of the soldiers at Carnton to Nashville. He'd said it to her, but she'd been so stunned to discover what was happening, she hadn't had the presence of mind to respond. Until he'd been walking away, roped to the other prisoners, down the long drive. She'd whispered it to him over and over then. But of course he hadn't heard her. And she'd regretted it ever since.

Lizzie sat on the little Poynor chair in Winder's bedroom— where she most always sat when writing Roland—and read back over what she'd penned to him. She wrote him every day. But for almost three months now she'd received only one response. And that nearly a month after he'd been taken. She kept the cherished letter with her constantly, tucked in her skirt pocket—his handwriting and words long committed to memory. She clung to the hope he was still alive, and that the Federals had taken him and the other men to a hospital and not a prison. His letter hadn't specified, and she'd internally— lovingly—scolded him for that oversight countless times.

She folded the stationery and slid her letter to him into the envelope she'd already addressed to the War Department, not knowing if her letters were even being delivered. With a last glance at the floor to the left of the hearth, the space Roland had occupied, she rose, memories of their conversations swirling inside her. Memories of him loomed everywhere she looked.

She crossed to the open window where the surgical table had stood, the blood-stained wooden floors bare of carpet, a nicety that was still unattainable. And unimportant in light of all else. A warm breeze blew in from across the Harpeth Valley. The McGavocks and the children had long since been reinstalled in their bedrooms. She'd slept in Winder's room with him and Hattie for the first two weeks, helping them readjust. She'd set her cot up right where Roland's had been. And as she'd lain there at night, staring at the room from a perspective he'd certainly grown to know well, she'd thanked God for bringing him to Carnton that fateful night.

She looked beside her at the chest of drawers and at the copy of *A Christmas Carol* that stood shoulder to shoulder with Winder's other self-proclaimed favorites, as did her copy of *Sense and Sensibility*. She ran her hand along the binding of Jane Austen's novel, under no illusion that Winder was ever going to read the story. But since Winder's discovery that Roland had read it, the boy proudly announced he would too.

She felt something protruding slightly from the pages of the Austen novel and looked more closely. Likely, it was a scrap of paper Roland had used to mark his place. She tugged it from the book, and her heart squeezed tight at the sight of the familiar handwriting.

Dearest Lizzie,

I don't know when you'll find this note. But since you shared with me that you reread this novel on occasion, I am certain you will. And when you do, know how appreciative I am that you shared this story with me. Not only did it provide hours of enjoyment, but reading the story through your eyes and knowing how much you love it was like being given a window into your soul. And may I say most unabashedly, it is a most beautiful view.

In deepest friendship,
Roland

Lizzie smiled even as tears rose in her eyes. Especially as she read the postscript.

P. S. I especially enjoyed Fanny getting her comeuppance. Still, I would have preferred the stockade.

Slowly her smile faded. *Please, Lord . . .* As much as she wanted to believe this was a sign that Roland would return to her, she knew that countless women had held similar hopes for their men over the past four years, only to have those hopes dashed. She tucked the note into her pocket, praying it wasn't one last memento of the wonderful man Roland had been. But of the wonderful man he was.

Eager to mail her letter in town, she checked on the children in the family parlor, then sought out Mrs. McGavock. She found her in the kitchen. Lizzie stopped at the base of the stairs. Tempy was back in the larder, judging from the sounds of crates and boxes being moved.

Lizzie cleared her throat. "Excuse me, Mrs. McGavock?"

Carrie looked up from where she sat at the kitchen table, her expression—once so easy for Lizzie to read—now cloaked and distant. "Yes, Miss Clouston?"

Lizzie motioned behind her. "Hattie and Winder are up in the family parlor reading. With your permission, I'd like to walk into town to mail a letter. I won't be gone long."

"That will be fine, Miss Clouston. Thank you for letting me know."

Lizzie held her gaze, mourning the rapport they'd once had. She knew this awkwardness between them was a result of what she'd done. She'd counted the cost when deciding to teach Tempy and George. But counting the cost of a decision and living with its repercussions were two very different things.

"We do not appreciate you doing this behind our backs, Miss Clouston," the colonel had said, displeasure weighing his tone. "And no matter the evidence that the North will indeed be victorious, your actions are still illegal. But equally concerning, from my perspective, is that you have placed yourself, Tempy, and George in a most perilous situation should anyone discover what you have done."

Carrie, her own expression one of surprise, had remained surprisingly silent.

"However, there's been so much upheaval of late," he had continued, features somber. "Too much. Especially for children so young. And more is guaranteed to come. Understanding that, you may remain in your position. For now."

Lizzie had been prepared for a swift dismissal. But that hadn't happened. Yet.

"Missus McGavock . . ." Tempy walked from the larder, holding a piece of paper. "I'm readin' the receipt of this cake from your mama-in-law you give me. The cake she used to make for the colonel when he was a boy. But I can't rightly make out what she's sayin' right here. Is that one cup o' sugar? Or one cup o' somethin' else?"

Carrie looked from Lizzie to Tempy, a shadow of culpability sweeping her face. But despite the stiltedness of their current relationship, seeing the two of them together like this warmed Lizzie's heart. Tempy deciphering a recipe written by the colonel's mother. So small a thing. Yet monumental.

Carrie studied the page Tempy held out. "It's sugar. But it's written in a very poor hand."

"That's what I thought, ma'am. But I wanted to be sure." Tempy turned. "Hey there, Miss Lizzie. Would you like a cup o' tea, ma'am? Got some hot water on the stove."

"No, thank you. I'm just headed into town."

Tempy smiled. "Mailin' the captain's letter?"

Lizzie nodded.

"Hope you told him Tempy says hi."

"I did."

Tempy gestured. "Me and the missus are going over menus for the next couple o' weeks. Gettin' it all written down so she can look it over real good."

Lizzie smiled and nodded again, then turned to go.

"Miss Clouston."

At Carrie's voice, she turned back.

"I hope you also included warmest regards to the captain from the colonel and me." A tender, familiar smile touched Carrie's eyes, and Lizzie felt the warmth of it in her own. "We pray for Captain Jones daily. And for his swift return. To you . . . my dear."

Lizzie took a quick breath, hoping her voice would hold. "Thank you, Mrs. McGavock. So very much." She nodded. "And yes, I included your regards. As always."

"Very good." Carrie sniffed and sat a little straighter. "Take your time in town, Miss Clouston. It's a beautiful day. Enjoy it."

Lizzie closed the kitchen door behind her and took deep breaths, the scents of honeysuckle and summer sweetening the air. Her heart felt lighter than it had in a very long time.

The kitchen door opened, and she glanced back.

"Miss Lizzie?" Tempy stepped out and pulled the door closed behind her. "I just want you to know, ma'am, that I done made up my mind 'bout what George said he'd do for me."

Lizzie waited, honestly not knowing what Tempy's decision would be. She hadn't offered Tempy counsel either way. For the first time in Tempy's life, the woman had the chance to choose her *own* path, and she deserved to do it without anyone intruding.

"I 'preciate George askin' me to come and live with him and his family out there in Mississippi. And with all them precious kids they got. But . . . Carnton is my home. Has been most o' my life." Tempy looked down the brick walkway that led to the gate, then around the front yard. "I reckon I don't have that many more years here, ma'am, 'fore the good Lord takes me home. And I love that Hattie and Winder.

I'd like to see them growed up a bit more, if I can. 'Sides . . ." The sheen of tears filled Tempy's eyes. "If I's to leave here now, how would a person who'd knowed me ever find me?"

Warmth flooded Lizzie's chest. She recalled Tempy mentioning that she had a brother and a sister. Lizzie grasped her hands. "I pray you all find each other one day, Tempy."

Tempy took a quick breath and nodded, then hugged Lizzie tight. Lizzie held on, drawing strength from Tempy's firm embrace.

"You go on now," Tempy whispered against her ear. "And mail that letter to your captain."

Lizzie smiled and continued on her way. The hinges on the front gate creaked as it closed behind her. As of one week ago, the war had officially been brought to its formal end. But the day the war ended in her mind was when General Robert E. Lee surrendered to Federal General Ulysses S. Grant on the ninth of April. A journalist's description of events in Appomattox, Virginia, had stirred vivid images. Grant arrived to the meeting in his muddy field uniform, whereas General Lee turned out in full dress attire, including sash and sword. Lee requested terms. All officers and men were to be pardoned and allowed to return home with their private property intact—most importantly, their horses, which were required for a late spring planting. Officers would keep their side arms, and Lee's starving men would be issued Federal rations. Grant had hurriedly written out the terms and accepted every one. Then, as Grant and Lee walked from the house, a band had begun to play in celebration. But with a quick gesture General Grant had silenced them. "The war is over," he'd been reported as saying. "The Rebels are our countrymen again." Still, for the next two months, news of continuing skirmishes had peppered the front pages of the newspapers. For all practical purposes, the war was over. But that hadn't ended the killing.

When Lizzie heard about President Lincoln's assassination, she'd wept. But as Tempy told her shortly after, at least the president had seen the war that had enveloped his years in office come to a close. In an article written after his passing, Lizzie read that Lincoln had believed God was punishing the land for its hand in slavery. That America was atoning in blood for its complicity in the wicked act. And she agreed. And had repented many times for her own silent complicity in it all.

In his farewell address to his men, General Hood wrote that he alone was responsible for the orders issued in the Tennessee Campaign. He'd penned that he had "strived hard" to do his duty. Lizzie would be the first to admit that she was not able to think about General Hood and his actions without being back on that battlefield. Without her senses recalling every painful, heart-wrenching detail. She took in a deep breath, held it, then gave it slow release. And as she had many times, she gave General Hood over to God, knowing she lacked the compassion—and the right—to pass judgment on what he'd done.

Because when *the* Judgment Day came and everyone's sins were laid bare, she knew that no nails would be left clutched in anyone's hands or stuffed in anyone's pockets. Including her own. That everyone would have driven their very last nail into the hands and feet of Jesus. So, yes, even as she struggled to move forward and seek understanding of all that had happened, she would leave Hood and this entire, horrible war at the cross of Christ.

As she made her way down Lewisburg Pike, she looked toward the fallow fields where so many were buried. She'd walked the field only once since she'd walked it that December first morning. The graves, hastily dug six months ago, were marked with crude wooden boards that bore the soldiers' names, ranks, and units. The men had been buried in graves roughly two and half feet deep and wide enough to lay two men side by side. She'd learned that when they'd buried young James. It comforted her to know that he was buried beside someone from his unit. A fellow Rebel.

But already the graves were showing wear, the heavy spring rains having beaten down upon the field as though trying to rid the earth of the memory of the blood spilled there. But no amount of water could ever wash away the memories. Not from her. Not from anyone who'd witnessed and experienced what had gone on here. She hoped people would remember the sacrifices. That they wouldn't forget. *Oh, Lord, please don't let it be forgotten . . .*

Missing Roland keenly in that moment, she pulled his well-read letter from her pocket and unfolded the stationery, already knowing each word by heart.

My dearest Lizzie,

Two weeks have elapsed since we left Franklin, and we are still prisoners. It is a short period of time, yet the anxiety and suspense of years seems concentrated in it. Those and only those who love deeply and devotedly can fully appreciate the torture of being separated from those who are far dearer to them than life itself.

I often imagine being transported back to Carnton, and fancy that I am resting in Winder's bedroom watching with restless impatience for the appearance of her who is dearer to me than the whole world beside. Such pleasing imaginings are short-lived, however, and sober reason whispers that circumstance shall for a time separate us. But as you say, my love, we have nothing to fear because we know who holds our lives in the palms of his hands. Those words are written on my heart, and I aspire to live by their truth a little more each day.

Hence, I console myself with the reflection that this state of things will soon be over, and that at no distant day I will be able to claim you as my own. And in ecstatic happiness that will then be mine, I'll forget all of these transient trials and sufferings. My dearest Lizzie, shall it not be so—I feel assured that no effort of yours will be wanting to bring so desirable a result.

Please give my kind regards to the Colonel and Mrs. McGavock, Hattie and Winder, and Tempy. But save the most treasured and intimate for yourself.

Yours forever,
Roland

She folded the letter and slipped it back into her pocket. When she rounded the bend, she spotted a man in the distance, limping, his head lowered, his gait afflicted. He walked with what looked to be a stick, the kind one found on the side of the road. She thought of all the young men who'd been wounded in the war, their once-whole bodies now broken and bent. Peace—fledgling and fragile as it was—had come at such a dear price, and she prayed that this still-too-divided nation could hold on to it.

She looked down the road again and squinted. Then slowed her steps. Her heart quickened. "Roland," she whispered, her voice scarcely audible. She said his name again, louder this time, and the man's head came up. He went stock-still, his posture strained as though he were trying to make sense of what he saw. But Lizzie ran for all she was worth, and saw that he too was hurrying toward her. She crossed the greater distance and raced into his arms, her tears flowing.

"My dearest Lizzie," he whispered against her hair, kissing her forehead, her cheeks.

"Oh, my love . . ." She held his handsome face in her hands. He looked older, wearier. Yet as she looked into his familiar gray eyes, she felt a stirring inside her that no words could capture.

He kissed her tenderly, then drew back as though wanting to take her in. A slow smile edged up one side of his mouth. "I've come to sweep you off your feet, Miss Clouston. If you'll still have an old, invalid man like me."

"Captain Jones, I'll have you any way I can get you, sir."

A brow raised. "Is that a promise?"

"Oh yes . . . It's a promise. For as long as we both shall live."

EPILOGUE

Lizzie sat at the writing desk—what was now *her* desk—in the sitting room off the master bedroom, pen in hand. She'd written this letter so many times in her mind, yet had never committed it to paper. It was time. The scratch of the pen against the stationery accentuated the quiet summer afternoon.

> August 14, 1866
> Oak Hill

> Dearest Susan, or should I say, Weet—
>   It is with a heart of gratitude that I write these words to you. Words you will never read unless, of course, those who have gone on before us are able, with God's consent, to look back into this earthly realm. Whichever is the case, I wish to thank you for loving your husband as well as you did. And for writing him so faithfully during the war. It is through those letters (which I've now read in their entirety) that I first fell in love with Roland.

Lizzie shifted in the chair, her back already beginning to ache. She rested a hand on her belly and smiled, eager for October to arrive. Only eight weeks until their first child was due. At least she hoped it would only be their first.

> Lena's and your untimely departure left a gaping hole in Roland's life, one I am earnestly and with great joy seeking to fill. At first I feared I would not be able to take your place. Then I realized how

foolish a thought that was. Not because your love was not wide or deep enough, but because our hearts are capable of far more love than we might imagine. When one love leaves, another never "take its place." Rather, I believe, the heart grows to encompass that new love.

The world is much changed since you left. But I believe those changes—at least most of them—are for the better. Especially here in Yalobusha. We still have far to go in how we view one another, but we are making great strides in that continued struggle. I believe you would be proud of Roland and the changes he has made to the farm. The changes he has made with George. George's wife, Sophia, tells me that you were always kind to them and their children, and from what I've come to know of you in your letters, I believe it.

Lizzie peered out the window, across the garden of lilies, to the long drive leading to the main road. Their guests should be arriving anytime, but everything was ready. She and Rachel had been preparing for days.

To Lizzie's delight, Ezra and Rachel, the couple who had served as the Jones's house slaves for so many years, had decided to stay. Roland was paying them a wage now. She was so proud of what he was doing here. While the first year of sharecropping had been successful, it had not been without its challenges. But as she'd once told George, everyone had to learn to walk before they could run. Which reminded her of Roland.

He'd insisted they not marry until he could walk down the aisle without aid of his cane. So they'd married almost a year to the day of the night they met at Carnton. And since they'd married in Carnton's best parlor, it was a very short aisle, as Roland had jested. Carrie McGavock had decorated the house so beautifully for their ceremony and reception following. The day was everything Lizzie had ever dreamed of. Granted, she and Roland hadn't wed in a field of flowers with only a preacher for a witness, as she'd envisioned her wedding as a young girl. But the happiness she felt that day—and now—was meant to be shared. And that she'd been able to share it with Johnny, who'd returned home to them safely—save a still healing shoulder wound—was an extra blessing.

She and Carrie had both cried the day she and Roland left Carnton for Yalobusha. Hattie and Winder too. Lizzie still missed those precious children more than she could say. Even Colonel McGavock had grown misty eyed as he'd bid her and Roland God's richest blessings. But it was what the colonel had whispered in her ear, much as her own father had done that day, that touched her heart the most. *Stay true to who you are, my dear. And always follow God's lead.*

A warm breeze wafted in through the window, and her gaze was drawn to a point in the distance where the fields dotted with wildflowers met the edge of the woods. And though she was far from Franklin, Tennessee, she thought of Towny and the last morning he'd come to her at Carnton. He was still so dear to her, and always would be. So it had thrilled her when she'd seen him in town shortly before she and Roland married. And in his company, a beautiful young woman who looked adoringly up at Towny as surely as if he'd hung the moon and stars. Towny and Becky had wedded about a month before she and Roland. She'd attended the wedding with her mother, and her heart had warmed when Towny slipped Marlene's ring—which Lizzie had long since returned to his father—onto Becky's finger, his gaze only for his beautiful bride. She wished them all the—

Lizzie sucked in a breath, feeling little Carrie kick. Roland was certain she was carrying his little namesake, but her instincts told her they were having a girl. And if they did, they'd already agreed that her name would be Carrie McGavock Jones.

Lizzie heard the front door open downstairs, followed by Roland's boot treads across the foyer, and knew she needed to hurry.

One last thing, Susan . . . Roland's mother and sisters have accepted me warmly into this home and into their lives. But I know Mrs. Jones still misses you dearly, because she speaks of you often. Very often. Every day, in fact. So if you're able, I would appreciate you putting in a good word for me on that end. Perhaps between the two of us, I will one day win her over.

Lizzie smiled to herself, not having intended to write that. The creak of a wagon brought her head up. Sure enough, their guests were coming up the drive.

Thank you, too, for planting the rows of lilies along the berm outside your bedroom window. I've always admired people who are gifted at gardening. They spend their time making the world a more beautiful place by what they do. And that is certainly what you have done for me. I look forward to meeting you and your precious Lena when I get home.

With deepest gratitude—

The bedroom door opened behind her, and Lizzie hastily signed her name to the letter as Roland's arms came around her.

He nuzzled her neck. "The sisters and Conrad are coming up the drive, Mrs. Jones."

Lizzie lifted her face for his kiss, ever grateful to have him in her life. "I know. I heard them."

He looked down at the desk, his eyes narrowing. "Writing a letter, are we?"

She turned it over. "Yes. One I'll let you read later on. But for now, let's go greet our guests! I'm so glad Conrad was able to come with them."

"Sister Catherine says he's doing well, and that everyone in Franklin brings their shoes to him." Roland leaned down and kissed her belly, running his hands over the ever-increasing swell. "Roland Junior, we'll see you soon, little fellow."

Lizzie swatted his arm. "Her name is Carrie."

"Whichever it is, I already love him or her with all my heart. Just as I love you."

"And always will?" she asked teasingly.

He answered with a promise that didn't need any words.

$\mathscr{A}$FTERWORD

Thank you for taking Roland and Lizzie's journey with me in *With This Pledge*. Civil War history has long been of interest to me, and when I learned about Roland and Lizzie meeting and falling in love following the Battle of Franklin—a pivotal five hours in the final outcome of the war—I knew I wanted to write their story. I also wanted to tell the story of what happened within the walls of Carnton both that dreadful night on November 30, 1864, and in the days, weeks, and months following.

I'm deeply indebted to the extraordinary folks at Carnton in Franklin, Tennessee, who invited me into the wealth of their historical knowledge, and to David Doty, the great-great-great-great-grandson of Captain Roland Ward Jones, and for granting me full access to family documents and historical keepsakes. I read through the shared family letters countless times (and sincerely hope Weet doesn't mind us sharing her letters so widely).

I'm also indebted to Eric Jacobson, CEO of the Battle of Franklin Trust (Carnton), for his years of extensive research about the Battle of Franklin and for his passion about informing current culture about this critical page in American history. Thank you, also, to Brian Allison for his extensive research into the specific soldiers who were at Carnton following the battle and who convalesced there for months following.

If you're interested in knowing more about the Battle of Franklin, Carnton, Roland and Lizzie, and the McGavocks, I invite you to visit the *With This Pledge* book page on my website (www.TameraAlexander. com). Click the link titled, TRUTH OR FICTION, and you'll open up a page chock-full of "insider information" about this book, as well as a list of recommended reading.

Among the "real" characters in the novel (based on people who truly lived) are Roland, Lizzie, John and Carrie McGavock, Tempy, Dr. Phillips, George, Hattie, Winder, Captain Pleasant Hope, James Shuler, E.M. Bounds, and many of the officers in the Confederate and Federal armies. With only two exceptions (entries from Towny and Levi), every document and letter in this novel is authentic. I deeply appreciate the opportunity to weave history into the fabric of my stories, but doing so in *With This Pledge* was especially meaningful. And challenging. Any mistakes are my own.

The texts I pored over and studied while writing this story are too numerous to mention here, but to say I'm grateful for the many historians who have written about this tumultuous time in America's history is an understatement.

Freedom. Choices. Promises.

These three themes run with vivid undercurrent through this story, just as they continue to run through our still too-divided United States. Far too many struggles of the late nineteenth century continue to plague the headlines of newspapers today, and only through the power of Christ can we overcome these obstacles and break down barriers and become one. The ground at the foot of the cross is level. We are each created in the image of Almighty God, and therefore are image bearers for his glory. It is my continued prayer that we'll strive with ever increasing fervor to see one another through this eternal lens.

Transatlantic slavery was an abhorrent evil. And as President Lincoln professed, this country had to bear a price for that wickedness. Yet there is more slavery in the world *today* than in the nineteenth century. If you would like to know more about fighting this evil in our world—and in your backyard—visit www.inourbackyard.org.

Lastly, much as Levi fought in the place of someone else, so we too have One who has fought—and is fighting—in our stead. You have a champion and his name is Jesus. He is everything you need. Reach out to him. He'll meet you wherever you are. And every promise from the Living Word of God is true and everlasting.

I'm grateful for you, friend.

Until next time,

$\mathcal{A}$CKNOWLEDGMENTS

To my family: from the depths of my heart . . . Thank you. Especially this time.

To Deborah Raney, my writing critique partner, and so much more: a thousand peanut butter twists.

To the Ladies of Coeur d'Alene: your brainstorming skills are stellar. So is your love and laughter.

To Jocelyn Bailey, my editor at HarperCollins: your insight and clarity made all the difference in this story. As did your patience as I wrote and rewrote. And rewrote.

To my fabulous team at HarperCollins (Amanda Bostic, Paul Fisher, Allison Carter, and Jodi Hughes): working with you is an absolute joy.

To Natasha Kern, my agent: you are an ever-present encouragement and strength. Thank you, dear friend.

To you, dear reader: thank you for taking yet another journey with me. You allow me to do what I do. You make it all worth it.

To Jesus, my beloved Rabbi: continue to take me down roads I would never choose for myself. Only let them lead me ever closer to you.

$\mathcal{D}$ISCUSSION QUESTIONS

1. Before reading *With This Pledge*, had you heard about Carnton in Franklin, Tennessee? Were you familiar with the Battle of Franklin and with the history of the final months of the Civil War?

2. Did you feel closer to Lizzie or to Roland in the novel? Which of them did you identify with most? Are you from the North or the South? How do you think your own personal heritage shaped your perspective as you read the novel?

3. Lizzie felt powerless to change her world due to the social mores and restrictions placed on women during the 19th century. Have you ever experienced the brunt of such restrictions? If yes, how did you meet those challenges? Did your situation change?

4. Roland Jones was a slaveowner in real life and held extensive properties in Yalobusha, Mississippi. How did knowing this about him shape your view of him and the opinions he so staunchly held?

5. Though we don't know the real name of the older black woman who served as cook to the McGavocks, we do know that she was "left behind" when the rest of the slaves were moved South during the war. What are your thoughts about Tempy's character? And if you could write the rest of her story, what would it be? (Stay tuned . . . There's more for Tempy in books two and three!)

6. As the battle unfolded that night and you ascended the stairs with Lizzie after the surgeon requested her assistance, what thoughts were going through your mind? How would you have responded in her place? Would you have been able to do what she did in the story?

7. Roland and Sister Catherine share a conversation in Chapter 18 that centers around faith, believing, and temptation. Did you relate to what they were saying? Sister Catherine comments, "Sometimes life on this side of the veil is far more difficult than I think it should be. Especially for those of us who belong to God. But then again, his promises do not eliminate suffering." Do you agree or disagree? Why?

8. In Chapter 20, Lizzie is faced with the choice of whether or not to be completely honest with Towny. Can you relate to Lizzie's motivation behind saying yes to Towny? Does her motivation translate in any way to today's culture? If yes, how?

9. We're introduced to Preacher E. M. Bounds in this story. Bounds really did accompany the Army of Tennessee into battle as portrayed in the novel. One of his favorite sayings was "Prayers are deathless. They outlive the lives of those who utter them." Do you agree or disagree? Has your life been changed because someone prayed faithfully for you? Have you seen an answer to faithful prayer in your own life? Please share.

10. In Chapter 30, Roland confronts Lizzie about her stance on slavery. What was the motivation behind his timing? Can you relate to Lizzie's reasons for the McGavocks not being aware of her beliefs? Do you think you would have had the courage to stand against opposing views on slavery during that time? What difficult choices have you made in your life in relation to standing for what you know is right?

11. In Chapter 38, Roland struggles to reconcile the fact that two men he greatly admired and who largely shaped his faith might have been immoral men. What faith legacy are you leaving to your family? Will it stand the test of time?

12. Did you enjoy *A Christmas Carol* being woven into the story? Had you read that story before? What parallels did you see

between Scrooge's life and Roland's? What lessons can we learn that we can apply to our daily lives?

13. In the epilogue, Lizzie writes a letter that's been "being written" inside her for a very long time. Who is the letter to? And have you ever written a letter like that to someone who's already passed? Do you believe those who've gone on before us can see back to this earthly realm? Can you give biblical evidence (or supposition) for this?

Come and see how a terrible battle became...

The Greatest Story of the Civil War

at Carnton in Franklin, Tennessee

BATTLE OF FRANKLIN
TRUST
The Greatest Story of the Civil War

615-786-1864
www.boft.org

Tempy's Skillet-Fried Hoecakes

Tempy hardly ever measured anything, so you don't have to be spot-on with this humble nineteenth-century recipe either. For each six to eight cakes desired, stir together the following, gradually adding more water until the consistency looks "just right." Similar to pancake batter. Not too watery, but not too thick. Use either white or yellow cornmeal, your preference. The amount of water will vary depending on the brand of the cornmeal, so start with a smaller portion and gradually add more if necessary.

Ingredients

1 cup white or yellow cornmeal

1/2 teaspoon salt

2/3 to 3/4 cup water, or more as needed

Butter, bacon grease, lard, solid shortening, or vegetable oil as needed

In a medium bowl, stir together the cornmeal, salt, and enough water to obtain a thin (but not too runny) consistency (how's that for approximation!). Let the batter stand while you heat a large cast iron skillet or griddle over medium-high heat until thoroughly heated. It doesn't *have* to be a cast iron skillet, but cast iron fries these hoecakes so beautifully. And it's what Tempy used! Add 2 tablespoons of fat for each four cakes prepared. (I prefer the combination of a little bacon grease and butter, but it's up to you.)

Continue heating the skillet until a splash of water sizzles when sprinkled on its surface. Using about 1 1/2 to 2 tablespoons batter for each cake, spoon out generous tablespoons onto the griddle or skillet (three or four at a time), making sure to keep them well separated. Gently spread the circles of batter out into thin rounds. The thinnest rounds will make the crispest hoecakes!

Cook until crispy and lightly browned on one side, then carefully turn with a spatula and cook until crisp and brown on the other side. This usually takes 3 to 4 minutes. Serve immediately with butter, honey, maple syrup, or jelly, if desired.

Makes 6 to 8 three-inch hoecakes. The recipe may be doubled or tripled as desired. Tempy would be so proud!

Lizzie's Southern Soda Muffins

This muffin "receipt"—what Victorians called recipes—originally appeared in *Godey's Lady's Book* in 1862, and represents a very common and quickly made muffin, which would have been important when feeding that many soldiers. It's light and spongy and is a great representation of an authentic nineteenth-century "quick muffin."

Ingredients
 3 large eggs, lightly beaten
 4 $1/2$ cups all-purpose flour
 1 $1/2$ teaspoons baking soda
 4 $1/2$ teaspoons baking powder
 $2/3$ cup sugar
 1 $1/4$ teaspoons salt (adjust to taste)
 3 cups buttermilk
 4 tablespoons butter, melted

Mix dry ingredients thoroughly, then gradually stir in the buttermilk 1 cup at a time along with eggs and butter. Beat well by hand (or with a mixer—although more love goes into the batter when you beat it by hand) until smooth.

These tender muffins can either be fried with the aid of "egg rings" in a buttered skillet (with batter poured to near $1/2$-inch thickness) or baked in muffin tins or in two loaf pans. For muffin tins, preheat oven to 350 degrees. Put a small dollop of bacon grease (or shortening, but bacon grease is yummiest!) into the bottom of each muffin tin cup and stick the tin in the oven until the grease is melted. Carefully remove the hot muffin tin from the oven, fill the muffin cups half full, and bake for 10 to 12 minutes or until golden brown. Serve hot and slathered with butter and honey!

Yield: 24 muffins or 2 loaf pans

Confederate Johnny Cakes

Ingredients

2 cups cornmeal

$2/3$ cup milk

2 tablespoons vegetable oil

2 teaspoons baking soda

$1/2$ teaspoon salt

Mix ingredients into a stiff batter and form eight biscuit-size "cakes." Bake on a lightly greased cookie sheet at 350 degrees for 20 to 25 minutes or until brown. Or if you prefer to fry them, spoon the batter into hot cooking oil (or bacon grease) in a frying pan over low heat. Remove the corn cakes and let them cool on a paper towel until warm to the touch. These are best served with butter and honey—or molasses, if you're truly Southern at heart!

Lizzie's Apple-Brandy Hot Toddies
(in memory of Second Lieutenant James Shuler's mother)

Ingredients
- 1 1/2 cups water
- 2 tablespoons plus 2 teaspoons honey
- 1/2 cup fresh lemon juice (bottled can be used, but fresh is tastier)
- 2 cups apple brandy (less or more depending on the desired strength; for teetotalers, substitute straight apple cider)
- 8 cinnamon sticks

In a small saucepan, bring the water to a boil. Remove from heat and slowly stir in the honey until dissolved. Next, add the lemon juice and apple brandy and mix until well blended. Slip a cinnamon stick into each of eight mugs (or heatproof glasses) and pour in that hot toddy bliss—then serve. Delicious! And definitely a drink authentic to the 1800s.

Tempy's Southern Tea Cakes

No matter how many times I make these, I still love them! They're more akin to a cookie than cake, and the story of where these cookies originated from varies depending on whose kitchen you're in. Likely, some frugal Southern cook found her cupboards on the meager side and whipped something up anyway. These cookies are—by nature and circumstance of situation in the Civil War—usually fairly bland. To dress them up, cooks would add either a little cinnamon or nutmeg or (my favorite) lemon zest. But I do encourage you to try these little jewels. They're especially delicious with—you're reading my mind, I can feel it—a hot cup of tea.

Ingredients

  1 cup (2 sticks) unsalted butter, softened

  2 cups sugar

  3 large eggs

  1 teaspoon vanilla extract

  3 1/2 cups plain flour

  1 teaspoon baking soda

  1/2 teaspoon salt

Beat the softened butter at medium speed with an electric mixer (or if you're feeling particularly toned, by hand). Gradually add the sugar and mix until well combined. Add eggs one at a time, beating after each. Then stir in the vanilla. In a separate bowl, combine the dry ingredients and whisk well. Gradually add the dry mixture to the butter mixture, beating at lower speed until the mixture is fully combined. Then divide the dough into halves and wrap in plastic wrap. Chill for 30 to 45 minutes.

Roll out the chilled dough on a floured surface. Using a biscuit cutter (or cookie cutter of choice), cut out the cookies and place them on a parchment-lined baking sheet. Bake at 350 degrees for 10 to 12 minutes or until the edges have started to brown. Watch closely so they don't burn.

Set during the Civil War at Nashville's historic Belle Meade Plantation, Tamera Alexander portrays stories about enslavement and freedom, arrogance and humility, and the power of love to heal even the deepest of wounds.

ABOUT THE AUTHOR

Author photo by Mandy
Whitley Photography

Tamera Alexander is a *USA TODAY* best-selling author and one of today's most popular writers of inspirational historical romance. Her books have earned her devoted readers worldwide, as well as multiple industry awards. Tamera and her husband make their home in Nashville not far from Carnton and other Southern mansions that serve as the backdrop for many of her critically-acclaimed novels.

Tamera invites you to visit her online at:

Website: TameraAlexander.com
Instagram: TameraAlexanderAuthor
Facebook: Tamera.Alexander
Twitter: @TameraAlexander
Pinterest: TameraAuthor
Group Blog: InspiredbyLifeandFiction.com

Or if you prefer snail mail, please write her at:
Tamera Alexander
PO Box 871
Brentwood, TN 37024

Discussion questions for all of Tamera's novels are available at TameraAlexander.com, as are details about Tamera joining your book club for a virtual visit.

Tamera hosts monthly giveaways on her website and invites you to sign up for her eUpdates and have your name tossed into the hat!